T0144620

The Advisor

by Carl Nelson

The Advisor happens to be set during the Vietnam War, but its message is universally applicable – the characters could be State Department, Peace Corps, or soldiers in Bosnia.

What sets The Advisor apart from the many other novels written about Vietnam? It deals with the complexities of being an advisor to foreigners in wartime: a clash of cultures, combat action and political intrigue. Played out through Viet Cong, as well as American and South Vietnamese characters, the book narrates both sides of that strange war.

More than just an action-adventure story, The Advisor is driven by historical intrigue, gripping drama, and haunting romance suffused with the mystery and seduction of the orient. It begins in the summer of 1972, the last year of the war, before the U.S. Military left South Vietnam and ends in 1975 when the last Americans are evacuated. This metaphoric novel challenges the Domino Theory – the premise of the Vietnam War, while spinning a tale of protecting the Long Tau Channel, the most strategic waterway in the campaign.

In 1972, U.S. Navy Commander Blake Lawrence is unwillingly thrust into the Rung Sat Special Zone, a place he does not want to be, among a people whose culture he doesn't understand, and a kind of war he is unprepared to fight. As the Senior Advisor, he struggles to sort out several moral dilemmas: Will he be court-martialed and lose his destroyer command? Who is correct: His boss Rear Admiral Paulson or his Vietnamese Navy counter-part Captain Duc-Lang? What should he do about the women in his life: His wife Beverly, who is fed-up with Navy life, and the temptation of infidelity with seductive Peg Thompson? What should he do about his naval career? What's more important: a North Vietnamese Colonel named Tu or the Russian AT3 rockets, his integrity or his destroyer command? What's the war about: Communism or Dynasties?

At the end of the book, Blake is at sea where he witnesses the final American withdrawal in 1975, and we learn what happened after his days as an advisor and why he is invited to return to fight.

THE ADVISOR
(CÔ-VÂN)

CARL NELSON

TURNER PUBLISHING COMPANY

TURNER PUBLISHING COMPANY

Turner Publishing Company Staff:
Randy Baumgardner, Editor
Shelley R. Davidson, Designer

Library of Congress Catalog Card No. 99-64660
ISBN: 978-1-68162-424-2

Additional copies may be purchased directly from the Publisher.
Limited Edition.

Poem "I miss you so"
courtesy of Monica Ann (Nelson) Askari.

"Cracklin' Rosie" by Neil Diamond
© 1970 Prophet Music, Inc.
All Rights Reserved. Used by Permission.

Cover artwork courtesy of John Mark Jackson.

DEDICATION

To those honorable men and women living and dead who served in the Vietnam War and their loyal families, including my own.

ACKNOWLEDGEMENTS

I extend my deep appreciation to all the friends in the Pearl Harbor, San Diego and Coronado areas, who gave freely of their time and remembrances to help make this book possible. I'm especially grateful to: Mike Barajas; Ann Marie Lindstrom; Colonel Richard Shigley, U. S. Marine Corps (Retired); Captain C. Jerry Wages, U. S. Navy (Retired); Colonel Peter Houben, U. S. Army (Retired); Captain Ralph Harms, SC, U. S. Navy (Retired); Olin Thompson, Arthur Fleming, James Kitchen, and various members of Marsh Cassady's writing group and all others who read, listened, critiqued and otherwise suffered through various revisions by this growing writer; and my wife, Barbara, who endured my growth as a writer.

I am also grateful for the support of Colonel John Carty, U.S. Marine Corps (Retired); Admiral Elmo Zumwalt, U.S. Navy (Retired); Vice Admiral Robert Salzer, U.S. Navy (Retired); Mr. Dave Turner, Publisher, Turner Publishing Company; and Mr. Randy Baumgardner, Editor, Turner Publishing Company; and Ms. Shelley R. Davidson, Book Designer, Turner Publishing Company.

AUTHOR'S NOTE

The only consistency of the American involvement in the Vietnam War was the advisors. They were there from the beginning in the early 60s until the pull-out in 1972-73. For them it wasn't an American war, it was a Vietnamese war and they were there to help.

Their participation was different, because to them it was always unconventional and it never changed during the twelve year involvement. United States advisors served with Vietnamese forces, whose tours of duty were for the duration and who allowed inexperienced Americans to tag along for 12 months until just about the time they knew what they were doing, they went home. Those professional American military men and women had the additional burden of understanding the culture and psychology of East Asia.

The Vietnam War did happen. The Long Tau shipping Channel, Rung Sat Special Zone, and Nha Be do or did exist. The underlying theme of this book is true, that cultures and dynasties were at play as well as the fear of Communism. The history of the period, the places, the events, and the chronology offered were either observed by the author or accurately researched by him (see A History of South-East Asia, by D.G.E. Hall, MacMillan and Company, 1964) and retain their essential authenticity. Because this is a novel and not a history the author has, for purposes of story line and plot, taken literary license. For instance, the Bokassa and Nguyen Anh stories are true, just as it is true that a North Vietnamese Colonel did walk, for one year, all the way from the North to command the guerrillas of the Rung Sat. However, in each case the stories and names have been adjusted to fit a fictional story. The men and women of this book are fictitious — created from the author's imagination. No similarity to anyone living or dead exists or is intended.

PROLOGUE

America did not enter the war in Vietnam until 1960 and even then by only contributing $1 Billion in aid and about 1,500 advisors.

Twelve years later, in January of 1972 the nation was still involved in what turned out to be the longest "hot war" in the history of the United States. By then the American people had little enthusiasm for it — the Armed Forces only a bit more.

In that month, President Nixon announced his intention to run for re-election. When Hubert Humphrey entered the race on the 11th of January he vowed to get America out of the war. On January 14th, Nixon countered by announcing that despite an expected Communist offensive in the spring he would reduce the number of Americans in Vietnam from 139,000 on the first of February to 69,000 on the first of May. But, he added, "If the enemy holds one prisoner of war I will not withdraw all forces."

Nixon's bargaining position thus became the residual U.S. military advisors whose mission was to remain in-country and continue the "Vietnamization" program begun in 1970. They were to turn over the military equipment and train the Vietnamese, so that when the last U.S. forces pulled out, and all prisoners were released, the South Vietnamese could fight on and win the Domino game.

The following excerpts and headlines from actual issues of the _Los Angeles Times_ printed during the winter and spring of 1972 reveal the mixture of blood, rhetoric and emotion of that period:

February 8, 1972   Presidential aide H.R. Haldeman accused American Vietnam policy criticizers of consciously aiding and abetting the enemy of the United States.

February 18, 1972   President Nixon embarked on a Journey to China for "Peace."

March 17, 1972	President Nixon announced he would visit Russia on May 22.
March 31, 1972	North Vietnamese Communists began an offensive.
April 4, 1972	The Allies launched a huge counter offensive.
April 6, 1972	Russia became the key Hanoi war supplier.
April 10, 1972	Nixon threatened postponement of his Russian trip if the Vietnam situation worsened.
April 11, 1972	Jane Fonda won an Oscar for her portrayal of a stylish and wily call girl in "Klute".
April 16, 1972	For the first time since President Johnson ordered a halt in November 1968, B-52's bombed the Haiphong area. It was the northernmost raid of the war.
April 23, 1972	At a rally in San Francisco, Miss Fonda told a crowd that their festive attitude was justified, "because the Vietnamese people and Cambodians are winning."
April 26, 1972	Kissinger secretly visited Moscow for four days.
April 27, 1972	Nixon announced withdrawal of 20,000 more troops but said he would continue bombing.
April 28, 1972	The flow of Russian built tanks and other weapons into North Vietnam increased.
April 29, 1972	40,000 Reds began a siege of Quang Tri; thousands of refugees fled south.
May 2, 1972	The fall of Quang Tri gave the North Vietnamese their first major victory, and it periled the city of Hue.
May 8, 1972	For the first time in the twelve-year involvement in the Vietnamese War President Nixon ordered the mining of North Vietnamese ports. Naval aircraft laid area mines which were to be activated at 3 AM Thursday, May 11 in Haiphong Harbor.

ONE

Blake Lawrence served as executive officer, navigator and CIC evaluator aboard the destroyer *Decatur*, directing gunfire support for U.S. Army, Marines and allies in the war he and most other servicemen thought was about saving South Vietnam from Communism. He had already been at sea in the war zone for the past six months and during the previous three months the ship had provided seaborne artillery along the Northern coast of South Vietnam. Fighting near the DMZ during the spring of 1972 had been savage, but after the Reds were pushed back, Blake's ship was ordered south to operate near the coastal city of Vung Tau. There they were to support anti-guerrilla operations.

On this evening, though physically exhausted by the strain of his shipboard duties, Blake was buoyed by the thought of going home. Before leaving the bridge he checked the ship's navigation, signed a few papers, then went below to have a cat-nap before dinner, his first in weeks.

He had hardly fallen asleep when a knock on his cabin door jarred him awake. He rubbed his eyes then glanced at his watch. "Yes, come in. Who is it?"

"Ah... ah, excuse me, sir."

It was Petty Officer Roark, who the crew called Red. He reminded Blake of the movie actor Mickey Rooney: short, freckled with two dominant front teeth and a grinny face.

Red pulled an envelope from his pocket. "Got a letter about the baby, Commander."

"Great. How's the wife doing?" Another of Blake's duties was to look after the personnel problems of the ship and he remembered that Red was a father-to-be. He marveled at the way the petty officer handled the helpless feeling of being so far away, fighting a war.

"Everything's look'n good, sir. Baby's due next month. Doctor said it's gonna be a girl."

"Don't we have you scheduled home on a flight out of Subic?" Blake's burly eyebrows pinched as he struggled to remember.

"Yes, sir! And in case I don't have another chance to say this, I do appreciate everything you've done, sir."

"Don't mention it." Blake shrugged. "Happy I could help." Then he broke into a full grin. "Besides, I'm gonna be on that same plane. Gettin' my own destroyer command."

Blake held up a picture of his family. "Go'n home to my kids, too." He pointed to his daughter. "This is what your baby girl will look like when she's ten years old."

"She's got your blue eyes, Commander, but she's beautiful like your wife."

After Red left, Blake flopped on his bed and drew the pillow under his head. Operations at sea had been grueling. Destroyers fired all day, re-loaded their magazines all night, then fired all day again. Four or five hours' rest was the norm; some lived on less. Most days on the gunline Blake was lucky to get three hours' sleep often broken into half-hour intervals. Now he was so tired he couldn't sleep. He stretched his long legs, then relaxed them trying to release the tension in his body. He dozed for a few moments, wakened to roll and toss, stare at the overhead and walls of the pastel colored compartment, and to listen to the splash of water and the creaking sound of bulkheads moving in rhythm to the rolling seas. A sour odor of unchanged bed clothes mixed with petroleum smells from the engine room below permeated the room.

Blake's mind wandered alternately from his duties on the ship to his wife and family. Determined to fight his over-tired condition he pulled the pillow over his face, pinched his eyes and then relaxed them. A light feeling replaced the stress. Drowsy, his mind drifted with the ship's roll.

He missed Beverly and pictured himself lying beside her. He smelled the scent of her perfume. They were naked and his hand reached out to touch her body. She was not as slender as when they first met, but the fullness felt good. He kissed her mouth then slowly ran his lips to her breasts. Her body responded to his touch and his hand moved down her back to the softness, the roundness. Their bodies melted. He pulled her to him. They were about to consummate his sexual dream when he heard the irritating squeal of his sound powered telephone. "Supper time, sir. You asked for a call."

The officers had already gathered when Blake entered the conservatively decorated destroyer wardroom. Some talked about odds and ends of business, while others studied the latest Esquire and Playboy magazines. The song *Cracklin' Rosie* played in the background over the stereo system. Two of the more senior officers, both lieutenants, played Acey Ducey at a corner table.

Conversations stopped as Blake moved to his place at the right hand of the Captain's chair, his wordless signal for the others to also take their places at the table. Filipino and black messmen moved about in final preparation for the meal. Lights were dimmed. Candles glowed across a formal setting. Even in the war zone, when not on an actual gunfire mission, this Captain insisted that the table for each evening meal be set for gentlemen.

When Commander Art Johnson, a prematurely gray-haired man in his mid-40's entered, the voice of a junior officer shouted, "Attention on Deck." The messmen, dressed in white trousers, wine-colored jackets, and bow ties took their invisible positions, hands clasped behind their backs.

Obviously accustomed to the differential treatment given destroyer commanding officers, Johnson slid into his seat at the head of the table and gave a slight nod. "Take your seats, gentlemen."

At first the officers were silent, but conversation soon picked up. At the junior end of the table Ensigns laughed and joked. In the middle, lieutenants talked seriously about tactics and the war. At the Captain's end, where most of the married men sat, there was jovial conversation about how good it was to be near the end of the cruise.

The Operations Officer took a sip of soup then commented. "It'll sure be different than this at home. Forget the candlelight suppers. It'll be 'honey take out the garbage — honey do this, honey do that'."

During dessert, smokes, and coffee, a harried looking Chief Petty Officer wearing sharply pressed khakis, entered the wardroom and waited for the right moment to interrupt.

"Excuse me, Captain. This just came in. Thought you and Commander Lawrence might want to see it right away."

The Chief handed a message to the Captain, who quickly scanned the paper and passed it to Blake.

"For you." He said in private tones.

As his eyes scanned the words, Blake felt his skin flush, his heart pound, and his stomach knot.

JUNE 20, 1972
CONFIDENTIAL
OPERATIONAL IMMEDIATE
FOR IMMEDIATE DELIVERY TO COMMANDER BLAKE
LAWRENCE, UNITED STATES NAVY.
ORDERS TO DESTROYER COMMAND CANCELED.
DETACHED IMMEDIATELY.
REPORT TEMPORARY DUTY U. S. NAVAL FORCES VIETNAM,
SAIGON, REPUBLIC OF VIETNAM TO AWAIT RESULTS OF IN-
VESTIGATION AND PARTY TO POSSIBLE COURT-MARTIAL.

My God! Blake said to himself. He stroked his freshly shaven face then ran his fingers across lines of near forty years etched across a broad forehead beaded in sweat. Thoughts poured. *Court-martial? Not going home? No destroyer command? In-country! A mistake.*

He read the orders again.

They seemed real enough, but...maybe it was a wardroom joke. Junior officers sometimes did that — dreamed up games like phony orders just to liven up an otherwise boring meal. After all, they did joke with him and call him the "Marlboro Man." They said his protruding brow, high cheek bones, dark mustache, and sturdy chin reminded them of the rugged, athletic looking man who posed for a popular cigarette billboard advertisement.

He ran his fingers through tossed salt and pepper hair then shrugged and said casually, "They canceled my orders to command. I'm going in-country — party to the gunfire investigation."

He waited for their burst of laughter.

The mood at the table did change, but it wasn't a joke.

Conversation stopped. Eyes dropped. Bodies shifted. Every face expressed sympathy. Junior officers didn't know much about in-country war, except that it was different than blue water sea duty. But they all knew a court-martial could ruin a career.

Captain Johnson attempted to ease the awkward silence by laughing off Blake's change of orders. "Oh, well. A slight navigational detour. No sweat. You'll be home by the Fourth of July."

Blake grinned, but inside he felt flat. In his game of Monopoly the roll of the dice specified do not pass go — proceed directly to hell. He had not only lost his command, but now felt the pressure of an investigation that could end his twenty-year career. He couldn't let his bitterness show. In the corporate world of the Navy one didn't snivel. Career officers were supposed to accept their orders — just salute and march off. He already disliked Vietnam — the little country that drained his energy and took him away from his family. The place where so many Americans had already died. The place that sucked away the best, and left only the bilge water.

Blake didn't finish his meal. On the pretense of pressing work he excused himself and went to the bridge. He stood alone in the darkness on a cat walk aft of the main deckhouse, where he often shot the evening stars using a sextant for celestial navigation.

His eyes followed a geese-like formation of returning Navy attack bombers passing overhead enroute to their aircraft carrier. One after another they broke sharply from their "V" shaped formation to form a single line that curved into a picturesque oval. Each caught a wire, wrenched to a stop with a final great roar from their powerful engines, then taxied quickly to a parking spot among life-less squadrons.

Blake then focused on his *Rembrandt*, another destroyer silhouetted against the red horizon. To him that was the most beautiful sight in the Navy. He heard the crack of her 5" guns and saw them flash as he watched her wake boil and her bow knife through the waves, as she raced by the Vietnamese coast.

He folded his arms across the bridge rail and raised his eyes to witness as if fathered by magic the evening stars blooming one by one from the darkening sky. It was that part of the day when the ocean blended with the heavens in a final burst of crimson — ordinarily the most pleasant time for the eternal sea-man — when they most deeply felt its beauty.

Slowly the heavenly bodies grew to their full and brightest, but Blake's thoughts remained dim and ugly. He had just lost his ticket to paradise. He wanted to curse, something he seldom did.

He should have felt the exhilaration of having orders to command his own destroyer — the first of his Academy class to get a ship — a major step in his career — a ticket to the top just like his dad.

It wasn't that he didn't understand what was happening in South Vietnam. As a result of his Annapolis training and discussions with his father, Rear Ad-miral Blake Lawrence II, he knew the Vietnam war was based on the "Domino Theory". The foundation of that concept was National Security Council Document Number 64, originated way back in February of 1950. It pro-nounced Indochina a key area of South East Asia, which was considered to be under the immediate threat of Communism. His father had showed him a copy of that secret memorandum, which predicted if Indochina fell to the Communists, Burma and Thailand would soon fall like the humpty dumpty kids version of the Domino game and the rest of Southeast Asia would be in grave danger.

Blake also knew America sent advisors to assist other countries fight their wars. In the case of the Navy it was usually in the brown water, but that was not for him. He was a blue water sailor — cruisers and destroyers all the way.

He stroked his fingers across weathered seaman's skin and believing he was alone said, "Why me? What about my destroyer? What about Beverly and the kids?"

"I know how you must feel, Blake." Captain Johnson had quietly joined his executive officer at *Decatur's* bridge rail. "For us, South Vietnam is the asshole of the universe, but they must need your testimony — why else the hurry up orders?"

"Why an investigation at all? It's a war — people get killed."

"It's that kind of a war and it's Admiral Frank Paulson's way. Watch out for him. He's nicknamed the Chameleon — goes back to Academy days when he was a company officer. Shouldn't say this, but... between you an me, he's an ambitious, hip-shooting sonofabitch, the kind who's always out to hang an imperfect world."

TWO

Maybe Blake should have known that instead of going home he would soon be fighting on the ground in the ugly swamps and rivers of the delta in a place called the Killer Forest for altogether different reasons than the Domino Theory. The clues were there. The incident happened. An American was killed and Rear Admiral Paulson had declared an investigation.

As Executive Officer of the destroyer, Blake's job was to coordinate the gunfire missions – make sure the projectiles got to their target and he remembered vividly the day when he authorized the rounds on top that had precipitated his change of orders and possible court-martial. It all began two weeks before, on June 6, 1972, with:

"General Quarters! General Quarters! General Quarters! All hands man your battle stations! All hands man your battle stations! General Quarters!"

On that day, as soon as he heard the clatter of the alarm and the Bos'n's cry, Blake left his cabin on the run. Sprinting up the starboard ladder, he almost tripped on the strings of his untied shoes. He arrived in the Combat Information Center only in a sweat drenched T-shirt and khaki trousers.

Breathing hard, he listened for the call-for-fire. "Fireburner, Fireburner, this is Moonriver, Moonriver. Emergency-call-for-fire! Fuc'n gooks're tr'n to overrun us."

Blake grabbed the radio handset and held it close to his mouth. His eyes focused on the hands of the clock which showed it was late afternoon. Billowing monsoon clouds would be poised to spew their routine afternoon shower.

"Moonriver. This is Fireburner. What's the situation, over?"

Petty Officer Roark, known as Red, grabbed a pencil and pad to record the next transmission.

The distant voice shouted again. "North Vietnamese junk infiltrated from the sea. Caught the bastards off-loading weapons on the beach near Can Gio. Had them cold 'til a bunch 'a fuc'n guerrillas jumped us. Got us pinned down. Need y'a t'a get the gooks off our backs then blow the boat, over."

The destroyer shook and bulkheads vibrated as her bow knifed through the water in response to the urgency of the mission. The ship's speed dial already moved past twenty-five knots on the way to flank speed. He felt the stern skid as it turned around the peninsula at Cape Saint Jacques to enter the narrow dredged channel. He knew Captain Johnson was monitoring the radio on the bridge and in order to get his guns within range for an emergency-call-for-fire wouldn't slow until the water turned brown.

"Roger, Moonriver," Blake answered. "We're on the way. We're passing Vung Tau at this time. Soon as we're in range we'll start shoot'n. Give us wind, bearing and coordinates, over."

The man on the other end of the circuit kept his transmitter keyed and Blake heard obscenities, foreign voices, and a language no one in CIC understood. Weapons fired. Finally the voice came again, "Here ya go, out there. Our position is North—Yankee, Sierra 125-495. Hurry. Start shoot'n, now! The fuckers are gonna overrun us if you don't give us something. Now!"

To Blake, the voice sounded like a high school kid revved up for a football game.

Red knew Blake's distaste for messdeck talk. It was seldom used by wardroom officers, let alone on a combat radio circuit. He grimaced and gave a half embarrassed, half apologetic grin. "Just some grunt, sir. Sounds like he's been do'n Cracklin' Rosie or Mary Jane."

Red pointed to position North—Yankee, Sierra 125-495, near the beach southwest of the village of Can Gio. He touched the chart with his finger and traced the channel as it narrowed near the village. He drew an imaginary circle around a large area of ugly brown and green swampland that extended almost to Saigon. Red raised his head and eyes just enough to be sure his words could be heard. "Advisors in the Rung Sat Special Zone, sir."

Blake nodded to Red that he had heard the name. He made a mental note to read up on the place called Rung Sat — later when things were quiet. *Decatur's* position on the chart was adjacent to the symbol of Nui Nho lighthouse high above the coastal city of Vung Tau on the Cape. They were passing the place where the merchant ships lay at anchor before taking aboard their pilot to begin the dangerous journey up the Long Tau Channel to Saigon.

Blake called the gunnery officer and told him the situation. The two officers agreed that the advisors under attack were beyond the range of the ship's explosive rounds, but they had to do something. They decided to fire Star Shells, the illuminating projectiles designed to explode in the air and float to the earth on parachutes. They would light the sky and ground as they fell and could be seen from a great distance. "Who knows," they agreed. "Maybe the VC will take the hint."

Finally the *Decatur's* 5"/54's were loaded. The ship was still out of range, but when the guns roared *whomp, whomp*, the entire ship shook.

"Got your Star Shells," came the voice from the beach. "That's cool. Fuc'n beautiful, but they want the real stuff, man!"

The ship vibrated as it crashed through the channel water closing the target. Blake ordered the ammo changed from Star Shells to explosive rounds; the kind that do maximum damage to personnel and other targets.

Finally *Decatur* came within range. Her great rifles fired projectiles at the distant target.

Again moments of silence then, "Not close enough. They're gonna fuc'n over-run us. Gotta get closer. Shit they're almost here. Give it to us — on top!"

A crackling noise and silence.

Blake grabbed the radio handset. The young voice had just ordered the ship to explode highly fragmentary projectiles over the heads of the advisors. It meant dead guerrillas; it also could mean dead Americans. Blake wanted confirmation. "Moonriver, this is Fireburner! Are you sure you want it on top? Repeat, are you certain you want it on top? Over."

No response. Only crackling broke the silence. He waited for an answer, then he tried again. Still silence.

"Did you hear him ask for it on top?" He asked Roark.

"Yes, sir. Think so. You think he meant it?"

Blake felt tired. His thinking processes slowed. Digging fingers into aching temples he questioned. *Were they already overrun? Had the radio been blown up?*

Red gave his boss a what-are-you-going-to-do look.

Blake stroked his stubbled chin. *What to do? Should he order rounds fired to where he knew American advisors were fighting guerrillas, or should he wait until he re-established radio communications and received confirmation?* His mind ached as it searched for the decision. His father, Rear Admiral Blake Lawrence, the second and his grandfather Captain Blake Lawrence would not have hesitated. His grandfather had always said that in war there was never time to think and feel. Just carry out your orders.

But, Blake Lawrence, the third was different. He did think and he did feel and he hated being another Blake Lawrence. He refused to use the symbol III and even resisted the nickname "Trey" bestowed at a boys prep school. For him every life mattered, it was the reason he served. He was not in the business to randomly kill. It was his grandmother Hildur, the Swedish girl his grandfather met and married while on duty in Europe, who had challenged him to think independently about things that mattered. "You may come from a long line of naval officers," she told him. "But, your duty lies with your conscience — always do the right thing. Think for yourself. Don't be a sheep and above all don't believe that your leaders, especially admirals, are always right. Ambition gets in their way. I know. Your father and grandfather have made their share of mistakes. Seek a civil society, one that values all life and when you fight a war make sure it leads to a more peaceful world."

If Blake waited they all could be killed but if he fired and he was wrong, he still risked American lives. He picked up the radio handset and held it to his lips, hesitating. Finally, shaking from fatigue he spoke, "Moonriver, Moonriver. This is Fireburner, transmitting in the blind. I roger your request for rounds on top. Take cover. I say again, take cover and standby."

He made another call to the ship's gunnery officer and quickly changed the bearing and range to the target. The ship's vibrations dampened as *Decatur* slowed from twenty-five knots, to twenty, then fifteen. Captain Johnson had held the speed until his guns were well within range of the American advisors. He had already risked churning the blades of the ship's screws into the mud; to continue without slowing now mean endangering his own crew.

Once more Blake said, "Moonriver this is Fireburner. I say again, take cover, here comes Fireburner's kitchen sink."

He gave the order.

He heard the guns go *whomp, whomp, whomp.*

The flight of the projectiles seemed to take a lifetime.

He heard the monsoon clouds burst. Rain pelted the ship's superstructure.

Humidity in the room increased. Everyone became drenched in sweat. His head ached from the stench of boiler gas and stale air that permeated the room.

At last he heard the crackle of the radio. A different voice said, "Give me that handset Marquell, you fuc'n pot head."

The deep voice blasted over the radio circuit, "Cease Fire! Cease Fire! Dammit you hit our own men. Cease fire."

Blake's shoulders slumped forward as the strength drained away. He pinched the soft space above his nasal bone, shook his head, then looked at Petty Officer Roark.

"Crap," Blake said shaking his head again.

"The fuc'n VC are pull'n out. Fire mission complete," The gruff voice boomed. "Can you hang around, just in case? Over."

Blake confirmed that his destroyer could stay in the area and questioned the voice about casualties. He learned a medevac chopper was on the way to take out a dead South Vietnamese and a wounded American Advisor.

THREE

Blake transferred to the nearby aircraft carrier by a helicopter that lifted him from the fantail of his destroyer in a horse collar on the end of a wire. Then he was on to Saigon by plane where he'd been summoned to testify about the gunfire incident.

"Check your seat belts. We're approaching touchdown at Tan Son Nhut airport. Time in Saigon is 0830 hours."

As he listened to the words, Blake twisted the stem of his $10.00 Timex. Buying the cheap watch and shipping his Elgin home to Beverly was triggered by the only pessimistic thought he had before leaving for the ship. "If I get hit I don't want a VC to get rich."

The controlled voice of the pilot continued, "The weather on landing will be approximately 96 degrees Fahrenheit, 80 percent humidity, with intermittent showers. Keep your seat belts fastened until the aircraft comes to a complete stop." His tone softened as he added, "Have a good stay in Vietnam... And keep your heads down."

As the plane made its approach the passengers stopped talking and when it touched down, as if on signal, everyone roared "ohhh" in unison. It sounded much like the *ohhh* children use when they ask, "ohhh, mom, do we have to?"

Blake didn't make the "oh" sound. Navy commanders who came from a long line of career officers didn't do that, but he felt the same way. He felt bitter for his own reasons. For not getting his destroyer command, for not having time to be with his family, for having his life changed so abruptly for the investigation, but most of all for having to come to this craphole of a country. *The timing's all wrong*, he thought. *Political bargaining, secret diplomacy — no one cares about it anymore, if they ever did. Bastards! After twelve years we're still debating this damn war. At least I'll be able to hang around Saigon until they sort out this investigation.*

At first glance it looked like any other airfield, but as the plane taxied along the strip behind the "follow me" truck, Blake saw bunkers and high observation posts manned by Vietnamese military police. Open bays made with sandbag walls paralleled the strip. He saw mountains of military hardware. Hundreds of transport airplanes idled in hangers alongside what seemed to be an endless line of H-1 Huey helicopters, some painted military green, others in camouflage colors, all waiting their call to battle.

None of the passengers moved for several minutes after the plane came to a stop. The pilot encouraged them by announcing, "You may now de-plane."

In strange silence they walked down the aisle as if their steps were testing for safe footing while moving through a dark passage in an unknown cave, each expecting a vacation in hell.

Blake surveyed the unfamiliar surroundings. The skies were gray and cloudy, the heat oppressive.

As he descended to Vietnamese soil, the humidity shocked his body. Sweat oozed through his skin and dripped across his clean shaven cheeks. His uniform clung to sticky flesh. He heard taxies and Honda motorcycles, and smelled pungent morning wood fires and Asian foods. It reminded him of the foul smell of Hong Kong when a ship first rounded the island from the sea.

I already miss fresh ocean breezes.

He suspected he looked like an officer coming from destroyer duty. His immaculate summer white uniform, with its short sleeved open-collared shirt contrasted with darker airport colors. He felt a bit embarrassed, in this land of warriors, that the only touch of color he wore were three theater and service ribbons pasted like sticks of gum above his left breast pocket.

Blake searched the faces, all strangers among a blurred sea of green. His gaze did follow the swaying hips of a pretty Vietnamese woman with black hair hanging to the waist of her green Ao Dai dress.

"Commander Lawrence?" came a deep voice from behind him.

The voice had a familiar sound. He had heard it before — but where, when? He turned to identify the speaker. Scanning the panorama of foreign faces. "Yes," Blake answered automatically.

"Over here, sir," the resonant voice said. A hand saluted. Blake's eyes focused on the motion of the hand and paused for a moment before going to the face. The lips emitted a familiar sound — like a gravel truck in first gear. "Major Mark Harris, U.S. Marine Corps — from the Rung Sat Special Zone, sir."

Mark's face reminded Blake of the actor Edward G. Robinson, round, thick lips, with "V" shaped eye brows. His hair was cut close on the sides, "white sidewall" style and, Blake surmised, because he couldn't see under Mark's green beret, there was only a shock of short hair on top. His eyes then drifted to a body that was built in the same style as the voice, strong, and rugged. Blake estimated that Harris was about 5 feet 8 inches tall.

"Blake Lawrence, Mark," extending his hand.

The Major stiffened at the familiar use of his first name.

A by-the-book Marine.

Mark offered a right hand that had two crooked fingers which, for Blake made shaking hands feel awkward. Several scars showed on his extended arm.

"Follow me, Commander," Mark said crisply. "Got a vehicle wait'n."

Two men waited by the jeep marked U.S. ADVISORY UNIT RSSZ. Mark introduced Blake to First Lieutenant John Strode and Gunnery Sergeant Benjamin Johnson, a tall, muscled black man.

Mark explained that Lieutenant Strode, dressed in a wrinkle-free camouflage combat uniform and wearing spit-shined boots, was a recent graduate of the Citadel and the District *Cô-Vân* (advisor) in the Can Gio District. The slender, bespectacled Marine officer had flown in to Nha Be that morning in order to drive to Saigon with Mark and the Gunny.

Blake reflected on a Marine wearing glasses. *Usually not sent to hot swampy places where they can fog up — maybe it's the nature of being an advisor, or else they're getting to the bottom of the list and every one else has been toured to 'nam already.*

"Gunny Johnson's our senior non-com. He's a career Marine. Almost got twenty years in the Corps," Mark briefed. "Try'n to convince him to stay for a promotion — maybe become an officer like I did."

So Mark was once a Sergeant, Blake thought. *Maybe that explains the by-the-book stuff.* He noted that the Sergeant's cammys were wrinkled. *Apparently not as careful as a new military school Marine like Strode.*

Mark pointed to Blake's luggage. "We'll leave Gunny here to get your gear checked through. He'll take your sizes, pick up some fatigues, then meet us at NavForV headquarters. That way we can get you in to see your new boss, Rear Admiral Paulson and get on to Nha Be before curfew."

"Nha Be?"

"Yes, sir. It's not far. Only about an hour from Saigon. The Admiral says you'll be stay'n in the boondocks with us."

"How will Gunny get out of here without transportation?" Blake asked, concerned that if he took the only jeep, the Marine sergeant would be stranded,

"Don't worry 'bout me Commanda. Ah gets around Saigon. The Gunny's got lotsa friends!"

For Blake the Gunny's sonorous voice portrayed neither the racial patois of inner city nor southern American negro. The idiom was a bit of both plus a mixture of Marine and lots of messdeck. "You sure you'll be alright? I don't mind waiting." Blake wasn't in any hurry to meet Rear Admiral Paulson.

"No, Sa. You go right on with the Maja. I'll be alright. Thank you, Sa."

"Mark, is there a telephone nearby? I need to call the States. My wife doesn't know I'm in-country yet."

*****

Blake waited near a row of telephone booths in the Hotel Caravelle. His call to the States placed with the operator only minutes before.

He scanned the battery of phones and watched as newsmen and servicemen alike scurried to make their calls to the States. He swept the folded handkerchief across his sweaty brow as he scanned the pock marks on the walls of the curio shops on Tu Do street, the only reminders of the '68 Tet offensive.

"Commander Lawrence — Booth 3."

He dabbed his eyes one more time before pocketing the damp cloth. After he squeezed in and closed the door, Blake glanced at his Timex. He picked up the phone just as the overseas operator was completing her question, "...collect call from Commander Lawrence. Will you accept charges?"

"Yes, Operator. I'll take it."

"Beverly? Its Blake, honey. I'm calling from Saigon."

"Saigon? You were supposed to come home. How did you get there? You were on *Decatur*."

Blake massaged his temple. He wasn't sure if he should mention the investigation and his possible court-martial. He decided to do so, but to play it down.

"I don't like it any more than you do — I have to testify for some investigation — it's routine." He didn't tell her how bitter he felt about losing the command, but he hoped she would sense it and offer a consoling word.

"Those Washington bastards!" Her voice screamed. The words sounded jerky as if she was sucking for breath. "Saigon?" Their marriage had become strained ever since he wrote about wanting to remain at sea to take command of his own destroyer. Beverly had declared strongly in several letters she wanted him home. But this outburst was uncharacteristic because she usually didn't over verbalize, she kept words inside — even her letters were short but often explosive in meaning. Her voice softened. "When will we see you? Ever?"

Almost in a whisper he said, "I'm sorry, honey. You have every reason to be angry. It came as a surprise to me, too. But it's OK. This won't take long. I'll be home soon. Probably by the 4th of July." He brushed a fly away from his nose

"Why? Why the change? You had orders to your precious damn destroyer command." She lashed out, "You should have been going to shore duty. I suppose you're eager to be in Vietnam." She finished coolly. "You're always ready for your next set of orders — like father, like son."

"I'm not eager for anything. Not this time. I feel like hell. " His tone softened and his words stumbled on incoherently. "I'd rather be home, but I don't have a choice. Everyone says Nixon's gonna pull us out. I don't care about the war anymore. I won't get involved."

She gave a sarcastic laugh. "You don't care about it? Won't get involved? You're naive like the rest of the Navy. This isn't that kind of war. Everyone's involved and no one cares! What choice do we have, the children and I?"

"I'm sorry, Honey. I told you the investigation came as a complete surprise. How are the kids?"

"Oh, they're alright. They miss you." It was as if she hadn't heard him the first time or that it had just registered because she added, "Investigation? That sounds terrible."

"Nothing, really. Just something that happened on the ship."

"Will you be flying in helicopters?"

"I doubt it."

"That's dangerous. The papers say helicopters kill most of our men."

He shrugged his shoulders as if she could see him. "Sometimes, I suppose..."

"We had every reason to expect you to come home. You've already been at sea for so very long. Will it never end?"

"I said I'm sorry. You don't understand."

"I don't understand!" she exploded. "I finally do understand! I understand the Navy comes first! I understand the Navy needs this war! I understand your family comes last!"

Blake heard a sucking of breath before she continued. "It isn't like you haven't fought in this war. You were supposed to come home. After shore duty you could have your ship, I would have understood that. What you don't understand is I'm damn tired of being mother and father! I'm tired of the responsibility for fixing cars, and being the only parent to meet the children's teachers! I'm tired of sleeping alone! Your mother liked it, but I hate the Navy and I hate this war. I don't want this for the rest of my life. You don't understand that!"

After that outburst she fell silent and Blake did most of the talking. He repeated, "Don't worry, honey. I'll ride a desk and be home soon, you'll see."

They talked for a moment longer, then she broke into a sobbing goodbye. For Blake there was no flag waving, no get-those-German-bastards, not even "I'll still be here when you return," just the sound of Beverly hanging up the telephone. The sound of plastic on plastic.

*****

Blake cleared his throat to choke back a tear then dabbed a handkerchief into the corner of his eyes.

A feeling of defeat crept over him. The conversation with Beverly, the tiredness he felt after his recent sea duty experiences, and the plane trip drained his mind. He felt like crawling back into the cave-like booth but that would give the wrong impression to the waiting Marines. He stepped out and stretched himself tall to give the look of a seagoing, blue water officer. He stood with an easy erect posture, hands at the seams of his trousers to add to the appearance he wanted to project, of straightness, tallness, and firmness. Only then did he step from the front of that phone booth at the Hotel Caravelle to march toward the waiting jeep, his new companions, and his meeting with the Chameleon.

FOUR

As they continued the jeep ride to call on Rear Admiral Paulson, Blake could still hear his wife's angry voice. "I hate the Navy and I hate this war." He asked himself, *Where is the war?* All he saw was a busy metropolis with smartly dressed business people, ragged peasants, and idle soldiers. He had expected bombs and bullets.

Near the Saigon River, Mark pointed to a giant statue of a Vietnamese man standing in the center of a small park. "One 'a their fuc'n heroes," Mark sneered. "A gook admiral named Tran Hung Dau."

He winced on hearing the Marine officer use the F-word. Wardroom officers seldom said that word. He wasn't sure about the word "gook" yet. He thought it was left over from the Korean war and everybody still used it.

The jeep stopped in front of a building apparently erected before 1954 while the French were still in Vietnam. It was a busy place with Vietnamese and American Navy men scurrying about.

Mark escorted Blake for short visits to several offices, one an introduction to the Chief of Staff, then finally to the Admiral's outer office.

Rear Admiral Frank Paulson wearing green fatigues rose from his desk and stepped forward to meet them. In his early fifties, his clean-shaven, unwrinkled face made him look younger. The Admiral was graying at the temples but otherwise had a full shock of black hair parted in the middle and brushed straight back from a widow's peak. A holstered pearl handled six-shooter hung on a hook behind his desk.

Considering the age of the building and war zone conditions, the Admiral's office was well-appointed with carpeted floors, comfortable furniture, and beautiful oriental lamps. A reproduction of Van Gogh's *The Starry Night* hung on one wall.

Behind the large mahogany desk maps and charts of South Vietnam showed the surrounding "off-shore" waters marked into sectors. Paper silhouettes of ships pinned on the chart showed the positions of the United States Seventh Fleet. A map of the Vietnamese peninsula similarly showed the "in-shore" operating sectors which had already been turned over to the South Vietnamese Navy.

Another map showed the river patrols of an operation called "Gamewarden" — Task Force 116 and 117 called "river rats" who guarded the thousands of shallow, brown water streams in the delta.

The Admiral motioned Blake to take a seat. "Welcome to Vietnam, Commander Lawrence. Major Harris has done a superb job holding down the fort since Commander Weeks got hit. Damn good man, Weeks."

Paulson remained standing and waved his hand toward the chart. His smile was broad and engaging. He spoke slowly with a syrupy tone. "You'll agree, won't you, Major Harris, that the Rung Sat is one of the most fascinating places in all of Vietnam, certainly one of the most strategic. What makes it important is the Long Tau Channel. Only deep water from the ocean to Saigon, and it passes smack dab through the middle of the Rung Sat. Ninety-five percent of all the supplies for this military region come from the sea."

Blake didn't want to hear that. *What I want to know is why the hell am I here? What about the investigation?* He remembered his destroyer C.O.'s cynical warning before he left the ship. "Watch out for Admiral Paulson." Then Captain Johnson had told the story of how the Paulson got the nickname Chameleon. "It was while on duty as a company officer at the Naval Academy. Paulson could be in smiling conversation with a Midshipman at the same time frapping him for ten demerits and two hours loss of weekend liberty. Loves you one minute then changes colors and knifes you the next. Fancies himself a cowboy. Rumor has it he wears six-shooters in Vietnam. Tread softly in his presence, Blake. He's been known to destroy the careers of some awfully good men."

Paulson's smile was disarming. Blake knew there was an explosive personality underneath, but so far the man seemed decent enough. In spite of the warnings, he thought, *Who knows, I might even learn to like him.*

Paulson pointed again to the chart. "Because of the strategic importance of the Long Tau the surrounding Rung Sat area was made a Special Zone. In a way it's a microcosm of our effort in Vietnam. Has its own force of Vietnamese Army, Navy, and Air Force organized as a Joint Command under a Vietnamese Navy Captain named Duc-Lang."

As if he was preaching or giving a pep talk, Paulson pounded his right fist into his left hand, then shook his finger. "The Long Tau channel's the lifeblood of Saigon. It must not be interrupted. It's the only link between Saigon and the ocean — and our American supply ships gotta get through. Our boys ain't gonna be stopped by no frig'n pajama-dressed gooks carry'n pitchforks."

A surge of futility seeped into Blake's mind. *What's the connection between the destroyer incident and all this background stuff.*

The Chameleon sat down in the leather chair behind his desk, then leaned forward. Until now he had been talking through his toothy smile, but now he pinched his words in tight-jawed, let's-get-down-to-business, intensity and motioned with his right hand, palm up. His words accelerated. "I'm worried about a couple of things, Commander. Major Harris knows. After the action where Commander Weeks was hit, we found evidence that some new — very sophisticated rockets were introduced into the Rung Sat. Soviet made. Wire guided — called AT3's. Don't know how many rockets they brought in, or if they stayed in the Rung Sat. We do know if they're used successfully against the ships on the Long Tau, that waterway could be shut down. Probably why they sent in those Russian jobs. Mark my words, now that we've mined Haiphong they'll give it their best shot."

Mark Harris grunted agreement with the Admiral and offered, "Should have let the Air Force nuke the frig'n Red River dikes while we were at it, Admiral." His gravel voice added. "Flood those bastards to their knees. We could still win this frig'n war, sir."

That was when the lights came on. Blake connected the deep resonant quality of Mark's voice. It was Mark who had grabbed the radio from the person called Marquell who called the rounds in on top. He was the one who stopped the gunfire mission that killed Commander Weeks.

"Anyway," Paulson went on, "in response to Mark's statement about the dikes, that decision's behind us now," He again motioned with his hand toward Blake and the words rattled. "I'm not at all satisfied with the Vietnamese effort to track down the rockets. Captain Duc-Lang is the problem. Major Harris tells me that Duc-Lang isn't aggressive. Acts like the Pope himself. Keeps talking about some character named Colonel Tu, but there's absolutely no intel about this guy Tu. At least no recent intel. Oh, we have some history on the man. Was once in the Rung Sat but that was a long time ago. First showed up in 1967, but by now he's either been killed or pulled back to Hanoi. Duc-Lang's either on the take or he's incompetent. Either way I want him relieved."

"The sooner the better as far as I'm concerned, Admiral." Mark Harris ad-libbed.

Then the Admiral said it, so off-handedly that Blake almost missed it. "That's why you're taking over as Senior Advisor in the Rung Sat. The detailers in Washington say you're the only one available on short notice — you're apparently command qualified and you have to be around anyway — for the investigation and — in case there's a court-martial. I really wanted Major Harris to stay on as Senior Advisor. After all, he has the experience — this is his second full tour in Vietnam and he's just received approval to extend for another six months. He even won the Purple Heart and a Silver Star during his first tour as a Company Commander in I Corps." His voice strengthened. "Do I have that right, Mark?"

Mark acknowledged the Admiral's words by nodding his head.

What in the hell do I know about the damn Rung Sat and the brown water navy? The only thing Blake remembered was from a naval reference he read after the gunfire incident. The book said:

Rung Sat Special Zone (RSSZ).

Mission: Protect the Long Tau Channel.

Topography: More that 3000 miles of interlocking streams in a complex area of forest, jungle and swamp. Literal translation: Killer Forest.

Blake had trained to go in-country once — even went through the Navy's SERE training, the acronym for Survival, Escape, Resistance, and Evasion. But every time a chance came to stay at sea, on a destroyer, he had jumped at it. Ever since graduation, he had a straight line to the top mapped out in his mind and it never included duty in Vietnam. Now he was stunned. Thousands of men had already served in-country, but Blake had spent his career at sea, on the rim of the land. He had no understanding of the relationships of war on the ground yet he was to become advisor to the Vietnamese Navy. And that meant land, rivers, and politics. A westerner in an Asian culture.

"Senior Advisor of the Rung Sat Special Zone? Me? For how long?"

"Yes, you. You're command qualified." He was repeating himself. "You were going to a destroyer. You have to be here for the investigation so Bupers made you available for this duty — to finish Commander Weeks' tour — until next March or when the war ends, whichever is soonest." Without hesitation, Paulson continued his explanation of the Rung Sat situation for Blake's benefit. "Mark could do the job but the Senior Vietnamese up here are sensitive to face. Duc-Lang doesn't want a Marine Major for his counterpart — so I need a naval officer, commander or above. You have to be here, so you get the job. Your challenge is to weed out the problem in the Rung Sat. Find those rockets, and get Duc-Lang out of there. The investigation of the gunfire incident at Can Gio isn't finished yet. Because a Vietnamese was also hit the investigation is up at MACV. They tell me it may have been the Marine radioman Marquell that screwed up. But, we're still looking into it. MACV will get in touch with you." Paulson added, "We don't kill our own. And...ah, Washington wants a full report."

Blake tensed and flushed at what he had just heard. *Damn Bupers. Some wacko detailer made the switch. Kill two birds? That's the way those bastards think. And this miserable... — the S.O.B has very casually told me, in front of Harris, that I'm his second choice to be Senior Advisor simply because an oriental Navy Captain doesn't want a Major as his advisor? Or is that it? No! Even though he's been told that the radioman named Marquell is to blame for the gunfire incident, he's implying I may still be at fault. I could have waited at home for the results of this investigation, but he's got me in a vice. He's holding a court-martial over my head to do his bidding. He expects me to find a few lousy rockets and help him get rid of a Vietnamese officer who puts face before the war effort. This is the Chameleon Captain Johnson warned me about.*

The Admiral stood again and continued, "There are other things that bother me. It's been too quiet around here, right, Major? As if the bear's in hibernation. Won't stay this way, so keep alert."

Quiet? Good, Blake thought. *All the better to ride it out.*

Paulson seemed unable to relax or quit talking. "The Advisory effort's been damn good but as we get closer to the end, we'll need to work all the harder. We've turned over almost all of our equipment and the Vietnamese training is getting better all the time. If we do our job right, when we pull out the Vietnamese'll be able to carry on professionally. Remember, you are an advisor. You're in Command of the other U.S. Navy and Marine advisors in your area. You have no Command authority in the Special Zone. but... you are in command — we let the Vietnamese think they are." His eyes changed and his lips closed over his teeth. "Let me warn you. I hold you responsible for the execution of the Rung Sat missions."

Blake felt his skin burn and his heavy brows pinch as he listened to Paulson give him his second threat. *He's already warned me about the results of the investigation, and now he's warning me I'm responsible to control the Rung Sat war zone but without any authority. This is probably why they call him the Chameleon — the way he leads: carrot and hammer.*

Paulson faced Blake and spread his feet, lacing his fingers at his mid-section he said. "Let me know immediately if you detect any relaxation of effort in the area. We know the VC and North Vietnamese are in there, don't we, Major.

They're just waiting for us to let down our guard." Then the Admiral paused, "So far I've done all the talking. Any questions?"

Blake thought a moment then asked a question he thought would get a short answer, "Yes, sir. I guess I'll have to learn quick, but truthfully I don't know anything about the Rung Sat and even less about the Vietnamese people."

Admiral Paulson's lips expanded into a wide white smile. "Good question. You will learn but it won't be easy. Here's what I expect." Sitting again he spun in his chair to look at the wall map and the rat-a-tat began again. "I expect each advisor to become the world's leading expert on the functional and geographical area of his assignment. Know the size, ethnic make-up, religion, and political breakout of the population. Know the major personalities including their family name, age, education, place of birth, strengths, weaknesses. Know the history of the area, its physical characteristics, potential for development, VC infrastructure, enemy order of battles. Leave anything out, Major?"

Mark smiled and shook his head.

Paulson spun back to face Blake. "Don't get discouraged. I don't expect it over night. But, I'd say you ought to have a good handle on it in a few weeks. Any other questions?"

Blake didn't want to hear another answer like the last, but now he felt even more bitter than before. Already all he could think of was going home. "There is one more thing, Admiral. I...ah, where do we stand on the peace talks? Does it look like the Americans'll be pulled out soon?"

"Not getting much more out here than what the papers say. I personally think we're making progress. Hope we don't give away too much of the farm. Agree, Major? Trouble is we've been here so long, hardly anyone remembers why or how we got here. Truth is it just crept up on us. Found ourselves subsidizing a French Colonial war against the Viet Minh, and backing Bao Dai against Ho Chi Minh. Kennedy wanted in, then by the time he wanted out it was too late. Here we are twelve years later trying to figure a way to get out."

Ask a simple question and you get a lecture on Vietnamese-American history. Should have learned from his answer to the first question.

Mark cleared his voice and grunted, "Hope the bosses in Washington don't forget the blood and bodies that went into this thing."

"Agree, Major," Paulson responded. "In any event, it's all up in the air right now. The drawdown of forces is going on at a steady pace. Be ready to pull out on short notice. This is an election year and the President is getting a lot of heat. Our involvement could stop quickly. Frankly I'll be surprised if the Vietnamese ever stop fighting. That's where you come in. If the VC are able to close the Long Tau Channel and cut off Saigon from supplies, the Reds could use that as a bargaining chip at the peace talks. Just as we're using the mining of Haiphong."

The Admiral's aide poked his head in the door and gave a signal.

"My horse-holder just gave me the sign. Have another meeting." The voice sped up and his words flashed another warning. "Remember, you have three responsibilities. Finish out the Vietnamization process — leave 'em strong. No American heroics — Washington doesn't want casualties. But above all, protect the Long Tau Channel. Oh, and a fourth — get rid of Duc-Lang"

Gunny drove and Mark sat in the back so he could talk over Blake's left shoulder. Strode sat next to Mark.

As the jeep left the teeming metropolis, Blake felt dull and listless. Mark pointed out the black market area with hundreds of people. "It's called the Sun Market, sir."

Blake only half listened to his new companions as he scanned the market. The midday heat, the dust, Mark's cigar smoke, and the blue fumes from hundreds of cars and motorcycles in bumper-to-bumper Saigon traffic burned Blake's eyes. Through the blue haze of Honda smoke he could see betel-nut-chewing women hawking goods set out for display on low tables. They protected the merchandise from the sun by erecting ponchos and canvas liners on poles, just high enough for a Vietnamese to walk under. He saw the taller Americans stooping and weaving among the tables and stalls, some in animated conversation, some just looking.

"That's Cholon over in there, Commander." Mark pointed to a section of the city off to the right. "The fuc'n Chinese live there. Where most of the whorehouses are. It's where the real money is. They say the fuc'n Jews are the bankers of Europe and the Chinese are the bankers of Asia. Probably where Duc-Lang hangs out — fucking a concubine."

Mark's hard-hat mentality and irritating language only added to the discomfort of the heat and the burnt petroleum smell Blake was inhaling. He thought of the differences between Vietnam and his blue water destroyer. He was used to the refinements of a wardroom, even in a war. It wasn't that he hadn't heard messdeck language before. After all it was often used by the sailors aboard ship, but he preferred not to use the F-word. He never thought using it equated to manliness. What startled him was that everyone here used it, officers, and enlisted alike, even the Admiral, in a variation, all the time — as an adjective for everything.

The other thing he noted was the thousands of Oriental faces who peered into the jeep. At first he felt nervous, because, coming from sea duty, he had been led to believe "they" were dangerous — ready to kill on the spot. So far all he had seen was normal curiosity. After a time Blake relaxed and thought about his predecessor, the AT3 rockets, and the firefight. He asked, "Major, what happened to Commander Weeks?"

Mark's chin jutted over Blake's shoulder and he gestured with his hand. "Well, we were in the gook village of Can Gio for an inspection — they always have trouble in that town — when we got a tip that the North Vietnamese were bring'n in a boat. Must'a been a setup, because we got there late and the fuc'n VC jumped us. Before we could get help they damn near overran us. Everybody agrees our radioman Corporal Marquell was high on something that day. Whatever reason, he called your frag in on top of our positions. We lost communications, and before we got it back you unloaded on us. Suppose your gunfire saved our ass, but it wasn't me that asked for it on top — may have been one of the VN Officers. Your rounds stopped their charge and took out the VC. We heard your warning and dug in. It was a fluke Commander Weeks and the gook officer took it. Rounds were explod'n overhead and a fragment must have ricocheted — Weeks lost an arm and a piece lodged in his chest. Took out the VN officer right away. Most blame Marquell because Commander Weeks got hit. But he was scared, and we haven't been able to prove he was on the weed. Weeks died during his medevac flight home."

Blake wanted to know more about the radioman who apparently had such an effect on his life, "What about the Corporal?"

"Noth'ns happened yet. Gunny's all over his ass. Sooner or later we'll catch him us'n the shit, and when we do..."

Slowly the traffic thinned and after a time they were on route 15 heading for Nha Be. On the way, they passed an area where Blake could see huge petroleum storage tanks.

"That's the Dutch World tank farm. Those fuc'n tanks hold the fuel for Saigon and the surrounding area. As the tanks go, so goes the war hereabouts. By the way, Dutch World is where the Marbos live. Nice people. Civilians. Work for the Dutch World oil company. You'll like them, Anthony and Joanna. He's the European manager. They have us over from time to time. An opportunity to relax. Always a welcome change."

Lieutenant Strode, the bookish looking Marine picked up the monologue. There was no doubt his dialect was deep South Carolina. "We'a almost to the Village of Nha Be, Command'a. In quiet'a times, it was an easy drive from Saigon for a aft'anoon picnic. It's a peninsula juttin' like a compass needle point'n Southeast, right through the middle of the Rung Sat and directly toward Vung Tau on the ocean. From h'a to Vung Tau's only 'bout 38 kilometers as the crow flies. They tell me in the old days Nha Be was like a fuc'n vacation place, quiet an restful. In those days, the chil'en played und'a the shade of beautiful trees 'long the riv'a. But that was befo'. Now it's too fuc'n busy. The rice paddies and wat'a buffalo 're still he'a, but the best pieces of prop'ty were fenced for our base a long time ago."

Gunny slowed the jeep for the first time since they left the outskirts of Saigon. They would pass through Nha Be on the only street. It was late afternoon now and the people were up from their afternoon naps. It seemed to be a pleasant place. Many, even men, were walking hand in hand. Blake could see that Americans were accepted and even welcomed because as the jeep passed, shopkeepers nodded their heads and he heard, "*Chao Cô-Vân My, manh gioi!* (Hello, American advisors, good health)." His companions returned the greetings with waves.

Young girls smiled shyly as they strolled in their traditional Vietnamese Ao Dai dresses. Children waved and shouted. They laughed and rapidly said, over and over, the only American word they knew, "Okay, okay, okay."

By then Blake's rapid entry into Vietnam had caused the tonal voices to mix with his memory of Admiral Paulson's warning. "Okay, okay — no heroics, but protect the Long Tau Channel — okay, okay."

FIVE

Like any mariner, Blake surveyed the morning with an examination of the sky. *Monsoon clouds*, he thought. *Drifting — could mean rain later today."* Next he scanned the horizon where instead of blue seas he saw jungle, rice paddies, and a few small huts. *What a contrast from destroyer duty. Here I am wearing camouflaged combat fatigues instead of khakis, the deck doesn't roll, I'm taking my first ride in a Huey, and it's brown water and green jungle as far as I can see. Where would I rather be? Almost anywhere. In command of my own ship — with the wife and kids — even a desk job in DC. Anywhere except this ugly swampland.*

The airstrip at the Nha Be base paralleled the river. Its tarmac glistened from the morning rain. A dark Huey gunship waited near a bunker where several Vietnamese airmen scurried about in the dim morning light. Some inspected the chopper, others loaded boxes of ammunition. A gaunt looking Vietnamese soldier wearing wire-rimmed glasses sat hunched against the sandbag bunker. His knees were bent and his feet were flat on the ground Asian style. His arms rested on the tops of his knees. One hand held a tin cup, the other rose and fell as if by habit to push ill fitting wire frames up to his eyes from the tip of his nose where they continuously slid.

The sound of an engine and squealing tires interrupted Blake's examination of his surroundings.

Mark Harris slammed on the brakes of a jeep and jumped out. Stocky and tough looking, he approached at a quick step. His camouflaged fatigues matched Blake's, but the beret was Marine green.

Mark snapped a salute. "Morning Commander Lawrence. Sorry if I'm late. Marines are usually on time."

"Not to worry. I came early. Wanted to get more of a feel for this place."

"You'll get plenty of that, sir. Now, if you're ready, let's get to it." Mark started to spread a chart across the top of the bunker, but stopped and shot a finger at the bespectacled Vietnamese soldier and said in resonant baritones, "*Manh gioi*, Sergeant Trieu."

The crouching man raised his head from the teacup but only nodded. He didn't get up and salute.

"Who's he?" Blake asked, detecting a touch of disrespect in the soldier's response.

"Sergeant Trieu's your translator when you go out with the gooks, Sir. Goes everywhere you go. Speaks good English." He lowered his voice, "Would you believe that fuc'n gook used to be a professor, history...or someth'n."

Blake walked toward the soldier and extended his hand. "Good morning, Sergeant Trieu. Look forward to working with you. Hope you're good at your job. I don't know much Vietnamese."

Trieu jumped to his feet, saluted then bowed. Before grasping the outstretched hand he pushed the glasses back to his eyes. "Oh, sir, I am fluent in your language, sir. You will see."

Mark moved out of ear-shot of Trieu and spread the chart. "My ground brief won't take long. I'll try to get you up to speed quick. Gett'n you in-country from sea duty didn't take long, did it? Only a little more than a month since Commander Weeks took it."

Ya, and screwed up my life to do it.

The two Americans huddled over the laminated map. Mark made a rotating motion with his hand. "This is the Rung Sat Special Zone — kinda pie shaped." Then with his crooked right forefinger he traced the long river from Vung Tau near the ocean all the way to Saigon.

"Reason the Rung Sat's a special military zone is it surrounds the Long Tau Channel. As the Admiral said, its the only river with water deep enough for the big tankers and ammo ships to get from the ocean to Saigon. Long Tau's actually a connection of three separate rivers, but since '62 it's been the only channel we've kept dredged. That's why we gotta protect it."

Guard a river surrounded by jungle and swamps? Not an easy job.

"Looks ugly and menacing on the chart," Blake offered.

Speaking through teeth that held a half burned cigar while pointing on the chart to the Southeast, Mark answered. "Let's hope you don't find out how menacing, too soon. Here's where you're to meet *Dai Ta* Duc-Lang...here...at the village of Can Gio. Strode, Gunny, and Doc 're already down there. You haven't met Doc yet — he's our Navy corpsman and a damn good one. He's on his second tour, just like me — was my company corpsman on our first tour up North. Awarded the Silver Star for action up there. Still don't think it's a good idea for you to meet Duc-Lang for the first time at that place. Town's always been a problem. There's been unrest there ever since Commander Weeks got hit."

"Couldn't very well say no." Blake shrugged. Fourth of July came and went and though he had already been at the base at Nha Be for two weeks his days had been filled with office work — getting to know the job and the men. "I still haven't met the man I'm supposed to advise. Met his deputy, Lieutenant Colonel Phat — he's sure strange looking — looks more Indian than Vietnamese. Besides, I'm told Americans need to get out and do more among the people. Accompanying Duc-Lang at that village's annual fishing celebration should do something for our image."

Mark stood erect to face his taller boss and shook his head. "True, but...well, I just don't trust Duc-Lang. Spends most of his fuc'n time in Saigon. Either he's play'n politics, got a concubine or running a black market operation. Or all of the above." Mark took the cigar out of his mouth. He tapped off the long ash. "Besides, he isn't aggressive. Don't know what's wrong with him. Lost face when Commander Weeks died. They're supposed to look after their advisors ya know — the senior ones. Maybe he doesn't think the spirits are right. He's a fuc'n Buddhist ya know. Practices Confucianism or something. Who knows what his problem is? We're always havin' to put up with the fuc'n Oriental mind. Don't trust 'em. Been lucky no shippin's been hit on the Long Tau recently. Advisors 're nervous. Too quiet — too long. Listen, Commander, the fuc'n VC are out there. You better believe they're out there and as long as we sit on our asses, they love it."

"What about these Soviet weapons Admiral Paulson talked about?"

"Same thing. We know they're out there. But Duc-Lang doesn't seem to give a damn one way or the other. I tell you, Commander, the first thing you gotta do is get Duc-Lang outa here. Get that fucker fired!"

"Why hasn't Admiral Paulson done it already?"

"Tried, but the Vietnamese wouldn't do it. There's somthing different about Duc-Lang – don't know what. Anyway, the recommendation must come from the field and Marine majors don't fire Navy captains. You gotta fire that fucker, Commander."

Blake felt his brow wrinkle and his eyes harden as they steadied on Mark. *How can I have him fired when I don't even know the man? I hate to be pushed. Especially about people. He's probably right. This is his second tour in-country. Bound to know something. But I already dislike this place and I don't need another harangue about Duc-Lang like I got from the Admiral in Saigon. And I'm already tired of all this messdeck language.* "Ok, Mark," he said quietly. "I'll watch him, but..." his tone hardened. "I'll decide about Duc-Lang in my own time."

Mark's shoulders bunched. Returning Blake's hardened eyes he said, "Won't listen will you? Admiral Paulson said it and I've told ya. What'll it take? You gonna let another fuc'n American buy it?"

Blake felt the hair at the base of his neck tighten. "Who the hell you think you're talking to, some boot? Sit on it, Mark! I just got here, but you may as well know... unlike you, I don't want to be here. I don't like this place... but I'll make the best of it. All I want is to get home to my wife and kids – and salvage what's left of my career. You have experience in 'Nam but there's a lot besides the tactical situation I don't understand: the country, the people, their culture. Neither you nor the Admiral's going to stampede me. You have the wrong guy. I'm no robot. Get off it — until I get my bearings. And I don't want to hear about Commander Weeks again. "

Ignoring Blake's warning, Mark groused, "Well, don't say I didn't warn ya."

"I won't forget, Mark. But I haven't even met the man. If you're right, I'll be the first to say so. Until then I need more time to learn what makes Duc-Lang tick. Drop it! And clean up your language."

Mark dropped his cigar and stomped it into the ground. "Still don't like the feel of that fuc'n village. It's real goddamn tense. I'd feel a whole lot better if ya let me stay down there with you."

Mark had retreated, even though he ignored the caution about foul language. It was as if he were the kind who tried to bully and only gave respect if you stood up to him. Blake accepted the change and softened his tone. "Thanks Mark. I know you're thinking about my best interest and safety, but I'll be alright. You need to be back here minding the store."

"Okay Commander, you win. But I hope you're right."

The chopper engine started with a whine. Above the turbine noise Mark shouted, "You'll get a better feel for the Rung Sat when ya see it from the air." Mark seemed more relaxed now. As if he'd got it all off his chest — done his duty. "You'll get used to these Huey choppers," he went on. "Vietnamese pilots have a tendency to hot dog, 'specially for a new advisor, but they settle down. They're pretty fuc'n good."

Blake strapped on his flight helmet, picked up his CAR-15, then followed Mark and Sergeant Trieu to the chopper. They climbed into the rear compartment, where two Vietnamese Air Force gunners stood next to miniguns. Sergeant Trieu joined one of the gunners and struck up a conversation.

Because of the *wap, wap* sound of the rotors and the whine of the turbines, Mark had to tap Blake on the shoulder to get his attention. "Pick an ammo box to sit on," he shouted. "Not very fancy, but it'll do. Plug your headset into the intercom system—over there."

Mark clicked on his lip mike and said, "Okay, Lieutenant Ha, let's climb out like we were on a regular recon flight, except let's stay at altitude today. I want to show Commander Lawrence the Rung Sat."

The Huey lifted about two feet off the ground then air taxied sideways to clear the open hanger. The pilots went through the check-off list as they maneuvered to a takeoff position at the end of the runway. The helicopter jerked and held a hover for one last respectful passenger check. "Everything okay, Sirs?" the Vietnamese pilot asked.

The two Americans gave the thumbs-up sign.

Blake felt the chopper jerk, surge, and move forward. As it picked up speed, the pilot changed the attitude of the helicopter so that the nose pointed on a slant toward the ground with the tail extended higher. In this attitude the aircraft continued to gain speed. As they approached the end of the runway, with the river just ahead, the pilot eased the nose of the chopper smoothly into a flat in-flight profile, then without warning pulled the chopper into a sharp vertical climb.

High over the Nha Be complex the pilot did a hot dog turn and dived for the ground. Caught by surprise, Blake found himself looking almost straight down as the chopper screamed straight toward the runway. His body tensed. He gripped the back of the co-pilot's seat and squeezed. *Now that's show-boat. Hope these jokers know how to pull out.*

The chopper gained speed and buzzed back across the runway where the ground crew waved to them.

As they zoomed by, Blake relaxed and remembered what his mind had captured at the apex of the chopper's flight. For the first time he saw the entire base at Nha Be, as well as the bend in the river. He saw the peninsula jutting like a compass needle pointing to the Southeast, right through the middle of the Rung Sat, directly at Vung Tau on the ocean. He also saw the Nha Be river swinging sharply from the North and joining the Vam Co on its way south to where it spilled into the ocean. He could imagine the old days when it was a vacation place instead of a war place. In those days it would have been quiet and restful, with children playing under the shade of the beautiful trees along the water.

Staying low the chopper headed Southeast skimming the water. The opposite bank rushed toward them. At the last possible moment the aircraft popped up, just high enough to clear, then fly a few feet above the rice paddies. In that nose-down attitude they were so close to the ground that the chopper appeared to touch the rice stalks just before they parted to make a path. The helo made a swoosh sound as it sped by farmers working in their fields and water buffalo standing knee deep in mud. Some of the people waved, some were indifferent, but most look irritated. The water buffalo reacted much the same as the people, plodding on, indifferent, irritated.

Cart paths wove their way between rice paddies and occasional wooden structures. Thatched roof farmhouses clustered to form a micro-community.

Ahead Blake saw the end of the rice fields and the beginnings of tall trees, and beyond, a dense forest. As they approached the wooded area the pilot again jerked the chopper into a steep climb and the next thing Blake knew they were at 1500 feet.

Mark nudged him and pointed to button 2 on the intercom, then said into his lip mike, "How do ya hear me?"

"Okay, Mark."

"We can stay up on this circuit and not bother the pilots. How do ya like the Huey so far?"

"The bird's okay. Not sure about the pilot."

"First time in a chopper?"

"No. I flew a few times in Navy helos. On those occasions I had an absolute feeling of trust — but with these young Vietnamese pilots I'm not so sure!"

"These fuc'n VNAF pilots can scare the shit out of ya sometimes. We usually fly low along the channel and check the banks for signs of infiltration. At least it keeps the VC heads down. Today, we'll stay high so you can see the whole place."

Mark switched frequency. "Okay Lieutenant Ha, let's head for Nhon Trach."

Wind creased Blake's face and dried his sweaty uniform as the aircraft now flew hot and straight.

"Look, off to your right, there, sir...where I'm point'n." Mark said. "That's check point five. See the PBR's with their bows up in the bank," Blake couldn't see the boats at first but by following Mark's arm, past his crooked finger, sure enough, there they were, two black patrol boats blending with the mud and the river.

As the chopper continued Northeast, for the first time Blake could see large portions of the Rung Sat Special Zone. From that altitude he saw the snake-like path of the Long Tau and the character of the surrounding swampland. The wide, brownish channel had a lazy look about it. Patrol boats idled as if they were on a holiday, and lethargic fishing junks moved near the banks, all with no apparent schedule.

Except for a few rice paddies the surrounding ground was a tidal swamp — barren of any roads or bridges. The entire area was interlaced with a multitude of streams and canals. It looked impenetrable.

Blake felt apprehensive about this country. It was the kind of caution that tells the brain not to drive too fast on an icy road. Here his gut told his brain, *Don't get lost in the Rung Sat.*

It seemed an unnatural place for people, yet for Blake it was strangely beautiful. It went through his mind that maybe God made the area so desolate and so forbidding because He wanted people excluded. But forbidden or not, people were here.

Mark interrupted Blake's thoughts. "Rung Sat translates 'Killer Forest', sir, but..." He pointed to the dense jungle ahead. "There's the real Indian country, Commander. It's the Northern boundary of the Zone. Called Nhon Trach. In the early 50s, the Viet Minh began their activity right down there. Been a haven for bandits and pirates throughout history. Nhon Trach's the roughest fuc'n country in the Rung Sat. But that's another story. "

Blake marveled at the forest he saw. A jungle of tall, dense mangrove and nippa palm umbrellas, laced with small streams. But the brightness of the greens really struck him. He'd never seen colors so rich — with so much glistening brilliance.

Continuing to point to the Nhon Trach region, Mark said. "That's where Dai Ta Duc-Lang thinks the mysterious Colonel Tu resides." Mark switched frequencies and told the pilot, "OK, head South now — follow the channel."

"How come neither you nor Admiral Paulson seem to worry about Colonel Tu?"

"The Admiral doesn't pay him much store because he figures if Tu's still out there since '67, he's ineffective. Too long in the Rung Sat jungle."

"Five years in that crap? If he's so ineffective, why the concern about my visit to Can Gio village?"

Mark didn't answer.

SIX

Two days before Blake took his first chopper flight over the Rung Sat, Do Van Nghi, bone skinny but tall for a South Vietnamese, sat hunched over, cross-legged on the ground, writing on an improvised table. His black hair spilled across shallow cheeks and eyes. Several strands of chin hair formed a modest beard.

Deep in the jungle of Nhon Trach, Do Van Nghi sat in a subterranean room no more than fifteen feet long and six feet wide. Carved out of bare dirt with sections of trees wedged as supports for the overhead the tunnel's damp walls and muddy floor gave off a raw, musty smell. A fading beam of light projected through a cavity onto a wooden bedboard where a piece of rice paper lay protected from the moisture and dampness of the mud pit.

Nghi's mind drifted from his task of writing a letter to Colonel Tu. He marveled that he, Do Van Nghi, was now the leader of Doi 6, for it wasn't that long ago that Nghi had resisted becoming a guerrilla. Born in the South in 1938, in the village of Binh Trung, he was drafted by the Viet Cong from his farm in August of 1967. The first two years were agonizing. He wished only to be a farmer. He resisted political indoctrination and his probationary period did not go well. He intended to escape at the first opportunity. The only thing that held him was his fear of Senior Colonel Tu. Guerrilla leaders told him the Colonel was a fanatic and ruthless man. Anyone who ran, sooner or later would be found and dealt with. Regardless of the threats, Nghi intended to escape.

It was in 1969, during the latter part of his training that the Colonel and two other guerrillas arrived in a small sampan. Tu walked into the base camp from the jungle wearing the traditional black clothing of a working peasant. A K-54 hung loosely around his waist. The other two men were armed with rifles.

Nghi pretended not to notice as the three men greeted the cadre leaders then spoke in quiet, serious tones near the dirt bunker which served as headquarters.

Later that day, the members of the cadre, all recruits from South Vietnam, were called together. They bowed and entered the crudely thatched covering in polite silence. Each sat in the traditional way, feet flat on the ground, body hunched forward, arms folded across bent knees. In this position they were relaxed and comfortable. They would not move again until the meeting ended more than two hours later.

The cadre leader introduced Senior Colonel Tu as the commander of Doan 12, and his companions as members of the Doan's political section.

Colonel Tu stepped forward and bowed slightly. Nghi expected a younger man. Because of the strands of gray through his moderately long black hair, he estimated the Colonel to be in his late forties. His beard and mustache were trimmed, giving the impression he had been trained to military standards. Nghi could tell he was a Northerner because he was taller than most guerrillas. Tu fit

Nghi's image of a guerrilla leader except for his speech. Tu's use of the language was clearly that of an educated man. He used formal sentences, sprinkled occasionally with words Nghi didn't understand. After only a few years in a French classroom, Nghi had no more than a rudimentary ability to read and write.

Senior Colonel Tu bowed a second time before reminding them, in father-like tones. "Our country's early development was influenced by both India and China. But we have always retained our strong individuality. Even under the long domination by Chinese rulers we developed a culture which preserved our own identity. Since the greatest of the Le rulers, Le Thanh-Ton, joined the two in 1471, the kingdom of Champa and that of Annam have been as one."

Senior Colonel Tu stroked his chin hair and continued, "Ever since the war that brought the Japanese, a long struggle has existed to reunite the North and the South. Ho Chi Minh, who is in Hanoi, has lived only to reunite all of Vietnam as one nation. Ho is the greatest leader in the long history of Vietnam. He brought Communism to the North and it has been successful. We have achieved self-sufficiency. The North has had great successes in industrialization. The people are happier now than ever before. Communism will also bring the South a new way of life. It will do for the South the same things it has done for the North."

Do Van Nghi remembered how impressed he was by Colonel Tu's confident style, the power of his words and a deep sense of sincerity. Tu's sunken eyes scanned the group of thirty-five probationers before he continued. "Ho Chi Minh's determination to be free from foreign influence resulted in forming the Front for the Liberation of the South. Communist cadres are now throughout South Vietnam and you are joining this elite force. You will be the leaders of a new Vietnam. You must unquestionably believe in the rightness of the concept of one Vietnam — without foreign domination or influence. You must believe in the will of Ho Chi Minh. Be patient," he pleaded. "An example of patience: I began my infiltration from Hai Duong Province in the North in January of 1966. I took the train to Quang Binh City. From there I began to walk. First I walked through Ha Tinh and Vin Lynh Provinces of North Vietnam. Then I passed along the chain of Trong Son mountains of Laos, Kontum and Cambodia. By late spring of 1966, the group I traveled with arrived in Kho Sanh, on the Cambodian border. From there I continued my march. It was not until the winter of 1967 that I arrived in the Rung Sat to take up my duties as Commander of Doan 12. More than a year after the journey began — patience!"

Colonel Tu extended his hands as if welcoming the probationers. "Join me," he said. "Our quest may take 50 years or even 100, but we will succeed."

After that speech, in 1969, Nghi no longer resisted the Viet Cong, and even resolved to dedicate his life to the Colonel's cause. Now, in 1972, he was a confident Doi Commander following, with the rest of his band, that same great leader.

He remembered the time when he first arrived in the Rung Sat to be the leader of Doi 6. He had found the guerrilla unit at a low state of training, but with the help of Colonel Tu's headquarters staff and special rocket training, it was now a much improved organization. His own attitudes about fighting the

Americans had been finally accepted, because, through patience and by example, he showed the men and women how they could live off the land, even the Rung Sat. It was a Spartan life, but they needed little.

It was time to leave to conduct his first attack using the new Soviet rocket against a ship on the Long Tau Channel. But Nghi was determined to finish the letter he was painstakingly writing to his Senior Colonel at his Doan 12 forward headquarters.

The rays that flickered across the paper provided just enough light for him to direct his pen as he wrote in Quoc-ngu, the Romanized version of the Vietnamese language.

Dear Comrade Tu:

Although I was able to transmit most of what I am now writing before our radio failed, I am sending this letter with Tam Ha to be certain that you received the information. It is my hope that Tam Ha will find the replacement radio parts in the village of Nhon Trach after he delivers this to you.

As you directed, I am now Commander of Doi 6. My movements from Long An to here were difficult and took a long time because of the need to remain concealed from the enemy.

Most of the base camps in this place have been hit and much rice has been lost. Thi, the previous commander, was killed by the Rung Sat Provincial Reconnaissance Unit.

I found morale and physical conditions serious when I arrived. Our strength is greater now. We have twenty-two personnel including fourteen women. Seven of these have been recently recruited and are serving probation. Morale is now higher and all comrades are aggressive and fearless. We are committed to our mission, and as soon as I complete this letter to you, I will depart to attack a ship on the Long Tau using the new weapon.

It was necessary to use 6,000 piasters to buy rice and other needed articles. I request that you send me that amount of money as well as an amount to sustain our welfare until Tet.

Nam Ho's wife gave birth to a boy in mid-August. His family is well. He has already departed to the place to conduct the assassination as you ordered.

I have nothing more to report. I send my greatest respect and look forward to your visit to this area soon after I return from this attack. Your presence at our victory party will greatly enhance morale.

Humbly signed,
Do Van Nghi

Nghi folded the wafer thin paper and wrapped the letter in folds of cloth. He placed it carefully in a worn U.S. Army ammunition pouch.

Then he closed his eyes, rested his arms across his knees, and turned the palms of his hands upward. From this position he recited to himself the message of the "the Enlightened one," Siddhartha Gautama Buddha.

"Man is born to suffer and he suffers from one life to the next. Craving is the cause of suffering. The cure for craving is non attachment. Non attachment is attained by the eight fold path of right conduct, right effort, right intentions, right livelihood, right meditations, right mindfulness, right speech, and right views."

This could be my last letter, he reflected, but if I die, I die. Life is in the hands of Buddha.

The sound of a woman's voice startled him. "Nghi, it is time to go."

Quickly closing the flap of the canvas pouch, he strapped on the symbol of his new leadership, a K-54 pistol. Nghi climbed the wood and mud ladder leading out of the small tunnel they had dug only two weeks before.

He looked around the base camp. The twilight of a full moon illuminated a handsewn Viet Cong flag. Faded and torn, half red, half blue with a gold star in the center, it hung from a nearby tree.

"Now we can move," he said. "The Rung Sat helicopters will be on the ground at Nha Be and the patrol boats will be gone from the back rivers. Are the boats loaded?"

Co Hang, the sixteen year girl who had called to him, stepped forward. She responded subserviently, "Yes, comrade Nghi. All is ready." Dressed in loose black pajamas like other guerrillas, she was set apart by a red bandanna wrapped across her forehead and tied at the back of her head. Ordinarily Nghi wouldn't let anyone wear bright colors on an operation, but Co Hang had told him it was her favorite color. He accepted it as a residual sign of her teen age and because red was one of the colors of their flag.

The women in his Doi ranged in age from 16 to 23 and were the ones trained to carry and use the heavy rocket and mortar weapons. They were expert at setting, aiming, and firing. Nine guerrillas would go this time, in three sampans. Only one would be a woman.

Co Hang seemed impatient and nervous. *Normal,* Nghi thought. *It's her first operation.*

There were several reasons why he had selected Hang from the other women to train for this special mission. Foremost, she was very bright with exceptional hand-to-eye coordination. Most of all she came from the village of Can Gio, where most people expressed fanatical hatred for the Americans. She was also strong and seemed reliable. All qualities necessary to test the new weapon.

Tam Ha, Nghi's lieutenant, stood nearby holding the broken radio. Built differently than most Vietnamese, Tam Ha had the sturdy, powerful body of a weight lifter or gymnast and legs that could run all day.

Nghi handed Tam Ha the ammunition pouch which contained his letter to Colonel Tu. They bowed, but no words were spoken. Tam Ha knew his mission — deliver the letter and get the radio repaired. He departed at a trot along the jungle trail toward Nhon Trach.

Nghi and the others went in the opposite direction. They also trotted, but along a different path under the heavy umbrella of nipa palms, where monkeys chattered and tropical birds cried warnings of invisible animals preying among the thick vegetation.

Co Hang, a man named Chi, and six others, followed by Nghi soon arrived at the small cove where the sampans were hidden. Nghi checked the fishing nets and poles needed to disguise their escape. These fishing boats were just like others that plied the Rung Sat rivers and streams, except for the one in which Nghi would travel. A fiberglass case and control unit for the new Russian rocket lay in the bottom. The other sampans each held a B-40 rocket launcher.

No one spoke as the girl climbed in first. The men followed and Nghi pushed off.

The lead sampan soon left the cover of the nipa palm as it entered the stream called Rach Dong. The other sampans followed.

The men poled the boats quickly to the turn at Tac Ong, which would take them to the Song Dong Tranh.

As they approached the river they hugged the long shadows of the shoreline. At one point they stopped and pretended to be fishing until they were certain there were no other boats in either direction. When all appeared clear, they turned right and paddled swiftly.

Ordinarily it would not take them more than a half hour on this short stretch, but it was almost dark and they were in the most vulnerable time period. It was not unusual for Navy craft to linger on the Dong Tranh late in the day to ambush VC traffic.

They carefully made the turn into the Song Dua, where Nghi ordered the three sampans to start their engines. He knew it would be dangerous, but, he told himself, "They had to take the chance in order to have better control in the current."

After a time Nghi began searching for the small inlet of the Rach Tac Be. Even though they had rehearsed the operation three times, small streams like the Tac Be were hard to find in the dim moonlight.

"Now — turn. Over there," he whispered and pointed.

Two of the boats cut their engines and eased into the narrow stream. The other one continued on in the main river toward the second ambush site: the place the Americans called "Hanging Tree Bend."

They arrived on the low tide when the swamp water was only about six inches deep. Nghi poled stealthily until his boat was just above the bottom. He knew on their return they might have to wade in as much as three feet of mud and water so he ordered them to lift the boats and reverse their direction in preparation for retreat.

Co Hang silently picked up two of the four rockets and strapped them on her hips, then in a practiced motion, eased the suitcase-like backpack over her shoulders and adjusted the load evenly.

Chi carried the rifle and took the point, while Nghi strapped on the other two missiles and followed. The three, in single file, followed by the men from the second boat, trudged along a ravine.

Nghi recognized the change from the odor of backwater to the smells of a brinewater mixture of fresh and salt. He motioned the others to spread out. He whispered, "We are near the main channel. Rest until it is time to take final positions,"

Nghi watched as Chi fell asleep easily, but Co Hang's eyes remained open.

Nghi cupped his ear to listen for ship noises above the splashing, gurgling sounds of the channel. Hearing none he told Nang, "It's alright — there are no ships. Sleep now."

They relaxed and soon dozed.

*****

In the morning, a crack of light on the horizon signaled it was time to move. "We must hurry." Nghi had been on many operations and knew the territory well. "The Rung Sat sun rises quickly."

As they approached the river bank, Nghi scanned the area carefully. He selected a piece of high ground set back from the bend. A place where they could see the Long Tau Channel in both directions. Much of the area had been defoliated, but the place he selected for the ambush was one that the American Air Force had missed. It still had considerable trees and vegetation.

Nghi's team worked together to dig a small pit with a thatch of fresh ferns. The other group took a supporting position and also dug in.

Co Hang unloaded her suitcase and assembled it so the railings on the lid of the case could be used as a rocket launcher. Silently she and Nghi readied the missiles. They wired the batteries, control stick, and periscopic unit as they had been taught by the North Vietnamese Sergeant from Doan 12, then Nghi ordered, "Co Hang, Chi take your final positions."

He walked around the trench trying to visualize how it would look from the air. His greatest enemy would be the Rung Sat helicopters. Once satisfied that the cover was authentic and their footprints brushed over, he climbed in and carefully pulled the last pieces of camouflage over the pit.

He quietly reviewed his strategy. "We will stay hidden in the dugout until the target is in range of the new weapon, then rise only high enough to fire and control the rocket on the wire. I do not know exactly when or what the target will be. I only know, from our Nha Be spies, that the target will be a large ship from the ocean, full of ammunition or oil."

Then he again took the Buddha position: knees crossed, arms extended, palms turned up and he said to himself, "I am a Buddhist. I am also a Taoist and believe in patience. I will carry out Colonel Tu's orders whether it takes days, weeks, a month or..."

SEVEN

Blake was still thinking about the North Vietnamese Senior Colonel named Tu, when Mark ordered the chopper's course changed to a Southeasterly direction generally paralleling the Long Tau Channel.

This whole setup is strange, Blake thought. *Tu could be out there, but our intel isn't sure. If he is, Admiral Paulson doesn't care, but Duc-Lang does. And Mark thinks it's dangerous for me to be in the village of Can Gio because of guerrilla activity, but he won't say why. Who's right?*

Mark interrupted Blake's thoughts, "OK, Commander. We're head'n South now. Want to point out a few more things before we land at Can Gio — and that'll wrap up my brief. During the second World War, the Japanese patrolled this same fuc'n channel and the adjacent sea. After the war the French Navy took control. They established a River Assault Group to stop the pirates that were knocking off commercial ships and boats moving to Saigon. About '49 they built forts and outposts along the Long Tau. Now we keep Vietnamese Regional and Popular forces positioned throughout the Rung Sat even in the villages. If you look off there to the left you can see the old French fort at Tam Thon Hiep. We keep a 105 artillery piece there."

"Are the VN soldiers any good?"

Mark shot Blake the thumbs-up sign. "Pretty damn good. Rough, but gett'n better. Their officers 're damn good — most professional I've seen in two 'nam tours. But the fuc'n grunts are still sloppy. That's the way it is throughout the country, but... longer we're here, better they get. Popular force platoons need a lot of training, but...gotta give it to 'em, they're brave. Remember, this is their fuc'n home. They're damn good mud soldiers."

Blake shook his head, "I don't see how ground troops can operate in that stuff."

"Ain't easy! Two high tides and two low tides every day about six or seven hours apart. I mean the high tides 're high. Average more than ten feet. Boats or choppers are the only way to get around in the Rung Sat. In practical terms — when troops 're in ambush along these streams they're waist deep in water for at least half the ambush period. Troops can't operate in this fuc'n terrain more than 48 hours without getting immersion foot or bad colds. Even when we operate in the higher mangrove areas, cross-country movement is hindered by the soft, sticky mud. Hey! It's rough! A big American can sink in as much as three feet."

Sergeant Trieu, who taught history before the draft got him, sat staring stoically out the choppers door. Blake tapped him on the shoulder and shouted above the wind and helicopter noises. "Sergeant Trieu. What are the people in the Rung Sat like. Where did they come from?"

The two men shifted their cartridge boxes so they could huddle together, yet see the ground below them. Trieu adjusted his wire-rimmed glasses and for a moment seemed to collect his thoughts. Then with his lips near Blake's ear he spoke above the rotor noise. "It is not an easy life they have — fishing, wood-cutting, paddy farming and trading, but the people of the Rung Sat seem to accept it." In wooden sounding English, more perfect than any American, he continued. "The Rung Sat people are generally pleasant, respectful and fun-loving. Most have even learned to tolerate foreigners. As for where they came from— there is not a great deal written. We know that Saigon was once the center for the ancient kingdom of Khmer and that there have always been river pirates in the Rung Sat.

"Probably the earliest settlers were a few Chams or Lin-yi as the Chinese called them, and we know that the first Chams go back to the second century of your Christian time. Vietnamese settlers of any consequence date back to about the 15th century when they pushed south at the expense of the Chams."

Trieu touched his glasses again and continued. "It wasn't until the 17th century that the first Chinese refugees came to the area — partisans of the defeated Mings. In the early stages of their colonialism some religious sects gave the French trouble, so they relocated some of the dissidents — people of the Cau Dai religion—from Tay Ninh Province into the Rung Sat. But there have always been refugees and transients, mostly fishermen and woodcutters from the Delta. After World War II even Japanese soldiers settled here. They refused to surrender and fled to the villages where they assumed Vietnamese identities to avoid prosecution. So you see the people are a strange mixture."

Blake nodded. He was beginning to understand. *Sounded like the Rung Sat people are the cast-offs from other wars and other times. A few of every sect and every group in Asia. I would suppose they have a love-hate relationship with the channel, like a Deity who gives and takes at will. The river brings them their livelihood, but they'd probably prefer to be left alone except for the money out-siders bring. On the other hand, except for the channel, no one else probably gives a rat's-ass about the Rung Sat. Because of the channel, everybody came— the French, the Japanese, then the French again, and finally the Americans. No wonder the people only tolerate the Americans. No particular advantage to change their way of life or their politics. After all the Rung Sat's their protection and who'll be ruling them tomorrow?*

There was a click of the intercom and the Vietnamese pilot said, "Excuse me, sirs. I thought you might like to know there is a ship ahead in the channel."

"That'll be the oil tanker China Fox," Mark explained. "Drop down and let's take a look," he ordered the pilot.

The chopper went into a low angle dive and leveled off about thirty feet above the water, then flew the contour of the Long Tau. They were at deck level when they passed the giant ship and Blake saw several men and a slender dark-haired woman wave as they flew by.

"China Fox," Mark said again. "She's full of oil. Headin' for Dutch World to off-load."

"There's a woman on board!" Blake exclaimed.

"Yes sir, Commander — more than one. The women are mostly radio op-erators. Taboo in our Navy but merchies don't worry about that stuff. Even take their wives with 'em. That blackhaired girl is Peg Thompson. Good look'n Australian honey. Probably wav'en at me. She's my girlfriend — the reason I volunteered to stay in-country an extra six months."

Must be one hell of a woman, Blake thought. *For anyone to extend his tour in this God forsaken country.*

"The village of Can Gio's on our right, Commander." Mark pointed. "And there in the distance directly ahead you can see the coastal city of Vung Tau — the 'Riviera' of South Vietnam."

Blake could see the mouth of the Long Tau Channel ahead where the brown water turned to green, then deepened into ocean. He felt like he was in jail and the blue water represented freedom. He could see it, pine for it, but was trapped in a cage of brown, green, and orange bars.

The chopper turned right, passing over the heliport and lighthouse at Can Gio, then flew along the coastline of the peninsula — the Southeastern crust of the Rung Sat pie. He had seen it once before but in the distance from the bridge of the destroyer *Decatur.* It was a grim reminder of the on-going investigation. Up close he was surprised to see such beautiful white sand bordering the clear shallow water where children played as if there were no war.

The chopper flew low just skimming the sandy beach and waving hands of the kids, then climbed out over a small streamlet.

"It was down there that the fuc'n AT3 rockets were introduced into the Rung Sat — where Commander Weeks got hit."

"Ya, Mark, I know. Remember — I was there. Hey, I've never felt so bad about anything."

As the Huey headed for the Can Gio heliport Mark added, "There you have it, Commander. You've seen the Rung Sat."

Blake nodded, then gazed out the chopper door to take in a total view. *Contradictions and contrasts. Dense forests, rivers, and rice paddies. Swamps, water buffalo and sandy white beaches. Grim-faced airmen, guerrillas, lazy-day fishermen, and playful children. I've got a lot to learn about the Rung Sat.*

The chopper settled slowly over the painted white cross that marked the center of the Can Gio heliport. A cloud of billowing dust swirled up and out, then hung in the dry late morning air. The crowd parted respectfully as a short man wearing the blue uniform of a Vietnamese Navy Captain stepped forward, followed by a young man in a plain gray safari suit and a small girl. They were followed by a taller man in an Army officer's uniform and several other senior Vietnamese military men. Blake climbed down from the helo, swung his CAR-15 over his shoulder, and stood for a moment brushing dust from his uniform.

Mark shouted as the chopper rose in the same cloud of dust. "I'll bring this bird back for you after the ceremony."

The people formed a semi-circle around Blake, but remained mute until the engine whine faded to the North. Finally a line of soldiers dressed in ceremonial uniform snapped a salute. On cue the girl wearing a green Girl Scout uniform bowed nicely and handed a bouquet of flowers to the new American advisor. Blake returned her bow and thanked her using the few Vietnamese words he knew, "*Cam On, Co.*"

He saluted the plump, stoic looking Vietnamese officer he surmised was

Duc-Lang. For a moment each sized the other. Blake's immediate reaction was that the man just didn't fit the image. Looks more like a Mandarin money changer than a seagoing naval officer.

Duc-Lang returned Blake's salute and said slowly, as if it were a rehearsed welcoming speech, *"Manh gioi.*. I am *Dai Ta* (captain) Duc-Lang. Welcome to South Vietnam and the Rung Sat Special Zone, Commander Lawrence."

Duc-Lang had large eyes and cheeks that puffed when he spoke causing his dimples to flatten and appear smaller than they were. The thing that struck Blake most strongly was not the man's fat appearance nor his dimpled cheeks, but what Blake's grandmother would have called good eyes: straight, honest, and true. They even had a sparkle of good humor. Blake thought, *Without some private time with this guy I'll never get to know what makes him tick.*

The young civilian accompanying Duc-Lang pressed forward and spoke. "The village is honored to have *Dai Ta* Duc-Lang, the Commander of the Rung Sat Special Zone, and his new *cô-vân* who represents the American government join us for our annual fishing celebration."

The two naval officers accepted gifts and shook the young man's extended hand. The *Dai Ta* seemed delighted to have an opportunity to give a speech to the village people. He rose to the occasion with a longer talk than his short welcome to Blake, but this one was in Vietnamese sprinkled with only a few words in English. When he finished the honored guests were led toward the village.

John Strode, in spit-shined Marine boots and a sharply pressed uniform, accompanied Blake as they followed Duc-Lang and the young civilian away from the heliport. Gunny Johnson and Hospital Corpsman Second Class Jesus "Doc" Crow strolled behind.

Strode walked in step with Blake. "The young civilian's the village Maya', Sah. And the otha' guy in the army uniform is the District Chief. They say the Maya's the nephew of President Thieu. Down he'a, they say, to get seasoned befo' he takes over some impo'tant Saigon job."

"How's everything going in Can Gio, John?"

"So so, Sah," Strode replied. "Gunny and Doc say the civic action stuff is going all right, but it's tense. The District Chief's not very popula' among the people of the Peninsula. Especially aft'a he slammed them with an early curfew and extra martial law sanctions aft'a that junk brought in the rockets. He accused them of clos'n they'a eyes, but the word is only a few people really knew what was going on. The other thing, ah suppose ah better tell you right off. We have a problem with Corporal Marquell. Gunny caught him stoned in barracks again. Ah talked to Maj'a Harris and ah'm prepar'n the papers fo' captain's mast. He's the radioman who called in the naval gunfire on top of our positions, when Commander Weeks got hit."

"What's his problem?" Blake asked.

"Gunny says he's still a spoiled kid — from some wealthy East Coast family. Got thrown outa an offic'a program then enlisted in the Corps. Paris Island just didn't take. Maj'a Harris think we may have to send him back to the States, Sah."

"Tell me, John. How well do you know Major Harris? What's his background?"

"I've been here in the Rung Sat only about as long as the Maj'a and I really don't know much about him. Doc knew him befo — up north."

Strode motioned Gunny and Doc to join them. "Doc, the Commanda wants to know about Maja Harris. You knew him up in I Corps didn't you?"

Doc Crow wore the lapel badges of a Navy Hospital Corpsman, but he had the look of a Marine. His boots were spit-shined and the lines of his cammy uniform sharp and straight. Doc registered in Blake's mind as a Hispanic because his hair was black, skin swarthy, and he had the heavy body structure of Mexican Indian heritage. Doc's smile was his dominant feature — lots of big white teeth that exuded friendliness even when his eyes did not.

"Yes, sir. You get to learn a lot when you share a fox hole. I was his company corpsman up north. I was with him when he got hit."

"Got hit?" Blake asked.

"Yes, sir. Shrapnel. His right arm and hand still bother him. You've seen the crooked finger on his right hand."

Blake nodded. "Where's he from — what's his background?"

"He grew up back East — on the south side of Pittsburgh and joined the Corps as an enlisted man out of high school. Came from a tough family of steel workers, but he told me it wasn't for him. After the Korean war he went back to steel town. Played a couple of years of football at Pitt but he decided to come back into the Marines before he finished. Did a couple more years enlisted and the Corps made him an officer. Don't know much more except he was married once. No kids. That's all I know, sir. Anything I miss, Gunny?"

"Hell, you know more about him than I do Doc," Gunny replied.

"One other thing, Commander," Doc said. "Major Harris was one hell of a company commander. We kicked ass up north."

Blake thanked Doc and Gunny and followed the District Chief's party to his headquarters which was halfway between the heliport and the village. There the dignitaries sat cross-legged around a long, low table as soldiers set various foods before them for lunch. The District Chief sat at one end of the table with the young Mayor at the other. Duc-Lang was on the Mayor's right. Blake on the other side across from Duc-Lang.

The Mayor asked Blake, "Do you speak Vietnamese?"

"No, not really. I understand a few words, but I hope to improve."

The initial table conversation was in English, polite but stilted as if it were a state dinner and every one there for the show. As host, the Mayor did most of the talking and spoke of benign matters such as the weather, which he warned had a good chance of raining before the day was out. He told a few semi-funny jokes and everyone laughed with the Mayor. Blake suspected that most of the men at the table didn't understand English any better than he did Vietnamese and in short order the conversation did shift to Vietnamese. Soon lost in the blur of strange words, Blake stole occasional glances at Duc-Lang whose almond shaped eyes danced back and forth from the Mayor to the other speakers. *So this is the guy I'm supposed to advise. No spring chicken. Must be about forty five.*

Looks experienced. Certainly more experienced than me in this brown water crap. Wonder if he's ever been to sea. Wonder where he was trained? Hasn't said much to me so far. Hope he speaks English.

Bowls of steaming rice were placed between large crocks filled with boiled whole fish and chicken, eyes, heads and all. Small plates of river clams, squid, and sea urchins were set next to smaller dishes of the Vietnamese sauce called Nuc Mam. Blake felt his leg muscles cramp. *My long legs'll never get used to this.* But he held the unfamiliar position and struggled with the chop sticks as he attempted to imitate Duc-Lang's every movement. *I wish I had a fork.*

Great pieces of fish and chicken meat were ripped from their carcass and individual bowls filled with rice. The Vietnamese used the sickly-smelling Nuc Mam on every food. Blake was satisfied to taste only once the liquid made by fermenting alternating layers of fish and salt.

*****

Sergeant Trieu called John Strode outside, where the two men began a heated discussion.

"No, dammit!" Strode exclaimed.

Sergeant Trieu kept his Asian composure. "But both the Mayor and the Dai-Ta believe it is best. They only wish to show the people that the leadership of the Rung Sat have come here in peace — only to take part in the village ceremony. Commander Lawrence would be without his weapon only during the activities on the open street and in the Buddhist temple."

"Ah said, No!"

"But they say it would be a symbol of confidence in the local government." Trieu pressed on. "Others will have weapons to protect them. You will be there with your weapon."

"Well, you tell the May'a and the Dai Ta, ah don't like it. Ah'll talk to Commander Lawrence. Ah won't guarantee anything."

*****

Strode came in from the bright sun, then waited by the door until the Mayor and the Village Chief finished their speeches. At an appropriate moment he quietly slid alongside Blake and whispered, "Excuse me, Commanda, could you step outside fo' a minute?"

Blake, grateful for the opportunity to stretch his long legs, excused himself and followed Strode outside.

"What's up, John?"

"Command'a, the Dai Ta and the May'a have asked that you leave yo weapon behind during the Village ceremony. Ah think it's too damn dangerous and ah know Maj'a Harris wouldn't go for it, but ah said ah'd talk to you about it. The May'a and Duc-Lang'll be unarmed. They want the people to know you came in peace."

"Well, it is a peaceful mission. I'm not intending to get into a firefight while I'm down here. What are your reservations?"

Strode scratched his head as if searching for an answer. "Well, Sa. It's noth'n you can put yo fing'a on. But we already lost Commander Weeks down he'a. It would strength'n the Cong's position in the Rung Sat if they got another American. It's the same thing I told you bef'o about the village. It's tense! We just have an uneasy feel'n."

"I'll be all right, John."

The young Citadel graduate shook his head, and gave a gesture of futility, but it was Sergeant Trieu who resolved the dilemma. He stood close and slipped Blake a snub nosed 38. He said quietly, "Take this, sir, and carry it under your fatigue blouse. No one will know."

Blake took the gun and slipped it into his belt at the small of his back where it would less likely be seen. *First Mark warns me, then Strode, then Trieu offers me a private weapon. There must be more to this town than meets the eye.* Blake decided then to be especially alert.

After lunch, the party left the compound and entered the main street leading into the village of Can Gio where the people turned out in great numbers. Along the way children shouting, "Okay, okay" waved sticks with small paper fish attached.

The procession continued to the center of the village adjacent to the basin where the fishing boats were moored side by side to a long pier. There the official program began.

The village people closed around the parade of dignitaries. The Mayor made another presentation to the Dai-Ta and the villagers dutifully clapped their hands. Then the teenager in the Girl Scout uniform again came forward. The first time Blake met her she was a blur. Now he had a chance to study her. She was beautiful with emerald eyes, high cheekbones, and short black hair tucked under a green tam. She bowed shyly, but her smile sparkled. In a way she reminded Blake of his own daughter. Martha had already shown leadership qualities. This girl was the spokesperson for all the local scouts, boys and girls, many of whom stood bashfully behind her. She presented a token of their handicraft to Dai-Ta Duc-Lang and to his American *Cô-vân.*

It was the sporting events that everyone had really come to see. The street was cleared and the bicycle and foot races began. In each event various parts of the crowd had a favorite athlete. They argued about who was best then laughed and shouted encouragement.

Duc-Lang and the Mayor took turns presenting prizes to the winners.

A show with jugglers and magicians came after the athletic events. They kept the village folk oo'ing and ah'ing as balls and sticks flew gracefully through the air.

As the events continued, Blake noticed the sky became puffy with large cumulus clouds. *The coolness of an afternoon rain'll be a welcome relief from this heat and dust.*

Near the end of the program, the Mayor and Duc-Lang introduced Blake to the village Elder who seemed the kind of old man who might be found in any village, in any country in the world. The kind that could quietly charm the most suspicious personality. He was obviously the town hero of an age gone by, and now the root wisdom of the people. A man who had always been there, as long as anyone could remember. He was small and slender and wore fisherman's clothes, but it was his face that fascinated Blake. It was etched with deep lines and highlighted by a white chin beard which had no more than two dozen strands of long hair. Blake liked the elder immediately and wanted to remember his name, but it was given so quickly he couldn't recall if Duc-Lang had said Quac Cam or Quac Loi. What he did remember was the young Mayor's gestures of deep respect for this man of humble background.

The party followed the Mayor and the Elder to the center of the street where the procession again formed. Out of respect for the Elder and the Mayor, the town's people cleared a path. Many of the town's fishermen now mingled among the dignitaries and together they all began the short walk to the Buddhist temple near the end of the fishing pier.

At the other end of the street, near the temple, a procession of monks formed and slowly came to meet the Mayor's party. As the two groups came together Blake heard explosions. He touched the pistol, just to be sure, but it was only firecrackers. At first the firecrackers were sporadic but soon grew in loudness until the two processions were surrounded with hundreds of cracking noises. The head of the monk who lead their procession was shaved. He wore brown robes of light-weight cloth wrapped loosely and tied with a single cord. Behind him, his entourage of lesser monks wore saffron-yellow colored robes, wrapped and tied in the same fashion, heads slightly bent in the pious meditation attributed to Gautama the Buddha.

When the two parties joined, the older monk bowed. He offered proper invitations, then turned and led the entire party toward the temple.

As they neared the building the clouds exploded and the afternoon monsoon rains came in a torrential downpour. Water flooded from the roof along the curved corners of the pagoda. The water soaked through Blake's uniform and felt cool on his skin as he ran with the other dignitaries through the temple doors.

Inside, chairs had been arranged with the places of honor in front facing a small raised stage. The Mayor, the older monk, the beautiful young Girl Scout, the village Elder, Duc-Lang, and Blake, with Sergeant Trieu at his shoulder, shared a small table of refreshments. Lieutenant Strode, Vietnamese soldiers, the lesser monks, and fishermen were seated on benches to the rear.

Villagers swelled through the doors filling every space in the temple. In order to see over the taller adults, the children climbed to high perches on the statues of jungle animals. As the bodies multiplied so did the temperature and soon the temple became like an oven, steaming from the heat and moisture. Sweat poured from Blake's body drenching his clothes. The room filled with a mixture of strange, sweet incense and the stench of a hundred human odors.

On the stage in front of a giant statue of Buddha, young monks hurried about making last minute arrangements for the play. The stage was decorated with papier-mâché dragons and tigers, brightly painted in oranges, blues and greens. Soon the crowd settled and a single monk in yellow robes moved center stage. He bowed and spoke in respectful tones as the tinkling sound of Oriental music played in the background.

Sergeant Trieu, who was kneeling next to Blake, explained. "He says the ceremony is to bless the fishing fleet and it will begin soon. They are honored to have such a distinguished group."

The Master of Ceremonies was followed on stage by three younger monks each carrying incense sticks. They walked slowly and solemnly as they pronounced blessings on those who went to sea as fishermen. Then came a group of young girls swaying and chanting an ancient folk dance. Next a troupe of actors in strange costumes came on stage, portraying fishing men in various aspects of their work. The tone and language of the play was stilted and Trieu explained that most of it was not to be translated literally. When the actors did a comic mimic of a seasick sailor, the village Elder and other fishermen laughed and clapped their hands and the crowd joined in. It was at the peak of the clapping and laughter that the play was interrupted by a cracking sound that at first Blake thought was just another firecracker until he saw the wooden table next to him splinter.

A voice shouted in Vietnamese *Coi chung! Ban tra! Sat Cong!* Then in English, "Watch out! Shoot back! Kill the Communist assassin!"

EIGHT

Co Hang waited anxiously to fire the new Russian rocket at a passing ship. She wanted time to go quickly, but one hour dragged with the next and the waiting in the camouflaged mud trench only annoyed her.

She knew Do Van Nghi was a Buddhist, but she also knew, like most Vietnamese, he practiced a mixture of religious philosophies. Taoism taught him to be patient but she was not. When he touched her shoulder to calm her and help her be a better Taoist she affectionately glanced toward the man who too often treated her like a sister even though she wanted their relationship to be more. To her, Nghi looked like their handsome leader comrade Colonel Tu. Nghi's beard and mustache were neatly trimmed like his; and Nghi was tall like the Northern Colonel. But Nghi's long hair was still black with only streaks of premature gray. The Colonel's was very gray, almost white.

At the moment her eyes left Nghi's face and returned to the river she saw a ship turn the bend. As it came closer she read the name China Fox on its bow and realized it was an oil tanker. It was coming fast — faster than any ship Co Hang had ever seen before.

Nghi saw it as well and said, "Prepare to fire when it is at its closest point."

Her heart beat fast and the new weapon shook in her hands. Before she aimed she checked the periscopic sight and control unit. When she looked back at the river she saw a patrol boat racing toward them. Her entire body began to shake and in a reaction to her fear she momentarily took her hands off the control box. By the time she found the control stick again and raised the periscopic sight to take aim, the great ship had passed and was moving away.

"Hurry, fire!" Nghi said. They both knew that the wire-guided rocket could reach no further than 3000 meters. He squeezed her shoulder and she squeezed the trigger.

The sound of the missile leaving the launcher brought a feeling of power and satisfaction, but her hands still shook and her touch on the slender control stick was rough. She couldn't hold the infrared light of the burning rocket in the center of the optics. The bird-like projectile flew up and down and sideways like a kite out of control, its wire snaking loosely behind.

*****

Master Angus MacKenna was awakened by a shout from a deck hand. "Look, it's following the ship!" The Master of the oil tanker China Fox rolled his head to a resting place on the other shoulder. He closed his eyes and said to himself, "the First Mate will take care of whatever is bothering the man."

The next thing Angus heard was a cracking noise like the sound of a car backing hard against a fire plug, the sound of metal tearing metal. After a short delay that noise was followed by a great explosion. The Master flew out of his chair and ran for the starboard bridge wing. As he passed the Vietnamese pilot he saw terror in the little man's eyes, and heard him say, "Right fifteen."

It was exactly the wrong order, but it was too late. Before Angus could countermand, he heard a grinding sound and felt the ship shudder as she went hard aground. Simultaneously he heard voices screaming and saw a ball of fire and billowing smoke.

*****

Because there was no immediate explosion, Nghi wasn't certain if the rocket had even hit the ship. But when he heard the noise he squeezed Co Hang's shoulder and ordered, "Load again! Quickly! Fire another rocket at the ship."

Free of her nervousness, Co Hang smiled and jumped out of the mud hole where they were hiding. She ran to the launcher where she loaded another rocket.

As the girl prepared to fire her second wire-guided missile at the ship, two things caused Nghi to decide on a new target: First, the giant tanker came to an abrupt stop. He said to himself, "We've sunk it. Our mission is complete with one shot from the new rocket weapon." The other thing he saw was the patrol boat firing its 50-caliber machine gun at them. The PBR was now between the guerrillas and the ship and heading directly toward them. Nghi saw a puff of smoke from the rear of the PBR and knew a mortar round had been fired. It soon exploded nearby causing mud and water to spray over their hiding place.

Nghi shouted to Co Hang. "Shoot at the patrol boat, instead of the ship!"

It was obvious she was no longer frightened. Her hand was now steady. Co Hang fired her second rocket and this time it flew smooth and straight. Although the boat was a much smaller target than the oil tanker she made a direct hit. The explosion caused the PBR to lift totally out of the water, twist, break into two pieces and in seconds sink beneath the boiling debris. Behind the volcanic splash of water Nghi saw two more patrol boats firing weapons as they raced toward the guerrillas. Grenades exploded around Co Hang and machine-gun fire ripped the mud.

NINE

Blake's eyes darted in every direction then focused on the blood splashing from a bullet hole in the Girl Scout's face. Another bullet ripped the wooden floor near Blake and the next hit the village Elder. Blood drained through the strands of the white chin beard as the old man collapsed on the table, instantly dead.

"Coi chung! Ban tra! Sat Cong! Duc-Lang shouted. He slammed his body into Blake and drove him from his seat to the floor. In English he repeated, "Watch out! Shoot back! Kill the communist!"

The music stopped.

The crowd spread quickly as screams and shouts ricocheted off the walls.

A mixture of fear, rage, and adrenaline pumped through Blake's body. He saw the lone gunman standing to his right partly hidden by a large temple pillar. The killer's weapon was raised, ready to shoot again.

Blake rolled toward the open space to his left and extended the snub-nosed 38. His hand shook as he aimed at the assassin and fired. The man staggered and leaned against the pillar still attempting to aim his weapon. A fusillade of rifle fire from the back of the Temple riddled the man and he crumpled to the floor.

The noise of screaming, crying, and shouting people filled the temple as the crowd swarmed over the killer and dragged his body into the street. Monks and village people rushed to the victims, while Vietnamese soldiers forced their way from their ineffective positions near the back of the temple to surround Blake and Duc-Lang.

"You had a gun? You shot him," Duc-Lang said.

"You saved my life when you pushed me to the floor," Blake responded, voice now shaking in the after-shock. For the first time in his life he had been shot at from close range.

Duc-Lang said, "I was his target, not you."

"Why?" Blake questioned, rubbing a shoulder now sore from Duc-lang's push.

"Colonel Tu sent him. Come. Follow me!"

The Vietnamese captain got to his feet. He shouted to the soldiers. "Do not let them kill him. We must interrogate him."

"Come," he motioned to Blake. "

Sergeant Trieu helped Blake to his feet. The taste of vomit swelled in Blake's throat as he watched them carry away the crumpled body of the beautiful teen-ager, her Girl Scout bandanna hanging loosely from a bobbing head.

The village Elder's body was surrounded by old women screaming and sobbing as they wiped red stains from his wrinkled face.

Blake staggered out of the building and onto the muddy street where John Strode caught up to him. "You alright, Commanda? Yo face sho is white!"

"I guess."

"Ah'm sorry ah couldn't get to that guy befo he fired. Too far out a ma pict'a, and ah was afraid a hitt'n the crowd from where ah was. Ya sure nailed him, sah. Good thing ya had that pistol."

"I'm not sure I hit him."

Strode shook his head up and down. "It was you alright. You hit him, 'm sure a that. Trieu says the guerrilla may not live. Would you believe the Maya was upset because ya had the gun. Shows ya what his priorities are."

By the time Blake caught up Duc-Lang was shouting "*Ngung* (stop)!" to the men and women who were beating the limp body of the assassin with sticks and rifle barrels. Duc-Lang pushed his way through the angry crowd and kneeled over the uniformed body. His dark eyes pinched and his jaw set tight as he slapped the man's face several times. Duc-Lang's voice and words were low, guttural, and harsh. The only thing Blake could understand was a question ending in, "Colonel Tu?"

Blake waited on the fringes of the crowd and watched as various Vietnamese were brought before Duc-Lang to answer his frantic questions.

Finally Duc-Lang came to join Blake. At first he said nothing. Blake knew the Oriental man had again lost a great deal of face, so Blake broke the silence. "Did he talk?"

"No. He's dead. Not finished with the interrogation. I'll be back." Before he left he remarked in a subdued tone, "Sorry *cô-vân*. My men couldn't get to him in time. Villagers say his name is Nam Ho — brother of one of the town's most prominent men — thought away in the army. No one suspected. Must have deserted. Joined guerrillas." Duc-Lang walked away toward the village, shoulders slumped, head down.

Blake stood by himself. He looked out across the Long Tau Channel and jungle beyond. His hands and body shook from rage. He could still see the faces of the guerrilla, grim and sneering, and the dead Elder and Girl Scout.

He raised his hands to the sky and spoke as if the listener was the Deity and could respond to his questions. "What else? Lost my destroyer command, possible court-martial, an angry wife, stuck in the Rung Sat, a place where men turn mean-sick and old men and Girl Scouts get killed in holy places? What else?"

John Strode came running toward Blake. His voice full of excitement. "Commanda, ah got bad news. Just gotta radio call that China Fox has been hit. She's aground somewhere on the riva."

A ship aground on the Long Tau? I wasn't going to get involved. Now I'm a part of it. Damn you Corporal Marquell!

Then he remembered Rear Admiral Paulson's warning: "Protect the Long Tau Channel."

Blake barked, "Strode. Get a chopper in here — now!"

TEN

Blake was waiting at the Can Gio heliport when he heard the chopper. It came at high speed and didn't slow as it dropped from the sky and screamed to its landing hover. The aircraft was still five feet above the white cross when Mark Harris sprang to the ground and sprinted toward them. "I heard about the shoot'n in the temple. You okay, Commander?" His voice accentuated his concern.

"Whatta you know about China Fox?"

"She's aground at the second bend, between check point four and five."

Blake looked at his watch. "When did it happen?"

"Just happened. Hit by a VC ambush. She's hard aground. I'm having a hell of a time getting information out of the fuc'n Vietnamese pilots. Took me some time to get the details about your problem in the temple. Christ, that was a close call. I told ya Can Gio was fucked up. The pilot didn't tell me about the ship being hit until I was almost here. Guess it's because it's been so quiet in the Rung Sat. Two incidents in one day's got the Vietnamese circuits all screwed up."

Mark squatted Asian style on the ground in front of Blake. His CAR-15 lay across his knees.

"How bad is she hit?" Blake asked.

"Haven't been able to find that out either, sir. Only thing I've learned so far is she was hit near the radio shack."

"Any casualties?"

Mark stood. "The Vietnamese Navy apparently lost some people on a patrol boat. Sure hope the ship's crew is okay." He began to pace. His body moved like an animal ready to attack. "The radio shack is where Peg works. I'm worried about her."

Turning to Strode, Blake asked, "Where's Duc-Lang?"

"Still in the vil', sir."

"Told ya." Mark sneered. "More of the same, Commander. Probably with a fuc'n concubine."

Blake ignored Mark's remark and directed his words to Strode, "Go! Find him. Tell him about China Fox and that I'm waiting for him at the chopper pad."

Even as he answered, "aye, aye, sir," Strode was galloping toward the village of Can Gio.

Blake stood and looked up the channel as if searching for China Fox. "What do you think the VC will do next?"

"Don't know. This is new, Commander. Every other time when a ship's been hit on the Long Tau she's kept going. This is the first time one's jammed the fuc'n channel since the Baton Rouge in '66. Usually the VC hit and run, but if they see 'er sitting there high and dry no tell'n what they'll do. Probably attack again."

Blake remembered the importance Paulson had placed on the channel. "Make sure the Vietnamese do it right, but above all keep the channel open." He wasn't in command of the Rung Sat, but things had to be done — immediately. His mind cleared and thoughts came to him quickly in a series of crisp questions. "What forces do we have in the area?"

"The nearest unit's Company 908 – 362's across the river." Mark's voice responded to Blake's urgent tone.

"How about PBR's?"

"Should be four. Two at check point four. Two at five."

"Break in on that circuit." Blake ordered in a tone that erased any doubt of who was in charge. "Order 908 and 362 to move out and surround the ship. Get the ship on the radio. I want to talk directly to the Master."

Mark walked quickly to the chopper waiting in the center of the white cross and spoke to the young Vietnamese Air Force pilot. They talked for a few moments, then above the noise of the whirling chopper rotors Blake heard Mark say, "Bullshit! Why not?" The discussion became animated, the situation tense. The pilot's hand went to his pistol. Mark's did the same.

Blake who had moved closer to take the call from the Master became inquisitive. "What's up, Mark?"

"He's givin' me a hard time Commander. Won't let me have the circuit. Claims it's a Vietnamese circuit not to be used for ship to shore traffic."

Blake could see the eyes of the young Lieutenant flash a warning — an alarm that could be read on any face anywhere in the world. He was protecting his turf. His body language showed he was flustered and tight.

"Tell him the senior *cô-vân* needs it."

Mark said something and the Vietnamese officer's grip on his .45 cal. revolver tightened. Knuckles showed white as he said, "*Khong duoc!* (no, it is not possible)!"

Face, Blake thought. *A hell of a time to let cultural differences get in the way of the mission. Got to defuse the situation.* He smiled, stepped in front of the bristling Marine and motioned Sergeant Trieu to join him. *If I ever needed an interpreter it's now.*

He bowed slightly to the Vietnamese pilot and using the few words of Vietnamese he knew purposely promoted the man from Lieutenant to Major. "*Da, Cam on Thieu-Ta.*"

"Trieu, tell him who I am and that I would like Companies 908 and 362 to move out and surround the ship. Then ask him to let me talk to the Master of China Fox."

Trieu smiled and spoke in his own tonal language, "*Xin toi can Dai-Uy, giup do noi tao. Trung Ta Lawrence Cô-Vân Mi.*"

Blake held out his hand for the radio telephone.

The combination of Blake's willingness to communicate in Vietnamese, the flattery of being addressed several ranks senior than he really was, and the effect of Sergeant Trieu's explanation seemed to calm the young man, convincing him not to challenge the senior *cô-vân*. Slowly the officer nodded his head. He broke into a grin as he said, "*Da duoc*." Then the young man spoke authoritatively over the circuit, obviously relaying the troop order.

When he was finished, he handed Blake the handset.

"China Fox. This is Moon River. Let me talk to the Master of the ship. Over."

At first there was silence, then the excited tones of a Scottish voice said. "Hello, Hello. Master Angus MacKenna of China Fox here."

"China Fox, this is Moon River. This is Commander Lawrence the Senior U.S. military officer in the Rung Sat. How do you hear me? Over."

"Well now, I was wondering when you Yanks would finally show up. I hear you very well. Can you help us? Over."

"What's the situation there, Captain? How bad are you hit? Do you have any casualties, Over."

The Master's voice sounded matter-of-factly as he explained the plight of his ship. "Yes, well, we were hit just above the fuel tanks. We are on fire. If we can't get the fires under control the ship could blow. Several of our crew are injured, one dead. Over."

"What's the enemy situation there? Do you see any activity? Over."

The Scotchman's voice responded, "I see some of the Vietnamese patrol boats shooting up the river bank. One was blown up by the guerrillas a bit ago. So far I haven't seen any troops or helicopters to defend us. I know this place, and the guerrillas are still out there. They'll attack again if you don't do something quickly."

Blake winced when Mark touched his sore shoulder to get his attention, "Ask about Peg, will, you Commander?"

"China Fox, this is Moon River. How badly are you aground? And who are the wounded? Over."

The Master's words rolled in a heavy brogue, "Really don't know at this time how badly we're aground. Back side of the high tide when we went on the mud. Actually, it was beginning to ebb. A bit late getting started from Vung Tau. If she's not holed she may float on the next high. We'll need some help to get off. Oh, and the wounded. Several of the radio people took shrapnel. One's dead—a woman."

Eleven

It was about thirty miles from Can Gio to where China Fox was aground. As they raced above the channel, Blake could see patrol boats below up on their step slicing across brown water going in the same direction as the chopper. Foam boiled and spray flew high in the air as rooster tails left a frothy swath rolling to both banks of the Long Tau channel, washing over river debris.

Blake wore a flack jacket. His CAR-15 with banana clips lay across his legs. Mark sat on an ammo box next to him, similarly dressed except that the color of his beret was green instead of black. Both nervously searched ahead for China Fox, each for different reasons. Blake's thoughts were about the ship, but Mark kept asking the pilot about the woman who was hit by the rocket attack, obviously concerned about the Australian girl named Peg Thompson.

Dai Ta Duc-Lang and Sergeant Trieu huddled on the other side of the gunship's rear compartment. Minigunners prepared ammunition as the pilots went through their check list to arm the rockets hanging from pods on each side of the chopper.

China Fox lay parallel to the flow of the channel with her bow in the mud. The current had swung her so that her starboard side was snug up to the river bank. She was so full of oil that her water line was invisible below the ebbing tide. Blake could see black smoke billowing as firemen sprayed water across the flames. *She'll blow if they don't beat the fires. Even if they do save her, she'll be tough to get off the mud. If the guerrillas are still out there she's an easy target and if that happens neither fires nor grounding matters.*

The chopper buzzed China Fox then climbed and flew a search pattern parallel to the river expanding farther and farther away from the ship.

Blake could see that the tide had reversed and the current was flowing toward the ocean. He knew the guerrillas would have rough going in their attempt to escape.

As the aircraft passed over a small ravine, Blake saw a smoke-trail climbing toward the helo. The pilot saw it also and violently jerked the chopper into a sharp diving turn away.

The enemy rocket passed so close that Blake could smell the smoke. His eyes were still following the rocket skyward when he heard a tearing sound to his right. He turned to see the skin of the helo shattered by bullets.

The chopper shuttered for a moment as if it would stall, then it went into a steep dive. At first Blake thought the chopper was out of control and going to crash, but he soon realized the pilot was attacking the guerrillas. Blake could see several dark figures moving along a mud bank. As the chopper dove toward the Rung Sat swamp Blake felt the aircraft shake and smelled burning powder as two rockets burst from their pods. Four more rockets were fired in the direction of the black clad figures. Blake's eyes followed the smoke as they flew toward the area where the enemy rocket had been fired.

The pilot continued his dive and pulled out no more than a hundred feet above the ground where he held a tight turn and circled slowly as the mini-gunners sprayed bullets. The explosions kicked up mud and water, but the guerrillas had disappeared leaving behind one body lying among the flotsam.

For another ten minutes the pilot searched for the guerrillas, then turned back toward China Fox.

It wasn't until Blake saw Company 908 already moving into positions surrounding the ship and Company 362 crossing the river in small amphibious boats and sampans that he felt a release from the pressure of Admiral Paulson's words, "above all protect the channel." Duc-Lang must have had the same feeling, because even though his eyes were still pinched in nervous concentration, a half smile flickered across his normally stoic face.

The chopper descended to an open area adjacent to the ship and held a hover. With its skids just touching the swampland, Blake, Duc-Lang and Sergeant Trieu stepped into the Rung Sat mud.

Mark started to follow the group, but Blake held his hands high to stop him, then shouted over the chopper noise, "No, Mark! Stay airborne. Keep comms with us on the ship. Help direct the troops toward the area where we last saw the guerrillas."

Mark's bushy, 'V' shaped eyebrows raised in protest. "Hey, Commander. That could be Peg that got hit."

"Know how you feel, Mark. But this is more important. Protecting China Fox comes first. I'm too new. You're the only one who can coordinate the land operation."

Mark nodded grimly and gave a reluctant, "Aye, Aye, Sir." But before the Huey lifted off he added, "Let me know if Peg's okay."

Blake and the two Vietnamese waded ankle deep in the Rung Sat mud toward the giant tanker.

"Ahoy, aboard China Fox." Blake shouted.

A blond-headed man leaned over the ship's rail and in an Australian accent asked, "Mate, you Commander Lawrence?"

"Yes. Request permission to come aboard?"

The First Mate hesitated apparently caught off guard by the nautical protocol, then answered in an apologetic tone, "We only have a ladder."

Shortly, several seamen lowered a Jacobs ladder and the two Vietnamese, with their American advisor, climbed carefully to the fo'c'sle of the tanker where they were greeted with a hearty hand shake and a heavy Scottish accent. "Angus MacKenna, Master here. Welcome to China Fox. 'Ave ya seen our little hole yet?"

"From the air. Much damage?"

"Fortunately they didn't hit the main fuel tanks. Do you think the bastards who did it are still nearby?"

Blake motioned toward the two Vietnamese: "This is Captain Duc-Lang and the other is my interpreter, Sergeant Trieu."

Duc-Lang bowed slightly, his eyes expressing concern.

Blake said, "I'm told this attack is different — the Rung Sat guerrillas have been quiet recently, but it looks like a hot war now and with this ship aground they could attack again."

"Dutch World headquarters in Saigon wants to know the situation," MacKenna said with a frown. "What can I tell them?"

Blake suspected that the oil company, which owned the ship, would bring pressure on the military. They would want assurances that aggressive action was being taken to protect the tanker. He answered for his new counterpart. "Tell them Captain Duc-Lang is aboard with his senior American advisor. Tell them choppers are patrolling the area and several infantry companies are deployed around the ship."

Blake put both hands on the rail and leaned over the ship's side to better see the way the ship lay in the mud. "By the way, Captain MacKenna, what caused China Fox to go aground?"

"Well..." the Master said in a blustery tone, "the bloody pilot became excited when he heard the explosion. Gave the wrong goddamn rudder order in the bend and we ended up here, on the mud. The bastard said, 'starboard' when he should have said, 'port.' I've already had the hull checked and we're not holed. I believe tugs can get us off on the next tide."

Blake knew that only in the Panama and Suez canals were sea captains exempt from responsibility for their ship. Otherwise they were to control the pilots. Blake thought he had smelled alcohol on the Master's breath when he first came aboard. *Wonder if a drunkard'll have a problem selling his story to Dutch World Corporate headquarters and the Navy in Saigon.*

Knowing this would be his first time to offer professional recommendations, Blake carefully chose his words. He was still uncertain of how well Duc-Lang understood English, so he spoke in short baby-like sentences, "Next high tide not for several hours. Take long time for Saigon tugs get here. Have long wait. VC could attack again — any time. Suggest you get communications with field units and choppers. Get them positioned to defend ship. When finished with radio let me contact Saigon. Get tugs and fixed-wing air cover."

Duc-Lang smiled but didn't comment. He just nodded and went directly to the radio.

While Duc-Lang talked to his Vietnamese forces, the First Mate led Blake aft to show him the damaged outboard bulkhead. The fire was out except for a few hot spots where sailors stood raking debris or spraying salt water.

"This is where the bloody rocket went in. You can see its not a very big hole, but let me show you the damage inside."

They stepped through a main deck door and into a passageway leading fore and aft.

"Look at this," the Mate said. Shrapnel and fire damage were everywhere. Every bulkhead, the wiring, and the furniture had been ripped and torn either by flying metal or by the fire the rocket ignited.

"It's a strange weapon," the Mate said. "One of our deck hands actually saw the rocket flying toward the ship. According to him it had a long wire attached to it and actually followed the ship before it hit."

"Wire-guided. Shaped charge." Blake said. "It's the AT3 all right. Fortunately whoever fired it didn't know much about ships. One of those in the right place could devastate a tanker like this."

After Blake had completed his inspection of the damage, the Mate led him across the ship to a small wardroom on the port side. A woman's body lay on a table covered by a sheet. Several men and a raven-haired woman worked over the wounded. When she saw Blake, the woman bounced to her feet. She wore jeans and a T-shirt. A dressing covered a scalp wound on her upper forehead. Blake estimated she was five feet nine or ten and her athletic slenderness made her seem even taller. Her face reminded him of the American actress Bette Davis because it was slender, with large eyes, high cheek bones, and the same motion of her head Miss Davis had when she smiled. His eyes traced a body that tapered upward from a narrowness at her belted pants to full breasts of classic proportions. Blake even noticed she was wearing lip rouge. He wondered how someone as appealing as she got aboard a merchant ship in the war zone?

"So you're the Yank 'o's come to save us from the bloody Commies." She said offering a half-smile.

"Now you've met the other Aussie aboard this vessel, Commander." The First Mate stepped forward to introduce them. "This one's a sassy bird. We thought she was dead, but it was actually only an ugly bump on the head. Tough bird as well. Vietnam may never be the same because of her! Meet Peg Thompson,"

"Sassy for the likes of you. Piss off," Peg said again with a subdued laugh as she extended her hand like a man. "So, you're the famous Com-aaan-der Lawrence. Major Harris told me about you."

Blake took a hand that was hard and firm. "It doesn't seem like we did a very good job of saving you from Charlie. How bad is that head wound?"

"Actually I feel quite well. Still get a bit dizzy. But... ." Retrieving her hand she said sadly, "One of ours bought it and several were seriously injured."

Blake matched her mood change and wanted to reassure her that he was doing things. "You're lucky to be alive. Sorry about your friends. We'll get the casualties ashore as soon as possible, but I need a phone so I can call Saigon. The Vietnamese are using the bridge phone."

"I have another one almost repaired." Peg said. "It won't take but a minute to finish."

"The radio room looked a mess from that rocket. Didn't think anything worked. Are you up to it?" Blake asked.

"A bit of blood never stopped an Aussie," Peg said with a flip of her head.

The First Mate gave a mock salute. "I'll leave you here, Commander and get back to my duties. I warn you. Be careful. This bird will talk your leg off if you let her."

Blake asked the Mate to send word to Mark that Peg was alive, then he followed her to the radio room where she immediately busied herself with a soldering iron and other tools. She seemed not to have time for small talk and it was Blake, impatient to make his call, who broke the silence. "How's it coming, Miss Thompson? Will I be able to get through to Saigon from here? The Vietnamese should be finished with the radio on the bridge by now."

"Peg, call me Peg," she said with a saucy smile. "I'll have this one fixed in a minute. I've had to hard wire this amplifier component into the rectifier circuitry. Don't know if the values are right. If it works, you can call."

Blake relaxed and leaned against a damaged bulkhead, "I thought you were just a radio operator."

"I am that. Also the best bloody radio-woman aboard," she said. lifting her head from her work just enough to give him a quick smile.

"Where'd you learn that?"

"Learn what?"

"Electronic repair."

Without stopping her work, Peg responded. "Australian Navy."

"Uh — How long were you in the Navy?"

Peg, who was working at a low bench now flipped her head again and gave Blake a full smile. "Six years. I left to get on with something else. Anyway, the Australian Navy doesn't pay as well as this, and where else can a girl find this kind of excitement?"

Blake was standing with his arms crossed, head down, listening without focus until he caught the motion of her head. For him it was a sensual movement. He could see she was bra-less and he followed the quivering firmness of her breast as it curved upward under the flimsy covering of the 'T' shirt. Then he noticed how her fitted pants pulled tight against her bottom. He caught himself attracted to this woman-sailor and it surprised him because he never thought of himself as a girl-chasing kind of guy.

Peg put down the soldering iron and said. "Well, that's that. Let's put some power to it and give it a bloody go!" She adjusted a few knobs, then spoke into a microphone, "Testing one, two. Testing one, two." No response. She made more adjustments with a screw driver and tried again. "Good as new. Here, you can try it now."

Blake stepped close to her. Their bodies touched lightly when he took the short-corded microphone. He inhaled her heavy scented perfume. He held the mike to his lips and said, "Navy Operations Center, Saigon, Navy Operations Center, Saigon, this is Moon River, Moon River. How do you hear me? Over."

There was no response, only the crackling of background noise and the click of someone keying a transmitter. The short length of the cord and the narrow passage between the work bench and the radio required Peg to lean across Blake to make more adjustments. Her body molded with his for a few moments — long enough for each to become aware of the other.

Peg in a whispery voice said, "Try again."

Blake felt a tightness in his groin. His cheeks flushed as her breasts rested lightly against his chest. Her lips were near and he felt the warmth of her lower body against his. His right hand moved automatically to lightly touch her left hip and she raised her chin, smiled slightly, and brought her lips close to his.

Blake's throat became too dry to talk on the radio. He had already been away from his wife for six months when his orders came to go in-country. By now he was hungry for a woman and he wanted to touch the roundness of Peg's breast, but he told himself, "Steady boy. This is stupid." Their lips were, for a moment, a breath apart when Peg said huskily, "You better make your call, Yank!"

Blake sucked air into a heaving chest then smiled agreement. As much as he felt the desire he knew better — it wasn't the time or the place. He held the microphone to his lips and said," Navy Operations Center, Saigon, N O C, Saigon, this is Moon River, Moon River. How do you hear me? Over."

Almost immediately he heard a clear response, "Moon River, this is NOC Saigon. Hear you loud and clear. How me? Over."

"Roger, NOC. I hear you the same. This is Commander Lawrence aboard oil tanker China Fox broadcasting in the clear. Urgently need to get the dead and wounded off. We're aground in the Long Tau Channel. Request tugs. Believe we can get the ship off the mud on the next high tide. " Then he added, "Troops and helos are patrolling the area, but we could use some additional air cover, over."

The operations center wanted more details, the ship's location, information about the wounded, and the precise composition of the troops. Finally they confirmed that several large tugs were underway and air cover from Tan Son Nhut would soon be overhead.

Peg's body still rested against him and Blake's mind continued with the struggle until he forced himself to say, "I better get back to the bridge."

"Okay, Yank," she said as she moved away. Then she added an invitation. "I'll be spending a few days at Dutch World's tank farm near Nha Be before we sail for Singapore and another load of oil. Come to see me, if you want."

Blake didn't answer, not because he wasn't already contemplating that meeting, but rather that he remembered that Peg was Mark's reason for extending in-country.

TWELVE

Blake joined Duc-Lang, his Vietnamese counterpart, on the bridge of China Fox. The *Dai Ta* had completed his radio telephone calls to organize the defense of China Fox. He now stood idly on the bridge wing nearest the shore.

Still uncertain about Duc-Lang's English, Blake continued using short, choppy pidgin talk sentences to brief the pudgy navy captain. "Got through Saigon. American side sending air cover and tugs. Be here one — two hours."

Duc-Lang smiled and only nodded. Looking out toward the Rung Sat he said, "Ah, you...couldn't know this." He sounded like he was struggling with his words. Blake supposed it was because he didn't want say the wrong thing. He had already lost face as the result of the Can Gio incident. "But, ah," Duc-Lang continued. "I have been to America to study and I am fluent in your language. There is no need for you to adjust your manner of speech. I understand you perfectly. Hopefully you will understand my humble attempts at English."

Duc-Lang's sentence structure and pronunciation were too perfect — too correct. For Blake it was as if the words were being read from a library book by new Americans trying too hard to prove their ability with the language. Blake felt embarrassed. He even smiled to himself at how he must have sounded using pigeon. With little thought, and probably because his own Vietnamese was so poor, he had assumed Duc-Lang needed help. Looking down at the smaller man, Blake said through a foolish smile, "Sorry, Dai Ta. It's me who will need help with your language."

Duc-Lang's almond shaped eyes brightened at Blake's response. He seemed more at ease and just as interested in Blake's background. "The day has not been dull, has it? It's good to have a peaceful moment. I suppose you have a family in the States?"

Blake thought of his encounter with Peg and he was struck with a pang of guilt. "A wife and two children. Living on our West coast."

"That's a very nice place. I was at your base at San Diego once. You have children? Boys? Girls?"

"A boy named Blake, he's fifteen, and a girl named Martha, she's only ten." Blake knew it was an act of Asian courtesy to ask about a person's family so he added, "And your family, sir?"

Duc-Lang smiled, "I have two children."

"Boys?"

Blake sensed a retreat to stoic Asian pensiveness. Duc-Lang's eyes glanced toward Sergeant Trieu, then dropped. His voice and eyes softened as he said, "Two girls."

Observing the change, but not understanding it, Blake attempted a joke. He said with a grin, "No sons," then paused, "yet."

Duc-Lang didn't respond, but he did glance again at Sergeant Trieu.

Blake wanted to change the subject, but didn't know exactly what to say. Obviously there was something about his counterpart's children that was secretive and unsaid.

Duc-Lang finally laughed and the expressive twinkle returned to his eyes. His cheeks dimpled. "Ha! Sons? Of course. Good joke. Maybe someday." Then it was he who changed the subject. "This is the first time we have actually seen wire-guided weapons used in the Rung Sat. We suspected they were still here ever since Commander Weeks was wounded in Can Gio. I have had our special Reconnaissance Unit searching, but the guerrillas have been very quiet and clever. Until now we have learned nothing."

So, Blake thought, *Duc-Lang has been trying to find the Russian rockets. Both Admiral Paulson and Mark Harris assumed he was doing nothing.* Blake saw a section of jets fly by then break-up as they began a search for the guerrillas. He looked out at the uncivilized tangle of brush and mud. *How little we Americans understand these Asian people and this country.* Obviously their situation was still dangerous, but realizing they faced several hours of inactivity Blake decided to pursue a line of questions that might enlighten him. He attempted to speak casually but his words still came out stiff-sounding, "The Rung Sat is certainly different than sailoring in the blue water of the ocean. It looks treacherous and unforgiving."

"It is a bad area, *cô-vân.* One of the worst in all of Vietnam. Do you know the meaning of the words *Rung Sat?*"

"Killer Forest?"

"Yes, you Americans call it that but it is not a good translation. The name 'Killer Forest' implies that a forest can kill, but we all know that trees don't kill; people do. A more accurate translation is 'Forest of Assassins.' The name Rung Sat goes back to a time when bandits lived in the jungles along the banks of these rivers, preying on fishermen and other transitors. These pirates often stopped the boats, robbed them, then murdered the people."

For Blake, his counterpart's English, although still brittle improved the longer he talked. He had no reason to debate the correctness of the translation, but he knew Americans wouldn't know the background of the region so for them their name would stick — always be Killer Forest.

Duc-Lang continued, "Over time the area developed the reputation of being a forest full of assassins, or Rung Sat. Even today, only the bravest venture through the region. Of course, the jungle on either side of the Long Tau channel is much less dense now that your Air Force sprayed it with Agent Orange, but the section of the Rung Sat to the North of us near the Nhon Trach remains as dense and dangerous as ever."

Duc-Lang's eyes became nervous and took on the look of an animal. "We have known all along that if the rockets were in the Rung Sat, they would be in that place, because Nhon Trach is known as the heart of the Forest of Assassins. It's a no-man's land and it belongs to whomever needs it."

Blake felt a chill even though the sun was high and the heat stifling. He was learning things most Americans never had a chance to learn and he wanted to know more.

Duc-Lang must have sensed Blake's willingness to learn about Vietnam. He again looked nervously toward the jungle. "Forgive me, *cô-vân*, but many of your countrymen do not understand the meaning of the struggle in my country."

He paused again, apparently to be sure Blake clearly understood. Then he began again, "They think it is simply a struggle against Communism, but if you understand the Rung Sat you will understand Vietnam. The struggle here is for South Vietnam. You see, whoever controls the Forest of Assassins usually rises to rule this country. That is why Colonel Tu is so dangerous."

Again he paused then said, "Excuse me, please." He signaled for Sergeant Trieu.

Blake's translator, who had been standing at a polite distance listening to the conversation, joined them. He saluted and bowed as he approached.

"Sergeant. You know our history and you are a much better storyteller than I. Please. Tell Commander Lawrence the story of Nguyen Anh, so he will understand the historical significance of the Rung Sat."

Trieu bowed deeply and very formally to Duc-Lang, as if he were addressing royalty, "It would be a great honor to tell the story. Of course, sirs, I do know it very well. I taught it in my history class before I was called to the Army." The Sergeant moved closer to his seniors and began, "This is a story of three brothers, a French priest and a young prince, and it is a true story."

The former professor stopped and adjusted his wire rimmed glasses before continuing. "It begins in the mid-1700s when the Nguyen's of Hue, (pronounced win) were the ruling Dynasty in Saigon. This family had been busy at war against their traditional enemy, the Trinh family of the North. You see, these two families always wanted to be dominant and their war against each other has been constant since the seventeenth century." Glancing at Duc-Lang he quietly added. "Even today."

"I don't understand the connection to a North Vietnamese Colonel named Tu."

"In due time," Duc-Lang said.

Blake nodded impatiently. "Hope we have enough time." Blake's mind flitted to their predicament. He looked nervously at the hands of his Timex.

Touching his glasses again Trieu continued. "At a time in the struggle when the ruling Nguyens were weak from their battle against the Trinh family, three dissident brothers from the Rung Sat began a revolt. The brothers, distant relatives of the Trinh family in the North, led an attack on Saigon. After their victory, they hunted down the Nguyen family and killed them all. One of the brothers even declared himself Emperor of Vietnam."

Trieu paused, took off his glasses, studied them, then put them back on. After he had gained just enough suspense, he said slowly, "But there was one survivor. A young prince by the name of Nguyen Phuc-Anh or simply Nguyen Anh. Only a boy of fifteen, he had escaped and hid in the Rung Sat. Close by, in a seminary, lived a French priest by the name of Pierre-Joseph-Georges Pigneau. The priest traveled to the Rung Sat and helped the boy escape to exile on the island of Pulo Panjang. At the very moment when Nguyen Anh was about to abandon all hope that he would ever regain his inheritance, he learned that the main body of the three brothers' army had left the Saigon region. Prince Anh with his French benefactor quietly slipped back to the Rung Sat, joined his supporters, then struck out and regained possession of Saigon. A long struggle began with the see-saw occupation of the capital city, until the young prince's forces were defeated with frightful losses. The three brothers then methodically made themselves masters of the South and by striking North they even pushed back the ruling Trinh family. Then they made peace, partitioned the country at its historical division near Hue. You see, there has always been two Vietnams, a North and a South. During those times the North remained under the control of the Trinh family."

Duc-Lang interjected. "That is true. Vietnam has always been two countries, even then." Confirming what the Sergeant had just said.

Blake glanced again at his Timex. *I guess this is one way of getting to know Duc-Lang,* he thought. *Maybe I'll learn what makes him tick. I certainly hadn't expected Trieu's story to continue this long. The Sergeant's nervous habit of adjusting his glasses doesn't help, but actually I'm enjoying the saga of Nguyen Anh.* Blake's own knowledge of Vietnamese history was nonexistent. He did remember that the 1954 Geneva agreement had divided the country into two parts. He also knew that the family name of Premier Van Thieu and Premier Co Ky before him was *Nguyen*, the same as the young prince. *American's think this war is only about the Domino Theory — stopping the spread of Communism. Could it actually be we've stumbled into an age-old fight between two feuding dynasties?*

Blake was beginning to notice little things about his new friends, cultural differences. For instance they smiled more than Americans and they always showed teeth before they talked.

True to form Trieu smiled then continued, "In the meantime, Pigneau and his young charge fled first to Phu-quoc island, then to Siam, and finally to Paris. More than fifteen years passed after the rise of the three brothers before Prince Anh was strong enough to strike again. You know we are a patient people. Time has less meaning for us than for Westerners. When he was a grown man, Anh returned to Siam. There he raised an army and again secretly re-entered the Rung Sat to begin a long struggle."

Duc-Lang added, "The powerful always rise from the Forest of Assassins."

The Sergeant waited respectfully to be sure that Duc-Lang had finished his comments, then continued. "Pigneau had stayed behind in France and then followed with shiploads of stores and hundreds of European volunteers. After stiff fighting, Saigon fell and the three brothers were killed."

Trieu now lowered his head and silently stared at the floor, oblivious of his listeners, apparently transfixed on some image of the dramatic history he was telling.

Blake broke the silence by shuffling his feet and clearing his voice, "Is that the end?"

Trieu raised his head, looked at the *Dai Ta* and then to Blake. He smiled as he said, "No, *cô-vân* Lawrence, there is more." As if he had a surge of energy he began again, "Because Pigneau was Nguyen Anh's *Cô-Vân* or Chief Advisor, the Prince officially bestowed his priest with the title of 'Great Master.' With the old French priest at his side, he fought North to the fortress at Qui-nhon. But victory was assured only at great personal loss to the Prince because his French friend died there. As a result of the pain of losing his close advisor, Anh became ruthless and ferocious in his quest. He defeated the Trinh Family, took Hanoi, then proclaimed himself Emperor of both Vietnams. At a great ceremony at Hue, in the name of his family and Pierre Pigneau, he again partitioned the country at its historical division, North and South."

Duc-Lang thanked the sergeant and after Trieu had returned to the pilot house the *Dai Ta* added, "There you have the story of Prince Ahn, the last seed of the Nguyens, the boy who rose from the Rung Sat to rule Vietnam. The true history of Vietnam is about two families that have always wanted to rule the entire country, but realize that the people in the two halves are so different they must always be governed separately. What Trieu didn't tell you is that Bao Dai, a member the Nguyen family, ruled all of South Vietnam until 1955. It was the Americans that replaced him with an outsider named Ngo Dinh Diem."

Blake accepted the story at face value. *Interesting folklore. Wonder if the U.S. Defense and State departments ever knew or considered the centuries-old hatred of the Nguyens for the Trinhs.*

"Dai Ta, I still don't get the connection to Colonel Tu."

"Well," Duc-Lang began, but at that moment the First Mate called from the pilot house. "The wounded and dead are being transferred to a boat that will take them to the Dutch World tank farm at Nha Be."

Blake was left to consider the intriguing thoughts in the vague fringes of his mind as he moved to the river side of the ship to watch the boat pull away and start on its journey to safety. Peg, who was standing in the back of the boat, was already talking to one of the American sailors. When she turned to wave goodbye, Blake felt a surge of sensual desire but he doubted he would ever see her again.

After the boat's rooster tail became a silhouette against the back-drop of the far river bank, Blake and Duc-Lang returned to the side of the ship where the attack was expected to come.

Seeming infatuated with the opportunity to tell an American about Vietnamese history, Duc-Lang began again, "It was during the Diem period that I first became involved in the Rung Sat. I had come South from Hanoi with my family in 1954 and as a young Lieutenant was assigned to a Dinassant, an French amphibious craft. The Binh Xuyen, a group of gangsters who opposed Diem, had been driven out of Saigon, so naturally they fled to the Nhon Trach region of the Rung Sat. From their base camp they countered Diem's forces with terrorist raids, using bombs and hit-and-run tactics. They also began to attack shipping on the Long Tau Channel in retaliation for government actions against them. In September of '55 my ship was ordered to join a large force to attack the Binh Xuyen stronghold. Army and Marine units surrounded them while the Navy blocked their retreat. After a long battle we were able to close the perimeter of our circle enough that the Binh Xuyen surrendered and their general was killed. So you see, if it's not the Nguyen Family, it's the Binh Xuyen, the Viet Minh or the Viet Cong. Some band of guerrillas has always occupied the Forest of Assassins."

Duc-Lang's expressive eyes pinched and a look of hatred spread across his face. "You see Senior Colonel Tu's full name is Trinh Pham Tu, and although he renounced his inheritance to become a Communist, we all know he is a member of the ancient Trinh Family, the enemy of the South, a venomous snake. His headquarters is somewhere in the Nhan Trach area, the heart of the Forest of Assassins."

Blake shivered. *So that's the connection. Colonel Tu is a member of the Trinh family and is confirmed to be hiding in the Forest of Assassins.* Now Blake wanted to know more about Duc-Lang and the Nguyen-Trinh relationship. He wanted to learn the connection this Navy Captain had with a North Vietnamese Colonel. He wanted to know why there was such hatred and passion. "Do you know Colonel Tu, personally?"

Duc-Lang never answered, because he was again interrupted by the First Mate who reported the tide had changed and the tugs were ready. Duc-Lang simply said, "I'll tell you about that another time."

Blake sensed the importance of the rest of the story and was disappointed, but he didn't press it. He knew he had penetrated the shell and already learned more about Vietnam and the Asian mind than most Americans. He speculated there were probably some things we never learn.

Blake and Duc-Lang watched as the ship's Master began the process of refloating the ship. When everything was ready MacKenna gave the signal and the tugs began their pull. The heavy oil-ladened ship was limber, but she didn't move. Too heavy. Wires were adjusted and the tugs tried again, but again China Fox wouldn't come off the mud.

Everyone's thoughts were on the impending darkness and the Viet Cong. Master MacKenna told Blake he would try one more time. If she didn't come free they would be forced to wait until morning and off-load some fuel. That would mean several more days of exposure. It was too dangerous to continue the salvage operation in the dark. This time the Master used every bit of engine power available and the wire ropes from the Saigon tugs quivered as the giant tanker began to vibrate, then inch slowly. Faster and faster she moved, and when she came free China Fox drifted midstream in a swirling cloud of dark silt. After a few moments, the Master cast off the tugs and ordered his engine ahead. She picked up headway to again follow the winding channel.

Blake, Duc-Lang, and Master MacKenna all knew that another danger point lay just ahead, at a place the Americans long ago nicknamed Hanging Tree Bend. It was a favorite place for guerrillas to launch an attack. Duc-Lang ordered the escorting PBRs to spray the adjacent banks with bullets as China Fox cruised on.

As the ship made its way toward this most dangerous area, ominous dark clouds formed and Blake felt the first drops of a rain storm. Light was fading, but he knew the ship's silhouette when passing Hanging Tree Bend would still be sharp against the horizon. She would be an easy target.

The sky darkened. The wind whipped and slashed out of the Southeast and the rain came shortly before China Fox passed Hanging Tree Bend. As the giant tanker swung a wide turn hugging the bank nearest the heavy foliage that made the place so treacherous, Blake heard a single rifle shot. At first it seemed no more than a token attack. Then there were several volleys; then rockets began splashing nearby.

Because of the weather, the fixed-wing aircraft from Tan Son Nhut had been forced back to base. Mark had stayed airborne in the chopper and was in communications with the ship. Despite poor visibility Mark pressed the attack on the guerrillas by spraying mini-guns along the banks. Duc-Lang's patrol boats fired mortars and 50-caliber machine guns.

Just when Blake thought the attack was over there was a massive explosion on the starboard side of the bridge, and the last thing he remembered was the Master's Scottish brogue, shaking from tenseness as he shouted, "We're hit! We're hit again!"

THIRTEEN

By the time the ship arrived at the Dutch World tank farm to make repairs and discharge her fuel gale force winds were blowing and rain pelted her superstructure. Master Angus MacKenna needed both Saigon tugs to keep China Fox from going aground again as he maneuvered her next to the narrow pier.

Blake watched as armed men guarded the dock area while stevedores hurried about connecting hoses, a prelude to off-loading the valuable petroleum from the ship into the giant oil tanks. He saw a Vietnamese Army driver hunched in a waiting ambulance. *Trung Ta* (Lieutenant Colonel) Phat, Duc-Lang's Army deputy huddled under a slicker in the front seat of a jeep. Mark Harris, who had apparently landed near Dutch World, was standing under a pier light shielded from the rain by an umbrella held by a civilian.

After the tanker was snugly moored, a fragile swaying gangway was set in place so Duc-Lang and Blake could go ashore. The *Dai Ta* lead the way as crewmen guided Blake in his unsteady condition, down the rickety ladder. His thinking processes were still somewhat dull and fuzzy as a result of being knocked down by the China Fox bridge explosion, but otherwise he felt alright. Once on the pier, Blake slowly walked under his own power toward Mark.

"You OK, Commander? What happened out there?"

"B-40 rockets..." Blake shrugged. "Hell of a day. Knocked down and shot at in a temple, then dinged at by a rocket and knocked down by the explosion — wrong place at the wrong time, again. Actually my shoulder hurts more than my head." He brushed off Mark's attempt to help him walk and when asked if he wanted to go back to the base in the ambulance, he brushed that off also saying, "Thanks, but I can make it. I'll be OK."

As Blake and Duc-Lang moved off the pier, *Trung Ta* Phat sprang from the jeep and stood at attention. The stevedores stopped their work and bowed deeply to the *Dai Ta*.

Duc-Lang paused at the jeep. "Are you certain you don't want to ride back to the base with me?"

"Thanks, but I'll go with Mark." Blake said good-bye to his counterpart, a man he was just beginning to know, and proceeded head down through the rain toward the civilian holding the umbrella. The man was older, maybe fifty and slender, and wore a tropical safari suit of dark cotton. The color matched his swarthy face.

Mark made the introduction. "Commander Lawrence, meet our neighbor Anthony Marbo, manager of the Dutch World tank farm."

"Tony. Call me Tony," Marbo said with an unmistakable English accent. He clasped Blake's hand warmly. "You must come by. You both look like you could use a tot. Mark told me you were injured aboard China Fox. Joanna, my wife, is a nurse — quite good you know. She was the one that changed the bandages on those blokes who were injured earlier. She insisted they be taken to the hospital in Saigon for a check up by a real doctor. She refused to come out in this bloody weather tonight, but she really should take a look at you before you return to your base."

"I suppose we do have a few minutes. If you don't mind the grubby way we look."

"Nonsense, you look just fine, come along then." As the jeep pulled away, Tony Marbo paused and stared after Duc-Lang. Tony had a quizzical look on his face. "Jove, my Vietnamese dock men treated that man with rare distinction. Who is he?"

"My counterpart. Captain Duc-Lang. Commander of the Rung Sat Special Zone."

"Hmm. Interesting. By jove, my boys usually don't kowtow that way to an ordinary captain. Duc-Lang must be an important one. Oh, well, let's get along now. Too dark to show you around the place. Save that for another time."

From the beginning, Blake had thought Duc-Lang received unusual attention from the people around him, but Blake had no means to compare. This was the first time anyone had confirmed that kowtowing was not done to all senior Vietnamese Officers.

"Probably kowtow to him because he owns the local whorehouse or opium concession," Mark said.

There he goes again. Who's right about Duc-Lang, Mark or me? I don't know. I just haven't seen or heard any facts that he's involved in funny stuff. Actually, so far I like him and not just because he saved my life. I'll keep my peace until I learn more.

To keep out the jungle moisture, the Marbo's house stood on large pillars about ten feet above the ground. It was a handsome Mediterranean-style villa leftover from French Colonial days. Storm wind rattled wooden shutters. A canvas covered balcony overlooked a garden and the Saigon river.

The shoulder Blake landed on when Duc-Lang pushed him to the temple floor was still tender and he had a bit of a headache. He winced as he placed his weapon near the front door. Rubbing the shoulder, he followed Tony and Mark up a stairway leading to the main room. As he climbed, a sweet perfume floated in a blue layer past his nostrils. Blake wasn't surprised to hear American music playing, but he thought it strange that an English couple had taken to the heavy aromas of the Orient. He wondered if the decor of the rooms would be consistent with the image transferred by the Asian incense.

At the top of the stairs he saw a ceiling fan in slow rotation. Wind caused ruffled silk drapes to flutter and spill. "We're expatriates from England." Tony Marbo explained. "Lived in many countries on assignments for Dutch World. Suppose our furnishings reflect the travel. They're a mixture of styles because Joanna is a bargain collector." Blake saw a German stereo system controlling a stack of records. Brass tables from India held collectibles from every country: dolls, bells, and vases. Capiz shell lamps from Malaysia hung above a chair in the corner. Based on what he saw Blake conceived an image of Joanna Marbo. He pictured a short, plump, broad-beamed, rosy-cheeked English woman, who wore colorless clothes, walked briskly in short-heeled shoes, and had a very direct personality.

He heard her high-pitched voice before he saw her. She approached from the kitchen still giving instructions to a servant. Blake turned to see a tall slender woman, with brown eyes and short, well coiffured hair. She was wearing high-heeled shoes and instead of drab clothes, her dress was made of a flattering colorful design.

Joanna Marbo walked briskly to him. She shook his hand like a man and said in a British accent. "Welcome Commander. Call me Joanna."

Blake's image of her was almost totally wrong. *She's direct,* he thought. *I got that much right — one out of six.*

Tony introduced. "This is Blake Lawrence. U.S. Navy. He's the new American in charge here in the Rung Sat. Replaced Commander Weeks."

The tone of Joanna's voice initially irritated Blake, but the annoyance soon faded as she spoke in a modulating conversational manner. "Replaced Commander Weeks - he was so nice - shame - Here, let me look at you - I understand you were injured aboard China Fox - can't lose you like John Weeks - so glad you are here. Blake - is it - may I call you that?" Without allowing time for Blake to respond she continued her flow of one-way conversation. "We've heard so much about you already - we have wanted to meet you before this - you would think that the base at Nha Be was a world away instead of being just three miles - we want you American boys to feel at home here - don't ever hesitate to come by to see us even on the spur of the moment - we just love company - don't we, Tony dear - and we love American music - do you like Neil Diamond - He is so popular, isn't he, Mark - The Vietnamese are so nice - but it's so good to talk to an American..." She laughed and her voice blended among Blake's thoughts. *She could pass for the English actress Greer Garson, red hair and a bubbly personality. He already felt a homeyness around her and in this home away from home. Wonder what motivates this odd couple to stay here amidst this crazy war.* "Are you married - Blake, do you have any children - Unfortunately, Tony and I are childless but I love them - just love to hear about the families of our friends - I volunteer two mornings a week to care for some of the most darling Vietnamese - they are orphaned you know, by this horrible war - but they are so lovely - Blake, do you like tea or do you want to drink with Tony - He likes his scotch, you know..."

Tony finally interrupted, "Now, Joanna, let me take care of the drinks. Besides you haven't given this bloke an opportunity to even say hello. Come with me, boys" Tony led them from the living room through two large doors that opened to an awning-covered balcony overlooking the garden. Joanna went off to find tea. "Take a look around, gentlemen, while I fix the drinks. What will you have?"

"Scotch for me," Mark answered.

"Make it two." Blake said offhandedly enjoying the quiet of the garden, a spot of Vietnam apparently untouched by the war.

Blake and Mark stood near the railing not two hundred feet from the Long Tau channel. Through the pouring rain he could see lights glowing on river junks moving quietly toward Saigon. Against the black horizon he could see the shimmering glow of the city. Blake spoke first, "Any ideas where the guerrillas went after the attack?"

"Lost 'em. Troops found a few signs but the rain washed away most of the tracks. The dead guerrilla they brought out was just like all the rest, a skinny body in black pajamas. The others must have got away in boats. There's a hundred little streams in there. How did it go aboard China Fox?"

Blake rubbed his tender shoulder as he answered, "I was a bit worried when she didn't come off the mud right away. Thought we might have to stay the night. Then I thought we bought it at Hanging Tree Bend, but the VC obliged us. Had a chance to block the river, but they blew it. Didn't use those wire-guided rockets on the second attack."

Mark turned and squinted at Blake as he lit a cigar. "Saw Peg before they took her to Saigon. Tells me she met you aboard China Fox. What'a you think of her?"

In the hub-bub of getting China Fox safely underway Blake had forgotten about Peg, but now that he was reminded he chose his words carefully. "Quite a girl — and talented. Fixed a radio so I could get through to Saigon. Know her well?... er...long, Mark?"

"Off and on for the past year." He paused for a moment. "I like her a lot."

Blake didn't know how to read the last remark. *Had Peg told him of their encounter? Was it a warning? After all there was nothing to it except a moment of arousal.*

Tony returned with the drinks. Before the conversation about Peg could continue he said, "Here you are, me mates. Scotch neat for me. Over the rocks, as you Yanks say, for the two of you."

Joanna joined them holding her tea cup over a saucer. She was followed by a pretty Vietnamese house girl who offered a tray of cakes, cheese, and sweets.

Tony lifted his glass. "Cheers and welcome to an expatriate's home away from home."

Joanna came to Blake and entwined her arm in his in a warm affectionate way, as if she had known him always. "Commander Lawrence, you must try some of these small cakes - I found them in a shop in Chalon - they're just delicious - don't you just love this house - the French couple that was here before us didn't do anything with it - and they left us that ugly couch, but we've made it livable - I do love the aroma of incense don't you?" Without taking a breath or allowing him to answer she squeezed Blake's arm and continued, "Everywhere we go we adopt some of the ways of the local life - burning incense is so lovely - do you have children - we know all about Mark's background but you haven't told us a thing...."

Tony's voice raised an octave, "Joanna, that's because you haven't given him an opportunity."

Blake actually liked her non-stop way of speaking. He supposed it could bother some, but for him it was just plain wonderful — no pretense, not overdone. One of those rare personalities who seemed comfortable with anyone. Blake wondered if her effervescent personality came from the loneliness of being without children. He took a sip of his scotch and smiled at Tony's attempt to control Joanna. "Nothing much to tell. Wife's name is Beverly. We have two children, a boy and a girl, Blake Junior and Martha. Blake's fifteen. Martha's ten. They're in California."

"What does Beverly think about you being away in this war?"

Blake's response gave no impression of the true situation back home or his feelings about being in Vietnam. "What does she think? I suppose she'd rather I was home, but this is what I do." Then shifting the subject. "Tell me about you folks. This is an oasis right in the middle of the war. How did you find your way here?"

This time Joanna deferred to Tony. "This house was built before World War II as part of a French plantation. The original owners were involved in rice and fruit farming, as well as export-import. Some time later Dutch World bought the place and built the oil tanks and piers. Joanna and I are among a long series of managers brought here to oversee it. We're the only Europeans; everyone else on the staff is Vietnamese..."

Joanna broke into Tony's explanation with, "Actually we've been expatriates for so long, home is where Tony's work takes us - I suppose we would call Roxsbury home, it's near London - you see Tony's parents are Greek but he was born and raised in Britain, on the other hand my parents were Belgian - we were able to get to England just before the war and never returned - so you see Tony and I are natural expatriates - but this is a terrifying place sometimes," she said cocking her head and touching Blake's shoulder. "A rocket landed right out there in the gardens about six months ago, fortunately no one was hurt - most days I actually enjoy it here - I'm not afraid and I come and go as I please - we have good friends in Saigon among the European community - and I've made friends with some of the local Vietnamese women - some are quite educated you know - and they love their children as I do - you must see the place in the daylight - it's surrounded with beautiful trees - we have a lighted tennis court....."

Tony interrupted. "Do you play tennis, Blake?"

"Only socially."

"By jove, right in our league. We'll have you here for a day of tennis soon."

"And dinner." Joanna burst excitedly. "Don't forget I want them to come for dinner also very soon - we will have a lovely time - we'll have some friends from Saigon - to introduce them to Blake and Mark, and the Master from China Fox if the ship is still here - maybe a few of the crew...."

Joanna was interrupted by the arrival of Master MacKenna. His tangerine-gray beard was freshly trimmed and he wore a tropical safari suit similar to Tony's.

Tony Marbo greeted the old seaman. "Evening, Angus. You made good time. Hooked up and pumping already?"

"Your boys did well. They had my new First Mate hopping to get at that oil as soon as we were tied up."

"Drink?" Tony asked.

"Scotch neat."

Assuming the two had never met, Blake said, "Master MacKenna, this is Major Mark Harris, Marine Corps."

Stroking his beard, MacKenna replied. "Ah, we already know Major Harris quite well. Often comes to see our Peg. Understand you were in the helicopter during that affair this morning. Most comforting, I must say."

"Angus," Joanna asked. "Tell us about your passage from Singapore and what happened on the river - have you talked to the doctors in Saigon about those people who were injured - will they be alright, must your ship be repaired - It must have been dreadful..."

"Give the man a chance to tell you, dear," Tony said with a laugh as he handed the Master his drink.

Holding his glass high the Scot said, "Cheers." Then he drank before answering. "Actually the trip from Singapore to Vung Tau was uneventful. Missed a good storm on the way but the events on the river made up for it. Bloody well exciting for a few moments. Wouldn't have been as bad, but that little bastard of a Vietnamese pilot ran us up on the mud. I'm still surprised we were only hit by one of those flying rockets. You familiar with them, Major Harris?"

Mark's mind must have been elsewhere because he didn't answer right away.

"Major Harris," The Master repeated. "Do you know about the flying rocket that hit China Fox?"

"Huh? Oh, the rocket? Yes, sir. Commander Lawrence and I agree it's the Soviet AT-3 wire-guided job. They have a couple of applications. We've nick-named the manpack version 'Suitcase Sagger'. That's the one I believe the Viet Cong have. It's got a hollow charge and can be launched by two people with a range of about 3000 meters. Frankly it's a level of sophistication we don't expect from guerrillas. The Russians are obviously supplying them."

Joanna became noticeably excited. She interrupted, "We've been hit by rockets here at the tank farm in the past - this one sounds horrible - do you think the guerrillas would use it against us, Mark - I don't at all like the idea that we could be bombed by that ugly thing...."

Mark responded to her question before she could continue. "I think it's unlikely. They'd have a hard time setting it up undetected near this area. Too populated. But we'll alert the local police, anyway."

"By the way," Master MacKenna said. "Before I forget, Joanna, I spoke to Dutch World's general manager in Saigon and the return trip to Singapore for repairs will probably be my last. They're letting me get home for a vacation in Scotland early this year. The company thinks I should leave the wounded crew members behind while the ship's gone. We leave tomorrow. Could you take a couple of house guests? That way a doctor can look after them. There are only two. Peg Thompson is suffering dizzy spells from her head wound and one of the men needs attention to his burns. I could certainly keep them in Saigon if it's any trouble."

Blake immediately remembered Peg's words aboard China Fox when she said, "come to see me, if you want." He also thought about Master MacKenna's early vacation in Scotland. *A reward for running his ship aground? Probably his swan song from sea command. There's a desk job waiting for him in London.*

Blake noticed that Joanna glanced at Mark before she spoke, "It's horrible that Peg was injured, isn't it, Mark, but how delightful - we have loads of room - I'll put those two courageous people in the guest cottages - I can look after their wounds and Peg can help me with a dinner party - we shall have a lovely time - what do you boys like? Never mind. Peg and I will shop in Saigon - we'll make it a surprise."

Blake glanced at his watch. "This has been a wonderful break for us, Joanna. We don't deserve to be in your lovely home in our muddy condition. It's late and we do need to get back to the base."

"Nonsense, a little mud could never hurt this place, we expect you to come often, you will come back for our dinner party, won't you?"

As a departing gesture to someone he had quickly grown to like, Blake took her hand then responded to her question. "Of course we'll come. Wouldn't miss your party for the world." But now he was thinking of Peg Thompson.

FOURTEEN

Do Van Nghi's attack on the giant oil tanker using the Russian rocket accomplished his purpose. His mission had been to test the new weapon, block the channel, and escape. When he saw the ship stop and apparently sink he thought, *The hulk will block the enemies shipping to Saigon. No reason to waste another rocket. Save them for the major attack Colonel Tu is planning.*

Based on previous operations, Nghi was well aware how quickly the helicopters came and how bullets and rockets rained as if the Americans had an infinite amount of ammunition. He also knew that parts of the Rung Sat swamps, those that had been defoliated, provided poor cover from the air. His small band would make easy targets as they passed through those areas on their return to the sampans.

Chi and the others were still firing at the attacking patrol boats when Nghi raised his hand and gave the signal to move. "Come quickly, follow me," he shouted. "We go now! Must get the boats into the deep water or we could be trapped to wait for the next high tide."

Without attempting to disguise their hiding places, Nghi's guerrillas took up their weapons and hurried off in a crouch. Their progress was impeded by the rising tide. They were almost to their boats when they heard the helicopter. It seemed almost on top of them when they dived for a crevasse between two mud banks. They were still in the open and they needed to gain time to continue their escape. Nghi gripped Co Hang's shoulder. "Run for the boat. Make it ready for us to escape — Quickly!"

He shouted to the crew of the other boat to run with her through the nippa palm jungle but ordered Chi to remain behind with him and shoot his B-40 rocket at the approaching chopper.

Nghi watched as the rocket flew on a direct path toward the helicopter, but just before it would have hit, the aircraft radically changed its flight path causing the rocket to miss. Then the copter dived spewing its own rockets at them.

Comrade Chi took a hit. Nghi dove to his side, rolled the bloody torn body onto its back. He asked, "How bad is it?"

"Go....without me...." the voice trailed off as his eyes closed.

Do Van Nghi attempted to pull his dead comrade toward the jungle. He struggled with the body, but it was awkward and wouldn't slide well in the thick mud. Nghi's mind vacillated. As the guerrilla leader his responsibility was to get his small band and the new weapon back to camp. Ordinarily it was his duty to bring out the bodies of his dead comrades, but he was already carrying parts of the new rocket launching equipment. He couldn't carry Chi and the equipment at the same time. He knew if he left him behind crabs and leeches would soon cover the body. Nghi struggled in his heart and mind. He trembled when he heard the chopper returning to the attack. Time was running out.

Pulling Chi's body to a bit of high ground, Nghi propped him in a sitting position with his rocket launcher pointing skyward. Nghi whispered, "Goodbye loyal fighter." Then he ran toward the jungle and the waiting boats, leaving Chi's body to give the helicopter a distracting target.

The sampans were still where his band had left them, hidden in an area of thick foliage, but now they were floating in about four feet of water. Nghi's guerrillas had to wade chest deep through brine that smelled of dead fish and urchins. They laid their weapons in the bottom of the boats and helped each other climb in, then began to paddle.

Nghi reminded his band of the things they had rehearsed many times, "Cover your weapons. Place the fishing nets and poles on top for our trip down stream."

Sampan motors made less noise than a Honda motor bike, but sounds magnified in the Rung Sat swamps. Wishing for a silent escape, but knowing a speedy departure was more important, Nghi gave the order: "Start your engines. We will take advantage of the tidal change. Run on the engine for the remainder of the flood. Then we will paddle and float with the slack and ebb until we blend with the other fishermen and woodcutters down stream."

Nghi's boat led the way and his comrades followed. He carefully watched the flow of the water and felt the movement of the boats. At the right moment he ordered them to shut off their engines and they began their drift with the ebbing tide, close to the bank.

In the distance Nghi heard the sound of helicopters, but he knew from now on it would be dangerous to hurry. Better to be Taoists and be patient. He said to the others. "From the air we must look like ordinary fishermen."

Nghi adjusted his fishing equipment and said softly to Co Hang, "Do not show fear if we are stopped by patrol boats."

To the guerrillas in the other sampan he said, "Spread out but stay in sight of this boat. Be good fishermen. Check your identification papers and have them ready."

They each had legal papers which showed them as fishermen, farmers, or woodcutters. The cards had been purchased from the Chief of Phuoc Khanh hamlet for $50,000 *dong* (Vietnamese piasters).

With the loss of comrade Chi, there were now only two people in Nghi's sampan. He stayed in the rear to operate the motor and steer while Co Hang sat alertly in the bow. Nghi adjusted his coolie hat, then spoke to the young woman, "You shot well. Colonel Tu will be pleased."

Co Hang turned her head, smiled, and bowed. Realizing she was still wearing her red bandanna, she quickly ripped it off her head before saying, "Thank you, brother Nghi. I am only a poor village daughter, unworthy of this great opportunity to fight the Americans. If I have shot well, it is because I have been taught well. Please, I wish to have another opportunity."

Nghi didn't answer but he knew she would have another chance, though not until Colonel Tu and COSVN agreed the time was right.

Later that night, in one of the heaviest rains of the season, Nghi guided the sampans out of a side stream where they had been pretending to fish. They paddled into the Song Dua and drifted slowly toward the dim lights of a village. They hugged the opposite side of the river. In the distance against the sound of flowing river water and rain, they heard the muffled voices of sentries talking. In the background they heard a baby cry.

Through the downpour they saw two flat-bottomed boats lying, bows in the mud, near a sentry station. The boatmen had taken shelter and were in conversation with soldiers as Nghi's boats drifted silently by.

Once around the bend from the village of Tan Than Hiep, the guerrillas relaxed, but Nghi knew the most dangerous part of their escape lay ahead because there were always two river patrol boats at the intersection of Song Dua and the Long Tau Channel. Those boats, unlike the ones they had just passed, were usually alert.

If they continued at the same speed they would arrive at this most treacherous place in the channel too soon. Conditions there must be just right.

By now light was breaking from the East. Nghi spoke softly, "It's too dangerous to pass in the daylight. We will pull into another side stream to wait for a more opportune time."

The small band of guerrillas stayed in the streamlet fishing and crabbing, and even left their sampans to make camp ashore where they cooked by the side of the stream. After a time, when the helicopters stopped searching and patrol boat activity returned to normal, Nghi ordered them back into the main stream and they continued their return trip to the base camp. Progress was agonizingly slow as they hugged the bank, skirting around driftwood and river debris. They moved into a side stream, slept, then returned to the main river. This time they inched along in the twilight careful that their noise was no louder than the slap of waves against the river bank. As they drifted with the current, they adjusted their load so their weapons were ready and within reach. At the place where the Song Dua widened into the Long Tau Channel the rain began to fall again.

"The time is right," Nghi said.

At first the moisture felt light and cool to his skin. It rolled off his peaked hat and dripped on his upper legs and knees, but soon the rain began to pelt in the second great storm in three days. One or two kilometers remained before they would be at the turn of the Song Dong Tranh where they could again speed away on their engines. The full moon that had helped them get from their base camp to the ambush site was now hidden behind dark, heavy clouds. Nghi said to himself, "Buddha is with us."

The sampans moved silently, reaching out for the bend of the Dong Tranh river. As they neared, Nghi heard the sound of boat engines. At first he couldn't see them, because their black hulls blended with the jungle background as they lay near the small regional force outpost. Then through the rain, as his sampan came closer, Nghi saw the crew moving about the decks. They were untying their craft from its nest with a second boat. The powerful engines revved several times, then moved ahead and turned sleepily toward them. Co Hang shivered when Nghi's hand touched her shoulder in warning.

As the boat approached, Nghi gave a signal for the two sampans to move parallel to each other so that the advancing patrol boat could not get between them.

A spotlight burst out of the darkness. At first it meandered around the water nearby as if it was out of control. Then like an arrow it streaked across the surface straight for the small boats. Back and forth it swept from one to the other until satisfied its great eye had seen all. Finally it stopped to shine on the nearest sampan.

Blinded by the bright light, the guerrillas sat motionless with their heads down and their straw hats pushed forward. The PBR approached slowly, its engine coughing in the cool of the evening. Nghi heard the sailors voices agree that the sampans looked suspicious. One crew member even urged caution.

As the patrol boat came alongside, Nghi's boats lay quiet in water rippling from the pock marks of pelting rain.

The three guerrillas in the other sampan responded as one of the sailors shouted, "*Can-cuoc.*" Nghi's men silently handed their ID cards to the bowman, who in turn passed them to an older sailor standing next to the spotlight in the rear cockpit. Because the rain was so heavy and visibility so foul, the senior petty officer could not read the cards until he held them in the glow of the spot light.

"This is not a fisherman's identification," he said. "It says woodchopper, and this one says farmer. Search their boat."

The nearest sampan, which by now had drifted away from the patrol craft was ordered back alongside. Nghi's men sat silently, heads down as their boat moved closer to the bobbing military craft. But when the sampan was so close that it was partially hidden under the flare of the PBRs bow, one of Nghi's guerrillas quickly stood up and rolled a grenade into the forward machine gun cockpit.

The noise was not much louder than a large Fourth of July firecracker until the 50-caliber ammunition and the forward gas tank blew. Then the explosion sounded catastrophic. The machine gunner's lower body was blown away and his vital parts splattered over the gun barrel. Fire and smoke filled the forward section and the bowman's head burst as if it were an overripe orange splattered against a wall. He fell to the deck edge, then slid over the side engulfed in flames.

The three guerrillas dove into the water. The reaction of their dive pushed their sampan even farther under the flare of the patrol boat's bow. The two boats lay bumping against each other for a few moments before another explosion rose up in a great gusher of water. The entire forward section of the PBR was blown away by the booby-trapped sampan. Parts of fiberglass ripped away and flew to the rear engine compartment.

The older sailor, standing near the spotlight, raised his M-14 and fired at the guerrillas in the water. Other crew members, now standing knee deep in river water, shouted, "The boat is sinking, swim, swim!"

Nghi ripped at the starter cord, but the motor only whined and coughed. He pulled again and this time the little engine growled and his sampan began to move. He did not try to rescue his three comrades swimming in the water, because in the darkness he heard the engines of the other patrol boat. It was racing in his direction.

FIFTEEN

FRIDAY, JULY 7, 1972, SUPPORT BASE AT NHA BE

"*Cô-vân. cô-vân,*" the feminine voice said.

"Um."

"*Cô-vân. Cô-vân. Da chao ong, toi doy. Cô-vân, Cô-vân.*"

"Um, Umm," Blake mumbled again as he became more aware of the sing-song voice and the hand shaking his sore shoulder. "Ow!" Pushing the hand away from his shoulder but not opening his eyes, He said, "Get away. Leave me alone!"

But when he turned away the voice became excited, "*Cô-vân! Cô-vân!*" The hand more insistent.

Rolling toward the voice, Blake rubbed his eyes and focused on the short, fat woman with a hurt look on her face standing next to him. She had pitch black hair flecked with silver gray strands and wore a faded black working Ao Dai.

"Um, " Blake said as he sat up in the chair and extended his long legs from their twisted position where he had fallen asleep the evening before. Every muscle felt tight. Particularly his left shoulder. His head still ached, but at least he wasn't dizzy.

"*Cam on, Cô-vân manh gioi khong?*" The woman said as she handed Blake an envelop and the letter he had been reading before he fell asleep. Obviously it had slipped to the floor from his lap.

Before taking it he weaved his fingers through tangled hair as if that made him presentable to his Vietnamese hooch maid. "Okay, Rosie, I'm awake."

Blake's room wasn't the Hilton but it wasn't the boondocks either. The decor was Spartan. The furniture early castoff. It was the kind of equipment military bases around the world kept stored in warehouses waiting for wars. The room had a standard Navy iron bed, a small desk, several chests of drawers, and a shower. The only comfortable piece was the chair in which he had fallen asleep the night before. It was cheap wicker from the Philippines.

Satisfied that Blake was finally awake, Rosie moved to the chest of drawers and took out clean undershorts, a green 'T' shirt and a pair of long woolen socks. She placed them next to a fresh set of utilities already laid out on the unused bed. Blake's spit-shined combat boots sat in the corner. Next the little woman stood in front of Blake and bowed low. Her Asian face broke into a big betel-juice grin as she held out her hands. "Give dirty goddamn clothes."

Blake rubbed his head and gave a pained grin. Rosie spoke very little English but it tickled him that she cussed in the language.

"Give dirty goddamn clothes!"

Shooing her away with both hands Blake groused. "Get out and let me undress."

"Give, give, give, dirty fuc'n clothes."

Blake stood his full height and shook his head. "OK, they're dirty but I'm not going to take them off in front of you."

He held his ground, but Rosie wouldn't go away. "Give, give, dirty goddamn clothes."

The tall, slender American faced the short, fat Vietnamese woman in a matter of will. Rosie unabashedly waited for Blake to get on with it. He finally did. He carefully slipped his fatigue blouse over the sore shoulder, then stepped into the shower. From his hidden position behind the door, he threw his undershorts to Rosie.

As soon as he started his shower Blake heard Rosie leave. Her shuffle faded as she hurried to the wash area. Blake smiled to himself. She'll probably tell the other hooch maids all about the new Senior Advisor, the one who doesn't sleep in a bed and has the habit of sleeping with his clothes on.

After his shower Blake slipped into fatigue trousers, then sat on the edge of the bed as he laced his boots. His body felt rough and sandy under his fresh clothes. He was never certain whether he was more clean before or after a shower. The brine water they used from the Nha Be river was mud-colored and almost as salty as the ocean.

As he dressed, Blake heard the rain begin. At first there were just a few splatters on the roof, but soon it grew to a downpour slapping the metal sides of the building like sticks on a snare drum. He glanced at the letter from Beverly. He hadn't finished reading it the night before, and although he didn't have much time now he again picked it up. When he opened the envelope several newspaper clippings fell out. He didn't read the clips, but he read the letter again.

June 23, 1972
Dear Blake,

Received your telegram that explained your temporary assignment as Senior Advisor in the Rung Sat Special Zone. Where is that? The word sounds mysterious — It'll probably help your career. When you called from Saigon you said you thought you would be home by the Fourth of July. What happened to your desk job and not becoming involved in the war?

I've decided to be my own person. I'm not going to be dependent on you or the Navy ever again. The Navy expects us to learn to cry on piers and watch our men try not to cry. I often wonder why any of us do it more than once.

I used to feel pride, but now I don't feel anything except rage. Who ever heard of sending a destroyer officer to fight in a place with a name like the Rung Sat — or fly around in helicopters? You don't know anything about fighting on the ground. You've hardly ever been on the land, always at sea. You don't even know your people let alone the Vietnamese. I mean real people, not Navy people.

Nobody wants this war, everybody's against it. The preacher at church is even speaking out against it. The damned politicians are worse — they're the ones who got us where we are. I've sent a few clippings that prove just how crooked they are.

I do hope the investigation results in your exoneration. Even if it does, will they let you come home — to your precious destroyer?

The kids are doing well. They don't understand why you couldn't get home, but they're enjoying ball games, swimming and summer fun. Your mother wants us to come with them, but we are going to stay right where we are until we know what's going on — until you have your next set of orders. I'll decide then what's best for them.

I've lost more weight and my figure is almost the way it was when we first met. My boss likes my work. He's already given me a bonus, and promised me a raise after Christmas. I'm going to a few office things. I know you won't mind if I go to an occasional evening get-together.

Love,
Beverly

He picked up the clippings and skimmed the headlines. The first dated 19 June 1972 from the <u>Los Angeles Times</u> read:

JAMES W. MCCORD JR., SUSPECT IN BUGGING OF DEMO-CRATIC OFFICE 17 JUNE, FOUND TO BE A GOP WORKER.

The second, from the 21 June 1972 issue seemed to Blake even more obscure in its meaning:

EX-CONSULTANT TO NIXON COUNSEL SOUGHT BY FBI IN BUGGING CASE.

Blake slammed the letter and clippings onto the nearby table. The clippings didn't bother him. He didn't even understand why she sent them. But the letter bothered him a great deal. Obviously written in a fit of pique. It was her stinging prose — just like her stinging tongue when she was mad.

What really upset him was her sarcasm about the destroyer and that she apparently had gone back to her career without even discussing it with him. To top it off she was going out. He thought she should stay home with the kids.

Sure, she had said, during that phone call several months before, the one when he called her from the Philippines to tell her about getting the destroyer, that she intended to change her life. But he didn't expect her to do it. She had said that right after he accused her of never having been keen about the Navy. To that point her voice had been reasonably calm, but that was the first time she began to verbalize her feelings. She said, "Not keen on the Navy? Keen is a dumb word and an understatement. I hate the damn Navy almost as much as I hate your damn war. The Navy is lonesome, it's drivel, and it's unfair. A few 'professional' military wives, who seem to wear their husband's rank better than they do may find Navy life keen. For me it's as dumb as the word keen."

"Now wait," Blake had said. "You knew it would be like this when we decided to make it a career—you went along."

That was a true statement. He met her when he was still a student at the Naval Academy. She had already graduated from Vassar College, a liberal all-girl school and had begun her own career in merchandising. Beverly was the kind of girl who stood out in a crowd: slender and aristocratic in tastefully conservative but modern clothes. She was also the quiet kind who would go braless to show her independence. She had told him then that the Navy was too narrow for her. The scope of the military mind too confining. She said she had never met a senior officer who had read anything literary, let alone understand it. Beverly was creative and wanted to continue with her career. She wanted to delay their marriage until he finished his required service and left the Navy. Nevertheless, they married the year after he graduated. She agreed to the marriage only after a romantic weekend in the Bahamas. Four years later when he wanted to stay in the service instead of a business career— she went along.

"We decided?" she had answered during that telephone call. "Oh yes, you told me and I went along. But I never knew it would be like this, that I'd never see you, that you'd never be home, that you would be at sea all the time. That the children would grow up without a father. That all you wanted was somebody to say good-bye to and to come home to."

"We've been over this a dozen times. A Navy career is demanding." Blake said raising his voice. "If you want to get to the top, you've gotta go for it and this destroyer command is my chance."

"Well, times have changed. We..." she emphasized. "We, don't have to go for it. My life just hasn't worked out like I thought it would. I'm a civilian and I hate this life." Then she mumbled, "I'm worried about our marriage."

"What about our marriage?"

"Our marriage is shot. Our family needs to be together! We need to be together. Now that's not possible. You want to stay at sea."

"Now, Bev, it's not that bad."

"It is that bad." She said raising the tone of her voice.

"You still love me, don't you?" Blake asked gently.

"Love? I'm not even sure I know what love is anymore." Beverly's outrage subsided, but it had taken its toll. Resignation had apparently set in and her voice became distant. He could tell she had steeled herself to his destroyer command assignment. She said she was resigned to unhappiness but before she hung up she said in sarcastic, sobbing tones, "Don't worry. Military wives become self-sufficient. They have to — their husbands are always gone."

Blake picked up his pen and scribbled several paragraphs. He wanted to splash the page in red ink with words that reflected his loneliness and disappointment. He wanted to write: *You think you're the only one who feels bitter. I could have been home with you and the kids. I could have been in command of my own ship. I don't like being here, but I can't bitch about it — it's what I do. Why don't you see the Navy the way I do? I guess it's because you can't feel what I feel. Why can't you feel the pride of being among the few wives who are strong enough to see us go, remain behind and be there when we return, no matter the circumstances? Why can't you believe what you do is necessary. That's the reason we men put up with the separation and loneliness. I'll probably never understand you, and I know you don't understand me.*

Instead he told her about some of the Rung Sat people. He described Duc-Lang and Sergeant Trieu, but he didn't mention a village called Can Gio; the shot that missed him and killed a Girl Scout; a guerrilla called Tu; the grounding of an oil tanker; or the pressure of the investigation. Nor did he mention the Australian woman named Peg Thompson.

*****

Blake left his partially complete response in the letter box — he would finish it later. Slipping on his poncho, he hurried across the muddy compound to the advisors' mess hall. He filled a tray and joined Mark Harris.

"I overslept," Blake said thinking of his busy schedule. "Rosie had to wake me this morning. Would you believe I fell asleep in my chair, still dressed? Rosie's something else, isn't she? Wouldn't leave until I undressed and gave her my dirty clothes — and what colorful language!"

Mark's booming laughter echoed across the Quonset hut. "So Rosie pulled her old 'gimme your dirty goddamn clothes' routine again. She can cuss alright. Her mess deck talk came from our guys. Sailors and Marines come and go but Hooch Maid Rosie stays and her repertoire of foul language grows with each tour of duty. She's been here so long she promoted herself to official caretaker of the Senior Advisor. Comes and goes on this base pretty much as she pleases. Says her husband's away fighting in one of the northern provinces."

"Guess you know Duc-Lang's gone again." Mark sneered over the top of his coffee cup. "That fuc'n gook took off right after the China Fox grounding and went straight to Saigon. Probably with his fuc'n whores."

True, he had gone to Saigon and he was out of his office more than he was in, always in Saigon on business. But he had saved Blake's life in Can Gio. The guerrillas apparently wanted Duc-Lang dead, and his work aboard China Fox was professional enough. *Why did he spend so much time in Saigon?*

Blake had other problems that morning so he passed over Mark's comment as if he hadn't heard it.

*****

The office of the Senior Advisor was on the second floor of a building shared with the Vietnamese Navy. It was simply furnished with several straight-backed chairs, a large desk and a small refrigerator. There was a table in one corner on which a captured B-40 rocket launcher and several disarmed claymore mines were on display. On the wall facing the desk was a chart of the Rung Sat Special Zone and another of South Vietnam. The only luxury was the window air conditioner.

That afternoon a bushy haired Colonel from MACV showed up. He said he had driven from Saigon to ask a few questions about the gunfire incident.

"You were the ship's gunfire coordinator?" The Colonel's words sounded like the "ra ta tat" of machine gun fire.

Nodding his head, Blake acknowledged his part in the affair with a simple. "Yes, Sir."

"Then, it was you who ordered the ship to fire on top of friendly positions?"

"Yes, Sir." Blake answered in a cautious tone. Just answer the questions, he said to himself—don't offer any gratuitous information.

Next the Colonel asked, "Didn't you know the risks?"

"Yes, Sir. I did, but..."

"But.... didn't you realize you could kill or wound Americans?"

"Yes, Sir, but the radioman on the beach asked for it — I thought they were being overrun. I heard the Vietnamese language in the background."

"You're sure they asked for it?"

"Yes, Sir. If they haven't been wiped we had tapes of the radio circuit and Petty Officer Roark heard it. He was with me. It's Navy SOP, ever since the U.S.S. *Maddox* affair and the Tonkin Gulf incident, for all ships in a war zone to tape their critical radio circuits."

"You say you had the tapes and a Petty Officer Roark overheard what was said on the circuit."

"Yes, sir."

"Okay, Commander Lawrence. Guess that's it. Got to get back to MACV. We'll be in touch. Oh, by the way, I already interviewed Major Harris and a Corporal Marquell."

*****

Outside in the hall by the yeoman's desk, Gunny stood with Corporal Marquell waiting for Captain's Mast to begin.

"Whataya think I'll get, Gunny?"

"Don't know." Gunny said adjusting his belt buckle so it would line up with his fly. "Could be the book. Could send ya back to the States. Don't know how Commander Lawrence thinks."

"I don't wanna get sent back, man."

Gunny shook his finger. "I told ya — An don't give me that 'man' stuff. Ya brought it on your own head. I told you to stay away from the shit."

Raising his hand, Marquell emphasized his plea, "Gimmy a fuc'n break, Gunny. I was just do'n some vodka I brought back from Saigon. You been on my case ever since we were almost overrun in Can Gio. I'm tell'n ya again, I might have said the wrong thing, but I wasn't on the shit. That investigator, the Colonel from MACV? He seemed real nice."

Gunny bristled. "Don't bullshit me. Ya been smok'n marijuana and I don't know what else. Hashish maybe? I smelled it. I can tell. Doc knows it and I caught ya. It ain't no secret."

"Ya, well there's no evidence. I was just drunk. I know I shouldn't a been in the barracks like that, but it wasn't like I was on duty or nothin'."

"Don't try ta sea-lawyer the Gunny. In 'nam you're always on duty. I told ya that."

Corporal Marquell's eyes clouded. "It'll kill my mom and dad if they find out I'm in trouble again. Come on Gunny. Just gimmy this one break. I'll straighten up. The officers listen to you."

Gunny Johnson looked hard at this blond haired, white boy in a Marine uniform. "If I'd been your DI, I wouldn't have this problem now. Don't know how ya got through PI. You needs yo' ass kicked and your daddy shoulda done it a long time ago."

The yeoman's voice broke over Gunny's, "You can take him in now, Gunnery Sergeant."

*****

After the MACV Colonel left Blake's office, Corporal Marquell marched to a position of attention in front of Blake, then spread his legs as he assumed the position of parade rest. Gunny stood at his side.

So this is Corporal Marquell, Blake thought. *The one I owe all this grief.* Marquell looked too young to be in the Corps. His was the kind of baby face that, to exaggerate a bit, would look 18 when he was 25, 29 when he was 40, and 39 when he was 50. It struck Blake that Marquell was actually only a few years older than his own son.

The charges were read. Marquell was asked for his plea and he gave Blake the same story he had given Gunny. He said he knew he was wrong, but held to the vodka story. He argued he could square away if he was given another chance.

Blake stroked his chin. His forehead wrinkled in thought. He recognized Marquell's voice. It was the same one that said, "Just start fuc'n shooting. Goddamnit, they're gonna fuc'n overrun us. Give us something now!" He particularly remembered the words, "Give it to us on top." Marquell's voice was that of a scared eighteen-year-old but had it not been for him calling in the rounds, Commander Weeks may never have died, and Blake wouldn't have had his orders changed. On the other hand it was Blake's decision to fire at the position, not Marquell's, and who knows, they all could have been wiped out.

Blake called a recess from the proceedings. He wanted to get Mark's opinion. After Marquell had left the room he asked, "What do you think about this case, Mark?"

"Except we had no direct evidence, I'd of busted him and sent him home right after the Can Gio incident. We still don't have any good evidence. Gunny thinks he smelled marijuana. The kid was out of it when Gunny caught him, but no one could find the grass. You can send him back to the States and the Corps will discharge him. If he's on drugs he won't get better in the States, he'll just blend with the cult and become invisible."

"How much time does Marquell have in-country?"

"A few months." Mark answered. "As far as I'm concerned the kid's an asshole, but it was Gunny who caught him and the Gunny thinks he can make a Marine out of him. If you decide to keep Marquell in-country, Gunny says he'll watch him close. I have mixed emotions. Not sure he's worth it, but if anybody can turn him around it would be Gunny Johnson."

Blake knew he couldn't be vindictive. On the other hand he was in a very awkward position. It was iffy and probably not within regulations that he preside at a Captain's Mast for a person who was also involved in the investigation of the naval gunfire incident. After all he was also a party but if he sent him up the line to a higher convening authority Marquell would surly be sent home. Even if he wanted to send Marquell out of country he wouldn't go right away. MACV wouldn't let him go until the investigation was settled. Blake knew that being sent back to the States early from a war zone was considered less than honorable and although it would never show on the record, the corporal would know it the rest of his life. Blake raised both hands in a sign of solution. The judgment came easy, "You say Gunny wants to keep him. Okay, we'll keep him — for the time being. But I know drugs are a problem in-country. There must be other users. I'll send them a signal. Marquell goes to Saigon for some brig time. It'll dry him out."

*****

Corporal Marquell shifted uneasily in front of the lectern. Gunny ordered him to attention.

"Let's make this short and sweet. I've listened to the evidence and I find you guilty. Reduction to Private First Class and one week brig time. After that he's all yours, Gunny — and Marquell, Gunny thinks you may still have the makings of a good Marine. Don't let him down." Only Blake knew there was more than one reason for his decision not to send him back to the States.

Gunny snapped to attention and nudged PFC Marquell to do the same.

Outside, the two walked side by side toward the barracks. Marquell's head hung low as he said, "The Saigon brig can't be all that bad, can it?"

Gunny stopped. "Stand tall, shit bird," he barked. "Snap out of it. At least look like a Marine. It may not be bad. You may even be able to get the shit there, but ya better be one squared away PFC when ya come back, 'cause your gonna work like you never worked before or I'll jerk you a new asshole. Before I'm finished with you, you're gonna be a Marine or wish Commander Lawrence had sent ya home ta your rich mamma and pappa."

*****

After the Captain's Mast, when he was alone with Blake, Mark said, "Commander, Gunny's got his hands full with another problem besides Private Marquell."

"What kind of problem?"

"He wants to get married."

"Didn't even know he had a girl."

"Yes, sir. They tell me he met a young Vietnamese girl down in Can Gio some time ago. Brought her to Nha Be. Uses every excuse to be with her."

Blake shook his head. Referring to the monastic life of most Americans in Vietnam he said, "You sure he doesn't just have a bad case of swollen gland?"

Mark half-smiled at Blake's benign effort to make a joke. "Gunny's no kid. Should know what he's doing. He's in the process of getting the paperwork for the marriage. Wants to take her home, but it's a slow process. He's asked to extend a couple of months to finish it. Not that I don't know the pitfalls of women near fighting men, but frankly if this was any other man my answer would be flat-ass no! But, Commander — Gunny's an outstanding Marine. He's saved my bacon more than once. I'd like to give him the extension."

Blake knew the Navy and the Marine Corps, all the armed services for that matter, discouraged Americans from marrying Vietnamese women. It was mostly a matter of statistics. The marriages didn't last. For one reason or another less than fifteen percent made it past the first year.

It wasn't that the Vietnamese were bad women or bad wives, it was just that a mixture of easy love, cultural differences, and social pressure both in Vietnam and in the States turned the marriages sour.

Blake told Mark he would approve Gunny's extension, but he added, "I hope this marriage'll be the one out of seven that makes it."

*****

When Blake left his office at the end of his working day the rain had stopped and the air had a fresh smell. As he made his way toward his quarters he heard a commotion behind the advisory compound. He diverted from his path toward the noise and as he neared he heard sounds of pig squeals and Vietnamese voices mixed with American laughter. He moved through a crowd of sailors and Marines to a place near the front. Blake took a sip from a can of beer thrust into his hand by an American sailor, then looked down from the knoll to see a large mud pit next to a pig pen. In the pit he saw Hooch Maid Rosie and another Vietnamese woman, neither of whom weighed more than 90 pounds wringing wet, with two massive hogs.

Blake shook his head and smiled thinking about America's last minute effort to develop the country economically. He was even required to have one of his officers assigned the collateral duty of assisting the Vietnamese raise hogs and chickens. The "Pigs and Chickens" officer had pens built on the base near the American compound where the art of animal husbandry was to being taught.

At first Rosie looked embarrassed. For her, mating the animals was serious business and she would rather the Americans left her alone. *If the truth were known,* he thought, *she probably hates the advisors for their intrusion.*

Nevertheless, her orders to the other hooch maid grew louder as Rosie maneuvered the boar. She pushed and pulled, shouting invectives until the male was behind the sow. With great effort, one hoof at a time she lifted the male's front end over the female. Rosie then turned so her back was against the rump of the hog and her legs were extended to gain leverage. She began pushing the male and exhorting the animal to exercise, but the male wanted nothing to do with copulation in front of the population and he wouldn't budge. The more

Rosie pushed, cussed, and shouted, the more the boar grunted, the poor sow squealed, and the more coaching she got from the beer-drinking Americans.

Rosie waved at the Americans and shouted, "go way sonsbitches."

But the crowd was having great fun watching as the other woman held the sow steady and Rosie attempted to guide the boar into position. At the top of their lungs various members of the crowd shouted, "Stick it to her studly! Get him up higher, Rosie. Push harder, Rosie. A romp in the mud is worth two in the bush!"

Someone shouted, "Who's taking bets. I'll give five to one on the hogs."

The two tiny women had their Ao Dai trousers rolled up. Their cone-shaped coolie hats hung from strings over their shoulders and they were totally covered with mud.

Finally, Rosie became a bit of an actress. She knew she had an audience so her instructions to her cohort began to include a few choice American cuss words for the benefit of the crowd. Every time she used the words "goddamn" or "fuck", the crowd broke into laughter and cheered her on.

Blake got caught up in the impossibility of it all. He shouted. "Good girl, Rosie, ya got 'em now."

Rosie shouted back. "Goddamn hogs, no fuck good!"

Blake grinned, waved, then moved away from the crowd. He could still hear the squealing and laughter but for a moment he just stood alone and reviewed his recent predicament. *What a place,* he thought. *And what a range of life: from bullets, to drugs, to pigs.*

His solitude was short lived, because a hurried voice shouted, "Commander Lawrence. Better get down to the chopper pad, fast! Admiral Paulson's com'n in."

SIXTEEN

FRIDAY, JULY 7, 1972, NHA BE

The Rung Sat sun scorched the peninsula where the Song Nha Be swirled sharply past the airstrip. There the river, foaming at its eddies, continued its journey to join the Cua Soirap.

The afternoon air was so calm even the sea gulls struggled in their search for survival. Sweat from the monsoon deep-delta heat soaked Blake's shirt. Droplets trickled from his cheeks down his neck and chest.

He heard the familiar gas turbine whine of a chopper, its rotor blades throbbing against the silent river. The blue V.I.P. helicopter stayed at altitude until it was high over the Nha Be base, then descended in a spiraling path to its target, a large white cross painted on the tarmac.

"Blake!" Admiral Paulson shouted through a toothy smile as he jumped from his seat in the back of the just-landed aircraft. Like a man hurrying to or coming from a high voltage conference, shoulders hunched, six-shooter flopping at his waist, he ran out from under the spinning blades. Blake sweltered, but if Paulson felt the heat he didn't show it. His boot toes were still mirror-bright and the sleeves of his fatigues were still rolled with a micro-precision that was mindful of photos Blake had seen of the immaculate General Westmoreland during his tours in-country.

Paulson extended his glad hand and shouted above the noise, "I followed the China Fox situation. You and your boys did a damn fine job."

"Thanks, Admiral." A hostile chill ran through Blake's body. Although it was nice to hear words of praise, he harbored a latent distrust of the Chameleon. After all he was haunted by a court-martial and the words of Captain Johnson aboard *Decatur*, "Watch out for him ... he's an SOB, the kind who's always out to hang an imperfect world."

"Would you like to run over to my office or the TOC? It's cooler there," Blake asked.

"Sorry — no time. Just dropped in for a few minutes on the way South. Can't talk over the phone."

They climbed into the front seats of the jeep.

"Blake," Paulson said above the noise of the engine, "I'm concerned about those wire-guided rockets. I was patient when the enemy was lying low, but now the bear's out of the woods. Sapper attacks have picked up. Fuel stocks and ammo dumps are blowing and we're low on everything. Something's building over near An Loc. May be a big attack on Saigon when the dry season gets here. That'd put pressure on the peace talks and the elections back home. Now that China Fox took a couple, it's really hit the fan. Got to get those rockets."

Even though they were sitting next to each other, Blake had to shout to be certain he was heard above the waiting chopper. "Admiral, I want you to know we're as concerned as you are. I'm working closely with *Dai Ta* Duc-Lang —

told me he had his people out on intelligence missions, but until now there just hadn't been anything to act on. The attack on China Fox was the first proof that the rockets were still in the Rung Sat. You said yourself that things had been quiet."

Paulson turned and wrapped his arm around Blake's shoulder. "Duc-Lang..." His voice took on a persuasive tone that reminded Blake of the kind Lindon Johnson often used in his television speeches. But the Admiral's jaws and eyes were hard as he said, "Got to get rid of Duc-Lang. He's asleep at the switch."

My opinion of Duc-Lang obviously differs from that of Mark and the Admiral, Blake thought. *Not sure why he spends so much time in Saigon, but in the past my intuition about people has been as good as the next guy.* Blake went with his gut feel and stuck to his guns. "I know you and Mark are down on Duc-Lang, sir — but he did save my life in Can Gio and he responded well during the China Fox situation. I've seen good things since I arrived here. Even Mark has been surprised."

"Well, Mark says he hasn't done his job." Paulson pulled back his arm and growled, "I'm not sure why the Vietnamese Navy keeps him here. I've asked my counterpart several times that he be relieved. For some reason the Vietnamese side is dragging their feet. I'm relying on you to get me some hard evidence about his dereliction. If I can learn what he's involved in, I'll have him out of here in 24 hours!"

Blake didn't want to sound disrespectful, but it had to be said. "Seems to me we should be more worried about this Senior Colonel Tu than Duc-Lang and the AT3 missiles. He's the guerrilla leader."

The Admiral's jaw tightened and his cheeks flushed. "The mysterious Colonel Tu? Our intelligence people say he's long gone — disappeared. If he's still out there, he's harmless. The rockets are our priority. Election day is just a few months away and MACV's getting a lot of heat from the White House. Nixon wants a cease fire and I want those rockets. Not going to wait much longer. I want action down here, and, Blake," Paulson extended his chin and shook his finger in Blake's face, "I'll get it one way or another."

*****

As he drove back to the advisor's compound, Blake could still hear the wap, wap sound of the chopper blades fading in the distance. Paulson's reputation was well known — ruthless with people to get his own way. The Admiral wanted Duc-Lang fired, but for reasons that no one understood, the Vietnamese side wouldn't agree. The meeting had ended abruptly with an ominous warning to find the rockets and get rid of the Dai Ta or else Blake's head would roll. Although he hadn't explicitly said it one didn't have to be a genius to understand the message: the gunfire incident and his destroyer were in the balance. All from a man Blake was beginning to think had a very shallow understanding of war.

The bitterness he felt when he first received his orders to Vietnam swelled again, even stronger. Now he had another or-else demand from Paulson. *Maybe I should throw it all in — resign. I've got my twenty in. Let Harris take over —*

Paulson would like that. I could be out of here in a week — save my marriage — join the other pukes who're sitting on their butts in front of a TV. That's a dumb thought, He reflected. *Maybe I'll do it after this is all over, but not until. Shake it off Lawrence! Get back to work.*

In his office Blake studied the chart of the Rung Sat. His finger found the place where China Fox had been hit. His eyes searched the surrounding area as his mind struggled for a solution. *How do you find wire-guided rockets in a jungle and swampland like the Rung Sat? Where did the guerrillas come from? How did they get away? Why didn't they do more damage when they had the chance?* His finger moved in one direction then another, pondering the various paths. He tried to put himself in the place of the guerrillas. *They must have come by boat. Blended with the surroundings, then set up at night for the shot We can't ambush every streamlet and river, too damn many of them.* Then he thought of Duc-Lang. *He knows this place. He's lived here and even fought the Viet Minh here. Why hasn't he been more aggressive? Is it because he knows the impossibility of a search? Is he on the take as Mark believes? Or does he do something else in Saigon?*

His concentration was so deep that he was startled when Mark said, "Heard you had a visitor, Commander."

As usual, Mark looked as if he had just stepped out of boot camp. His fatigues had sharp creases, and his boots were so shiny they reflected his hard-jawed face and countersunk eyes. Mark always addressed him as Commander, no matter how often Blake suggested he use his first name. *Maybe it was the disagreement about Duc-Lang or maybe he knows about the incident with Peg aboard China Fox, although I doubt that. On the other hand, maybe it's just because he's a rigid, by-the-book Marine.* In any case, Blake had gotten used to his formality and shrugged it off. "Ya, Admiral Paulson flew in to talk about the wire-guided rockets and I've been analyzing this chart to get some idea where to look."

"Maybe we won't have to look after you hear the news."

"What news?"

Before Mark continued Blake motioned the Marine to a chair then took a seat behind his own desk. "Two interesting things have happened, Commander. First, a Vietnamese Navy boat got shot up." Mark's crooked forefinger pointed to the wall chart. "It happened here at check point two. From the dope we got from the VN's it was some sort of sapper attack. It's hard to figure, though. There were two sampans and the guerrillas didn't do anything until they were stopped. One of the sampans was loaded with explosives. Blew the entire bow off a patrol boat. Sank in about thirty feet of water. Three slope heads escaped by swimming ashore. The other sampan took off."

"Anybody killed?"

"Two sailors. I understand they were blown up pretty bad."

Blake stood and moved closer to the chart. "Where exactly was the boat hit — the location?"

Mark moved from his chair and drew a circle on the chart. "The intersection of the Dua, the Dong Tranh, and the Long Tau Channel."

Tugging his chin, Blake pursued. "Which way did they go — the guerrillas — after they blew the PBR?"

"One of the VNs who survived says they swam ashore here," pointing to a peninsula at the intersection. "The other fuc'n sampan went North, up the Dong Tranh."

"Maybe they weren't sappers. Could be the same ones — the same guerrillas that attacked China Fox. Just trying to escape."

"Could be, Commander. It fits with the way it happened. Seems there were two PBRs on station down there. Only one got underway to investigate the sampans. That was stupid! But if they were sappers the guerrillas would have blown both boats. The VNs in the other fuc'n patrol boat didn't get underway until after the explosion and then they didn't follow the sampan up the Dong Tranh. I hear Duc-Lang is pissed."

Blake ran his finger along the Dong Tranh. "Have we searched this area?"

"Would you believe Duc-Lang's already got boats and aircraft over there? First time that fat little bastard's shown any interest! He's sure changed. They won't find anything though. That boat could be up a thousand little streamlets by now. They'd look like woodcutters or fishermen."

"At least it's better than doing nothing," Blake said, already feeling better about defending Duc-Lang to the Admiral. Then, as he handed Mark a Coke, he asked, "The other thing? You said there were two things that happened over the weekend."

"Commander, this is the big news. We got ourselves a fuc'n VC prisoner."

"Prisoner?"

"Yes, sir. The PRU captured him."

"Wait, Mark. You know I haven't been here all that long. What's a PRU?"

"Provincial Reconnaissance Unit. Rag-tag bunch. Mostly ex-junk force sailors. Every one of them has *Sat Cong* tattooed somewhere on his body. Work for the CIA, and do what they're told, most of the time. The CIA pays them — we don't ask questions. Anyway, a squad of them were in the village of Nhon Trach when they got a tip that some guy was trying to buy parts for a radio. They have him over in their compound, but the best part of this story is that when they picked up this guy, they found a letter on him. Lieutenant Cox says its from the Commander of Doi 6 to Colonel Tu."

"Tu's alive? We've got hard intel he's still out there? Damnit, I wish I'd known that when the Admiral was here."

"Wait, Commander. There's more. The better part is there's a good chance Tu already has the information that's in the letter. In his letter the Doi 6 Commander, a guerrilla — lemme see. I got his name right here," Mark thumbed a note pad. "Ya here it is. Name's Do Van Nghi, explained that the letter is only a follow-up to a radio message he had already sent. Reason this guy... what's his name?" He glanced again at the note pad. "Ah... Tam Ha was looking for parts — that's the prisoner's name, Tam Ha, the guy the PRUs captured — was because the radio broke sometime during the transmission. No shit, it's in the letter. Still better, unless we miss our guess, the author is the same guy that hit China Fox! In the letter he invites Colonel Tu to come to his base camp for a fuc'n party after their return from an attack using a new rocket — must be the AT-3. The PRU are working on this guy Tam Ha, to find out the location of the base camp."

As Mark Harris explained the news Blake began to chuckle; then he burst into laughter and Mark joined in. "Jackpot! Hoowee! This could be the break Duc-Lang needs to get Colonel Tu."

Mark frowned and his voice vibrated as he said, "It would be better if you didn't talk about this to anyone, Commander, over the telephone, that is. We've thought for some time there's a spy in the Rung Sat. Some believe it may be one of Duc-Lang's staff. Operational security's got to be tight on this one."

"Okay, Mark. When do you think we'll know something more?"

"We may never. Charlie has some tough guys. Sometimes they break. Sometimes they don't. It's never easy, but if anyone can get to this guy it'll be the PRU. If they break him, we may be able to put together the most productive operation the Rung Sat has ever seen!"

Blake felt exuberant over learning so much about Colonel Tu. The information from the captured VC overtook any residual bitter feelings he had after his conversation with Paulson. He off-handedly said, "I think I'll stop by to take a look at the prisoner."

Mark almost choked on his cigar. He blurted, "You're better off not to, sir. It's not that we Americans don't care, but this is grim business. Less you get involved with the PRU the better. He's their prisoner. You might see something you're better off not to see. Let the Orientals deal with the problem in their own way. Besides, the rules on treatment of guerrillas are fuzzy. We usually let the intel officer check it out. He won't let the PRU go too far."

Blake looked out the window and thought about what Mark had just said. *I've heard about this sort of thing. Seen it on television in the States. Everyone knows about Mei Lai and the famous TV shot of a Vietnamese officer shooting his prisoner in the head. I want no part of that.*

Blake warned, "Mark. I'll stay away, for now. But I'll tell you right now we don't need headlines."

*****

Blake returned to his room and took off his combat boots. He kicked each into a corner where Rosie could find them in the morning. Next he peeled heavy wool socks off tired feet and sailed them into a pile with the boots. He picked up several of Beverly's letters that had finally caught up to him from *Decatur*. They were three weeks old and he had read them all twice before, but he reopened the one with the latest post mark and read it again.

Dear Blake,

Junior is still playing baseball, but has begun to hang out with some of the wrong kids. I hope he doesn't get into drugs. Martha has moved from beginning to intermediate level in her tennis group and is playing the guitar. She says she wants to be a singing star like Diana Ross. She's even writing her own poetry. Wants to put it to music.

Blake thought of Marquell when he read the line about drugs and he ached to be with his son. He smiled as he thought about Martha. She was talented and pretty and it fit that she would want to write songs. Bev's letters never sounded loving anymore. This one was particularly short. The last paragraph bothered him.

> I've taken a job with Sak's La Jolla. I'm getting back into my old field of merchandising. My diet is working and I've already lost ten pounds. The boss is an interesting man and he thinks I have talent.
>
> Love,
> Bev

So that's what she's done. Gone to work at Saks. And in the latest letter she said she's going out. She's searching for something and if she finds it the marriage'll be over. There isn't anyway I can stop her. To try would only make matters worse.

Blake took his half-finished letter from the writing box and continued to compose. His descriptions of the war were usually limited to an occasional anecdote about the lives of the advisors or about some barracks event like Hooch Maid Rosie. This time he subconsciously reacted to his own bitterness and to Bev's unrest. It was as if he wanted to get even when he wrote about the invitation to Marbo's dinner party.

> The Marbo's home is an oasis here in the Rung Sat. Joanna Marbo is not a typical English woman. Mark and I've been invited to have dinner there soon.

Blake had just finished the letter when he heard a knock on his door. Mark entered and doffed his beret. He was followed by Lieutenant Jerry Cox, the Advisory Unit intelligence officer. Cox stood awkwardly at attention next to Mark.

"Got some good news. Tam Ha broke," Mark said.

Blake licked the seal on his letter to Beverly then asked. "What did he say?"

"Show him, Jerry."

Cox, a prematurely bald man adjusted thick glasses, then spread a pocket map across a table. "If we can believe what he says, the rockets are in a base camp right in the middle of Indian country," he pointed. "Tam Ha says he's the assistant Company Commander of Doi 6, and according to him the reason Doan 12 has been so quiet is there's been a big reorganization in the Rung Sat. Says they're getting ready for a major attack. I mean this guy really spilled the beans, Commander. This is the best intel we've had in months — maybe ever! He confirmed that Tu is alive and is still the leader of Doan 12. Said Colonel Tu is now a BTO with COSVN and they're planning a big guerrilla attack. Even gave us a description of him. He's tall, for a Vietnamese, has long graying hair, and wears a neatly trimmed chin beard and mustache. Says he doesn't know where he is but thinks he's somewhere near the rubber plantations over by Nhon Trach."

Mark interjected, "Tam Ha's in pretty bad shape. They're trying to get him to tell where Tu is hiding."

"Do you think he knows?" Blake asked.

"Of course he knows, but they'll play fuc'n hell getting him to tell."

"Did you see him, Jerry?"

The young officer shifted uneasily. "Yes sir — But not for long. Just got a glance. The PRUs tried to keep me out. Not sure he's going to live!"

"Did you see him, Mark?"

"No sir," the Marine responded defiantly. "But when Jerry told me, I went straight to *Trung Ta* Phat, the deputy, and told him about it."

Blake's words chopped, "You don't think they'll kill him, do you?"

"Phat didn't seem too interested in saving him."

Despite his own feelings about the war, some things were right and some things were wrong. This had the smell of another ugly incident like Mei Lai. It was time to step in. "Guerrilla or not," Blake barked. "He has the rights of a prisoner. I'm no bleeding heart but there's got to be a limit. The dope we have from Tam Ha sounds good. We need to check it out then go after the rockets. But we can't let them kill him, especially if he knows where to find Colonel Tu."

Mark shrugged. "Then you better see Duc-Lang. He's the only one that can get Tam Ha out of the hands of the PRU."

Blake walked to the corner and retrieved his green wool socks. "You better come with me, Mark. Jerry, you stay with the PRUs. Tell them I've gone to see Duc-Lang. Keep the pressure on them to keep Tam Ha alive."

As he began the task of getting back into his combat boots, Blake tried to recall the relationship of the guerrilla and international law. *I remember plenty about the law of the sea, but the guerrilla?* The word humanity kept flashing in his mind. *It's the underlying principle of the Geneva Convention.* Blake stood up, adjusted his fatigues, put on his black beret, then said grimly, "Okay. Let's go see Duc-Lang."

Blake, with Mark at his side, walked quickly through the base. American and Vietnamese alike stood out of their way.

In front of the Commander's office, a South Vietnamese flag with its yellow background and three horizontal red stripes hung limply from the flag pole. As they approached, the two Americans saw a Vietnamese boy kneeling at the foot of the pole with his hands tied behind his back. His chin was pulled high by a rope from his forehead to his ankles. He was dressed only in jockey shorts, and his head was shaved.

Not used to seeing people humiliated in public, Blake slowed his pace and asked Mark, "What's that all about?"

"A VN sailor. Had a fuc'n hippy hair cut. It's Colonel Phat's way of punishing him — sends a message to all hands. The Vietnamese have a different set of rules than we do. He's been here all day. Probably be there 'til late tonight." Mark then added, "It's not in our book, Commander, but it's effective. You may have to adjust your think'n out here."

"I doubt anything could change my mind about that."

They passed between two cement buildings into an open area where several freshly painted concrete block houses stood against a back drop of the Long Tau Channel.

"Duc-Lang lives in the building on the right," Mark reminded Blake.

As they approached, a tall dark-skinned army officer came toward them. He nodded and gave a reserved smile. Phat had a Vietnamese name but his blood line was obviously Indian, probably predating most Vietnamese in the country. He was a handsome man with delicate features and large brown, moon-shaped eyes that darted quickly when he spoke. "*Chao Trung Ta* (Hello, Commander)."

Greeting him in Vietnamese Blake said, "*Chao Trung Ta*. Is *Dai Ta* Duc-Lang in his quarters?"

"I'm afraid he's gone, *Cô-vân* Lawrence. Can I help you?" The lean Army Lieutenant Colonel asked.

"Where'd he go?"

"*A Saigon*. (To Saigon)"

Mark and Phat stood facing each other, hands on their sidearms. Mark turned his head and gave Blake an 'I-told-you-so' look.

Phat remained impassive. His Indian round eyes never blinked. "Maybe there is something I can do?"

"Something you can do?" Mark spat. "Have you taken custody of the fuc'n VC officer like I asked you? The one the PRUs captured?"

Phat's expression never changed. "I'm sorry, Major. I told you that is a matter only for *Dai Ta* Duc-Lang. I cannot interfere."

Blake felt his face flush. "I have a report that the PRU are killing the prisoner. You're the deputy here! It seems to me you could act in the Duc-Lang's absence."

Phat shook his head. "There is nothing I can do."

"When do you expect the *Dai Ta* to return?" Blake snapped.

"I'm sorry, *Cô-vân*. I do not know."

"Then you must do something about the prisoner."

"What can I do?" Phat shrugged his shoulders. Then calmly, as if he were attempting to divert Blake from the issue, he asked, "Won't you come in and have something cold to drink?"

"No," Blake snapped. "This is an urgent matter. I want you to take custody of the prisoner Tam Ha. Take him from the PRU and give him proper medical treatment."

Phat's eyes changed and his jaws tightened. "I have no jurisdiction. The man is a criminal, no more than a common gangster."

"He's admitted being the assistant Company Commander of Doi 6," Blake said as he raised his hands in exasperation. "If that's the case, he comes under the leadership of Senior Colonel Tu and Doan 12. Therefore he has rights under the Geneva Convention of 1949!"

Phat's face paled. His voice shook and escalated, "Geneva Convention? When has the Geneva Convention meant anything? Tam Ha is a guerrilla! A whoreson! His fate should be no less than summary execution!"

Blake sensed hatred spawned from years of guerrilla warfare. "But that's no excuse. Listen, *Trung Ta*. We're military men, not gangsters. Our job is to preserve humanity, not revert to barbaric methods. Yours isn't the first nation that's been up against guerrillas. It won't be the last."

Phat's voice became quiet, "I'm sorry. I have no authority."

"For the last time. I ask you to take custody of Tam Ha." Blake said.

"Did you wish to discuss anything else, *Cô-vân*?" The tone of Phat's voice reflected doom for Tam Ha as certain as the clichés: an explosion of a grenade; the curtain had fallen; the show was over.

Blake's mind raced to find the solution. *Does a guerrilla by the name of Tam Ha really matter? Does one peasant's life make a difference? This is one of those decisions too often passed off for an easier way and I'm not going to pass it off.* The words came slow and easy, "Sir, if this man can tell us how to find Colonel Tu, *Dai Ta* Duc-Lang would want him alive. I hold you responsible if he dies. I'm going to call Saigon to talk to Duc Lang, but if I can't get in touch with him, I'll call in Rear Admiral Paulson — and another thing — that boy tied to the flag pole. That's inhumane also. I better not see him there when I come back."

Phat's eyes shifted and he shuffled his feet slightly. Blake had the trump card and Phat had read him wrong.

Mark stepped forward and said quietly to Blake, "Commander, could I talk to you privately?"

The two walked past *Trung Ta* Phat to the farthest end of the small lanai where Mark said, "You got him in a corner, Commander. He doesn't want Saigon in on this one. I suggest we back off. Give him a chance to save face."

"Save face?" Blake couldn't believe his ears. Mark Harris, the gook-killing Marine, wants to allow this spineless Vietnamese to save face? "Bullshit, Mark. There's a time for face, and there's a time for action. I'll give him a half-hour. Tell him if he doesn't take custody of the prisoner by then, I'll do it myself."

Seventeen

Two guards stood side-by-side at rigid attention blocking the passageway. From a distance they looked harmless, but as Blake and *Trung Ta* Phat approached they bent low, their M-16 rifles at a hip-thrust position with bayonets fixed, as if to attack. These defenders of forbidden space were fierce-looking men who wore the silver combat helmets and the gold aiguillettes of Duc-Lang's elite headquarters guard. Blake froze until Phat gave the safeguard. On hearing the secret words, the sentries returned to the position of attention, then slammed their bodies against each wall to allow the visitors to pass into the sinister-looking inner corridor. Blake and Phat stopped at the end of the passageway and stooped to see through a small barred peephole into this prison within a prison which had no windows and no lights. Phat fumbled with a crude lantern, then focused its beam into the cell. A bed and a pan of water were visible near one wall. A body lay on the bunk. When the light hit his face the man moaned and rolled away.

"How is he?" Blake asked in icy tones.

"The pig may live."

"You made a wise decision, *Trung Ta*." Blake offered his obviously patronizing remark knowing that Phat had reluctantly taken custody of the prisoner from the PRU and placed him in this high security cell under the care of an Army Doctor.

"Do you wish to see more?" Phat snapped, ignoring Blake's comments.

"Of course." The sound of Blake's voice reflected his continued disdain for Duc-Lang's Army deputy. Phat had conceded immediately after Blake left Duc-Lang's quarters, but he delayed allowing the Senior Advisor to see the prisoner until the next morning. Blake assumed it was because the man had been severely tortured. Phat bought time by having the Doctor treat him.

"Unlock the door and let me examine him."

Phat called to the guards and one of them came with the key to the cell. The door hinges creaked as it swung open wide enough for Blake and Phat to enter. Once inside, Blake knelt next to the body lying close to the wall. He touched the man's shoulder. Tam Ha cringed and his breathing increased. Carefully Blake pulled the shoulder until he could see the man's face and upper body. There were dark marks on his throat and across the bridge of his nose. Black flesh about his eyes contrasted with the corpse-like pallor of the rest of his face. One of the man's arms slid across his body and limp fingers rolled open to reveal bloody pulps at each tip where a device had squeezed through skin and bone. It was clear the man had suffered severe torture. Some of the fingertips were bandaged and all showed signs of medical treatment. "Okay, I've seen enough. Treat him well and allow him to gain his strength. We will question him later."

Having fulfilled his desire to personally examine Tam Ha and still thinking about the tortured man's fingers, Blake returned past the sentries. He departed the black passage into the sunlight leaving *Trung Ta* Phat behind to save face anyway he could.

*****

On return to his office, Blake found Mark Harris pacing the room. He stopped only long enough to bellow his displeasure. "The sonofabitch is still in Saigon. Probably overseeing his fuc'n black market operation or ball'n his concubines. I told you about Can Gio but you had to learn for yourself. I've told you about Duc-Lang before. Now you see why Rear Admiral Paulson and I want the bastard fired."

"Wait a minute, Mark," Blake said. *Here we go again. Mark's on another one of his tears.* He slumped into his chair and kicked his feet onto the desk top. "I sent Sergeant Trieu over to Duc-Lang's office to find out when he's coming back. Trieu should be here anytime. Sit down — relax."

Mark took a seat facing Blake's desk. "Relax? Hell, if this Vietnamization shit is going to work, we need a full time Rung Sat Commander. And we need to do something about the intel we got from the prisoner. Somebody's gotta get out there and get those rockets. If we were still run'n this fuc'n war, I'd a blown the shit out of that place an hour after we learned the rockets were there. Admiral Paulson told you there's heat from Washington to get those weapons. I say we have to attack — right now, and Duc-Lang should be here to plan and direct the operation."

Sergeant Trieu peeked cautiously through the half-open door. "Excuse me, *Cô-vân.*"

Blake waved him into his office. "Come on in, Trieu. What did you learn?"

The slender Vietnamese man bowed to Blake and gave another half bow to Mark Harris as he entered, then stood facing the two Americans. He adjusted his ill fitting glasses, and spoke in a very differential manner. "The *Dai Ta* has been delayed in Saigon on personal business, but he will be here later today."

"Personal business? You mean fucking his girlfriend."

"Now, Major," Blake reproached.

Trieu's body stiffened at Mark's words and his eyes hardened. In an uncharacteristic show of emotion he confronted the Americans. "Don't you know why he goes to Saigon?"

Ignoring Blake's warning, Mark sneered again. "Sure, to be with his whores and get rich."

Blake had never quite figured out why Mark was so hung-up and nasty about Duc-Lang. He assumed part was because, after Commander Weeks was hit and while Mark was acting Senior Advisor, Duc-Lang, a Navy Captain, hadn't paid much attention to him. Part because Mark was only a major; and part because the Duc-Lang hadn't charged after the rockets the way Mark wanted. On the other hand Mark could have some underlying prejudice against all Vietnamese, a cultural distrust. Many Americans felt that way, particularly those who were toured up north near the DMZ and thought of it as an American war.

Regardless of the reason, Blake was about to slam Mark with a verbal barrage when Trieu's eyes flared even more. His voice sounded hostile as he said, "Do you think someone of *Dai Ta* Duc-Lang's family and station would lower himself to the black market or be a whore keeper? The only reason he goes to Saigon is for his children. Surely you know by now that the *Dai Ta* has two daughters. One is nineteen and the other only four. He tries to spend as much time with them as his work permits. The oldest girl is a student at the university, but the little one must have special care. She has many problems because she was born crippled and disfigured when Duc-Lang's wife was murdered."

Blake's feet came off the desk. He shot Mark an incredulous look. When his eyes returned to Trieu he exclaimed, "Duc-Lang's wife was murdered?"

"Yes, and his only son as well."

"A son?" Blake remembered Duc-Lang's sad response, aboard China Fox, to his earlier questions about sons.

"You and *Dai Ta* Duc-Lang have become such good friends, I assumed he would have told you." The skinny former teacher said. "This is very personal and I am just a sergeant who has already exceeded the limits of my position when I talk about his family. Don't you know that *Dai Ta* Duc-Lang's wife died during the Tet massacre of 1968 — killed by Senior Colonel Tu?"

Blake stood, placed his hands on the desk and leaned forward, "Killed by Colonel Tu? How?"

"I shouldn't tell you this. Please do not let him know where you learned this." Trieu hesitated as if he had already said too much. "The *Dai Ta's* home was among a small group of Navy houses near the Vietnamese shipyard in Saigon. On their way to capture the palace, Colonel Tu and his band of guerrillas attacked the military compound. They massacred everyone — women, children, old people, everyone. A grenade was thrown into the living room of the *Dai Ta's* house. Duc-Lang's wife was hit, but she didn't die right away. They say what really killed her was seeing her son and old mother chopped dead by the machete of one of Tu's young guerrillas. She was still alive when Duc-Lang found her. Before she died she told *Dai-Ta* Duc-Lang how Colonel Tu watched the entire affair from the door."

Mark Harris leaned forward and asked in a disbelieving tone, "How would she recognize Colonel Tu?"

Trieu stiffened at Mark's inference of disbelief, "She knew him,"

"Duc-Lang's wife knew Colonel Tu?" Blake said, shaking his head in wonder.

"Yes, from the North. Duc-Lang married her after he graduated from the Hanoi Military School in 1952. It was a small class and Tu was among the graduates.

Blake remembered the unfinished story aboard China Fox when Duc-Lang almost told about his relationship to Tu. Now Blake had to know more. "What else should we know about Captain Duc-Lang and Colonel Tu?"

Trieu touched his glasses. By now his facial expression had relaxed and his body language returned to the normal differential demeanor of a sergeant. "The guerrillas killed everyone else in the house. But when Senior Colonel Tu recognized Duc-Lang's wife he allowed her body to be abused by his young guerrillas. Even then he would not let them kill her. He wanted her to live long enough to deliver a message to her husband. She was pregnant and by the time Duc-Lang got to her she was almost dead. Doctors saved the baby, but his wife eventually died."

"My God! ....That sonofabitch!" Blake's voice shook with rage. Then he asked the obvious, "What was Tu's message?"

"That Duc-Lang was a traitor to the Vietnamese people by fighting with the Americans. That Duc-Lang's son, the last of his seed, is dead. That the Trinh family will overcome the Nguyens and the North will overcome the South. Tu promised that one day Duc-Lang's death would be even worse than that of his family."

Mark Harris gave Blake an embarrassed look. "Christ! That son-of-a-bitch!" Then to Trieu he blurted, "I should have been told."

Sergeant Trieu hesitated before he responded, then he bowed and said respectfully, "Like Americans, the Vietnamese are a proud people. *Dai Ta* Duc-Lang would only confide his personal affairs and problems to his closest and trusted friends."

*****

After the revelation, Mark Harris and Trieu left his office and Blake was left alone with his thoughts. He felt vindicated in his judgment of Duc-Lang, but, more important he now understood why his counterpart hated Colonel Tu.

Blake idled the rest of the morning, attempting to finish some paperwork and was still within his thoughts when Duc-Lang was shown to his office door. Blake stood and offered him a seat then returned to his place behind his desk. Duc-Lang began by saying, "You were right to intercede with Lieutenant Colonel Phat — about the VC prisoner. I would not have allowed him to die at the hands of the PRU. Tam Ha knows where to find Colonel Tu and that is most important."

Blake shrugged. "It's OK. It worked out. We can continue the interrogation as soon as he's stronger."

Duc-Lang's head sagged and he dropped his eyes. It struck Blake that he was carrying some unusual burden. *I suppose*, he thought. *Even Vietnamese Captains needed to occasionally confide in someone.*

"I have come to you with bad news," Duc-Lang half mumbled. "The prisoner is dead."

"Dead?" The news particularly jarred Blake because the significance of Colonel Tu's importance was just beginning to gel in his mind. He wanted to react like Paulson often did, by shouting or slamming something, but his relationship with his Vietnamese counterpart wouldn't allow any explosiveness. He contained himself. "He was alive earlier today. I saw him."

Duc-Lang shook his head. "Yes, I couldn't believe the news at first either, but he was killed by one of our own soldiers, one of the guards. Trung Ta Phat caught him coming out of the cell. But when Phat tried to capture him the guard attacked Phat and he had to be killed. We have suspected for a long time that a spy had infiltrated our Rung Sat forces and it turned out to be one of my own headquarters guards."

Blake scratched his head. "Damn it! Well — fortunately, we have enough intel to go after the rockets."

Duc-Lang's voice raised and he made a fist as he said, "But I want Colonel Tu."

"I now know why Senior Colonel Tu is so personally important to you, but our side places more importance on the rockets."

"What do you know about Tu's importance to me?"

"That he ruthlessly killed your wife and son."

Duc-Lang looked surprised. "You learned about that? Who told you?"

Blake wouldn't break Sergeant Trieu's trust, so he looked away as he spoke his white lie, "I'm not at liberty. Just say a friend of mine — in Saigon."

"Then that friend doesn't know anything, because that's not the main reason. What you don't understand is Senior Colonel Tu does not belong here. He is a Northerner, a dog eater. The Communists would have you believe that Vietnam has been one nation ever since the Annams defeated the Chams in 1471. But this has never been one nation. I told you aboard China Fox that the Nguyen Dynasty has almost continuously fought the Trinh family of the North. Certainly there have been long periods in our history when the North has occupied the South or the South has occupied the North, but we have never been one Vietnam. They are Annamites, Trinh and Bac Ky. We are Chams, Nguyen and Nam Ky. That is why the two great walls north of Hue were built in the 17th century."

Duc-Lang's voice rose and his fat jowls tightened as he continued. "That was the wisdom of partition at the sixteenth parallel after World War II and at the seventeenth parallel after the Geneva Convention in 1954. Tu is much more important than Russian rockets, because he is a Trinh and represents the North. Of course we should go after the rockets, but you Americans will leave and more rockets will come. There will always be more weapons, but there is only one Colonel Tu. Unless we can kill or capture him, he will be here long after your part in this war is over."

Could these be the real reasons for the war? Blake had heard Duc-Lang say it before, but then he had clung rigidly to his assumption that the war was only about Communism and the Domino Theory. It was true that his own analysis of the war and its root ideas were shallowly drawn, if at all. Things political at home were straight ahead, logical. *Here nothing is as it appears. Everything is illogical. Duc-Lang is emphasizing that on the surface the war is about a struggle against Communism when it really is like a fight between the Hatfields and the McCoys. Could this war, at least in the minds of the Vietnamese elite, really be an intriguing age-old struggle between the Nguyens and the Trinhs?*

Blake and Duc-Lang agreed a plan had to be developed and action taken based on the intelligence gained from the guerrilla. They decided to meet later at Duc-Lang's headquarters after the staff had a chance to work on a plan to gain both objectives: capture or destroy the rockets and capture or kill Colonel Tu.

Blake and Duc-Lang met in an old French building where maps of the Rung Sat were prominently displayed in a central area. They proceeded into a larger room lined with desks. Vietnamese officers sat working in deep thought. Others scurried from partition to partition like ants, carrying letters, maps and orders, all necessary to prepare a formal battle plan.

Mark Harris and Lieutenant Colonel Phat stood in front of a large map in conversation with a group of Vietnamese officers.

"Just covering some of the details of the plan. Be finished in a few moments, Commander," Mark said.

As they idled, waiting to get briefed, Blake studied the order of battle for the operation. Written in long hand on rice paper, the Vietnamese clerks had listed, in both languages, every unit and every element in the Rung Sat Special Zone, giving estimated strengths of each. Other lists showed the numbers of weapons required, the kinds of boats and helicopters needed to carry the troops and the number of patrol boats required to protect the transports.

Other lists showed the number of gunships needed to soften up the landing areas, and on still others, Blake saw the crazy names of American support aircraft like Spectre, Stinger, Spooky and Night Hawk.

Mark and Phat finally excused themselves from the discussions with the Vietnamese planners and joined Blake and Duc-Lang. Mark said, "You can see, we'll need everything, maybe even the kitchen sink."

Blake scratched his chin. "Seems like an awful lot of forces to go after just a few hundred Cong,"

"It's the way it has to be against the guerrilla," Duc-Lang said.

Mark took a long stick from a nail on the wall and pointed to the Northwest corner of the Rung Sat map, almost directly east of Nha Be and southeast from Nhon Trach Village. "This is the area where the prisoner said we'll find the rockets. It's Indian country — Doan 12 country. Tam Ha said Doi's 4, 5 and 6 are in there. The ground's firm, but it's some of the roughest forest in the Rung Sat. Three sides are surrounded by streams. The other side is heavy jungle and nippa palm, all the way north to the hamlets and villages along Route 319."

Duc-Lang's eyes glistened, his cheeks dimpled. He seemed excited when he said, "It's the same area where I fought the Binh Xuyen in '55. It's the heart of the Forest of Assassins. Whoever holds that area seldom stands to fight. They fade into the jungle. More likely they escape in sampans, if you let them. We must corner them. Force them to fight."

"Agree, Dai Ta. To keep them from escaping we're putting in an airmobile-blocking force to the North. We'll have them put on a phony demonstration, well in advance of the operation, just enough to contain the VC in the river area. We'll need to insert waterborne guard posts as blocking forces on the two streamlets. Then we'll make an amphibious landing, sweep through the area forcing the fuc'n VC toward our ambushers. The tricky part will be getting the river-blocking forces in position ahead of the landing without giving away our intentions."

Blake held up his hands, as if he were a police officer stopping traffic on a busy street. "I'm admittedly inexperienced in ground warfare planning, but it seems to me that an operation this big won't work unless we have two things — good intelligence and good security. The intel we got from Tam Ha seems good enough to me, but aren't there too many people working on the plan? The fewer who know what we're up to, the less chance for a leak."

"You're right, Commander. But it's the way the Vietnamese planning is done. Right, *Dai Ta*? To counter the possibility of spies getting the word we've set up a deception operation. Only a trusted few know the location of the main attack. It's going to be tough to pull it off without a leak, but it can be done if we're careful."

Duc-Lang, who had been studying the map as he listened to Mark's briefing, spoke next. "I know this place very well. There's no doubt we have a good chance of capturing the Soviet weapons if they are there, but to get Colonel Tu we need better intelligence. Right now we don't know when to attack. I want to know when Tu will be at the guerrilla celebration— the one that was mentioned in the captured letter. We need to send in a recon unit, don't you agree Major?"

"That's risky, *Dai Ta*. Could give away the entire op if the insert went sour."

"We could send in the PRUs." Duc-Lang persisted.

"I agree we could use better intel, but that CIA bunch is undisciplined. They'd just fuck it up and you'd lose control," Mark shook his head. "No, whoever we send in had better be damn good."

"What about your SEAL's?" Duc-Lang countered.

Mark frowned. "SEALS? Shit!"

Blake hadn't much previous contact with SEALS, except to admire them whenever he passed their training base near Coronado, California. On the other hand, he knew more about them than the average American with an interest in things military. Several years before, when he had undergone his special SERE training, his class had included a few SEAL's. They were a rugged lot, who found foraging in the mountains and desert for food, and then escaping from a mock P.O.W. camp, a picnic. Compared to their own "Hell Week," SERE training was a piece of cake. Blake knew of their mystique — they were known as fearless men who were selected for their physical and mental toughness and then taught to swim like fish and sky-dive like birds. They were the Special Forces of the Navy.

"What do you think, Mark?"

The Major shook his head.

Mark was stalling and Blake suspected it was because Marines typically thought they could do what SEALS did and twice on Sunday. Blake, wanting to be supportive of Duc-Lang and his goal of capturing his invisible enemy said, "I think it's worth a try. But I'll have to go to Saigon to get the Admiral's permission and that may be a problem."

Blake didn't relish the idea of convincing Paulson to allow him to send in the SEALs on an intelligence mission instead of just going for the rockets. Here he was an instantaneous advisor, in-country less than a month agreeing with his Vietnamese counterpart over the objections of his own Marine advisor. He knew, if he was to succeed Mark would have to be on his side. Or the Admiral would, out of hand, say no.

"Mark," Blake said. "I'd like you to come along. You agreed with the *Dai Ta* that we need better intel. Help me persuade Paulson."

Apparently sensing the squeeze play, Mark's face flushed. "There are a lot of things I could do right here to help get this plan off the ground."

But Blake's game plan included Mark Harris. He said again. "I'd really like you to come. Besides," Then Blake played his ace. "The plan can move along without you for an evening. Remember — this is the night we're to go to the Marbo's for dinner. We could stop there on the way back from Saigon. Frankly, we both need a break from this place and unless I miss my guess, Joanna will have organized a good supper. Anything's better than hot dogs and Nouc Mam in the Rung Sat."

Mark smiled, then nodded agreement. "That'll give me a chance to see Peg."

EIGHTEEN

The sampan turned from the Dong Tranh and re-entered the Rach Cai Go. Do Van Nghi sat in the stern, head tipped forward, eyes raised only when necessary to steer. He felt depressed. His thoughts returned to Chi's death from helicopter bullets and the loss of the three comrades who had to swim to shore after the Navy boat stopped them. He would have brought them home in his own sampan if he had not had to speed away to escape from the second patrol boat. Nghi's own sampan might have been captured had he not turned into a streamlet so shallow that the patrol boat couldn't follow.

Then a feeling of elation seeped into his mind. The guerrilla band had successfully fired the complicated new Russian rocket and they had even escaped with the weapon. Colonel Tu had told him under no circumstances were they to let one fall into the hands of the enemy. Nghi had been prepared to dump it in the river, because he knew there were others in the camp.

Despite his good feelings he was baffled by Co Hang's changing attitude. She should have been as happy with the results as he, but when he asked her to adjust some of the equipment she said, "No! Do it yourself!" Then slammed her paddle against the side of the sampan. After a few minutes she began fussing with the fishing nets sullenly doing what she had been told. Later, Nghi heard a quiet whimper. Her mood seemed to swing and he didn't know what was wrong. Maybe it was the sight of seeing her friend Chi die. It could be some female thing, who knows? Women.

He moved forward in the boat and touched her head, her shoulder, and the red bandanna around her neck. "You did well. Your rocket sank the ship! Do not fret over the loss of Chi or the safety of the others." Co Hang had conducted herself bravely and showed concern for the welfare of her comrades. Nghi consoled her by telling her that her comrades were clever, resourceful men and the jungle was their home. They could find their way back to camp; although, unless they were able to steal a boat it would take weeks of swimming and wading through the Rung Sat mud.

The touch seemed to work. She tilted her head. Her eyes softened and she gave a pleasant laugh.

Her smile is different, he thought. Women. Who knows what they think? She's only sixteen. She's been through a great deal. He nestled her head against his legs and asked. "Is there anything wrong?"

Co Hang rubbed her head against his leg. "No. Everything is wonderful, now." She began to hum.

Do Van Nghi returned to the stern to prepare for the return trek through the jungle to the base camp. He shut off the engine then guided the small boat into a swampy area where he let it glide through the stale water until the bow ran into the mudbank. He and Co Hang sat silently for several minutes listening to jungle sounds, trying to sense the slightest change that would indicate an ambush. As they waited, Nghi's elation dimmed as he again remembered he had started with three boats and was now returning with only one. Comrade Chi was dead, the three in the other boat were somewhere in the Rung Sat, he had no idea of the whereabouts of the other boat — the one he had sent to the place the American's called Hanging Tree Bend.

When all seemed right Nghi and the girl picked up their weapons and left the sampan tethered on a long line to a mangrove root. He would send someone for it.

Nghi led the way and the girl followed with the rocket launcher strapped across her back. He kept his gaze on the narrow path, searching for signs of the pits and traps set for the hated PRU who from time to time invaded the Forest of Assassins to ambush Nghi's men.

"*Ngung* (stop)!" Nghi whispered and pointed toward a section of the path. The girl came closer and stared at the ground. At first she shrugged as if she could see nothing unusual. Nghi showed her the outline of different colored grasses and leaves. He moved his hands in a circular motion and then up and down indicating that there was something sharp below the ground. "*Nguy hiem* (Dangerous)*" then led her around the hidden pit filled with sharpened sticks.

At the base camp Nghi learned that the men from the third sampan had already returned.

Guerrillas from the other Dois came to see the Russian weapon that had fired rockets on a ship. They crowded around asking questions.

"Who fired it?" one asked.

Nghi pointed. "Her, Co Hang."

"How far did it fly?" A guerrilla asked the girl.

Co Hang dropped her eyes as she responded, "Far enough to sink a passing ship on the Long Tau."

"How much damage did it do?"

Nghi felt his chest swell. "The ship sank and blocked the channel."

One of Nghi's men who had returned in the third sampan from Hanging Tree Bend said, "But, Comrade Nghi. We fired on a large ship on the night of the great storm."

Nghi then realized that his rocket had not shut down the channel as he thought. "Well, we claim victory anyway." To save face Nghi said, "Let us enjoy a party with Colonel Tu as the guest of honor." Nghi began making assignments and detailing arrangements when another of the men from Nghi's Doi asked to speak to him privately. They walked a few feet away from the crowd and the man whispered, "Tam Ha has been captured and killed."

"How? Where was he captured?" It was like a knife thrust to his heart. Nghi's eyes searched the men's faces as he asked, "Who captured him? Where was he taken? Who killed him?"

"We only know what we have heard from Doan 12 headquarters. Somehow Colonel Tu has learned that Tam Ha was captured in the village of Nhon Trach. He was taken to the Navy base at Nha Be where he was tortured, then murdered."

Do Van Nghi's skinny body ached from his rage. He immediately began to think of revenge. He stroked his chin beard then led his followers away to a thatched lean-to built under the nippa palm trees. There he sat in the traditional way with his feet flat on the ground, arms folded over his knees. The others gathered about him like children waiting for the telling of a fairy tale. But Nghi would not tell them a story. They would tell him.

"Where in Nhon Trach would Tam Ha have gone?"

"To the store where they fix radios."

"How would the PRU learn he was there?"

"Someone would have told them."

"Why? Why would they tell?

"For money." The men responded in unison, all nodding agreement.

Nghi's eyes closed as if he were visualizing the answer to his next question. "Who would turn in a guerrilla for money?"

There was a pause, then one said, "A villager."

"Who would they tell?"

"The National Police."

After Nghi heard it all he said. "The village of Nhon Trach needs a lesson." It was like the slice of a sharp blade. "We will pay them a visit."

NINETEEN

The jeep's engine sounded rough as it rumbled through the turn out of Nha Be village onto Route 15 and headed north. Mark changed gears and pressed the accelerator to the floor. "I'm going to rev her up to 40 or better from here to the Rach Doi bridge, Commander. Don't want to take any chances on getting ambushed in the unpopulated area. The trip from Nha Be to Saigon only takes about two hours and it's normally uneventful, but no one feels at ease on these roads."

Blake was learning how volatile it was, especially now because no one was certain what was happening. To the uninitiated it seemed just country, peaceful and quiet. One day there was talk of peace and the next, war forever.

In Saigon the two advisors went directly to Admiral Paulson's office. After about a half hours wait the aide showed them to the door. Inside, without looking up from his work, the Admiral motioned them to take seats across the desk. The Admiral continued to read a document and gave no sign of interest in the two. Finally he looked up and said, "OK — Busy. What's up?"

Blake began by telling about the prisoner. He showed the Admiral the place on the map where Tam Ha had said the rockets were located. Then he explained Captain Duc-Lang's idea to send in a SEAL recon group.

The Admiral maintained his silence until Blake finished. Then he exploded. "Send in the SEALs? You got that hair-brained idea from Duc-Lang? What the hell do we need a recon for? If we know where the rockets are, go for it! Bomb the place. A telephone call will do it. I'll just call in a B-52 strike."

Blake shivered. *I could have predicted Paulson's by-the-book, over-kill. My own military mind might ordinarily come to the same conclusion, but I'm learning fast that there's more to this kind of war than meets the eye. I believed in Duc-Lang. He isn't a Saigon crook, and I was right. Now my intuition is that Duc-Lang's approach is the better. Got to convince the Admiral.*

"But, Admiral. There are villages and hamlets in the vicinity. Besides, if we blow the place up we may never have the proof that the Russians are supplying the AT3's to the VC and we will never know if we got Colonel Tu."

"He's nothing. I've told you before it's the rockets we want. Forget Colonel Tu."

Mark Harris came to Blake's rescue. His resonant voice offered the solution. "Admiral. If we do it Duc-Lang's way we have a chance to get both the rockets and Colonel Tu."

Blake felt a warmness toward his new Marine associate. He wasn't sure why Mark was all at once supportive of Duc-Lang. He wasn't the kind to be falsely cooperative. *Maybe he's changed and agrees with Duc-Lang, that Colonel Tu really is important. More likely he's feeling guilty about doubting Duc-Lang's motives. On the other hand, maybe we're starting to click as a team.*

Focusing his eyes quizzically on Mark, the Admiral said. "You were the one that wanted Duc-Lang fired in the first place."

"Yes, sir, but..." Mark paused a long time then said in a subdued tone, as if he had a hard time saying the words. "I was wrong. The SEALs should do this job." His pitch strengthened as he said, "It needs to be done."

"Well, it's risky. A saturation bombing run would do the job just as well. But...ah...alright. When would you need them?"

"Monday," Blake responded.

Rear Admiral Paulson stood. His face reddened as he blustered his warning again. "Blake, I want those goddamn rockets."

*****

When Blake and Mark drove south on route 15 late afternoon shadows were peeling from their objects and farmers were returning from their rice paddies. Blake watched a small girl walking next to a water buffalo. She carried a long switch and every once in a while she cracked the animal across its hind quarters. The buffalo took a few quickened steps as if to amuse the tot, then settled back to its end of the day pace. The peasants walking behind the child were dressed alike: black baggy pants, collarless blouses, and straw hats; they carried curved knives used to cut their rice crop. After a day in the paddy dikes their hair was stringy and their faces streaked with mud, but they laughed and chatted during that problemless moment when the work day ends and evening begins.

"Seems funny to be going to a dinner party wearing camouflage fatigues and carrying machine guns, doesn't it, Commander?"

Blake glanced away from the Asian farm scene and smiled. Above the noise of the jeep he said, "For me it seems funny to be going to a dinner party at all in a war zone. Before I arrived in country, I thought it was all toe-to-toe combat out here. Then I learned the staff bunnies in Saigon have evenings like this all the time."

As they drove, Blake's thoughts drifted to Peg Thompson, the other person besides Senior Colonel Tu he had found difficult to forget. His memory of the scent and feel of those moments aboard China Fox were still with him. He tried to shake them but he couldn't and the sharply worded letters from his wife only compounded the paradox.

Mark slowed to negotiate the turn onto the side road that led to Dutch World. He slowed even more when an armed guard stepped out of the brush to check out the jeep. Recognizing them as Americans, he waved them on.

Due to darkness and rain on the day China Fox moored at Dutch World, Blake hadn't seen the petroleum farm. Now the eight oil tanks, arranged in two rows close to the river seemed like a colossus compared to the small Vietnamese dwellings nestled nearby. The Marbo's villa was a virtual palace in relation to the Vietnamese homes. Their French style plantation sat in its own grove of banana palms. It included a tennis court, several sets of guest houses, and quarters for servants.

"Looks as though the Saigon crowd's already here, Commander." Mark said as he parked the jeep next to several Mercedes and a black Cadillac.

Strains of American dance music drifted from the main house. The two paused near the door long enough to set their weapons out of the way. A heavy scent of incense still floated in the air, although tonight it was mixed with perfume.

They were met by Tony Marbo wearing a tailored tropical suit. "Ah, Commander Lawrence and Major Harris. Glad you could make it. And in time for cocktails. Come join the group."

The guests were on the balcony overlooking the gardens, enjoying the evening beauty of the Saigon River as lights from passing boats shimmered across the rippling water.

Joanna Marbo disengaged from a conversation with a young couple and strode quickly to them. "Good evening, Blake and Mark — how lovely you could come — we were worried some horrible thing would happen in that terrible Rung Sat and you wouldn't be able to make it, you both look wonderful — Vietnam must agree with you — I just love the green and brown shapes they have designed into these uniforms you wear — you simply must meet our guests and make yourselves at home..."

Joanna would have continued her bubbly extended sentences but Tony interrupted. "Just a moment Joanna," he said in a patronizing tone. "Neither of them have a drink yet. Why don't you let these two warriors have time for some good whiskey?"

Joanna laughed. "Of course darling — give their order to the bartender — they can meet our guests while their drinks are being made..."

Mark glanced at Blake. "Order me a scotch, will you, Commander?" Then excused himself and melted quickly into the blur of unfamiliar faces on the balcony.

Tony went off to order the drinks and left Blake with Joanna. Taking his arm she said. "You must come and meet these wonderful people." Then to the crowd. "Everyone! Everyone! This is Commander Blake Lawrence and over there, for those of you who have not already met him, is Major Mark Harris." Mark had already found Peg Thompson and was holding both of her hands while absorbed in conversation. In her buoyant British accent Joanna continued. "As you all can see, Blake is a Naval Officer and Mark is a Marine so we are totally safe for the remainder of the evening — we will be defended from the land or the sea — they're both charming Americans."

The sight of them together caught Blake off guard. He knew Mark had been seeing Peg, but even so it jarred him. The thing on board China Fox was spontaneous — no meaning, but he had to admit, she had been in the back of his mind ever since he had learned she was to stay behind after China Fox sailed.

Peg looked strikingly different than aboard ship. The bandage was gone and her ebony hair was pulled away from her forehead into a style too elegant for the Rung Sat. She wore a sheer dress pulled tightly at the waist to accentuate her slim athletic body, long legs, and classically shaped breasts.

As he completed his examination, Blake felt the same sexual nervousness he had felt aboard China Fox. Peg gave Blake a Betty Davis smile — with that same upward, twisting, movement of her head he found so sensual. Joanna guided Blake from couple to couple, chatting for a few moments with each, but as he went through the pleasantries he kept glancing toward Mark and Peg.

Blake met Tony's boss, the Dutch World Operations Manager down from the Saigon office, and his wife. They were both from England but had been educated in America. He also met Tony's chief petroleum engineer, an intellectual-looking Vietnamese man who stepped forward boldly and shook Blake's hand while his small, quiet, and matronly wife remained timidly in the background of her pushy husband. Next Blake met an American civilian, an ex-Army warrant officer who had retired and returned as a private oil trucking contractor. His Vietnamese girl friend clung to him, her head resting against his shoulder, both arms entwined about his waist.

As Blake and Joanna completed the rounds and approached Mark and Peg, Blake heard the Major say, "You're like the roses in May."

Joanna smiled at Mark. "You are a rascal — I see you've already found Peg — Isn't she lovely — and such a brave girl to go to sea — and her wound is better now — Blake I don't think you've met — unless it was aboard China Fox — this is Peg Thompson — the woman wounded in that horrible attack — her companions are in Saigon tonight — I suppose they prefer the company of the Vietnamese ladies...."

Blake extended his hand. The scent of Peg's perfume and the touch of her fingers sent a zing straight to his loins. He greeted her in a non-committal acknowledgment of their earlier meeting. "Evening, Peg, good to see you."

"Well, it's Commaaander Blake," giving mocking emphasis on the last syllables. With a twist of her shoulders she continued, "The Yank who came to save us. It's good to see you again." Then she turned to Mark and with the flip of her head, "How is it the U.S. Navy beat the Marines to China Fox?"

Mark raised Peg's hand to his lips. He kissed it lightly and in joking, overgalant deep-echoing tones said, "Where the Navy goes, the Marines have already been."

Joanna announced dinner and asked, "Blake, you will be my dinner partner, won't you?"

"I'd be honored."

"And, Mark, would you mind escorting this lovely Australian bird?"

Mark's eyes brightened. He dropped Peg's hand and held out his right arm. Then in Gone with the Wind formality, he said, "Allow me, Madame."

Peg responded in imitation Scarlet O'Hara, "You Yankees are all alike — just sweep us Southern girls right off our feet!"

"You've read Margaret Mitchell's book?" Blake asked.

"Please, Commaaander Lawrence — hasn't everyone?"

Blake and Joanna led the way to a round table set in elegant style with candelabra and sparkling silver. After the ladies were seated, Tony Marbo dimmed the lights until the room glowed only in flickering candle light. There was the usual awkwardness of napkin shaking and water sipping for lack of something clever to say. One of the Vietnamese servants offered Tony the wine. He examined the bottle, then waited patiently while it was opened. He held the glass to the light, swirled it, smelled it and tasted the sample. Then he tasted again, this time with a quiet slurry, waiting for the aroma to penetrate. Finally he nodded his satisfaction and the wine was poured.

Joanna's voice pierced the clumsy silence of the beginning moments with patter that soon stimulated conversations among herself, the Operations Manager's wife and Peg. She occasionally included the two Vietnamese women, but they were shy. She allowed no more than a few words and a smile, before she turned her attention in another direction. The conversation warmed to Joanna's graciousness and soon everyone was involved in lively casual talk, sometimes across the table and sometimes with partners on either side.

The meal would have been fit for Prosper Montagne the famous French Master Chef. Joanna openly admitted she could not have done it without the black market in Cholon.

During the meal Blake's eyes drifted frequently across the table to Peg who was in almost continuous small talk with Mark Harris. On the few occasions that their eyes met, Blake was rewarded with a teasing smile. Each time it happened, he felt an increasing sense of jealousy.

It was one of those evenings when everyone was in a state of celebration. The talk was endless and interesting, the service imaginary — things just appeared and disappeared from the table. Time seemed eternal and for Blake it was like the words of James Montgomery, "a moment standing still forever."

The pastries came, then the fruit and cheese, then the coffee, then in the distance the rumbling sound of artillery fire, probably from Tam Tan Heip and the moment was lost. The reality of being on the fringes of the Rung Sat, and being a part of the war wrapped about them like graveclothes. The conversation drifted from literature and art to international affairs, profits, and war.

Blake sensed the change at the same time that Joanna said, "Tony, why don't you take the boys to the bar for an after dinner drink, while we girls freshen up."

"Cognac or Grand Marnier? Who's for a cigar?"

The men chatted aimlessly for a few moments, observing how the starlit sky had clouded so quickly with the threat of rain. Several agreed it was not unusual during the swing period between the wet and the dry seasons.

The Dutch World Operation Manager asked, "Commander Lawrence, have you heard any more about the Americans pulling out?"

"I'm afraid we don't know much more than you do. In fact, you may know more."

The Englishman took a sip of brandy. "The rumors are endless. The latest, and the one with most credibility, is that your President Nixon is trying to get the war over in time for his re-election. You do have elections soon, don't you?"

"In early November. The seventh to be exact."

The Operations Manager next turned to Tony's Vietnamese petroleum engineer. "What about Vietnam? What do you think will happen to this country when the Americans are gone?"

"Why, we will fight on against Communism, of course, just as we have done in the past." The slender Asian man answered in excellent English. Then he hesitated. "Of course it will be necessary to receive help, at least in the form of arms and logistics,"

The Operations Manager persisted with his questions. "Major Harris, what do you think? Will the South be able to hold Ho Chi Minh's followers at bay by itself?"

"I'm a Marine. Like Commander Lawrence, I'm not a politician." Mark took a puff on his cigar. "Can't speak about political stability, the will of the people to resist, or any of that stuff. I can say, based on a comparison of what I've seen in two tours in-country, the Vietnamese armed forces are more professional now than they were when the first Americans came. Leadership's good and they've mastered our weapons, which are as good as any in the world. The Rung Sat, as an example, is basically secure. Villages are operating fairly free of communist pressure. Ah, I know we still have a few pot shots at the ships," Mark shrugged, "But the military forces here are capable of holding their own. I'd say, if the Rung Sat is typical of the rest of the country, the South can do well."

The Operations Manager who was obviously tipsy baited the Americans. "Don't you think the grand strategy of this war can be characterized as a futile attempt to weaken the resolve of Ho Chi Minh's followers to bring about unification? You Americans have a rigidity about Communism and no understanding of Vietnamese history and nationalism." Then he turned to the petroleum engineer and asked, "After all, you Vietnamese have always hated foreigners, isn't that so?"

Before the Vietnamese man could answer, the ex-Army warrant officer, who was also drunk, took up the challenge. "Now wait a minute! I may have a contract with you, but I don't have to listen to your soft talk about Communism. Democracy and Capitalism are firmly a part of South Vietnam. That's unlikely to change. These people have had a taste of freedom. They'll fight to stay free of the Communist North. We haven't foisted ourselves and our ways on them. They wanted us here."

The English Operations Manager scoffed and in stilted language born of too much to drink, he said, "You Americans are all alike. You can't see past your ideals." He lifted his chin as he laughed. "I tell you this, if you were to give them a chance to decide for themselves, 20% would vote Communist, 20% would vote against Communism and 100% would vote for whoever is winning at the time; whoever promises them peace and security. You military men do what you feel. War in this little country has made madmen of you all. It's been a war of stale ideas, run with the mentality of your Harvard Business School. The North Vietnamese won't agree to a cease fire unless they believe they can eventually win. They want to run you out of the country, just as they ran the French out."

Mark's jaw tightened. He moved toward the Operations Manager, but Tony Marbo stepped between the two before Mark could do him harm. "Gentlemen. Gentlemen. Why don't we change the subject? Here, let me turn on the radio to the American station in Saigon, so we can dance."

Mark stepped back after he was politely pushed by Tony, but barked, "Change the subject? Dance? I'm gonna set that Limey straight..."

Mark was still arguing with the Operations Manager as Blake started down the stairs. The evening was too pleasant to become involved in a stupid argument with a drunken man. As his head cleared the landing he heard Peg's voice call to him softly, "Leaving so soon, Blake?"

"Oh, no. Just going for a short walk. Had to get away from Tony's loudmouth boss."

She inhaled from a long cigarette and asked, "Mind if I walk along, Yank?"

Blake was silent as they strolled the stone path. The sounds of the men arguing about the war faded as Neil Diamond's voice floated across the garden. "Cracklin' Rosie get on board. We're gonna ride till there ain't no more to go. Takin' it slow. An Lord, don't ya know......"

Peg broke the silence. "Why so quiet?"

"No reason, just my mood, I guess."

"You know about Mark and me."

"Sure, Mark told me."

Peg slipped her arm around his. "It's not that serious."

"Does Mark know that?"

"Does it matter?" She took another drag from her cigarette.

Blake shrugged then looked up. "The sky looks messy. It could rain any moment."

The music continued to a strumming beat, "Cracklin' Rose, you're a store-bought woman. But you make me feel like a guitar hummin'...."

Peg tugged his arm. "Penny for your thoughts?"

"Just enjoying the music."

"You know that song?"

"No." He grinned. "But I've got a hootchmaid named Rosie, any connection?"

She laughed. "It's a hit. About wine being a substitute for a woman. You believe that?"

"For some men. I'm not much for wine."

"Try this," she said as she held her cigarette to his lips.

"Don't smoke, thanks."

"Just once — go ahead, it's different."

Blake inhaled, then choked a cough. "Forget it. What is it?"

"Just Marijuana. Everybody uses it — never mind."

They both fell silent as they stood by the river where the sounds of rushing water drowned the words of the song. Their hands brushed for a moment; then she turned toward him and smiled. She leaned against him. He touched her cheek. She placed her face against his chest, and he held her. They stood there like that, looking out across the shimmering water. Beverly's letter flashed momentarily across his mind, the part that said she was going out to parties, and he reacted by tilting Peg's chin and touching his lips to hers. He felt intoxicated — not from the marijuana, but from the music, the garden scene, and the dinner wine and scotch. Her scent flooded through his body. Blake crushed her to him and they kissed passionately as his hands moved and her body responded. She arched her back to press her body against his. Blake's hand swept down and gently slid under one leg and lifted. She responded by wrapping her calf around his thigh. He cupped her breast in his hand and let his tongue wander from lips to cleavage.

But at the moment their passion reached its fury it was quelled with the first sprinkles of rain. They drew apart and held out their hands to feel the drops.

The two ran laughing for the house, arriving just before the downpour, and blended with the wives as Joanna and the other women were returning from the powder room. As Blake and the ladies made their way to the balcony he noticed Tony had the Operations Manager in a corner trying to sober him up. Mark, now talking to the American contractor, shot a glance in Blake's direction. To dampen any suspicion Mark might have about his absence, Blake pretended to be continuing a conversation with Joanna. Speaking loudly, he told her the meal was superb. "Joanna. You must be a magician to have found the things to put it together here in Vietnam."

Joanna's unsuspecting voice was pleasant and agreeable. "I'm glad you enjoyed it — actually my Vietnamese girls are the magicians, they are excellent cooks and they can find anything in Saigon — it's exciting for me to walk through the open stalls and barter with the shop keepers, they all know me now and they expect me to barter — in fact I think they all enjoy seeing me come — you know, that English woman who will argue over one piaster — now have you all decided who will play whom in tennis tomorrow — that is, if this dreadful rain stops in time for the courts to dry — they do dry quickly in the sun, all we will need is an hour or so in the morning and they'll be alright — Tony have you told them that brunch will be at 10 o'clock — that's a civilized hour — and you can play your tennis before the heat of the day — why don't we all dance, ..."

Peg, who now moved between Blake and Mark, asked, "Will you both be returning for tennis tomorrow?"

Mark turned to Blake and, referring to the Dutch World Operations Manager, said out of the corner of his mouth, "If I played tennis with that sonofabitch, I'd run the ball right up his you know what! I'm afraid I have some pressing work to do."

Blake, who instinctively waited to find out how Mark would respond to Peg's question, smiled as he said, "Well, that leaves me. It does sound like fun. I suppose I can break away for a few hours, but I warn you, I haven't played in a long time."

"We have the morning all settled. It will be Commaaander Lawrence and me against all challengers!"

Joanna bubbled. "Sounds wonderful — Are you good at doubles — Blake does your wife play well — You and Peg will be a marvelous pair...."

Blake didn't look at Peg when Joanna blurted the news about Beverly, but out of the corner of his eye he could see Peg glance his way.

Tony asked Mark if he wouldn't change his mind and join them, but Mark explained he had some important planning to do at the base.

The Dutch World Operations Manager stepped closer and asked, "Are you planning an operation in the Rung Sat?"

Blake didn't want Mark to get into it again with the man from Saigon. He also wanted to cover up any idea that they were planning a special operation, so he said, "Oh no, Mark's work is routine. It has to do with his Marines."

"Thought you were finally doing something about that new wire-guided rocket that hit China Fox. I've already been to see your Rear Admiral Paulson. The Dutch World Corporation is upset. I certainly hope the Vietnamese are able to do something soon."

"We're just as concerned as you." Blake answered. "The Vietnamese are doing their best." Then he quickly changed the subject, "Peg, how long will you be here — at the Marbos?"

"Until China Fox returns. I'll be well enough to join her. Then it's back to sea for this sailor!"

The evening came to a close when Blake explained they must hurry back in order to beat the Nha Be curfew. They were gathering their weapons when Tony commented, "By jove there was one thing I meant to tell you, Blake. Remember my curiosity about your Dai Ta Duc-Lang the evening we first met? Well, I asked some of my Vietnamese friends in Saigon and they told me he's a member of the Nguyen family. In fact, they said he is one of the last males in that dynasty, maybe the last. He could have been the ruler of this country except that you Americans insist on democracy. No wonder the coolies bow and scrape to him."

For Blake, this news explained even more of the riddle. Duc-Lang had said that Tu was of the Trinh Family from the North and now he had learned that Duc-Lang was the last of the Nguyen family. He remembered the story of Nguyen Anh and wondered if history would repeat itself.

"We will see you tomorrow morning, Commaaander."

"If he can't make it, we'll send a message." Mark said. Then he took Peg's hand and kissed it. Obviously meaning to again be over-gallant, but in a serious tone he said, "I'll see you again — soon, my lovely."

*****

The jeep ride to Nha Be was quiet. Mark mentioned how beautiful Peg was. Blake couldn't get her out of his mind either, but there was a lot he couldn't get out of his mind. In the beginning he thought differently about the war. He was just going to ride it out. He told Beverly he wouldn't get involved. That was before he came to this place called the Rung Sat with its mystery, intrigue and beautiful women.

TWENTY

"She ain't no whore, Doc. You understand? She ain't no whore."

On the same evening Blake and Mark attended the Marbo's dinner party, Doc Crow made his way through the Village of Nha Be toward Gunny's place in the vil. He remembered his Marine buddy's words of caution the day he helped the sergeant find the tiny apartment. To Doc it didn't make any difference whether or not she was a whore. *She's Vietnamese and marrying her, that's stupid.*

Pausing on the wooden sidewalk outside a small shop Doc looked up through the broken evening light at the billowing gray sky. Warm rain water seeped along lean shoulders where his poncho was loose at the neck. He hoped to see clearing signs, but the clouds were like morning fog over the Channel Islands in the spring, dense and heavy. In the distance he heard lightning mix with the war sounds of artillery pounding out harassing and interdiction fire into some desolate jungle region.

He walked only a few more paces before powerful Southeast winds brought one of the most severe monsoons of the season. Hurrying the final steps into the store, he bowed politely to the owner, slipped out of his wet slicker, took off his black beret, and ran a comb through thick black shocks of Mexican-Indian hair.

He sat on the bottom step leading to Gunny's apartment to remove his shoes. As he sat there his mind drifted to the day in Can Gio village when Gunny first met Co Tahn. It was when they flew in with Major Harris for an inspection of the district advisory team. Gunny's job was to check out the pacification effort in the area and the newly constructed maternity clinic.

To that point Gunny had been just a happy-go-lucky Marine, but he changed when Doc introduced the senior non-com of the district to the polite, but very shy health worker. Through a combination of sign language and broken English, Gunny learned that Co Tahn had grown up as a farm girl in the local hamlet of Hung Thanh. She came to work in the new clinic after she finished the village school. She was known for her skill in helping sick people, using nursing techniques she learned from her mother and the other hamlet women.

As he sat his shoes next to Gunny's, Doc thought, *It must have been love at first sight, because here we are almost nine months later Gunny's shacked up with her in Nha Be and she's pregnant. Never believed it would go this far. Hell, Gunny doesn't need a mixed-blood baby and a teenage Asian wife. Jeesus! Only 16 years old? She could be his daughter. Ought to leave her behind like the rest of the Americans and find some nice black girl in the States.*

"That you, Doc?" Came a voice from the landing above.

Doc finished arranging his shoes then climbed toward the muscled Marine sergeant. Gunny held aside bamboo curtains. He wore a brightly colored African sport shirt over fatigue trousers. Sounds of jazz came from a radio tuned to the Armed Forces station in Saigon.

The wiry hospital corpsman grasped Gunny's extended hand. "Hey Gunny! How ya do'n, amigo?"

He clowned with Gunny doing an exaggerated ethnic hand shake the two had developed just for the fun of it. They liked each other and had become best friends. Doc buddied with the Gunny because he was the kind of Marine who teased the village kids by rumpling their hair and allowing them to search for, then find the candy he always hid in his multi-pocketed fatigues. Doc figured Gunny made friends with him for two reasons: He was impressed with Doc's Silver Star, which he had received during an earlier tour with the Marines near the DMZ. But more probably he liked him because whenever Doc said something, which wasn't often, it was straight, no bullshit. Nevertheless Gunny often pushed their friendship to the edge by getting on Doc's case about getting promoted. He told him, "You're probably the highest decorated Corpsman in 'nam with nine years in the Navy and still only a Second Class Petty Officer."

Gunny did defend him in front of others. He told them the story about why he hadn't been promoted. "Before Doc had a chance to figure out the Navy, he was convicted of beating up a shipmate. Some white boy called him a spic or a beaner or something like that."

Doc always laughed it off saying, "The only thing that really pissed me off was the guy didn't call me a redskin or injun. I got more Indian than Mexican blood — damn proud of both."

"Good! Do'n good, Doc! Come on in. Make y'self at home."

Doc could see the room had changed since Gunny first set up their nest above the store. The bed with the mosquito netting was the same, but the table, now set with a cloth and dishes, was surrounded by four straight-backed chairs instead of three. A chest of drawers had found its way from the advisors' compound to a place against the wall near the bed. Co Tahn had carefully placed her things alongside the few items that Gunny kept in town. A table, a reading lamp, and a lounge chair had been placed within reach of a small refrigerator.

Gunny pointed to the large French wicker lounge. "Take that chair, Doc, and relax while I get you a beer."

"Oh, no! That's your chair. I'll sit here by the table."

"No," Gunny insisted. "You sit in it. Want you to let me know if that ain't a man's chair. Like the big overstuffed one I'm gonna have when we settle down and retire back in the world. Gonna put it right in front of a TV."

Gunny opened the refrigerator. He took out two bottles of beer and popped the caps with an opener hanging from a string on the wall. "Hope you like Ba Moui Ba '33', or would you rather smoke."

"Hey, bro no marijuana for me, but beer's beer — except for Corona. " Doc replied as he settled into Gunny's favorite chair, then added. "Where's Co Tahn?"

"In the kitchen put'n final touches on the meal. She'll be here soon." Gunny proceeded to pour beer over large chunks of ice in two tall glasses.

"Got the place fixed up nice."

"Yah, not bad." Gunny responded as he handed Doc one of the glasses. "She's been a busy girl. Just got back from visiting her ol' mom in Can Gio. She's even goin' back tomorrow morning." Then he touched Doc's glass and added. "Enjoy."

At that moment there was a quiet knock outside the bamboo curtains. Gunny parted them to find Sergeant Trieu who had entered the building and silently climbed the stairs. The small man wore a tiger-striped uniform of the Vietnamese Army and steel-rimmed glasses that blended with his gaunt face.

"Come on in, Trieu. Doc's here already."

Trieu bowed politely and extended his right hand which held a beautifully wrapped gift. Gunny also bowed as he awkwardly extended the other beer glass and accepted the heavy box at the same time. Trieu greeted the Americans in Vietnamese, "*Manh Gio, Khong?*" Then he repeated it in his over-precise English, "How are you?"

"Hey Trieu, Buenos noches, Amigo. How ya do'n?"

"Take that seat next to Doc, Trieu."

Water pelted the hooch's tin roof so loud that Gunny had to turn up the radio before he took his seat on a wooden crate. Extending his beer bottle he said, "Mud in your eye. Glad you both could come over."

"Mud," Doc repeated. And the three friends bumped their drinks to consummate the toast. They then sat quietly for a few moments to listen to the music. Each was still drinking in deep swills when Neil Diamond's final chorus filled the room, "Cracklin' Rosie, make me smile. And girl, if it lasts an hour, that's alright. We got all night. To set the world right. Find us a dream that don't ask no questions, Yeah...."

Doc broke the silence. "Hey, that's a great song. Wouldn't have missed this party. How you and Co Tahn do'n?"

"Good." The Marine tilted his head and swilled from his bottle. "She sure is someth'n else. You know I ain't never been married. Had plenty of women, but never married. This one knows more about how to care for a man than the whole bunch back home put together. Oh, we have our ups and downs. She's got a temper and when her mood changes she can be a bitch. She doesn't want to leave Vietnam. We fight over that. I'm still try'n to convince her to come back to the States with me."

Doc wanted to tell Gunny that was good news — that she didn't want to leave — made things easier. But he kept his peace.

"Is the paperwork for the marriage complete?" Trieu asked.

"No, and that's the other thing!" Extending his arms in a what-am-I-gonna-do sign. "There's more damn red tape in Saigon than I ever seen. I keep pay'n money under the table, $2000 piasters here and $5000 piasters there. Before this is over, I'll be broke. Sure do appreciate your help with the Nha Be District chief, Doc. That turned out to be the easiest step so far."

"He take any money from you?" Doc asked.

"Only $2000 piasters."

"That Bastard! He owes me. I've been help'n in his clinic. Even treated his daughter once."

"It's okay, Doc. At least he didn't delay us like some of the others. Gettin' things through Saigon is jus' plain slow. It's as if everyone up there wants to talk me out of it. I get pissed!"

Co Tahn entered the room wearing a bright red Ao Dai. Although she was pregnant, it didn't show and she slid across the room, erect and smooth like a Paris model. She was a strong looking girl, not pretty by Vietnamese standards, because her cheeks were full and set wider than most. Doc figured Gunny only saw her ass and big tits. She bowed to Gunny, then turned to face Doc and Trieu. She bowed again then stood erect brushing straight black hair that reached below her shoulders. Speaking very slow and deliberate in perfect English she said, "Good evening."

Even though Doc didn't think Gunny should marry her, he did understand why he liked her. Her smile was attractive and she wasn't brash like the Saigon whores. "Hi, Tahn. That Ao Dai is sure pretty and you speak American good, too."

She blushed, then bowed again and even more precisely said. "Thank you very much."

"Ain't that a pretty Ao Dai, Doc? Had it made for her — red's her favorite color. Honey. Look what Trieu brought us."

In Asia it was impolite to immediately open a gift without the giver's permission, so Gunny asked Trieu in the traditional Oriental way, "May I open it?"

"Yes, please."

Gunny peeled the beautiful wrapper, trying carefully not to tear the paper. He lifted the lid and unwrapped white tissue from one of the objects.

"It's beautiful," Gunny exclaimed holding high a small green, gold trimmed, porcelain elephant.

"There is another," Trieu said through an eager smile.

Gunny carefully unwrapped the second elephant and handed the pair to Co Tahn, whose eyes brightened as she placed one on each side of the door.

"LUFE's." Doc exclaimed with a grin.

The two advisors laughed because they knew them irreverently as BUFEs and LUFEs which stood for Big and Little Ugly Fuc'n Elephants, acronyms long ago bestowed as an inside American joke.

Co Tahn gave Trieu a puzzled look and from her expression Doc could tell she knew the Americans were making fun. She thanked Trieu in her own tongue and scolded her black sergeant, "they will bring good fortune to the house."

Gunny sobered immediately to Tahn's sharp words. "Oh, I know. We didn't mean anything. And I'm pleased. Thank you, Trieu."

The men were quiet as Gunny's girl went about setting the table and making final arrangements.

Returning to the matter they were discussing before Co Tahn entered the room, Doc said. "Hope your marriage works out OK. With the news about a possible cease fire, time may be run'n out. By the way, hear we're get'n ready for something big. Is it OK to talk about it or is it too hush hush?"

"It's OK, Doc. You're right — it's gonna be a good one. Goin' after those fuc'n rockets!"

"You're gonna take me along, ain't ya? You're gonna need an American corpsman out there." Then so as not to offend Sergeant Trieu he added. "Not that the Vietnamese Corpsmen ain't as good. Listen, Gunny, you know I wanna go," Doc insisted. "I haven't missed an op since I've been in-country and I sure don't wanna start now!"

"Why you wanna go? You'll just get yourself shot up."

Doc knew what Gunny was thinking. The Marine Sergeant had confided to him earlier that for the first time since he joined the Corps he wasn't enthusiastic about going on this operation. He had less than two years to do before he could retire on twenty. Now he had Co Tahn and enough money saved from his Vietnam tours to put a down payment on a house back home. He had gone to one year of college before he joined the Marines. Now he wanted to finish and start a small business. He told Doc it wasn't fear; it was just that now he could see something beyond the Corps, and the war was ending. He didn't want the "honor" of being the last American to die in Vietnam.

Doc emptied his beer glass and puffed out his chest. "Shit, Gunny. If I ain't bought it by now, it ain't gonna happen."

Co Tahn seemed to float from the room making less noise than the rain pelting on the roof above. After she was gone, Gunny looked embarrassed. "She's the boss already — she sure has learned fast, Doc! I've been teach'n her American and she understands everything! She's a little bashful about trying to talk yet, but when we're alone she just prattles away."

The three friends told jokes and drank beer for a few minutes, until Co Tahn returned with the local shopkeeper's wife, who had been helping in the kitchen. Each carried bowls of steaming food which they placed on the small table, then hurried away for more. Soon every bit of space had dishes of one kind or another. The shopkeeper's wife disappeared and Co Tahn moved to the other end of the room.

Doc asked. "Ain't Co Tahn going to eat with us?"

"Oh, sure man." Gunny responded. "In this country women eat with their men-folk. It's only the rich who hide their wives and concubines. Ain't that right, Trieu?"

The slender sergeant smiled but didn't answer.

Co Tahn looked after a few last minute details; then when the men were seated she slipped into the empty chair. The meal was served Vietnamese family style. Each person had a pair of chop sticks, a large individual bowl, a small dish filled with Nouc Mam and another of salt and pepper over which lime juice was squeezed. In the center of the table, where all could reach, were several bottles of beer and many pots. A larger one was full of rice and another had an entire fish cooked in Nouc Mam sauce. The men drained their glasses, then poured each other more beer, never allowing the glasses to get empty. The toasts became a game for the three. The more beer they drank, the more their cheeks flushed, and the louder their laughter and talk became.

"New toast," Doc giggled. "To the new perfume called Nouc Mam."

"Easy, Doc." Gunny cautioned.

"Ah, I'm just hav'n a little fun. You understand, don't you Trieu?"

Sergeant Trieu toasted his glass and responded good naturedly. "Okay, Doc. We drink to Nouc Mam. But for me it is perfume."

Co Tahn didn't drink with the men, but she watched without emotion as Gunny presided over the meal.

Doc pointed to a medium-sized bowl of a dark substance. "Gunny, what's in this dish?"

"Don't know. Honey, what is it?"

"A special gift from the shopkeeper's wife. It is called duck's blood soup. It makes men potent and women have stronger babies."

"Potent! Hurry, hurry! I'll try it! I'll try it!" Doc said.

The men laughed.

"Doc, pour some of that soup for Co Tahn. We want our boy to be a great football player!"

"How do you know you're going to have a boy?" Sergeant Trieu said.

"Told you before. We know so! Don't we, Tahn?"

Co Tahn blushed and smiled but said nothing.

Doc knew the problems of mixed blood children in Vietnam. They were treated like non-people. He knew that many French and Americans left their women and children behind, and the mixed bloods were treated as the lowest class. Most became street urchins. The alcohol caused him to blurt in drunken speech, "Duck's Blood shoup ain't gonna help the baby. Mixed blood kids ain't any better off in the States than they are here."

"You're wrong, Doc!" Gunny spoke angrily. "Anybody can make it in the States. Just a question of what you want, then go after it!"

Trieu blurted uncharacteristically, "Boy or girl, the baby will be a Bokassa." Then he glanced uneasily at Co Tahn and lowered his eyes because she obviously understood the reference.

"Bokassa? What's a Bokassa?" Gunny asked.

Trieu poured himself more beer, then touched the glass to his lips before he said, "I will tell you a story that will explain what the word Bokassa now means in Vietnam. This story has become a Vietnamese folk tale and is about a black man, so I shall begin with: once upon a time, a black man." Trieu paused to adjust his reading glasses and to explain to Co Tahn in Vietnamese. Then he began again, "Once upon a time a black man, a sergeant in the French Foreign Legion, was stationed in a small town, not far from here. He met and fell in love with a beautiful Vietnamese woman. Of course they had a beautiful baby, a girl. They should have lived happily ever after, but..."

"But what?" Gunny asked.

Trieu's voice changed from Trieu the sergeant, to Trieu the history professor, the storyteller. He adjusted his glasses again and extended his hands. For reasons unknown to Doc he changed the location of the story. "In 1966, a Colonel named Jean Bedel Bokassa -- a tall, strikingly handsome man returned home from duties in the French army to a small African country. He soon rose to become Commander in Chief of the Army and led a *coup d'etat*. Bokassa then promoted himself to General and was elected President in 1968. Shortly thereafter he named himself Bokassa I, Emperor of the Central African Republic."

Gunny's eyes were as big as a child hearing a fairy tale when he slurred, "The sh'ame black Sergeant that was in Vietnam?"

"The very same — but that's not all." Trieu sat back in his chair knowing he had piqued their curiosity. "Some seventeen years after Bokassa left Vietnam with the defeated French Army, he wrote an official letter to the head of the Vietnamese government and asked that his sweetheart and daughter be found. He wanted them to come and live with him. But neither could be found. Rather than lose face by giving an improper response to a head of state, some unscrupulous government officials substituted another mixed blood girl of approximately the same age. She couldn't read or write, but she learned enough of the story to pass as his daughter. Bokassa was told that the mother was dead and the girl was sent to the African Republic, where she lived in Bokassa's beautiful palace. But one day the Emperor, who had become somewhat suspicious of the girl, showed her a photograph of his sweetheart. When she didn't recognize the photograph, Emperor Bokassa knew he had been duped. Now he was angry and more determined than ever to find the Vietnamese woman he loved and their true daughter. This time he sent his personal representative to Saigon to lead the search. The daughter and the mother were found alive, but living in abject poverty near the same small town."

Gunny became irritated when Sergeant Trieu sat back, and slowly poured more beer. The American moved to the edge of his chair and said, "Well? Is'h that all?"

Trieu carefully raised his right forefinger to his glasses, tilted his head, and smiled. "The mother refused to leave her country and the life she had made for herself during the eighteen year interlude. However, she knew life for a half-caste girl in Africa, or anywhere else for that matter, would be better than in Vietnam. She convinced her daughter to join her now wealthy father. When the girl finally arrived, Bokassa knew immediately that she was his daughter, because she knew details of the story only her mother could have told. He made her a princess and a member of his immediate household."

Sergeant Trieu savored the response from his American friends. Gunny was captured by the romance of the story and laughed at the theatrical way his friend had told it.

But Doc said sarcastically, "Ya, but how much better off was she? A half-caste in Vietnam is still a half-caste in Africa."

Like a child, Gunny asked. "Is that a true story?"

Trieu smiled and nodded his head. "Bokassa is, this very day, emperor of the country called Central African Republic, and the word Bokassa to the Vietnamese means those born of mixed Vietnamese and Black blood."

"I'll be goddamned!" Gunny exclaimed.

Gunny was a little slow and sometimes missed the point so Doc mumbled. "Hope you got the message and know what you're do'n, amigo."

"Whataya mean? What message? The story had a happy ending!"

Doc leaned close to his black friend, "Ya, but only because Bokassa's rich. Leave Co Tahn and the baby behind. They ain't go'n to be nothing but trouble in the States. You heard the story. Now ya know the word Bokassa is'h like the word nigger. The prejudice here is bad, and it ain't much better in the States. Hey, buddy, won't be no piece of cake."

Gunny jerked back from Doc's confidential words. "What kind of man you take me for, Doc? I don't even wanna hear no bad talk about it."

"Suit yourself." Doc said.

Co Tahn timidly entered the men's conversation. She measured every word as she said, "Gunny, what is it like in America?"

Gunny Johnson looked at Doc and Trieu. "Didn't I tell you she was gett'n pretty good, Doc? She's even learned to ash'k the hard questions."

"Ya. How ya gonna answer it?" Doc sneered. "She wouldn't like my answer. You gonna tell her it depends on whether you're colored or white?"

"Oh, I can answer it, if I ain't too drunk."

Gunny went to the refrigerator and brought back three more cold '33' beers. He filled the glasses, sat down and looked at Co Tahn. He looked off into space for a few moments, then back to his girl as he began. "This'll be my way of answering. Tahn, you got to understand other Americans might answer different. Trieu, will you translate for her, if I talk too fast?"

The small Sergeant nodded and Gunny began. "The land in America is mostly different than the land in Vietnam — colder too. But there are a few places, a few times a year, when you would think you were here. Ain't that right, Doc?"

Doc nodded agreement. "Florida, for sure."

"But even the land is different from one end of America to the other," Gunny went on. "In some places there are roll'n hills, other places have high mountains, and still others are just hot, flat, sandy desert. And the people, they're as different as the land. It's not like here in Vietnam where everyone, or nearly everyone is Vietnamese and looks alike — at least to us Americans. In the States it's like God just picked up a handful 'a people from every place in the world, threw 'em up in the air, mixed 'em up, and they all landed scattered."

Gunny paused for a few moments because he realized he was beginning to talk too fast. He waited as Trieu explained to Co Tahn.

"Some 're black, like me," Gunny finally continued. "But others 're Indian and Asian and lots are from Europe. There 're even some that came from the islands surrounding America and even more from south of us, like from Mexico. That's another thing about America. There ain't no borders. Not between the states there ain't. People wander anywhere they want. There ain't any checkpoints or curfews to make sure they're where they should or shouldn't be. Because they're allowed to be anywhere. There are borders North and South, between Canada and Mexico, but I'm not sure why—people come and go as they damn well please anyway. It's not that America is perfect, Lord knows it's got its share of problems. If it ain't unemployment, i'sh race relations, everybody ain't happy all the time, but somehow most people are satisfied. I guess it's the freedom we have that attracts everybody and keeps them happy. Am I mak'n any sense, Doc?"

"Ya, but Tahn won't understand." The corpsman responded.

Trieu questioned the girl in Vietnamese and Co Tahn bowed her head as she said in English. "I understand, Doc. Sergeant Trieu tells me everything."

"Okay, if you're sure. I'll finish," gunny said. "Funny thing about us Americans is that we're more alike than different. We like to be left alone. Now here's someth'n that nobody really understands about us. We got the spirit of freedom. It's inside every man and woman. It's more important than comfort, or race or religion. An' they don't want no one mess'n with that freedom. Another thing about Americans is we all have a bag. My granny never wanted me to talk nigger talk or jive for that matter so I don't and the word 'bag' used to be jive. Now-a-days everybody uses it. You must have a word like it in the Vietnamese language, Trieu. A bag is a story. It's the story about where ya come from, your way of life. A lot 'a guys in America today just wanna sit around and smoke pot and drop their bag, complain'n how bad they have things, instead of gettin' on with life. If they're rich, their bag is to tell about how hard they worked to get it. If they're middle class, they wan'na tell ya how rough it was when they were poor. An' if they're poor, an' there ain't many poor in America, not like you Vietnamese know poor. They wan'na tell you how the rich people and the government did them bad and owes them.

"My bag is that I come from Detroit, in Michigan, one of our states. Like one of your provinces. I've always seen America as a dream. One of those dreams that rises out of your sleep, sort of wispy. You're never sure if it was good or bad. I always took it for granted that the American dream was good. But you got to realize in this world there's some things you can't do nothin about.

"When I was young I wanted to be white, I'm not. I wanted to be rich, I'm not. I wanted to be smart, I'm not, but what I am is I'm free. I got a chance. I never took Whitey for granted, and I've made it. Now that I been out here, I'm gonna do it even better in the future. I know I'm as smart as the white folks and I'm go'n after it."

Gunny's eyes got a bit misty. He choked, "You see, that's what's so crazy about America. Unless you've been somewhere else, you can't realize how good it really is. It's got this freedom."

Gunny took a swallow of warm beer to clear his throat and leaned toward Co Tahn, "I guess I said that before, didn't I honey. But people ain't machines in America. People just do what they wan'na do and say what they wan'na say. That's why I want you to come back to the states with me, so our Bokassa can grow up in freedom, and have a chance."

Gunny sat back in his chair.

Co Tahn hadn't understood every word, but she sensed how Gunny felt and her eyes were filled with pride that her man could talk with such strength about his country. She thought about the great loss of face she had brought to her family when she left Can Gio and came to Nha Be, and the additional pain she would cause when she had his baby. She loved Vietnam as much as Gunny loved his country. She didn't want to leave, but now she knew America was a better place for their child to grow up. To most Vietnamese the word Bokassa meant prejudice, but to her it was a good word because Gunny reminded her of the African man. Because of that she said. "Can we name our baby Bokassa? It will be a good word in America."

"Does that mean you'll go to the states?"

Co Tahn nodded yes.

"Doc, Trieu! She's come'n home with me! Nothin' wrong with that name for the baby either. It's the thing for us blacks to take African names." Then he repeated it, to hear the ring. "Bokassa — no! Bo Johnson, son of Benjamin Johnson."

TWENTY ONE

SATURDAY, JULY 8, 1972, NHA BE BASE

"Wish I had a smoke," Private Marquell said to himself. He had roving sentry duty and that meant he had to hang around the Tactical Operations Center until midnight when his watch was over. It also meant he had to stay on base until the duty day was complete at noon the next day.

"Wish I had a smoke," he repeated. "The kinda smoke that can get me out of 'nam even for a few hours."

He picked up a copy of <u>Stars and Stripes</u> and opened the pages wide to cover his face. He slouched in a chair in the corner of the darkened room hoping to escape his last round. He hated a night watch on Saturday — especially this Saturday. Commander Lawrence had restricted him to the base and he was to be transferred to the Saigon brig Monday afternoon.

Guard duty meant going through the barracks, checking for security and fires, and seeing the sailors and other Marines dress for the show that he couldn't attend. Walking the base perimeter and checking the wire fence was even worse. The fuc'n gooks stare like you had no business being on their turf. Not sure why Commander Lawrence makes us check the perimeter anymore. Vietnamese stand the guard duty.

"Private," The duty officer said. "Isn't it time for your last round?"

"Ah, yes, Sir," Marquell responded sluggishly. He glanced at the clock. It was eleven. Only forty five more minutes and his watch would be over. Marquell made his way out the door. The rain had stopped but the night was simmering hot. Once outside he looked around to make sure no one could hear then said aloud to the darkness, "Bullshit."

Marquell entered the American compound and passed several Navy advisors hurrying to the club. The last show started at 2330 hours. He walked slowly through the corridor, glancing absently into the empty rooms. At the end of the building he exited through the rear door slipping a wedge of paper into the latch so that the fire door couldn't lock behind him. That door was often the way he got back in after an unauthorized night in the vil.

He skirted the compound, glancing occasionally at the fence line, then began the mile and a half trek around the perimeter of the base. He walked briskly, keeping his head held high, giving a military appearance to anyone who might be looking for the watch, and especially in case Gunny was checking on him. He passed several guard posts and waved to the Vietnamese soldiers who were, in most cases, just as bored as he.

When he arrived at the boat repair base Marquell stayed close to the water, looking for signs of infiltration. It was the one place where he felt he had to pay attention. He had been told VC were known to attack by water and he didn't want it to happen on his watch.

Near the helo pad he stopped and checked a small tool box bolted to a stanchion where he had hidden a lid of marijuana. It was still there. He wanted a smoke, but at first he thought it too risky. Then he remembered that everyone was at the show and said to himself, "Fuck it. Go'n to the brig anyway. What else can they do to me? Send me home? Why not." He glanced around to make certain he was alone, then hid behind a bunker, quickly rolled a crude cigarette and lit it. Smoke oozed through his lungs and into his blood stream giving him a dull listless feeling.

He thought of Gunny and how the black sergeant had taken him to C.O.'s mast only to back him in his effort to stay in country. Actually, except for his parents, Marquell would have preferred going home early. He hadn't wanted to come to Vietnam in the first place. But it was one of the few times in his life he thought about the effect of his actions on his parents. Screwing up in high school and college was one thing, but his dad seemed to forget all of that when he joined the Corps. To him, serving honorably for your country was the most important thing an American could do. To be sent home from a war zone would kill the old man.

Marquell stayed hidden cupping the lighted end. He smoked the joint until it almost burned his fingers. Finally, he dug the butt into the dirt under the heel of his boot and continued his rounds. He ended up back at the TOC at exactly 2340 hours, five minutes before he was to be relieved. Before resuming his position on the chair in the corner, he made his report to the duty officer. He mumbled, "All secure, sir."

"Okay, Marquell. Oh, and don't forget, you are the duty driver tomorrow morning. Take Commander Lawrence to Dutch World."

"Aye, Aye, sir."

At exactly 2345 p.m. his relief showed up. A sailor named Garfield who looked like he had just awakened from a nap. He rubbed his eyes and yawned, "What-a-ya-say, Marquell. Anything up?"

"Nope, same old shit," The Marine handed over the webb ammo belt and an AR-15.

Garfield examined the weapon, opened the breech, counted the bullets in the banana clip and said, "Okay. I got it."

Marquell strolled out into the night intending to return to barracks and turn-in, but as he was about to enter the American compound the door of the club opened and he heard the sounds of the show blast into the night. He changed direction and arrived just in time to watch the warm-up act for the main show. A skinny assed dancer with mammoth tits, took off her 'G' string and begin sensual gyrations close to the faces of the drunks in the front row.

The club's air-conditioning felt good as it flooded over the moisture Marquell's skin carried from the hot night air. The place was packed. It was almost show-time. The Filipino band had already set up their instruments. One member was strumming a Janice Joplin number. Two dark skinned girls were behind the stage practicing their steps.

A couple of Marines who had arrived early and were already crocked sat at the bar. One said, "No vil tonight?"

"Got the fucn duty."

"Bet your Co'll skip out with a sailor."

"Fuck you."

Marquell was still wearing a .45-caliber pistol strapped over camouflage fatigues and the club manager, a friend of Gunny's — a Chief Petty Officer who didn't like him growled, "You stay, you take off the fucn .45."

"Not stay'n long, Chief."

Saturday nights in Vietnam were no different than anywhere else — boring when there was nothing to do. The advisors usually went to a show at the club. But the shows were all the same. A small band played rousing drinking music; country or rock until it was time for the girls to sing and dance. The advisors and their Vietnamese guests drank until closing time, shouted dirty words at the strippers, then staggered back to barracks to sleep it off.

Marquell smiled to himself, because his Saturday nights were usually different. He went to the shows like everyone else, but when they were over he slipped out to the 'vil' for a little extra, a lift and to be with Co Voi, the girl he was shacked up with in a small apartment next to the Boo Goo.

He ordered a bottle of 'Bud' and leaned against the back wall of club. He felt smug because it was okay to have a couple of beers coming off watch and the coldness of the liquid felt good as it blended with the effects of the earlier joint. His eyes moved to the "red lady" behind the bar. She was everyone's favorite — like a mascot. It was a picture of a naked Vietnamese girl with a beautiful body painted on red velvet. The artist had made her eyes almost as big as her tits.

He looked around for Gunny, then remembered the sergeant had moved in with a Co in the vil. On a Saturday night he would be out there.

The room was filled with a cloud of blue cigarette smoke, and everyone was screaming for another dancer to take off her 'G' string just as the other girl had. She kept running her hands under her bare breasts, rubbing her ass, and signaling for the audience to throw more money on the stage. Two Marines had to pull back one of their drunken sailor buddies who kept trying to chase the girls with an extended tongue and a hand full of dollars.

Marquell finished his second beer and left about the time the crowd had thrown enough money on the stage to convince the girl to take off her "G" string. As he left the club he heard the roll of the drums, signifying it was time for the same old dull U.S.O. show, tits, ass, and rock and roll.

The painting of the red lady behind the bar and the dancing girls made him feel horny. Even though he was off watch, he knew he was still on duty. There was something he was supposed to do in the morning, but by now his mind was in continual motion from the effect of the beer and marijuana. He was unable to connect and hold a thought and couldn't remember what he was supposed to do. All he wanted was to get to the village. There he could get laid. There he felt free.

He skirted the Advisors barracks and casually walked across the main base road toward the water then disappeared into the shadows of the buildings. He hugged the walls and hurried until he found the fence that separated the base from the village. It extended out into the water, but Marquell easily climbed out to its edge then back to the village side as he had often done before. The wire was bent from the foot holds of the many Americans and Vietnamese who had also used this method to get ashore without leave.

Once again on dry land, he ran a few paces until he was in the shadows of the village. Marquell stayed away from the main street until he came to the Blue Lagoon.

The Boo Goo, as the old timers called it, was the place where his girlfriend worked. He thought of her as his girl, but he knew she slipped out with several other advisors when he wasn't around.

He glanced from the shadows onto the street. Clear. He entered. The place had wooden floors and a small bar, behind which a gray haired mama-san wearing traditional work clothes poured warm beer into a glass filled with ice. Blue florescent tubes on each side of the bar provided the only light for two tall Americans draped over their Asian girls, dancing lazily to a record of <u>Purple Haze</u> by Jimmy Hendrix. Another couple sat dreamy eyed at a corner table smoking a reefer. Between puffs, the sailor's right hand massaged his girl's left breast, while she rubbed the inside of his leg and crotch.

Marquell slid into a seat at the bar, ordered a beer, and asked for Co Voi. The mama-san gave him an embarrassed look as she poured and said she would have to send someone to find her.

"Before you go, let me have a joint, mama-san."

Marquell took the crudely rolled cigarette from the older woman, lit it, and took a long drag.

The music stopped and the two advisor's, one a sailor and the other a Marine left their girls and came to join Marquell.

"Thought you had the duty?" Jones, the Marine said.

Marquell didn't answer. He just gave a half smile and took a sip of his beer.

"Better not let Gunny catch you out here," Jones said.

"Fuck, Gunny," Marquell responded.

"Where'd mama-san go?" Smitty, the sailor asked.

"To get my Co. She'll be right back."

"Don't be disappointed if mama-san can't find her. I think I saw her leave with another swab," Jones said.

"Hey, that's okay. Come on over and join us. We got some good stuff tonight." Smitty said.

The three Americans and two Vietnamese girls sandwiched into a half-moon shaped lounge. One of the girls pulled out her hand bag. She extracted the contents, a pipe, tubs of acid, some hand rolled cigarettes, a bag of hashish, and other paraphernalia, then dumped some white powder on the table. Smitty snorted grains through a straw. Jones decided on the pipe.

"You can get hooked on that shit." Marquell said as he lit another cigarette.

The three advisors talked for a few minutes, but soon the other two became occupied with their girls. They left the table and went upstairs where there were small rooms with beds shielded by mosquito netting.

Left alone, Marquell returned to the bar. By now he had enough beer and marijuana that his eyes were half closed and his mind wandered.

"Hey, where's my girl?" He mumbled. No one paid any attention.

A little man came in from the street and held out a plastic bag full of hashish in one hand and some tablets in the other. Marquell told him to shove-off, then shouted above the music, "Hey mama-san. Where's my Co."

"Maybe here later, Joe. She come and go many places. Maybe she think you have duty."

"Fuck it," Marquell said. "Give me another beer. Hey, mama. Maybe you, me have good time."

The blond headed Marine heard the mama-san say something to the effect, "too old," as she sat the beer in front of him, but his thoughts were already back in Virginia. He was stoned, and at that stage he often had moments of fleeting clarity mixed with surges of guilt. "Ya know Mama-san, my own mama's such a lady she would die if she knew some of the things I do."

The Vietnamese woman didn't even look up from her work behind the bar.

Marquell's head bobbed as he continued his monologue, "She's a good lady, mama-san. She stood behind me when I had trouble. But ole dad, the ole school Virginian. He's always so fuc'n right. 'The Marquell's,' he says, 'have led our country and county for a century. You, boy had better shape up.' Would he have a fit if he knew about the gunfire investigation? This is absurd. I'm here in Vietnam — in uniform. In college I was in the anti-Vietnam shit and here I am try'n to please daddy again." Marquell's head rolled to one shoulder and he smiled as he remembered getting stoned his freshman year in college and raiding the girls dorm. "Hey, that was fun," he said aloud. His mind could clearly see the time he and his buddies were chased by the police after breaking into a liquor store and they crashed Marquell's car into the monument of the school's founder. "That's when the cops found the stash of drugs," he mumbled. "Wonder what old Gunny would say about that, if he knew. That was why they sent me home my junior year."

His mind could clearly see himself in officer candidate school. "Like every Marquell," his father had said. "Shit, it wasn't going to work from the beginning," the private said aloud. "I hated the fuc'n war, and I didn't have a degree. The physical shit wasn't the problem, it was the bullshit — them expecting me to stay in and study — and all the leadership shit. When I got kicked out Daddy insisted I do my duty. "Be a man," he said. He even got some of his Washington friends to convince the Marines to give me another chance.

"Ya know mama-san, Paris Island was shit. Anyway, here I am. Fuck it. Where's my Co?"

"Maybe she not come tonight. Maybe she go Saigon. Think you have duty. You want other girl, Joe?"

"Shit, no," he mumbled.

"You come. Give mama-san ten dolla. I take you see special fuck show," the gray haired Vietnamese woman said, pulling his arm.

"Bullshit. Fuc'n ugly bitch," he said under his breath. Marquell had already seen the peep show. Once before he had followed his girl upstairs and down a dark hall to a dark room. There she had him sit on a bench opposite a hole in the wall where he could see into another room that had dim lights. He had watched a Vietnamese man and girl come into the room naked and go through a real life porno show.

"Come, come. You see show," Mama-san said.

But he shook his head. "Not again. Too kinky for me."

Instinct told him he better get back. He couldn't risk being seen by Gunny in town, day or night. Besides there was something he had to do in the morning, but he couldn't remember what. He staggered to his feet, cursed Co Voi and headed for the door. He disappeared into the shadows and headed for the fence and slowly climbed back into the base. He again hung close to the walls of the buildings and walked quietly through the compound until he came to the back door. The wedge of paper was still there. He slipped into the dark passage.

He knew he was bombed and didn't want Gunny to catch him that way, so he slipped into the hootchmaid room to sleep it off.

TWENTY TWO

The morning after the Marbos' dinner party turned out to be beautiful. Only an occasional puffy cloud moved across the sky and the thundershowers left the air fresh and clear.

Blake went briskly through his Sunday morning routine. He had coffee at the advisors' galley, visited the Tactical Operations Center to check on the Long Tau Channel, and made a quick stop at his office to read the latest messages from Saigon. A letter from Beverly lay on his desk. He was already late for tennis at the Marbos' so he quickly opened it and skimmed the words. It didn't take long because it the words were terse and biting.

> Dear Blake
>
> Everything is alright at home, except for Blake Junior. He's become surly and isn't minding as well as I'd like. I'm not comfortable with the friends he's chosen.
>
> The kids have started the new school semester. I attended both "open houses."
>
> My new job is wonderful. My boss gave me a promotion and I'm having fun — my life is finally changing.
>
> > Love,
> > Beverly
>
> PS. This is a poem Martha wrote for you. She titled it, "I Miss You So." She told me she intends to put it to music. She wants to sing like Diana Ross.

A folded sheet of school paper fell out of the envelope. Instead of reading it then he slipped the child's note with Beverly's letter into the pocket of his fatigue jacket. "Read it later," he said to himself. He had a helpless feeling because he couldn't do anything about his boy. "Hope whatever is brewing won't develop into anything serious before I have a chance to be with him."

Blake returned to his room where he packed a towel, and tennis clothes into a gym-bag and grabbed his CAR-15.

The jeep wasn't on time. After waiting a few minutes he called the TOC to ask the reason for the delay. "He should be there by now, Commander. We told private Marquell last night he was to be your driver for the trip. I'll check on it, sir."

Blake paced the floor of his room, wishing he had asked about the driver when he had visited the TOC earlier, instead of waiting until he was ready to leave.

Shortly there was a knock on the door and a voice said, "Commander, your jeep is ready."

Blake climbed in next to a petty officer. A sailor wearing a black beret and an M-16 across his lap rode shotgun in the back seat.

"Sorry about the delay, Sir."

"Thought Private Marquell was to be the driver," Blake said in acid tones.

"Couldn't find him, sir. Don't know what happened. I was just told to take you to Dutch World right away."

Marquell gone? He was only a private and only one of the many enlisted men in the advisory unit, but because of the gunfire incident and his decision to keep the young Marine in-country, Blake thought more about him than the others. *Was he on drugs? Had he pulled out and gone A.W.O.L. to avoid the brig, to blend with the Saigon masses?* Blake was already late for the tennis match, but he had the driver stop the jeep at Rung Sat headquarters where Major Harris was helping with the Op Plan.

"Mark, did you know that Private Marquell's missing?"

"No, sir. Hadn't heard. I'm not surprised, that fuck-up!"

"He was assigned to be my driver this morning, but never showed."

"Don't worry, I'll have Gunny start looking. I'll have his ass when we find him. Guess you're on the way to Dutch World. Say hello to everyone for me." Then Mark's eyes tightened. "Especially my girl Peg."

Blake's jeep passed along the deserted main street of Nha Be. It was early and the village was quiet.

Dogs here must not bark in the morning, he thought. Then he heard a rooster crowing an early message. *Probably a warning. Like Mark's remark about Peg.*

Sunday mornings in the vil were usually lazy and because the roads were empty it seemed no time before the jeep arrived at the Marbos' home.

Tony Marbo must have seen the jeep coming shortly after it turned off Route 15, because he was waiting for Blake. "Come join us. We're all gathered by the tennis courts."

"Be right there," Blake said as he pulled his dufflebag clear and told the driver, "Have the jeep back here about one o'clock."

The driver grinned. "Okay, Commander. Have fun." Then gunned it down the road leaving a cloud of dust.

Blake winced at the driver's innocent remark. Playing tennis on a Sunday in a war zone didn't seem right, but he rationalized it was done all the time in Saigon. Besides, Peg was to be his partner.

Tony guided Blake toward a patio near the tennis court where players in white clothes had already gathered around two circular tables sheltered by straw umbrellas.

Blake's eyes quickly found Peg. She sat under one of the umbrellas, wearing a tennis dress and a scarf to keep her raven hair away from her face.

Her legs were pulled under her, but as Blake approached she seductively extended one leg and crossed it to reveal ruffled pants. "Come, Blake, sit by me," the Australian voice said. "Have you eaten anything? We're having eggs benedict or omelets. Which would you prefer?"

Blake slid easily into a sunchair next to Peg. "Omelet and some juice, please."

Tony repeated Blake's order to one of the Vietnamese servants, who quickly disappeared into the main house."Where's Joanna?" Blake asked.

"Still in bed — seldom rises before noon. She's a talkaholic you know," Tony said with a laugh. "Has to recover from over indulgence at her parties."

"I see everyone's ready for the match," Blake said.

The British Operations Manager looked hungover. He took a sip from a Bloody Mary before saying, "There's already been some warm-up hitting. Turns out that your partner is quite a player."

"I did play group tennis in Melbourne when I was quite young," Peg said. "And I try to keep fit. Except for an occasional cigarette," pointing to one burning in an ash tray. "Did you bring tennis clothes?"

"In my bag. Where can I change?"

Tony pointed. "The main house if you like, but do be quiet until Joanna is up and about, won't you."

Peg picked up her cigarette and pointed it in another direction. "My cottage is closer and you won't disturb her. Why don't you just change there, Blake? It's that one over there. Come let me show you."

The Operations Manager winked at Blake and smiled lewdly.

"Okay, I'll make a quick change while the cook is putting the food together."

"It's a bit of a mess. I hope you don't mind," Peg said. She pointed to a door leading off the bedroom. "You can put your clothes in the closet, and there's a bathroom and shower in there."

Blake sat his weapon in a corner and emptied his duffel on the bed.

Peg came close to him. "I'm glad you came this morning."

"I am, too." He felt sensual nervousness creep through him.

Peg moved closer and with that same upward twisting motion of her head, kissed him quickly on the lips. Blake's hand reached to the small of her back and pressed her to him. He smiled as he looked down then kissed her forehead. His lips roamed her cheek and nose before the two kissed hungrily. They held their embrace, but soon she moved away and said, "Silly Yank! First things first. I expect us to win handsomely." She backed toward the door. "Now get yourself changed."

Blake's heart pounded at Indianapolis speed. "May not be able to concentrate on tennis."

The conversation at courtside was light and relaxed while Blake finished his meal. His eyes sought Peg's and she responded with the same half smile and tilting head that had become so suggestive to him.

On the court Peg was everything they said. She had strong basic ground strokes and was light and quick on her feet. The extraordinary part of her game was her net play, where she slammed volleys at the feet of her opponents or down the vulnerable middle, forcing error after error. Peg played with the competitive intensity of most men and Blake soon found himself sharing court responsibilities equally and often deferring to her. Although the men played well, the games went quickly because Peg was far superior to the other women. The set scores were lopsided 6-1, 6-2.

The tennis players became exhausted quickly in the hot Asian sun, so the teams changed often. Soon Peg and Blake found a place in the shade of the straw umbrellas.

As they sat sipping cool drinks and watching the others play, Blake commented to Tony. "Quite a player, isn't she?"

"Not bad for an Aussie."

"Thank you, Commaaander," emphasizing the end of the word with her Australian accent. "You're not so bad yourself. I guess we showed them. We're the undefeated champions."

"Wait until next time. We'll practice before then," the Operations Manager said.

Blake glanced at his watch. Time had passed too quickly. He was enjoying Peg's free spirited ways. "Have to shower and change. My jeep'll be here soon."

"Use my cottage shower if you like."

"Ah ha, going to trap him in the shower. Typical Aussie trick."

"I haven't let you catch me in the shower yet, you bloody Limey."

"Not that I wouldn't try, Peg Thompson." The British Operations Manager winked at Blake.

Peg responded in a saucy tone, "Now I know why they say the sun never sets on an Englishman. It's because God and women don't trust the bastards after dark."

Tony was still laughing when Joanna Marbo joined them from the main house. "Joanna, our house guest is getting picked on by this Aussie bird!"

Joanna wore dark sun glasses and held a wet cloth to her head. She picked up her monologue from the night before. "Well, enough of that — but he probably deserves it — for having talked about so many uncomfortable things last night — have you all had enough to eat — We have much more being prepared — what are you all drinking — I do believe I need a Bloody Mary — it must have been the wine last night — I'm a little dull this morning — how was your match....?"

"Excellent tennis, but I'm afraid Peg and Blake gave us all a bit of a lesson." Tony motioned a Vietnamese servant to get Joanna a drink.

Blake stayed to chat with this bubbling lady he had already grown fond of. Joanna regained the conversational lead and rambled on in her country Englishwoman way reviewing the evening before. Several Vietnamese children who had been watching the tennis matches from a distance came to her. She hugged each of them and they clung to her as if they alone understood her humanity. Blake guessed her babbling non-stop conversation was her way of avoiding the problems of the world. She concentrated on only those things she could control: talk, happiness, friends, and her love for children and she conveyed a peacefulness not otherwise felt in a war zone.

Blake glanced at his Timex and excused himself. In Peg's cottage he stripped and showered quickly. He was slipping into his uniform trousers when Peg came to the door. "Are you decent?"

Blake's heart took a heavy beat. "It's okay." He'd hoped she would come.

Peg handed him a glass. "Thought you might be ready for another gin and tonic. If you don't mind, I'll save some time by changing now."

Peg disappeared into the bathroom. As he sipped the drink he heard the shower water start and stop. When she stepped through the bathroom door she was wearing a robe tied loosely at the waist. Her breasts were partially exposed.

"Blake, be a darling and hand me those undies from the top of the dresser."

He picked up the soft things and carried them the few steps to Peg. As he approached he felt the tightness grip him. She was beautiful, standing there with her hair rumpled from toweling.

As she extended her hand the waist cord slipped and the robe fell open revealing twin mountains, firm and curving toward peaks of pointed brown nipples. "Thank you, kind sir."

Peg's body was no longer a fantasy and he couldn't resist. He didn't want to resist. He took her in his arms and they kissed passionately. Blake kissed her this time with all the fury and frenzy of a warplace. His pent up loneliness exploded in the need to touch flesh.

"Oh, Blake, it's so good," the Australian woman whispered.

Until then they had touched and even kissed, but now he knew he could have her. Momentarily guilt erupted, flushing away all other feelings. His mind played ping-pong between Beverly and the urgency of the moment. He struggled to be released from Victorian rules and blurted, "You know I'm married."

"Silly Yank. It doesn't matter." Her response was accented with the coldness of war and it was what Blake hoped she would say.

It was enough. His fingers slid the robe from her shoulders as the controlling bonds of guilt fell away to let in loneliness and passion. His hands followed the robe downward until they slid under the roundness of her buttocks. He lifted her easily at the same time her legs encircled his waist. With her fingers digging into his back and their mouths washing in sucking sounds, he carried her to the bed. She lay staring at his chest as her breasts heaved. His eyes ravenously caressed her. His hands explored her upward sloping breasts. He was fumbling with his clothes as his mouth roamed breasts and belly and kissed the soft flesh of her legs.

There was a knock at the door. A voice said, "Commander Lawrence, your jeep is here."

Blake sat upright. A mixture of irritation and draining emotion flooded his mind and body. *Oh, what timing.*

"Send them away. Stay with me." Peg whispered.

"I'd like to. But I must get back. Important things are happening."

She whispered again. "Come back this evening."

Blake kissed her gently. "I'll try." Then to the voice on the other side of the door he said, "Be there in a moment."

Blake gathered his bag, weapon, and tennis racquet and slipped out while Peg finished in the bathroom. Tony and Joanna were still lounging by the tennis court. As he came by on the way to the jeep Blake said. "Thanks again for a wonderful supper last night and the fun morning."

Joanna smiled and waved. "You know you don't need an invitation — Blake, just drop in on us anytime — we're always here — Mark Harris comes often you know."

Blake climbed into the jeep and as it sped away along the dirt road his mind was still in the cottage, thinking about Peg. *In war time affairs happen,* he rationalized. *Lovers never know when they'll be together again.* Blake wasn't sure if this was infatuation or if it was more. When he thought of Peg, he felt jealous of Mark.

He thought of Beverly and again was caught up in guilt. His hand instinctively found the letter. Although he had already read it, he skimmed it again. The guilt compounded when he read Beverly's PS and even more so when he unfolded the piece of school paper and read the child's note.

PS. This is a poem Martha wrote for you. She titled it, "I Miss You So." She told me she intends to put it to music. She wants to sing like Diana Ross.

I Miss You So
by Martha Lawrence
Sometimes in the night I get
up and look around,
I see my love.
He looks at me and said,
I've missed you so.
How I wish you had not gone,
But I'll still love you,
Until the end.

Blake turned his head, looked out across the rice paddies and then at the sky. He swallowed hard but even so a tearlet gathered in his eye as he again thought of his son and re-read his daughter's scribbles. He smiled at the child's mistake of tense. She used "and said" instead of "and says." The thoughts of Martha's poem mixed with Peg's whispery voice that said, "Come back this evening."

TWENTY THREE

Do Van Nghi intended to take only men with him to the village of Nhon Trach, but when Co Hang returned from the place where she lived with an American GI, she pleaded to go. Her fearless work on the river had proven her courage, but he remembered during the later stages of the rocket mission her moods became mercurial, one moment child-like and the next maniacal and he was reluctant to take her. But when she professed her strong desire to find the man who gave up her friend Tam Ha, Nghi agreed she could come.

Once out of the jungle they stayed on the rubber plantation roads because those roads eventually blended with the rice farmer roads and they led to the village. The guerrillas carried machetes and wore the garb of country people, but under their blouses, in case they became trapped and had to fight a regional army patrol, they had knives, pistols and grenades.

Near the village of Nhon Trach, as if on a country stroll, they casually left the road. They sat behind a row of dense bushes hidden until the evening when other people began moving about.

As they waited, Nghi unfolded his strategy. Two men would meander into the village and go into the store that repaired radios. Nghi and Co Hang would observe from the back.

When the sun had dropped sufficiently low that the shadows were long and people came out of their homes to stroll hand-in-hand, Nghi signaled his two comrades to begin moving along the wooden sidewalk of the village of Nhon Trach.

Nghi and Co Hang crept behind the buildings paralleling the two men and the river Song Sau. They darted from one small out-building to the next stopping only when townspeople came to relieve themselves at the river privy.

They saw their two companions go into a building which Nghi assumed was the radio store. He and Co Hang checked their weapons then crept close to the rear door of the place. Again they waited.

A little boy, eight or nine years old, came dashing out of the back door. Nghi grabbed him. Pressing his hand across the boy's mouth so he could not make a sound he dragged the boy into the growing shadows. There he gagged and tied the boy. Nghi then crept close to the door and pushed aside the curtains. He peered in and saw a dark-haired, middle aged man wearing western dress haggling about the price of some object with one of Nghi's men. The other guerrilla idled near the front door.

Nghi stepped into the building and spoke sharply, "Close your store for the night. Do not give us away or I will kill the boy."

A frightened look spread across the man's face. Quickly he went out, pulled the bamboo curtain across the front of the store then returned closing the wooden door behind him.

Nghi ordered the man into a small room in the rear of the store where electronic parts were scattered on a work bench. It was not until then that Nghi smiled and spoke in a friendly tone. To reassure the storekeeper of their compassion and peaceful intent, he pushed the boy into the man's arms. Nghi said gently, "The boy will not be harmed if you cooperate. We are from the rubber plantation and only wish to learn about a friend that came to the village several weeks ago. His name was Tam Ha, a strong and burly man. He came to have a radio repaired. Have you seen my friend?"

The storekeeper hesitated then said, "I do remember a man such as you describe, but I don't know where he went."

Co Hang surprised even Do Van Nghi by springing across the room. She pulled the boy from his father's arms and jammed a pointed stick against the throat of the child. Digging it into flesh of the child she screamed. "Liar! Tell us or I will let blood ooze from a hole in this neck. Quickly!"

The child cringed and tried to go to his father, but one of the other guerrillas stepped forward and stood in the way. Nghi stepped closer to the storekeeper. *Another change in the girl, he thought. I miscalculated her ruthlessness. I hadn't planned she would threaten the child, but it falls nicely into my method.*

In gentle tones Nghi said, "You know we are really Cong, and our camp is near this village. We know our friend was captured, and we know you are not guilty. All we wish to know is who in the village is the spy for the Provincial Reconnaissance Unit. Tell us what you know and the child will not be harmed. Surely you know."

The storekeeper hesitated then in frightened tones said, "Please don't harm the boy."

Like a kind father, Nghi said, "Of course your child is innocent, but you can tell us what happened to our friend."

The storekeeper remained silent.

Do Van Nghi put his face close to the man and whispered. "You have a wife and other children do you not?"

"Yes."

"We will not harm them either, but you must tell us what happened to our friend."

"I know nothing. Believe me, I know nothing."

"Come now," Nghi cajoled. "We are your friends, surely you understand we are nearby in the jungle and will rule this village when we defeat the Americans. It is better to be with us now. We will remember. Did the PRU capture him here, in your store?"

"Please, I know nothing."

Nghi calmly turned and in passionless tones said to the other guerrillas, "Should we kill the boy now?"

Without question or other reaction, Co Hang impassively ran the stick to the boy's throat piercing the skin just enough that a trickle of blood ran down her arm.

"Nooooo. Ahhhhhhhhhhhh, I'll tell," the storekeeper moaned. He started for Co Hang, but the two guerrillas grabbed him and threw him to the floor. There he writhed, beating his hands against the wood, whimpering and crying curse words.

"Gag him, until he quiets." Nghi ordered.

The two men wrapped a rag about his mouth, but after a few minutes Nghi ordered the rag removed. "You remember now? Tell us what happened to our friend."

"Ahhhhhh, leave us..." But before he could finish the sentence the heel of a bare foot slammed into his kidney and he rolled to his back.

"Tell us!" Nghi barked.

"All right. He came with the radio. Here, to my store."

"Yes."

"I could not do otherwise. We villagers must tell the National Police. It is not my fault."

"What National Policeman did you tell?" Nghi asked gently.

"Vo. Vo Van Dinh. He's the one that knows everything in Nhon Trach."

"How much did Vo Van Dinh pay you?"

"Ahhhhhh," The merchant groaned. As before, a kick, this time to the stomach, quickly put a stop to the whining.

"How much?"

"6,000 piasters."

One of Nghi's guerrillas screamed, "Only 6,000 piasters for Tam Ha? Let me cut off his balls and turn my machete in his ass."

But Nghi said, "No, bring him. We go to see Vo Van Dinh, the policeman."

"What about the boy?" Co Hang asked.

"Leave him tied and gagged."

By the time they left the store, night had fallen across the village of Nhon Trach. Two of Nghi's comrades dragged the storekeeper through the back alleys until they came to the home of National Policeman, Vo Van Dinh. There they waited while Nghi circled the house. Inside a small electric light glowed above three small children and a man. A woman scurried back and forth responding to the man's guttural demands. The man sat cross-legged in his underwear, at a low table picking at rice with chop sticks.

Nghi took his K-54 pistol from under his blouse. He then signaled Co Hang and the two men holding the storekeeper to cover the back door while he went to the front.

Before going to the main door, Nghi scanned the darkness in each direction. Once assured the street was quiet, he burst into the house and pointed the pistol at Vo Van Dinh. "Make no move or it will be your last, as well as your family."

Vo Van Dinh had a hard face with scars on the left side under his ear. The wife and children were surprised and frightened, but Dinh showed little emotion. "Don't be foolish," he said. "Put the gun down and I will settle what ever problem you may have. I am a member of the National Police. I can help you."

At that moment the other three guerrillas pushed the storekeeper through the back of the house and into the dim light glowing over the table. One of the men quickly separated the children and the wife from Dinh. The other man forced the merchant to sit across from the policeman. Pistols were held to the temples of each man.

"What is it you want," Dinh asked, his voice rising in a growing display of fearless temper.

Nghi again used quiet, gentle tones, "We want to know how much the PRU paid you to turn in Tam Ha."

"Mad man. Who is Tam Ha?"

"Our comrade." Then Nghi said to the storekeeper, "Refresh the policeman's memory. Tell him. Quickly, we don't have all night."

The merchant hesitated until Co Hang whispered into his ear. Then the merchant choked, "No, please, not my family." To Vo Van Dinh, he said, "Tam Ha was the man I told you about who came to my store to repair his radio. Remember? You called the PRU and they came and took him away. Don't you remember?"

"Liar! Liar!" The policemen growled. "I know nothing of what you say. This man is a nothing. He eats dog meat and he lies. If the PRU took your friend, he..." Pointing to the man across from him, "made the report."

Nghi shivered with hate. The Vo Van Dinh's of South Vietnam stood between the Viet Cong and the Communist goals which Colonel Tu told him they must achieve.

The storekeeper whimpered, "It was he. It was he. He paid me."

Nghi moved behind Vo Van Dinh and stroked the scars on the side of the man's face as he said, "How did you come by these scars?"

"In the war. I have others. You like scars? You want to see them?" The hard faced man sneered.

Nghi's hand slid down Dinh's cheek and under his chin. He pulled it until he was looking into the unfearing policeman's eyes. Nghi exchanged his pistol for a knife and slid the blade next to the fat flesh of the man's neck.

"So you were a soldier, were you."

"Everyone is a soldier, sooner or later."

"It was you that turned in Tam Ha. Isn't that true? How much did the PRU pay you? Confess!" Nghi spat.

"Confess? Confess to what? Being a policeman? or a soldier? I don't remember Tam Ha, and I confess to nothing."

Nghi then said to the guerrilla standing next to him, "Tie one of his hands behind his back and hold the other flat on the table."

While Dinh's hand was being bound, Nghi held the knife to his throat and began to talk quietly. "Even though we don't live in this village, it is under our control. The people need to know that we are fair. Everyone deserves a trial. Let us begin. Who will be the first witness?"

At first there was silence, but soon Co Hang said, "I will be the first. Because I knew Tam Ha very well. He was a good man and he was my comrade.

"Anything else?"

"No," she said.

"Well we need more evidence than that," Nghi said. "Did he have a family?"

"Oh," Co Hang said in after thought. "Of course. And four children."

At the same time Nghi slammed his knife across Vo Van Dinh's hand cutting off the man's small finger and part of the next. "What do you say to that?" Nghi said to the Police Officer.

Dinh jerked and moaned, but the guerrilla held the hand firm on the table in the puddle of blood, next to the pieces of bloody fingers.

The policeman's wife burst into a pleading monologue and the children began to cry.

Nghi wrenched Dinh's head backward and whispered, "Oh, we have only begun, traitor — American sympathizer. The evidence is clear. Tam Ha was a good man and you turned him over to the PRU. You therefore killed Tam Ha." Then to his band of guerrillas he said, "Jury, what do you say?"

"Guilty!" they responded in unison.

With that Nghi slipped the knife under Vo Van Dinh's right ear and ripped upward leaving the meat attached and hanging by a piece of slender skin as red blood flowed down his neck and shoulder.

Do Van Nghi spat. "Confess! you eater of dog meat slime."

"Never," Dinh groaned as he slumped forward. Nghi kicked him in the back with his knee and cautioned, "Sit up, you pig." Then to Co Hang he said, "Take one of the children. Do as you did before."

Co Hang grabbed a male child from the mother and pulled him into the light next to the storekeeper, opposite the policeman. Again, without hesitation, she took her stick and held it a moment under the chin of the child then rammed it upward into the skull. The blood spurted in a stream, falling across the table top near the policeman's torn hand.

Vo Van Dinh winced at the sight of his dead baby slumped on the floor. The mother wrenched away from her captors and fell across the child sobbing.

Nghi sneered, "This is only the beginning, dog. Confess to the death of Tam Ha."

"But I am a policeman. It is my duty." Dinh gurgled.

"Shall it be another child?"

At that both Co Hang and the mother grabbed for the other small boy. There was a momentary struggle until Co Hang beat the woman with the stick and pulled the child from his sister and into the light.

"Confess, shit of a pig." Nghi barked.

"Ahhhh," the man groaned. "It was my duty. Don't kill the boy."

"So you do admit to it!"

At that Nghi ordered the mother to be brought forward into the light to stand next to the storekeeper. "You heard the confession. If you tell the townspeople anything less we will return and...you both have other children. Tell them that you heard this policeman confess to the murder of a Viet Cong. Do you understand?"

The two nodded they would comply. They were pushed away into a dark corner.

"Now then, what shall the sentence be?" the guerrilla leader asked.

"Kill him," Co Hang said immediately, and the others nodded agreement.

With that Do Van Nghi slipped his knife back into its sheath and took a machete from the guerrilla holding Vo Van Dinh. The policeman's bloody hand was pulled behind his back and his head forced forward until his forehead rested on the table. In one powerful slice Do Van Nghi drove the blade through the back of the man's neck and the head rolled sideways, severed from the policeman's body. The ugly face stared toward the dimly glowing light bulb. The body jerked, then slumped to the floor.

Nghi grabbed the head by the hair and ordered, "Come, leave them."

"What shall we do with the dead boy?"

Nghi didn't hesitate as he spoke in ruthless tones, "Take him to the river. Hang him where the village shits. That way they will remember that Cong control this village."

Nghi's band of guerrillas exited the back of the small home and went quickly through the night to the edge of town where they stopped only long enough to hang the head on a stick next to the road where all the townspeople would be sure to see it the next day.

Later that night, after they had returned to the jungle, Nghi's band stopped to rest. Each took a position isolated from the others so they could listen but escape separately if they were followed.

Do Van Nghi laid down on the mossy sponge, against the root of a mangrove tree. He began thinking about his report to Colonel Tu; how they had avenged the death of their comrade. His mind swam with the thoughts of the pride he would feel when he heard Colonel Tu's praise. He felt a body nestle close to his. He knew it was Co Hang cuddling to him, but he was so exhausted he didn't open his eyes. His arms closed automatically about her as they had before. Gently he pulled her to a female mounting position where she rode his hardness and they released the tension of their day.

In the morning, refreshed, the small band returned to their camp where the other Doi commanders met Do Van Nghi. He quickly told them of the events in the village of Nhon Trach and they, in excited tones, told him about a message from Colonel Tu. "Our spies in Nha Be have learned that a recon group is coming into the jungle to search for the new rockets. Colonel Tu has ordered us to move the Russian missiles. He sent his regrets to you, and said that your victory party will have to wait."

Inside he was disappointed. He wanted to tell Colonel Tu about Tam Ha. He wanted to hear the praise, but Nghi was now the most experienced of the Doi commanders and he spoke thoughtfully, "Coming here? To the Forest of Assassins? Of course the victory party will wait, but we will have another kind of party — just for the Americans."

Before he set the plan, Nghi ordered Co Hang to return to her village. "Be ready when we need you for another rocket shot."

"No!" she spat the word. Then as if she knew she was wrong she bowed and told Nghi, "I would rather stay with you and fight.

"What's wrong with you?"

"I want to stay with you — I'm going to have a baby."

Nghi touched her face. "Pregnant? Now I understand the reason for your mood swings. No! You cannot stay with me. We will need you later to operate and fire the rocket launcher. You serve us better in the village."

He sent her on her way with a gentle touch and called to the other members of the Doi, "Quickly! Let us move the rockets — but let us also set an ambush and kill the Americans."

Twenty Four

SUNDAY, JULY 9, 1972, NHA BE BASE

"Marquell! Get up! Get on your goddamn feet!

A rat's squeal broke the moment of silence.

"Ahh."

"Where you been?" Gunny barked. "Goddamnit, Major Harris is pissed. You were supposed to drive Commander Lawrence to Dutch World this morning. What you doing in here? No one could find you."

The storage room ordinarily used as a hooch maid hang-out had only two chairs, a few ash trays, and a chest-high stack of mattresses. Morning light knifed through the broken seams of a black cloth rigged across the only window. The normal musty odor of stale barracks air was cut by a mixture of cigarette smoke, and the stench of vomit.

Marquell struggled to sit up. He opened his eyes to find the giant body of Gunny Johnson standing before him. Doc stood to one side. His mind was still dull from drugs and booze from his night in the 'vil. His words came slowly, "I, ah... I came in here to read after watch. Musta fallen asleep."

Doc grabbed Marquell. He pulled him to the floor from his bed on top of the pile of mattresses, then slammed him against the wall. His right fist ripped into his belly and doubled the young Marine, then his knee rammed into his face. Blood squirted from his nose to the floor.

Gunny, who towered over his Mexican-American buddy, wrapped an arm around Doc's chin and neck and pulled him off Marquell. "No Doc. That ain't the solution. It ain't right. You ain't no Marine."

"Bullshit, Gunny. Smell the bastard — look at his fuc'n eyes. Don't give-a-shit it's a Marine problem. Let me teach him a lesson. Noth'n they can do to me — won't make Chief anyway. You do it and this fuc'n pot-head'll fuck up your career. You got a lot to lose, almost nineteen years in the Corps and that Bokassa almost hatched. Let me kick his ass, blood."

"No. Get out. I'll take care of it." He held the Corpsman away.

"What's he worth? He's shit. He's an asshole. He'll fuck you over, Gunny."

Doc reluctantly left the small room and Gunny pushed the private into a chair. "Don't move. We're gonna have an understanding. You know what I mean by an understanding? I talk, you listen. Now, I know where you were last night. I know you were in the vil — in the Boo Goo and you got stoned."

Marquell draped himself over the chair. "Hey, who says? I been here all night. You ain't got any proof."

Gunny slapped Marquell across the face. "Shut up, shitbird! Don't need no proof. Got your ass right here!" Holding his cupped hand in front of Marquell's eyes. "Listen to me. Last night one of the Vietnamese guards got knifed as he was coming off duty. A Cong musta got in from water-side. It happened on the mid-watch. Ordinarily it wouldn't be none of our business. But Saigon wants to know about our security and I don't want no Marines implicated... and you, you're a fuc'n Marine even if you don't got no respect."

Marquell's head slumped. "But Gunny...."

The palm of Gunny's hand shot out and hit Marquell's forehead causing his head to jerk erect. "Sit up like a man. Don't want to hear your shit... You ain't got anything to tell me that I don't already know. I know what you do. I know where you go. I'd squash you like a fuc'n grape, but this ain't the time. I don't want the Marines involved in this thing. You were here in the barracks last night, understand?"

"Yes, Sir."

"Don't sir me!"

"Yes, Gunny."

At that point Gunny's eyes swelled in fury and he shook Marquell's shoulders causing his head to bob. "This is the second time I've covered for you, bucket of shit. You ain't even a private. You shouldn't be wear'n no stripes. You were a Corporal and in the Corps that's a leader. Now you ain't shit. And you keep fuc'n up. Everybody says you're useless. You're going to the brig tomorrow and when you come back you're my project, and this is the last time."

As Marquell's chin slumped toward his chest, Gunny again hit the top of his forehead with the heel of his hand. "Sit up and act like a Marine!" Before Gunny left the room he said, "What do I have to do to get you squared away? When you gonna act like a man?"

Private Marquell watched the tall black sergeant leave the room, slamming the door behind him, then drooped forward in his chair, hands resting on his legs, head down. He felt like shit. His head hurt from the beer, and he felt dirty. He raised his head and caught the shimmer of sunlight glancing off glass. In a tall mirror, hung crookedly on the back of the door, he saw himself, disheveled uniform, baggy eyed, and unshaven. He wished he had a smoke or a beer. Marquell stared at his image and he saw himself — the way he really was. He closed his eyes, but the image wouldn't go away. He felt shame as he thought about Gunny's last words, "When you gonna act like a man?" The same words his daddy used.

TWENTY FIVE

MONDAY, JULY 10, 1972, NHA BE BASE

On Monday morning, just as Rear Admiral Paulson had agreed, two Navy men, dressed smartly in pressed green fatigues tucked carefully into spit-shined combat boots entered Blake's office. They marched rapidly together to the front of his desk where they stood at attention, side by side. One was in his late thirties, tall and rugged looking, the other so young he could be taken for the taller man's son.

More slender than the older man, but in obvious hardened physical condition, the younger spoke for the two, "Lieutenant Junior Grade Morris reporting, Sir."

Blake scratched his head as he listened to the junior officer make his report. *The Admiral said a Lieutenant Junior Grade would be the leader of the SEAL team, but I never expected a fuzzy-cheeked kid. There must be a misunderstanding.*

"Relax," Blake told the two. "I'm Senior Advisor here and this is Major Harris, my operations officer."

The J.G. whose blue eyes and crew cut gave him the look of a Nazi brown shirt, introduced the taller man as Chief Petty Officer Ace Magrue, assistant SEAL team leader. Given the order to relax, Ace, a hard jawed man with a scar across one cheek, now stood with his hands clasp loosely behind his back. Blake supposed the scar was from some earlier action. As he inspected the two, his eyes first riveted on Ace's big ears, scanned the vertical wrinkle in the center of his forehead, and then his straight black hair. *He looks more like a Marine Colonel than a Navy CPO.*

Blake reached across his desk and shook their hands then asked the J.G. "What's your first name?"

"Eric, Sir"

Mark also stepped forward and shook their hands. "How many men you bring?"

Now standing at parade rest in front of his seniors, Eric responded. "Just the Chief and five others, Sir. We were told this would only be an intel mission. We left the rest of the platoon at Cat Lai. We also brought along two LDNN."

"LDNN?" Blake asked.

"Vietnamese equivalent of our SEAL's," Eric answered.

Blake motioned for them to sit. "Anyone told you about the operation yet?"

"No Sir, but that's okay. I'll decide if we're gonna do it after we hear the details."

Blake knew the SEAL's always had the final say. He also knew they seldom, if ever, turned down a mission, but they often took strong stands about the means to accomplish the job. Even Admiral Paulson with all his authority couldn't command them to do something they couldn't do. The idea was to keep some asshole from sending them to hell for the fun of it.

Blake explained how the AT3 missiles had been brought into the Rung Sat. He told them the PRU's had captured a VC and during the interrogation the prisoner had given them the general location of the rockets. He also told them about the letter they had found on the guerrilla which indicated that the leader of Doan 12, one Senior Colonel Tu, would be visiting the camp. Then he explained, "In order to have a chance to capture Colonel Tu, the timing of this operation has to be perfect. Need you fellows to take a couple of the PRU with you." Then, pointing to a spot on the large wall chart, "Get in there, to about this area. Verify the location of the rockets, and if possible find out when Colonel Tu is arriving. We want Tu and those wire-guided rockets."

Color crept from behind Ace Magrue's floppy ears and spread across his cheeks. He slid forward to the edge of his chair as he said, "That's a goddamn tall order, Commander. We're not fuc'n miracle workers you know. That area of the Rung Sat is probably infested with Charlie."

Blake was taken back by the sharpness of the remark. But he wanted Colonel Tu so badly he didn't want to risk jeopardizing their co-operation. Instead of rebuking the Chief he went on as if nothing had happened. "This insert is critical. We need information, but it must be done in such a way that it doesn't give away our operation."

Ace's voice rose as he spat, "Obvious you don't know much about this kind of mission or you'd know the fuc'n PRUs're the wrong guys to go in with us. Damn good, mind you. Worked with them down in Four Corps, but they're wrong for this. They're civilians. Work for the fuc'n CIA, and they're undisciplined. They'd just end up getting us killed. Best guys to go with us are the LDNN. Been trained by us and damn tough jungle fighters. The other thing!" Chief Ace moved to the chart. "There's no guarantee once we get in there," pointing to the spot Blake had designated, "we won't make contact. Hang'n around to get dope on this Colonel Tu's crazy! Charlie puts out guards around his camps just like we do. Contact could happen at any time without any fuc'n ceremony."

Blake's jaws tightened. His face felt flushed. *Never ran across a smart-ass Chief Petty Officer like this before. In the blue water Navy a Chief who smarted-off like that would have been dismissed out-of-hand.* Blake had let it go too long already. He was about to lower the boom, but before he could say the words....

"Ah, Sir," Eric spoke softly. "Ah... What the Chief means, Sir, is that on this kind of mission sometimes the hunter becomes the hunted. We can't afford to have any screw-ups. Chief Ace is a little outspoken but he's one of our most experienced SEALs. Highly decorated. Been on more operations than any one. Just wants you to be aware of the risks involved."

Eric's words had a calming effect on Blake. He still wanted this mission to go. "Now look," Blake said. "I admit I don't have all the answers. I'm very new at this type of warfare. That's why we asked you guys to come down here. Hey, I'm even willing to go with you on this operation."

"You go with us?" The Chief sounded off as he rose from his chair. "Christ, Commander, these are my boys. You wanna get em killed? We may have to go three, four, maybe five days without talking or sleeping and almost no water.

You couldn't last a half fuc'n day out there. Besides you guys probably already leaked the operation. The gooks'll get you, and losing Navy Commanders ain't the order of the day."

Mark Harris came out of his chair, his voice booming above its normal gravel pitch. "Now wait a minute, Chief. Careful how you speak to Commander Lawrence. We didn't invite you here to take a lot of shit from you. We're happy to go over every detail of the operation, but don't try to hustle us." He paused, looking hard at Chief Magrue then he continued, "I agree — the Commander shouldn't go and if you don't want the PRU's along that's your business." Then moving nose to nose with Ace Magrue, Mark said, "Normally, I don't explain details to a Chief and I don't take any shit from them either. As far as operational security is concerned, we've got a lid on this one as tight as a drum. There was a break-in the other night — a guard got knifed, but that's all. Nothing's missing. Only three copies of the OPORDER have been prepared, and those were typed by one of our most trusted men. Two copies in Vietnamese. One translated into English. That should give you some indication of the effort we're going to, to keep this thing quiet."

Eric got out of his chair and stood beside Magrue as if to protect his man if things got out of control. Speaking quickly, his voice on the rise, he said. "What Ace is trying to say, Major. If Charlie finds out before we get there, he won't be there. On the other hand he might be there with goodies for us."

Blake was struck by the situation. A Marine Major nose-to-nose with a CPO! He remembered the words of the Brit — the Operations Manager for Dutch World, when he said, "War, in this little country has made madmen of you all." *Thank God Eric could interpret what his wise-ass Chief meant. Otherwise we might have a small madman war right here between the Marines and the Navy.* "Gentlemen! Sit down! That's an order! And Mark, back off!" Blake waited for a moment until the three were seated. "Now, we're going to have to work together on this thing. Let me try another approach. What can we do for you and your men, Lieutenant?"

From his chair next to Ace, Eric replied. "A couple of things, Sir. I'll need isolated quarters. Big enough we can all sleep in the same room, or in several rooms close together. I'll also need to do an air recon. After that Ace and I'll decide if we'll take the mission or not. Do you have regular flights over the area?"

It was the second time Eric had said he would decide, as if Blake hadn't gotten the message the first time. Blake's skin burned and for a moment his eyes pinched. He wanted to lash out at this impertinent junior, but the SEAL's were the key. He didn't want them to turn sour, so instead he confirmed, "Ever since we learned the rockets were in the Rung Sat we've been running searches over the area hoping to pick up unusual activity."

"Good enough, Sir. We prefer a flight that's not unusual. When can I get a chopper?"

"Any time. You say the word. Work it out with Major Harris. One more thing, Eric, I'd like to take you to meet Captain Duc-Lang so he knows who you are and what you're up to. As a matter of fact, why don't I come along with you, meet your men right now, then you and I can go right over to see the Dai Ta."

Besides the Chief, the SEAL unit was made up of two senior petty officers and three juniors. The two seniors were no more than a year older than the others. Blake knew these 19- and 20-year-old sailors were the crazy life's-blood of the U.S. Navy's Sea Air and Land teams, but it wasn't until he was among them that he became aware of how special they were. At first they came off like happy-go-lucky, grab-assing, kids, but pride and comradeship soon became clear.

As Blake scanned Ace's boys, he suspected their tightness as a team was the result of having survived the toughest military training in the world. Their hats were the only sign of individuality. One wore a baseball cap, another a golf hat, one had a bandanna tied across his forehead, and one of them had an Australian bush hat. Only one man wore a regulation GI jungle hat, and that one had the brim rearranged in a unique pattern. They were so loose, it struck Blake they must not read their own press clippings. On the other hand, there were never many clippings about the SEALs. There ops were black — what they did was usually so classified, even when it was over, nobody could talk about it. He had heard before he left the States that the SEAL's were the most under-decorated men in this war, for what they did. It was because they don't blow their own horns, and nobody else knows what really happens out there in the many small battles. There weren't any Bastones for the SEALs.

Gunny Johnson showed up about the time Blake finished meeting Eric's men. Marquell was with the Gunny, but he looked more like a marionette than a Marine. He was scheduled to begin his punishment at the Saigon Brig that afternoon and Gunny was obviously keeping him on a short string. When he couldn't be found to take Blake to Dutch World the morning of the tennis match, Blake had been told that Marquell had fallen asleep in an empty barracks room. Since the driving assignment was unofficial, Blake didn't press the matter. Whatever the real story, the sallow-faced Marine now followed the giant Sergeant wherever he went, moving in sync with every move and standing at ramrod attention when Gunny stopped, always just one pace to the left and to the rear.

Gunny went with Chief Petty Officer Magrue to get the SEAL team settled while the three officers went to visit the Rung Sat Commander.

The meeting with Duc-Lang was short. The *Dai Ta* was delighted when he learned Eric spoke fluent Vietnamese. He reviewed the plan and emphasized that the objective of the mission was to verify the location of the rockets, but also to learn when Tu would arrive for the so called victory party so they could coordinate the attack and capture the North Vietnamese Colonel.

As they returned to the American compound, Eric commented, "You guys are really hung up on this guy, Tu, aren't you?"

"Senior Colonel Tu is the key to success in securing the Rung Sat," Blake said defensively.

Eric's words also sounded defensive. "I want you to know my feelings, Commander. I know I'm a very junior officer, but when I'm in the jungle, I'm in-charge and the safety of my team comes first. You may as well know now, because this is an intel mission to locate the AT3 rockets, I won't risk my men for Colonel Tu. He'll only be of secondary interest to me out there. In fact, if we go, I don't intend to tell my men anything about that aspect of the plan. I'd like to take the chopper ride tomorrow morning to recon the area and pick a landing zone. If everything looks okay, I'll put together my warning order the day after tomorrow and kick it off the following morning."

The next afternoon, after his visual reconnaissance flight of the target area, Eric Morris met with Blake and Mark. "I took Chief Ace with me and we spent about an hour around the area. We were careful not to fly any patterns. That's real scudzy terrain over there. Had a heck of a time finding a decent landing zone, but we finally settled on a couple of old bomb craters at a point about two clicks from the suspected base camp. Chief Ace thinks this mission will have to go perfect to get in and get out without contact.""What do you think, Eric?" Blake asked.

"We'll have to patrol our way in from the LZ through some very tough ground. It'll be difficult to remain undisclosed, but we're trained to do this job." Eric didn't vacillate. He made his decision and simply said, "We'll go."

*****

Ten gray lockers lined the faded green walls of the barracks assigned to the SEAL team. Nude centerfolds from <u>Playboy</u> and <u>Penthouse</u> were already posted on the doors. Weapons and field equipment hung on metal bunks.

Ace Magrue stood in the center of the room surrounded by his boys. With a twinkle in his eye and a half smile he barked. "All right. Which one of you jokers is queer for snakes? Whoever brought Herman the python down here from Cat Lai, get him the hell out of this barracks."

There were belly laughs from around the room.

"But, Ace, I'm in love," someone said.

Above the sound of boyish giggles, Ace said. "Love, my ass, get that thing out of here." Then the Chief's voice changed and his boys got serious as well. "All right hold it down, you guys. The boss'll be here in a few minutes to issue the warning order. Before he gets here there's a couple of things I wanna say. I want you fuc'n guys to remember this. When you're loading your M-16's, re-member to load one round less than the full twenty, so the spring'll feed the rounds up. When you need that weapon, and let's hope we don't need them, you can't afford to have it hang up on you and missfire. Now, another thing I have to say before Eric talks. Get some rest tonight. This is gonna to be one tough fuc'n mission. We ain't gonna have time for many pit stops. Get your batteries charged. We're in now 'til we go. No club, and no vil', and check your gear."

One of the SEALs shouted above the noise of boos, hisses, and stomping of feet, "You mean I can't go out to see Co Three Fingers? But I love her! I love her!"

There was another roar of laughter, and someone said. "Yah, you'll love her when you get the clap."

To get their attention again, Ace shouted above the laughing and grab-assing group. "Hey, Hey. OK, hold it down for Lieutenant Morris."

Lieutenant (J.G.) Eric Morris had eased in quietly during Ace's talk and stood leaning against a wall waiting for his Chief to finish. Now he stepped forward and waited for the team to quiet. "Let me talk to ya for a minute." The six American SEALs and two Vietnamese LDNN crowded into a semicircle.

Ace stepped back and watched as the men quieted and focused on the slender, man-boy who had the reputation of doing almost everything better than any one of them. Throughout their SEAL training and the work-up for their deployment away from the U.S., Eric had shown the mental toughness and determination to lead in almost every activity they undertook. Ace knew Eric wasn't as experienced as he, but the kid from New York was smarter. Eric was educated — Yale University — fluent in Vietnamese, and he was an expert in every weapon. Ace's confidence in him came from knowing Eric had the qualities innately necessary in a SEAL leader: he was street smart, a survivor, and he always seemed to land on his feet.

Eric began quietly, "Tomorrow we kick off a tough mission. One which will test us to our maximum. It'll be dangerous, but that's not new for you guys. Nevertheless, I would like to emphasize the importance Ace has put on preparation of your weapons and getting adequate rest."

He continued talking, pausing only to hang a chart of the area on the hooch wall. "Maps. Everybody gets one of these maps," He signaled for Ace to pass them out. "Gunny Johnson had them laminated. Be sure you fold them and unfold them a few times so they don't crackle out there. Okay, the warning order: Reveille 0330 for a lift-off at 0530. Be dressed out and have your weapons at the helo pad no later than 0500 for final briefing. Chow will be served for us between four and five. Eat carefully. This will be a chopper insert, but for security reasons I won't brief you on the specifics until tomorrow morning just before we go. Prepare for a four-day mission. Take long range rations, bandages, and plenty of water. The target for this patrol will be about two clicks from the LZ and the Azimuth will be 315 degrees magnetic. The rally point will be here." Eric pointed to the specific location on the chart. "A small fishing boat will come by there every mid-morning. It will be marked with a small red bandanna hanging just above the Vietnamese flag. This will be a maximum stealth operation, so get it in your minds there will be no talking for at least three and maybe four days. Okay, now for equipment. Radioman, you got the PRC-77 ready?"

"Yo, sir," said Mackie, the kid from Philadelphia, wearing a baseball cap.

"Grenadier?"

"Yo," responded Taylor, the Tallahassee man in a golf hat with a PGA emblem.

"You take the M-79 and a bandoleer of M-79 grenades. Machine gunner? Who's the gunner on this op?"

Combs, a petty officer of medium height. He wore a black stocking cap. Obviously the strongest man in the group, he said. "I've got it again, Sir."

Ace shook his head in agreement because he knew Eric Morris was right about the M-60. It would be the M-60 that would lay down the base of fire with greatest hitting power.

"You're my main man if we get in trouble, Babe. Take 350 rounds."

Eric added. "All others, M-16s with ten magazines." Velluchi, from Chicago, wearing the G.I. jungle hat and the two LDNN acknowledged with a, "Yo."

"Smitty, you got your Stoner light machine gun?" Again Eric knew his weapons. There was controversy about the Stoner; some liked the M-60 and others preferred this lightweight weapon. It was like pianos; some like Steinways, some like Baldwins. Smitty, in the Australian bush hat, and one of the most experienced men, liked the Stoner.

Ace's Steinway was a Swedish K, one of the most efficient machine guns made.

Eric glanced at Ace as if he needed assurance of his support, then as if Ace had sent him a wordless message he added. "Okay, a few more things. Drink lots of water and try to get as much rest as you can. Chief Ace, make sure they have plenty of fresh combat dressings in case we get into trouble out there. Remember why SEALs are doing this job and not the Marines or Special Forces. We're operating in and around water — when in doubt get in the water and do what you know best — SWIM! Did I forget anything, Ace?"

"No, Sir. Covered it all, very well."

Accepting Eric's smile as his reward for the kind words, the older leader ended the meeting. "OK, you guys. Briefing complete. You're on your own until we kick off in the morning."

*****

That evening the SEAL's were like different men. The joking stopped. There were no more happy-go-lucky kids, no more grab-assing and no more laughing. Ace watched as each went through his own preparation, a ritual that couldn't be taught. At different times each wandered out by the river, sighted in, then test fired into the water. Some spent more time with it than others. They all checked and rechecked their equipment and recalibrated their night vision devices. Some just field stripped their weapons, but others tore them completely down, cleaned them, oiled the parts and put them back together. Smitty, Combs, Velluchi and the two LDNN unloaded their magazines of all bullets, then carefully put them back, one by one. There would be less chance for misfire. All tried on their backpacks to ensure a comfortable fit and all loaded up on water. Southeast Asia is hot and humid, and the Rung Sat was the worst of it. Canteens could be noisy and even if they stopped there would be precious little opportunity for more than a short mouthful, enough to ward off dehydration.

Ace knew the lucky and the fearless were able to sleep, but most were uneasy. The thought of being in a jungle where there was no visibility and where the enemy could come upon them without warning brought out whatever anxieties were in their characters. Time seemed to stop for them. Many lay on their bunks just staring at the ceiling. Others paced the compound until tired enough to drift off fitfully, only to be wakened by the slightest noise. Alarm clocks were set for the hour of reveille, but most were awake before they went off. Breakfast was accepted because it was on the schedule, but for most it rested like a lump in the pit of their stomachs.

Ace Magrue waited for his boys by the helo pad. He personally checked each one as he reported in for the final briefing. These were his men, and he left nothing to chance. Except for their hats, they all dressed similarly in camouflage utilities and standard jungle boots, with a neck scarf of loosely woven material. One of the last things each did before reporting to Ace was to have a buddy smear a careful application of Elizabeth Arden, the green, black and brown camouflage war paint. Ace checked to make sure it was applied to break the outlines on their hands as well as the creases of their faces.

Ace called to Mackie. His tone was like a bossy father overemphasizing with a challenge yet teaching at the same time. "Come here, goddamn it!" Ace, also from Philadelphia said with a half smile. "You Philly boys ain't slow, but if I've told you once, I've told you a thousand times. Now, by the numbers," he said. "Smear it into the bone structure below both eyes." Mackie tugged his ball cap, gave an 'ah-shit' look, and presented himself in front of Ace who applied a bit more grease paint in precisely the right place.

They stood idly around the helo bunker for the few moments before Eric Morris came, each making his peace in his own quiet way. Then they gathered with their maps in hand as Eric gave the last briefing. "The mission is to covertly patrol from the LZ to an area in the vicinity of YS1175. We are to penetrate sufficiently to verify the location of some special Russian wire-guided rockets in a base camp believed to be used by several units of Doan 12. We should, to whatever extent possible, determine the composition of the units located there and any other intelligence we can pick up, then get out so the main attack can begin. During this mission it is important that we remain covert. Avoid any unnecessary contact and don't leave any bodies behind. Last night I held a coordination meeting with the Rung Sat Advisors and key Vietnamese personnel. The choppers that take us in will remain on five-minute alert for the first hour after they return to base. After that they'll be on half hour standby in case we need to be pulled out. Fixed wing out of Tan Son Nhut will also be on call to support us. You already know the patrol azimuth and the rally points. Any last minute questions?"

The wap, wap noise of choppers exploded out of the North. Bright landing lights pierced the dark as four helos dropped out of the sky. The team formed two lines and boarded. Element one with Taylor, Combs and the two LDNN in the lead chopper. Element two with Mackie, Smitty, and Velluchi in the second.

Blake and Mark came to the pad to see them off. There were last minute discussions among the leaders; then it was time to go. They shook hands in silence.

It was still cool by the river when Ace climbed into the lead plane with Eric in the second, but by the time the chopper taxied and lifted off, the sun was breaking over the Rung Sat. As they climbed, wind cut across their faces, soothing the discomfort of their layered clothing and heavy loads. Ace could see the third helo, a gunship, following well behind. The fourth was at high altitude.

The choppers flew directly at first, but as they neared the objective the pilots diverted and flew an indirect path, eventually approaching the LZ at low altitude where they made two fake insert passes at locations somewhat remote from the actual one. As they proceeded toward the final approach the Vietnamese pilots questioned, "Are you ready?"

"Roger, let's do it," Eric said.

Ace felt the adrenaline pumping at even higher rates. Even the most brave knew fear.

One of the gunships climbed to about 2000 feet to observe and control the other pilots, then the two troop-carrying choppers went in, one behind the other, at tree-top level. At the bomb craters the two choppers with the SEAL elements aboard dropped down and hovered only a few feet above the ground. It took only a moment for each fire team to roll over the sides and disappear into the jungle.

The fourth helo had dropped down and buzzed at tree-top altitude toward the LZ. Just as it passed over the insert position, the two troop-carrying choppers lifted off simultaneously and fell into formation behind the passing fourth helo. The intent was to confuse any ground observers by canceling out the noise, and by giving the illusion there had been one continuous flight. There was no room for chance in Ace and Eric's plan.

They were now at the first danger point. Silence was the watchword as they waited in the dark jungle on the fringe of the craters. After what seemed an eternity Eric carefully reached out and took the headset from Mackie the radioman who knelt beside him. He made two clicks on the on/off switch, an encrypted message heard aboard a support boat on the river and relayed to Blake in the TOC. The insertion was complete and the SEALs were preparing to move out.

TWENTY SIX

MONDAY, JULY 10, 1972, NHA BE BASE

On the day the SEALs arrived for their recon operation, everyone on Nha Be base engaged in furious preparations for Duc-Lang's attack. They knew something big was about to happen, but because of tight security no one knew exactly where, when, or what.

It was Duc-Lang who came up with the brilliant idea to throw off the guerrillas. Everyone, including the VC, knew that the South Vietnamese Army had the bad habit of standing down after a major field operation. Some Americans thought it was because their diet didn't give them the energy to bounce back. Whether habit or diet, Duc-Lang decided to take advantage of this apparent weakness by combining a rehearsal with a feint. By giving the impression that the rehearsal was the main operation the guerrillas would learn about it and relax afterward. If the real attack kicked off immediately after the feint, Duc-Lang's forces would have the advantage of surprise. It was heady stuff, but he knew his Rung Sat troops would need every advantage if they were to overcome Colonel Tu's guerrillas.

Blake accompanied his counterpart on inspections of ground units, test-runs on boats, equipment inventories and weapons checks. Duc-Lang roved everywhere, and Blake, as his cô-vân, was constantly at his side offering suggestions and recommendations. Blake and Sergeant Trieu attended endless briefings with the Dai Ta. They flew to inspect an infantry company scheduled for integration into the main force for the attack. They had a meeting with a District Chief to reassure him his borrowed forces would be back on the job in a few weeks. Blake and Duc-Lang began to take their meals together, alternating Vietnamese and American food.

They executed the rehearsal in an area South of the Binh Khanh District not far from where China Fox went aground. The intent was to be very visible and very believable. Compared to Blake's blue water experience it was a sloppy operation, but it did happen and it did serve its purpose.

Duc-Lang kept his enthusiasm after the rehearsal even though the operation showed serious flaws. Driven by the vision of capturing his enemy, Duc-Lang stayed with every problem discovered by the rehearsal until corrected. He demanded perfection.

Company commanders and river boat squadron commanders worked around the clock to meet his deadlines. He asked a thousand questions and expected immediate answers.

"Where is the replacement ammunition? What is the status of boat repairs?"

Duc-Lang held meetings, and meetings, and meetings.

At one point Major Harris came to Blake and said, "I realize Duc-Lang's been working long into the night himself, but you need to intercede. If he's not careful, his unit commanders are going be too tired for the main operation. He's gonna burn 'em out."

Duc-Lang disregarded Blake's words of caution. "We'll give up rest in order to have success. Nothing can be left to chance. They can rest for a long time after we capture Colonel Tu."

Subordinate Commanders were called to a secret meeting. "You have corrected your mistakes," Duc-lang told them. "Now gather your troops. Tell them to remain in barracks and have their equipment ready for the real attack. It could go any time — no more than a few days. We only wait for the final intelligence report. Operational security is of utmost importance. Tell your troops only as much as is necessary to have them ready to go on short notice."

The level of excitement on the base rose. Advisors checked their gear and cleaned their weapons. Troops temporarily housed on the base no longer sat around in groups, but spent their time restowing their backpacks and snapping in rifles.

Blake stood alongside his counterpart as they scanned the base and its activities. "There's anticipation in the air, *Dai Ta*. The men feel it — they know."

Duc-Lang's dimpled smile twinkled satisfaction as he responded in his brittle sounding English. "They know just enough. It is good they feel the excitement. Now we wait for information from our SEAL friends."

TWENTY SEVEN

WEDNESDAY, JULY 12, 1972, NHAN TRACH JUNGLE

Time doesn't matter when you're not sure if you're the hunter or the hunted. There are no limits. Wait, then wait some more until you're certain you're alone. Eric knew the operation would take at least two days, maybe three, or even four. His mission was to get in and get out undetected and bring back the exact location of the rockets — maybe learn something about a guerrilla leader named Colonel Tu.

In the jungle, Eric's team waited. The jungle heat was heavy and oppressive; the mosquitoes ferocious. Steamy moisture and humidity rose from the ground around them like an epidemic seeping through a great city.

Finally, he whispered transmission to the lead pilot of the circling chopper, "Okay. We're moving out." Then he signaled Ace.

Much of the Rung Sat jungle was still marshy from the monsoon rains, but as the wet season merged with the dry there were spots where the elephant grass sounded like Rice Krispies. As one, the team crept, single file, each man stepping in the footprint of the one in front, American Indian style. Ace was followed by Combs the machine gunner. Then came Taylor, Smitty, Veluchii and the LDNN. Mackie the radioman was in the rear followed by Eric. They took five steps then listened. It was the only way to hear the enemy before they heard you. It was agonizingly slow, but this was a game of patience and stealth. They traveled for only a half hour before Ace signaled "stop and move out on line." Eric agreed with his point man. They needed an early rest period to relax and gain their second wind. No sense burning out right away — stay strong and ready for a sustained fight if it came.

As they waited, Eric's plan unfolded in his mind. *I'll take the team as far as today's conditions allow. Hopefully we'll find base camp activity before nightfall. If not, try to find a dry area to spend the night. When the base camp is discovered we'll spend a day observing and making sketches. Then at night, we'll work in close to locate the rockets.*

The thirty minute breather over, Ace signaled them back into column. Staying off the trails they walked only where fern growth and vegetation lay thick under the nippa palm umbrella. The only sounds were monkey chatter and the rustle of invisible jungle animals. Occasionally there was a snap when a branch stung one of the SEALs. The environment was stifling but they kept on, five steps, then listen.

For Eric, each rest period seemed shorter, even though Ace timed them precisely. He estimated the team had gone about a thousand meters. Cracks of light turned gray. No sign of the camp. Eric signaled Ace to stop for the night. The crafty Chief Petty Officer had been paralleling an old trail. Now he directed them away to an area where they could form a perimeter, yet be close enough to observe movement on the path.

For SEALs, happiness was a dry arbor, and Eric watched as each man searched for a few precious inches. Quietly they sipped water, then settled into the most comfortable position they could hold for the remainder of the night. If they moved, it was done very carefully, inch by inch, because sounds in the jungle magnify as if from rock band amplifiers. It was too dangerous to sleep. To avoid temptation they took Dexedrine.

Later that night there were noises in the direction of the trail. Eric and his men froze. Heads and eyes moved with the sounds as the doppler of two shuffling people grew, then faded. They knew the base camp was nearby.

The SEALs followed the two Vietnamese men until it was too dangerous to go further. They held their positions throughout the night. In the morning, Ace signaled them to move; their progress was even more deliberate, more patient, because they could come upon the camp before they knew it.

Ace suddenly stopped. Eric heard it also. A faint sound. He couldn't define it. But it came again, in the distance, from ahead. Sharp and resonant, it had the tone of metal on metal, like someone cleaning a utensil after a meal. Eric was grateful for such noises. They make the difference for those who moved in silence.

The SEALs inched forward until Ace froze again and pointed to an almost invisible piece of monofilament line tied to a tree limb. A grenade trap intended to warn the guerrillas of intrusion. Petty Officer Combs pointed to another trap; then Smitty spotted another and Taylor another. Eric knew they must go no further until they defeated the obstacles. The team spent the rest of the day deactivating some and marking the rest. Survival depended on knowing the limits and boundaries of the explosives.

Moving carefully forward, they arrived at a position from where Eric could see the fringe of a camp. Witnessing what he supposed were guerrillas moving about and a stock of small wooden crates, he moved close to Ace. There were Russian labels and writing on them, but they couldn't be sure if the boxes held rockets. Despite the danger Eric had to get closer, he also wanted to find out about Colonel Tu. *I told Commander Lawrence I wouldn't risk my men to learn about Tu. But I'm so near and men in camp always talk. Who knows... I'll only go close enough to listen.* He wrote a note with grease pencil on his laminated chart and handed it to Ace. "Going in with Smitty and LDNN. You stay. Get the others out."

Ace's frown expressed his disagreement, but he shrugged and accepted Eric's decision.

It took them two hours to get near the VC bivouac. Each step that touched the ground was eased to full pressure only after they were sure no crackly leaf or branch was underneath.

Eric surveyed the camp. Two Vietnamese had a small fire burning in a clearing near the boxes. So little activity made him feel more secure. Slowly he and his small team inched forward until they were not more than twenty feet from the men huddled by the fire. The two talked quietly. They were not guerrillas, only cutters searching for wood to sell in the village. Eric felt uneasy because of his error in thinking they were VC.

After a while the younger man moved off toward the crates. The older continued to poke at the embers.

After finishing his call of nature, the younger man, apparently out of curiosity, lifted the top of the nearest box. Grenade traps attached to the lid fired a series of explosions. Shrapnel laced his body and blood oozed from a severed shoulder.

At the same time a fusillade of gunfire roared from the previously silent forest and Eric's team was trapped, cut off from Ace and the rest of the team. Rifles blazed from the jungle into the campfire area. The world seemed to erupt. On hearing the shots, the older woodcutter jumped away from the fire and crouching low ran toward the SEALs. Eric signaled Smitty. As he came near, the unsuspecting old man was collared and wrestled to the ground where he lay pinned under elbows supporting a Stoner.

Protected by roots of a mangrove tree, Eric searched for a way to get his men out. Obviously the guerrillas had set a trap. But he wasn't sure they knew the SEALs were there. Eric's plan was to back his small band clear but not break silence to get Ace's help. *Who knows, he thought. We may pull this off without their ever knowing someone else was in the jungle besides the woodcutters.*

The firing died down and just as Eric was going to steal away, he heard Ace shout, "Now, Eric. Now!" Ace had broken the silence. *Damn,* Eric thought. He signaled his small band and they sprang to their feet. Dragging the skinny woodcutter with them they raced in a weaving path. Before Eric could stop him, Ace ripped the forest with his Swedish K and the others unloaded their weapons at the invisible enemy.

A bullet nicked the calf of Eric's right leg but he continued in a limping stride, dodging and weaving until he was among Ace's group.

Now the SEALs were the hunted. Moving quickly, swinging their weapons in wide arcs they retreated over the same ground they had entered, maneuvering around the grenade traps, fading into the jungle as the shots continued. After a time the weapon sounds died away. *So far we've been lucky,* Eric thought. *But the guerrillas will follow.*

Their progress took them to a small stream which Eric recognized as the Rach Cai Go. It would lead them to the intersection at the Dong Tranh and safety.

As they approached the stream Eric, with Mackie the radioman at his heels, hurriedly limped past each man in line. As he did, he gave each a touch on the shoulder. Veluchii and Combs acknowledged by nodding their heads and giving a half smile. Taylor and the two LDNN remained expressionless — heads down and serious. The woodcutter appeared to be all right, probably too frightened to make a sound. To be certain, Eric signaled Smitty to gag him. Then breaking the rule of silence he whispered, in Vietnamese, a reminder: "Old man, value your life with silence or die." Then he stroked a forefinger across the woodcutter's throat.

Arriving at the front of the column, Eric made a signal to Ace. Moments later the line of SEALs slipped past Ace as Eric and he traded places. Eric now became the point; Ace, the trail position. At the small streamlet, Eric followed the bank until the water appeared to be deep enough to swim. Again he made a signal. The SEALs stopped. Eric decoyed away from the stream into the jungle maybe twenty paces, then stepped backwards in his own tracks. At the water's edge he took off his combat boots, tied the long laces together, then draped the boots around his neck. Signaling each to do the same, Eric led the way. He quietly rolled off the bank into the water then drifted with the current. Ace checked the area, brushed over their tracks, and joined his boys. Like crocodiles in the Everglades, only the tops of their heads and weapons showed as they worked their way down stream to deeper and deeper water.

Eric signaled a warning not to drink the water. Dehydration tempted them, but it was brackish. Forsaking their self-discipline would contribute to their death faster than the pursuing guerrillas.

After a time Eric swam toward a small clearing on the shore and pulled himself onto the mud bank. He then helped Mackie, the next in line. When all were in the jungle they established a defensive perimeter and waited another night in silence. Eric knew the team was exhausted and desperately wanted sleep. Without rest and down to their last drops of food and water, some could be overtaken by a strange combination of sleepiness and the premature comfort of a mission complete. He had been taught that this killed more SEALs than anything. Even though Eric's leg wound was festering and Ace's legs were unsteady the two leaders knew that to survive their team must maintain their mental toughness. They moved among them encouraging and coaxing each one to take more Dexedrine and remain alert.

Once during the night, the SEALs heard movement in the direction of the base camp, but their training had strengthened them to master the corrupting influences which might have caused untrained men to bolt and run. The Bible said "yesterday and today and forever," but Eric knew forever is the jungle, the thirst, and the guerrillas. Got to get them out or they'll lose it — got to get them out.

Even before it was light, Eric had them back in the water. The line of heads bobbed among the morning shadows of the eastern shore. At the intersection of the main river they worked deeper against the cut-bank. They waited hidden under debris and foliage because Eric knew as the stream got wider there was greater chance of being discovered by crabbers or woodcutters who would have their boats in the stream.

Above the noise of the rushing water, Eric heard the putt, putt sound of a diesel engine. Leaving his team, he eased himself into the main stream to get an early look at the approaching boat. He treaded water. Holding himself against the late flooding tide he searched for a red bandanna above a yellow and red striped flag. The bow grew larger. He saw the superstructure. Finally he sighted the flag and at the same time he saw Commander Lawrence and Major Harris. Eric gave the signal and his men moved toward mid-stream where they could be picked up. Smitty and the captured Vietnamese woodcutter were the last to be pulled over the gunwale of the small craft. The SEALs lay exhausted on the deck, after four days of silence they all began to talk at once.

Taylor groaned, "fuc'n Rung Sat."

Veluchii said, "Get me back to the fuc'n world."

Blake moved among the young SEALs offering chocolate and cool drinks. Off-handedly he said to Eric, "Thought you left with nine guys?"

"We did." Eric scanned his men shaking a finger at each in his count. It was difficult for him to believe they had gotten that far only to discover one was missing. He grabbed Smitty by the collar of his soggy fatigues. Pulling him off the deck, his face only inches away, he said in a ruthless tone, "Damnit where's Ace! You were right in front of him!"

"Easy, Eric," Blake cautioned.

Smitty choked, "I don't know, Eric. I thought he was with us. I was busy with the woodcutter. I thought he came in the water this morning. I just don't remember, Sir."

"You thought? You don't remember?" Then Eric looked at each man and said through tight jaws and pinched lips. "Don't any of you remember? Think!"

They all shook their heads.

Eric dropped his head into his hands, then looked up at the sky. "It's not your fault — it's mine. It's my job to know and I took Ace for granted. Damnit!"

Blake asked, "How dangerous is it to go back?" He already knew the answer. Guerrillas could be waiting. To linger on the river was just as dangerous.

Before Blake could retract his dumb question Eric said, "We gotta go back, Commander."

"We're going back." Blake ordered the boatman to swing the junk around and head for the Rach Cai Go.

At the point where they had entered the water, the SEAL team readied their weapons. Staying low they peered into the jungle but there was no sign of Ace.

The boat swung sharply ramming its bow into the mud bank. Armed only with a knife in his belt, Eric, followed by Smitty with his Stoner, sprang ashore. When they reached the edge of the jungle the only noise they heard was the quiet chug of the diesel engine holding the boat against the current. Eric pointed to the mud tracks where they had moved about in the morning and confirmed it was the right place.

Before the two SEALs moved out, Blake turned to Mark and said, "I'm going with them. You stay. Someone has to get the rest out if something happens."

Mark's normal baritone voice squeaked as he said, "You're what? Bullshit, Commander. You don't know what you're doing in the fuc'n jungle. This is SEAL or Marine business. If anyone goes, it should be me. But they were the ones that screwed up — this entire fuc'n mission could be compromised because they didn't bring everyone out the first time. As far as I'm concerned, they got themselves in it, they can get themselves out. I...."

Before Mark could finish Blake leaped from the boat into the mud and ran into the jungle. He caught up at the fringe of the area where the SEALs had made their perimeter the night before. Eric's face showed a combination of irritation and disbelief as he whispered, "What the hell are you doing here? I can't order you back, Commander, but you're interfering and if anything goes wrong..."

"It's okay Eric. Let it be on my head. I'll take the chance. You're both tired. I can help."

Eric shrugged then pointed to tracks leading off into the jungle. Keeping low to the ground, they slowly followed the boot prints listening for Ace and sounds of guerrillas. At first the level of jungle noise receded, then it rose again as birds began to chatter and sing.

They followed the path until they came to a sight that jerked their guts. Apparently Ace had taken time to try the same trick Eric had used the night before. He decoyed his footsteps in another direction intending to backtrack. Seeing a small trail running parallel to the stream he decided to merge his fake tracks with those of the path. But when he stepped on the adjacent ground it gave way and he fell. There he was, impaled on stakes embedded in the bottom of the hidden pit. Obviously, Ace had struggled, for he now was part way in part way out, wedged on his side, but still alive.

Nothing in his career prepared Blake for the sight of blood oozing from this silent SEAL. Struggling to hold back the rage, he swallowed hard and wiped moisture from his eyes.

As if to warn them the jungle noise quieted. Monkeys and birds ceased chattering. Guerrillas were near. They had to work fast. It took their combined strengths to pull the heavy man out of the pit. Eric attempted to drag Ace by himself, but he was too tired and the body left a trail. Blake who was bigger and fresh motioned Eric to stand clear. Carefully placing his shoulder into Ace's belly he lifted the CPO over his back and moved quickly toward the waiting boat. Eric had Smitty cover the hole in the exact way it had been, then brushing the tracks as they went the three backed out to the stream and lifted Ace aboard the waiting boat.

As Mark helped them aboard he said to Blake, "You got more balls than any sailor I ever knew."

The usual exuberant feeling of a mission complete was gone. Blake, Eric and Smitty were covered with Ace's blood. Blake ordered the boat to withdraw. The other SEALs lay in silence; partly from exhaustion, partly from questions about what had gone wrong, but mostly from the sight of Eric holding their fearless, blood-covered Chief in his arms.

Twenty Eight

It was late evening before the fishing junk returned to base. Ace Magrue died on the way. A medevac chopper had been waved off mid-transit. Nothing could be done. Too many wounds.

Idle soldiers lined the piers gawking at the exhausted, mud-covered men. Taylor and Veluchii, in quiet sullenness, shouldered their way through the on-lookers clearing a path for Combs and Mackie who gently carried Ace's body covered by a makeshift shroud of fatigue blouses. In silence they laid the body onto a stretcher then hoisted it aboard the waiting ambulance.

Eric climbed aboard and kneeled beside his dead buddy. Blake took a seat near the back door. As the vehicle pulled away Blake watched the SEALs and LDNN, except Mackie, drift away to their borrowed hooch for a shower, a bunk, and a mental release from the stress of their days in hell. Blake last saw Mackie, the kid from Ace's home town of Philadelphia, walking toward a clump of trees along the river, head bowed, arms cuddling his weapon against his chin.

Blake spoke very little to Eric during the return trip from the Forest of Assassins. Now as they sat next to the torn body it was the same: neither talked, they just stared at the floor or out the window. Blake finally broke the silence. Speaking to the air, he said, "I understand Ace better now than when he first came to my office. His brusque manner bordered on disrespect, but it was just a defense. A warning to me not to take advantage of his boys. Can't fault Ace's leadership instincts, but it may have led to his own demise." Blake touched Eric's shoulder. "He didn't call for help. He died to protect his boys."

The ambulance stopped at the base dispensary and Blake climbed out. His voice wavered as he hurried his words to beat the slamming of the ambulance doors. "I'll make arrangements to evacuate his body to Saigon, then back to the States. Make sure Doc takes a look at your leg."

The next afternoon, after the Rung Sat mud had been washed away, and their bodies had recovered, the SEALs began their return to normalcy. Blake watched them move around the compound and mess hall. Before long much of the sullenness faded. For Taylor, Veluchii, and Combs the transition seemed instantaneous and complete. Mackie and Smitty still looked strained. None would laugh and joke quite the same as they had before.

Ace Magrue's body had been taken to Third Field Hospital where a service would be held before it was shipped out on a Pan Am flight back to the States. Eric would give the eulogy.

Blake and Eric rode together to Saigon. As they bumped along the winding road and through the villages, Eric talked about what had happened in the jungle. "Don't know. It just happened. We must have practiced that maneuver a hundred times. It was my fault. I should have got a head count before we moved into the river. I was too worried about finding the boat and getting the team out.

I thought Smitty would check, but Smitty was tired. We were all tired. That's no excuse. I blame myself. It was my fault."

A chaplain prayed. Then Eric stood beside the casket. Jaws tightened. Eyes squeezed. Bodies shook as they listened to Eric's sensitive words, "You know, he's a hero. He never cried out. Ace knew how sounds carry in a jungle." He choked as he said, "We all loved him."

After the service, Blake, Mark and Eric remained in Saigon to explain to Admiral Paulson what had happened.

Blake knew it wasn't going to be pleasant. He figured before they left there would be an ass chewing and he expected it to be his.

When they arrived at NAVFORV headquarters the Admiral told them his schedule was tight — he had an important meeting at MACV headquarters. His growling voice said, "Make it brief."

Eric looked tired as he told about the mission. He set the scene by describing the insertion and giving credit to the Vietnamese pilots for their precision flying. Obviously still distraught over the loss of Ace, he said. "I tell you, somehow they were tipped. The place was booby trapped. Not with claymores but monofilament and grenades. I should have known it was a set up. When the ambush began we were surrounded, but, but..." He choked. "Ace got us out." Regaining his composure he began again, "The intelligence you got from the VC prisoner was essentially correct. Weren't able to move around enough to survey the entire area, but that base camp is quite large. Estimate at one time there were about two hundred in the camp. They're gone now. Haven't heard the results of the interrogation of the woodcutter."

At that point Blake picked up the brief, "The old man was turned over to the Vietnamese. They questioned him for a long time. Wanted to know where Colonel Tu had gone, but the old man didn't know anything. The woodcutters had been trading with the VC. Been in and out of that camp over the past several weeks. According to the old man the VC just faded about a week ago and took the rockets with them." Blake added angrily, "There must to be a spy and Tu turned the tables on us. Used the rocket crates as bait for our ambush instead of his."

Paulson sat back, apparently sifting what he had just heard. Finally he said, "We're a little better off than we were before. At least we now know the rockets were not moved from the Rung Sat to another area, but gentlemen.".. He paused for emphasis and more sarcasm. "now, we no longer know where they are." Then Paulson stood and dismissed Mark and Eric with, "I'd like a few words with Commander Lawrence — alone."

After Eric and Mark left the room, the Admiral began to pace. His eyes became like two steel balls. He cleared his voice. "Goddamit Blake, you screwed up — again. I told you before I wanted those rockets. I meant it. You've lost your perspective. We're trying to disengage from this country, not chase some make-believe guerrilla who, if he's out there at all, has been in the jungle forever. We've lost another good American and an opportunity to rid ourselves of those rockets. Not going to sit well in Washington. I know them! Those bastards'll be on the phone. I went along but... against my better judgment." Paulson stopped his pacing long enough to emphasize, "It's Duc-Lang. He influenced you, didn't he? All the more reason to get him out of there. He always finds some way to screw up. For all we know, he's Cong. Doesn't he understand this is war? The build-up to the West, near An Loc, is taking more ammo and fuel than we expected. Stocks are low. MACV thinks they'll attack just before the election to embarrass Nixon and drive a wedge between us. We'll need the Long Tau. Lots of fuel and ammo. Things are getting hot..." He stopped in front of Blake. Pointing at him the Chameleon said, "I've run my string. I want those goddamn wire-guided rockets. Find them. And I want Duc-Lang to go away. And you make sure you keep that river open. By the way, even though the court-martial Convening Authority shifted from me to MACV, based on the final investigation report I still make the recommendation whether to convene. And of course you want your destroyer don't you? You got the picture?"

Admiral Paulson didn't wait for Blake to answer. He charged away to his MACV meeting leaving him alone in the office.

Blake walked to the window. He put his hands in his trouser pockets, leaned forward, put his forehead against the window glass and stared out. Hundreds of Vietnamese were moving about the streets of the Saigon. If any of them glanced at that window, at that moment, they would have seen a man in a childlike pose, forehead against the glass, and nose pushed over. *Wish I knew what's in that report of the gunfire investigation,* he said to himself. *It's still hanging over my head and now Paulson blames me for Ace's death. On top of that, he's threatened to fire me and take away my destroyer command if I don't find the rockets and fire Duc-Lang. Is the Dai Ta on the take? Is Colonel Tu unimportant? My dad always told me that Admirals are supposed to be 'big' people who accept their mistakes and didn't pass them on to subordinates, but Paulson's private sessions are always without grace. Wonder what my granddad and my dad would do in this situation? Would they trade a Duc-Lang for a command? Funny, Paulson glossed over the spy problem as if he wasn't interested. Could Duc-Lang be a spy? Makes no sense! Could there be more than one spy?*

Finally he left the window and joined the other two.

"What was that all about?" Mark asked as they walked toward the jeep.

"Nothing much. Some classified dope about the An Loc problem. Tell you later." To avoid any more discussion, Blake changed the subject. "I suppose you and your men will be returning to Cat Lai, Eric."

"Yes, Sir. Returning there for now, but — wanted to talk to you and Major Harris about that. The team's discussed it. We'd like to come back if those VC show up again. Wouldn't be a bother. Be willing to split up any way you like."

"Don't see any problem with that, Commander," Mark offered. "I don't have enough Marine advisors to go around anyway. Could fill in on some back river ops. On that basis I think I can get Saigon to clear it."

Blake was surprised that Mark spoke up for the SEALs so quickly, considering he had once said that Marines could do anything SEALs could do and twice as well on Sundays. Everything isn't Marine green after all. It isn't normal for SEALs to operate with regular forces, but this would be different. Mark could use them for intel and ambushes.

Blake gave the okay, but added, "Clear it with Cat Lai and the Admiral."

As Eric got in his jeep he said, "Thanks Commander. No John Wayne stuff, but — with the loss of Ace we'd like another crack at 'ol Colonel Tu."

TWENTY NINE

It was Blake's <u>Bad Day at Black Rock</u>. Sad thoughts of Ace's memorial service were still with him and the Chameleon's accusations and threats only compounded his feelings. He wasn't ready to go back to base and pursue the elusive rockets. On the spur of the moment he suggested to Mark that they turn at the road to Dutch World.

They were escorted into the house by a servant just as Tony and Joanna were finishing supper.

"How lovely you should stop by — won't you join us — we have plenty — if you don't mind waiting a moment for it to warm — tell us all about the exciting things that are happening — Blake, what do you hear from your wife and those lovely children...?"

Blake cut her off. "We didn't mean to disturb your meal hour. Just passing. Can't stay long." He had learned to interrupt Joanna's bubbly way or she would continue without answers to her own questions.

"Why don't we have coffee on the balcony?" Tony suggested.

Lights from the river traffic shimmered across the water as Joanna chattered on. The comfortable setting took Blake's mind off Ace, the rockets, and the Admiral's threats. Joanna asked about Beverly and the children again, and then began talking about Peg. She reminisced about the fun they had at the dinner party and the tennis match. "She's a lovely girl — don't know how she tolerates being on that ship all the time — all Australians are good at tennis you know — you two made a good team — and you seemed to get on so well together — she talked a lot about you after you left...."

At that point Mark's eyes squinted and took on a quizzical look. Blake looked at Tony, wanting him to interrupt.

But Joanna kept talking. "We did see Peg off on her flight to Singapore — she decided to join China Fox during her repairs and be on board for her return trip — sends her best to you Blake and asked me to give you a message: she said she hoped you keep your naval appointments better than you keep your social appointments — don't know what that means, but message delivered..." Again Mark tensed and again Joanna talked on, "We've known her quite some time — whenever China Fox comes to Nha Be — of course that's when we see Mark — her wound is healed, isn't it, Mark — she's as good as new and back on her old job — Mark came up to see her off, she'll be returning here again with China Fox...."

Blake's face remained impassive, but inside his heart tugged. *Mark went to Saigon to see her off? Why should I be jealous of Mark? Was it because I needed a woman? Had I instinctively come to Dutch World to listen to Joanna, or was it to learn about Peg?* He looked away pensively and when he turned back he avoided Mark's eyes.

Tony Marbo had been sitting quietly enjoying his coffee and listening to his talkative wife, but he glanced at Blake when Joanna spoke of Peg. "Quite a girl, isn't she?" Tony said to both men.

Mark responded immediately, "My kinda woman."

Avoiding the bait, Blake said, "Certainly knows how to liven up a party."

"Did I mention China Fox would be returning, she's repaired. Going to pick up the schedule of one of our other vessels. Just received the dispatch today, actually." Then as an afterthought, Tony whispered to Blake. "Have you heard anything about a major battle?"

"Something's brewing over near An Loc, but that's a long way from the Rung Sat. I wouldn't worry about it, Tony."

"Well, our Dutch World office told me we could be asked to provide additional petrol. They say your General Haig flies in and out of Saigon often. Our London office sent word that the Paris talks have broken off between the North Vietnamese negotiator and your American — what's his name? Kissinger?"

Then Tony pulled Blake off to the side and whispered again. "Don't want to worry Joanna, but our London office thinks something big is going to happen."

THIRTY

Beautifully plumed peacocks, parakeets, and golden-fronted jungle birds cawed, sang, and flew from tree to tree. They seemed oblivious of the small band trekking to join Colonel Tu near the village of Nhon Trach. Do Van Nghi led the way. The gay voices of his flock blended with the songs of the birds.

Senior Colonel Tu had sent a messenger to Nghi, the leader of Doi 6, with a special invitation. "Come to a meeting. Bring those that survived the rocket operation and any you think might be ready for a leadership position."

Barefoot and dressed in the black costume of the peasant, members of this group had been selected by Nghi for their special skills and craftiness at jungle fighting. Included were Co Hang and the three men who had blown up the patrol boat. He brought those three because he knew Colonel Tu would decorate them in the presence of the other Commanders of Doan 12. He also selected the young man who had replaced Tam Ha as his Lieutenant, because he had deserted from a South Vietnamese artillery battalion assigned to protect Saigon. The young ex-ARVN officer knew the local region, and understood how to survey-in large artillery pieces.

On approach to the plantation, Nghi spoke above the peasant songs, "Continue to sing and act like woodcutters returning from the forest. Do not become alarmed if we are challenged by the Doan 12 guards. They will be cautious."

Not long after his warning, the group entered a clearing. Four men camouflaged to blend with the jungle, and carrying automatic machine guns, stepped from nowhere.

"*Ngung!* State your name and your purpose to be in this rubber plantation."

Nghi stepped forward, hands high. "My name is Do Van Nghi. We are only woodcutters. Are you not expecting us?" Nghi knew the leader would toy with them until he was certain they were Viet Cong and not PRU or enemy soldiers disguised as peasants.

"From where do you come?"

"The Rung Sat. Do you know a woodsman named Tu?" The use of the Colonel's name in a sentence was part of the secret password.

"I will ask the questions! Give the sign!"

Nghi turned to face the speaker and held his right fist to his left breast while he spoke the rest of the words of the disclosure, "*Da duoc* (all right). *Hoa-luc* (fire power)."

With that the four guards relaxed and their leader smiled. "Welcome, comrades. You may   proceed. Senior Colonel Tu is waiting for you in the small building near the main house."

As they neared the plantation, Nghi saw a large French-style home surrounded by banana palms. Smaller houses nestled next to it. In front of the building nearest the forest two uniformed men lounged against their rifles. One guard leaned his head toward the door and spoke to an invisible person in the shadows of the room. Soon a tall slender man stepped forth. His long gray hair was neatly trimmed as was his mustache and beard; his only identification of rank was a holstered K-54 pistol.

Colonel Tu's face expanded into a grin. "Do Van Nghi, Do Van Nghi. You are a welcome sight. Are these your courageous followers? Welcome, welcome, Comrades. I know about the great achievements of Doi Six." Then he said to Nghi, "I was sad to learn of the loss of comrades Chi and Tam Ha. Chi died a great hero to our cause. But Tam Ha — well, a different story. We will talk of that another time. Come, let me show you where you will stay." Then privately to Nghi he said, "You and I will talk soon."

Silent in the great man's presence, Nghi's band followed Colonel Tu at a humble distance toward the smaller houses. Nghi felt pride that Colonel Tu not only remembered his name, but even seemed to have taken him into his confidence.

Near the smaller houses were several straw lean-to's where other guerrillas had gathered. Representatives from each Doi of Doan 12 lounged, eating rice and drinking Coca Cola stolen from the Americans. Some had come from Can Gio and An Thoi to the South and East. Others came from the island of Long-Son and the forest of Thanh An. Like children they flitted from one group to the other learning what each Doi did and who among each band they might know.

Not long after they were all settled, one of the Colonel's staff called the leaders to a meeting in Tu's quarters. Nghi along with seven or eight other company commanders entered the small house and sat cross legged around a long, low table. Tu alone sat in a tall-backed wicker chair.

Nghi noticed the enormous influence this Colonel from the North had over his fellow guerrilla leaders. Now a living legend, Tu's reputation for patient toughness was the pattern they all sought to emulate. Most of them even tried to resemble him by wearing a mustache and chin beard. The only difference, in many cases, was the men's size and their skin texture. Colonel Tu's facial skin was beginning to wrinkle and develop dark spots.

After they were settled and sipping beer, Colonel Tu called for their attention. "Later we will have a party to honor the performances of the brave comrades you have brought with you. First we must discuss our plans for the future. As many of you know, I am a member of COSVN. Much of my time is now taken to coordinate our efforts with those of the other Doans in South Vietnam. Your work is well known at the highest levels. It is considered vital to our eventual victory. Before I tell you of the new plan, I wish to hear from each of you. Tell me about your activities and successes in the field. I'm afraid I don't get away from staff work as much as I like."

The company commanders were reluctant to speak until Colonel Tu encouraged them: "Feel comfortable among your fellow company commanders." He pointed to the man on his right, signaling for him to begin. That Doi commander, whose scar crossed his nose and down his right cheek, rose and spoke about the exploits of his unit. "My Doi disrupted transportation routes and blew up a village meeting place."

Another, wearing a U.S. Army fatigue jacket said, "My Doi attacked two fuel depots, and an ammunition storage area."

A bulldog-faced man spoke in serious tones, "My unit has had major losses because of raids by South Vietnamese regulars and their American advisors. But," he bragged, "they hate the Americans and all in my unit conducted themselves with great personal bravery."

Several complained about bombs dropped occasionally from American airplanes, but a skinny man from the seacoast said, "That is nothing. American ships bombard day and night using their great rifles. There is no end to their ammunition."

By the time it came Nghi's turn to speak he was a bit light-headed from the beer. He wanted to impress the other Doi commanders, so he stood, then cleared his voice while he thought. Although Colonel Tu already knew of the rocket attack on the giant fuel ship, he wanted to be sure the others knew that story. *After all, only I, Do Van Nghi am the expert on the use of the new Russian rockets. Only my Doi has successfully fired one of the rockets on a wire.*

"The new Russian rocket flew straight and Co Hang is a very brave girl." Giving credit to others brought great face, so he said. "It was she who became the expert at shooting the new weapon."

Nghi bragged of the daring escape on the back rivers and of blowing up the PBR and of how three of his best men swam ashore and escaped. Pausing as if he might be finished, he almost rejected the idea of telling the truth about what really happened on the river, but even though he might loose face he continued, "My rocket did not sink the ship as I first thought. After we escaped, I learned it sailed on and even a second attack using B-40 rockets did not stop it. The lesson is that it will take more than one rocket to sink a ship. Of course the new rockets easily blew up the enemy patrol boats."

At that point Colonel Tu interrupted him, "The new rockets will remain hidden. They are not to be used again until COSVN decides. However, thanks to Do Van Nghi's experience, when we do use them the new tactic will include multiple shots from more than one location."

Sensing that was all Colonel Tu wished to say, Nghi bowed to acknowledge the face Colonel Tu had just bestowed, then continued his report. "We went into Nhon Trach and avenged Tam Ha's death. That village will again be loyal to our cause."

Lastly Nghi told of the young man who escaped from a South Vietnamese army artillery unit. "This new man has been trained in the United States at one of the American officers' schools. He was a Lieutenant Colonel in charge of Saigon defenses."

Colonel Tu didn't interrupt again but his eyes widened when he heard about this new addition to Doi 6.

Nghi took his seat feeling puffed by his self importance. He didn't hear the remaining reports because he was still thinking about the last point he had made in his speech, about the ARVN artillery man who had defected to the guerrillas. His skills could be of great help to Colonel Tu in the future.

Nghi remembered Colonel Tu's artillery background that he had learned about during his probationary period three years before. He remembered that was the time when he first raised enough courage to speak to the Colonel. He had cautiously asked if Tu would tell the probationers about himself. In the traditional Vietnamese way, the Colonel told them he was unworthy. "Nevertheless, I will tell you about my military background. That might interest you." He picked up a piece of fish with his chop sticks dipped it into some Nuc Mam and when he was finished chewing he began, "In 1942, when I was seventeen, I joined the resistance against the Japanese. It was exciting. We fought in the hills west of Hanoi between the Red and Black rivers. Later, I had the additional good fortune to study at the Military School in Hanoi. In 1951, I was commissioned a Lieutenant in the Army." He paused to drink some beer. "I quickly deserted to rejoin the Viet Minh. There I rose quickly to the rank of Major and was with General Giap at the great siege of Dien Bien Phu. As the commander of the artillery battalion, it was I who rained shells upon the French and drove them from Vietnamese soil. See, nothing much of interest — just the life of a wayward patriot."

Nghi jerked back to the present when he heard Colonel Tu congratulate the Doi Commanders for their excellent, complete reports, then toast them with a sip of beer, "You have been aggressive in your fight for the Communist cause. Well done."

Standing on a small platform at one end of the room, Colonel Tu began his own presentation. "As you all now, we have been preparing a major attack. The first steps have been taken. Each of our units in the Rung Sat have been reorganized — so has COSVN. This all took time and during that period we only conducted low level actions." He smiled. "The Americans believed they were winning because we were so quiet. That phase is over now. A higher level of action has begun. Now we must prepare carefully for the final phase."

He signaled one of his staff to unveil a map of South Vietnam. He leaned forward, spread his hands across the paper, then turned. "Our war in the South became stagnant after our Northern forces were repulsed last spring. Therefore, we have devised a new strategy. Our new plan is to stage an attack to coincide with the fall elections in America. Their President is a man named Nixon. He is a vain man who, unlike their President Johnson, wishes to be re-elected at any cost. Negotiations have begun between our Le Duc To and an American Jew by the name of Kissinger." Pointing with a long stick to the capital city he continued, "Regardless of the outcome of the negotiations, our new strategy will be to attack Saigon at just the right time before their elections. Of course, that coincides with the beginning of our dry season." He raised the stick and pointed to his audience. "Even if we are repulsed, our attack will bring great political pressure and we will achieve our ends — the withdrawal of the American armed forces. Once that is accomplished we will easily defeat the South Vietnamese."

Using a stick again he pointed to the city of An Loc on the Western border. "We are massing an army in Cambodia. On signal from Hanoi it will strike through An Loc, then along the Saigon River valley to the heart of the capital city. Once the South Vietnamese army commits to defending against our forces, the Doans surrounding Saigon will attack and take away their logistics support."

Colonel Tu pointed to the fuel and ammunition depots marked in red. "These will be Doan 12's targets and each must be destroyed on my signal. The Americans will attempt to re-supply from the sea, but you have all heard Do Van Nghi tell about the new rockets our Russian comrades have sent to us. It will be Doan 12s responsibility to use them to stop the ships on the Long Tau. Without supplies the South Vietnamese army will collapse."

Having satisfied the need to show his guerrilla leaders the over-all plan, Colonel Tu returned to his place at the head of the table, continued his talk in a less formal manner. "You all know that I am a senior artillery officer in the army of the North. When our forces are within striking distance of Saigon, it will be my great honor to execute the final phase of the South's downfall. I have been told that I will be given command of all the artillery. I will position it for the final bombardment of the city. I alone know this region. Nhon Trach is the perfect place to position the artillery. Because from there it can reach every inch of Saigon." He paused, and asked, "Do you have any suggestions or are there any questions?"

Nghi marveled at its simplicity. It's the mark of military genius to devise the simplest yet most effective plan, particularly one which included the coordination of regular and irregular troops. Nghi was curious about one thing and he was no longer bashful about talking to the great man. "How will we know when and where to position for the attack on the resupply ships from the sea?"

"Ah," Colonel Tu smiled, then responded. "That is a very good question, and it is a reminder that everything we have talked about this afternoon is very secret. You must not tell anyone unless they need to know, and then only tell them that which is essential to their individual mission.

"Now, to answer Do Van Nghi's question: How do we know when and where to attack? As many of you know Doan 12 has agents in Nha Be, on Duc-Lang's staff, and in other places. COSVN has many in Saigon. The agents will learn the enemy's plans. It is easiest in Saigon because of the decadent life the Americans lead there, playing tennis, golf, whoring, and drinking. It is more difficult in Nha Be, but our agents there are in excellent places to gain information and have been very effective. Some of you may remember Tam Ha, the one who was captured by the Rung Sat Provincial Reconnaissance Unit. He had to be killed because he was a coward. He gave the enemy too much information. It was our agent in Nha Be who told us about the American intelligence operation, which we successfully ambushed in the jungle. Another example of Duc-Lang's rigidity. I know him. We were students at the Hanoi Military School after the war with Japan. He was a bright student but he hasn't changed. He tended to be too rigid. He will not be a threat to our mission. Just in case, our agent will learn the American plans and reach us with them in time. Well, anything else?"

Silence.

Nghi was startled to learn that Tam Ha had been killed by Tu's spy. But he, Do Van Nghi had avenged his capture, and his death. *Well — if Tam Ha had given away secrets, then I have nothing to say. Tam Ha deserved to die.*

Hearing no questions Colonel Tu said, "Good, let us adjourn. Get ready for the party."

*****

That evening the guerrillas gathered by camp fires under the stars. Chickens, ducks, and fish, prepared all day by local farm women, filled bowls and dishes. The pungent smell of Nuc Mam filled their nostrils as they drank Johnny Walker Black Label and Ba Mui Ba beer. Members of each Doi sat together teasing and challenging adjacent Dois. The girls didn't drink as much as the men, but they sipped enough to feel happy and drunk. Their mood was joyous as their voices blended with the men in songs of victory over the Americans and the eventual success of Communism in the South. Do Van Nghi was especially happy because celebration had been rare since he had come to the guerrillas. They were always too busy moving and hiding in the jungle.

Senior Colonel Tu joined the party after the food was served. He moved among them, first sitting with one Doi then another, showing no partiality.

At one point, after Tu had spent what seemed to her too much time with a nearby group, Co Hang impulsively jumped to her feet and ran, giggling and laughing like the teenager she was to the old Colonel. Grabbing his hand and tugging so that he had to stand she said, "Come, it is time to visit our Doi. Comrade Nghi has a present for you."

Colonel Tu laughed and apologized to the Doi from which he was being dragged by the woman wearing the red bandanna.

Do Van Nghi sprinted to meet them and pushing Co Hang's hand from Colonel Tu, he screamed, "Have you no respect? Stupid woman. This is Colonel Tu! Such informality. You are a soldier. Behave like one!"

But Tu made a joke of it by saying she reminded him of his wife back in Hanoi, "They are all the same. They always get their way."

Members of Doi 6 gathered around Tu, offering him food and drink, chattering about the fun they were having and how different it was for them in the jungle. He, in turn, congratulated them for their success and told them how important their work was to the Communist cause. Then he shouted, "Where are the three who escaped by swimming?"

The three, by now very drunk, stood and wobbled forward. As they came, Colonel Tu signaled for his aide to hand him a box. From it he took medals and pinned one on the chest of each man. He also pinned medals on Do Van Nghi and Co Hang.

Having already forgotten the reprimand by Do Van Nghi and giggling from the effects of the beer, and the euphoria of the evening, Co Hang shouted. "Give it to him, give it to him."

From a canvas bag, Nghi produced a long object, gift wrapped in beautiful paper, which he presented to the leader.

Colonel Tu thanked them and as all Asians would do, sat the package aside to be opened later. But Co Hang pleaded, "Nghi, please let him open it now."

"Of course. Colonel, please open it."

Tu did as he was asked, carefully unwrapping what appeared to be a long roll. He was too slow for Co Hang as she exclaimed, "Here, let me show you." From the wrappings Co Hang withdrew an old hand-sewn red and blue Viet Cong flag with the symbol of Doan 12 marked in the upper right hand corner alongside the symbol of Doi 6. As she gave it to Colonel Tu she exclaimed pridefully, "It is Doi 6's original battle flag, but I have sewn a new one." Then her mood changed as she said, "Carry it for the good fortune. To kill Americans." Her words were in Vietnamese except for the last words. "To kill Americans."

Colonel Tu asked, "You speak English very well."

"Well enough for my purposes," Co Hang responded shyly.

Senior Colonel Tu got to his feet. He held the torn and tattered rag flag high for all to see. "Everyone," he said. "Everyone, look at what Doi 6 has given me. It was their battle flag, but I shall make it my personal Doan 12 flag. Ho Chi Minh would be proud of you. Our mission is to close the river, control the people, and support the movement of our own logistics through the Rung Sat. The success of Doan 12 can only be measured by your individual determination. We must all join together and rise up against the Americans. We must throw them out.

"This flag will lead us when the battle begins."

THIRTY ONE

Two months passed quickly. Days turned into weeks. Now it was the swing season between monsoon and dry. The weather oscillated from gusty rain one day to bright and clear the next. Showers followed sunshine.

The disappointment of not capturing Colonel Tu and the rockets brought frustration. The aftermath of Blake's ass-chewing by Rear Admiral Paulson left him in a mental funk.

On his return to Nha be, Blake had met with Duc-Lang to emphasize the urgency of finding the missing rockets. To disguise any body language which might have portrayed his feelings of defeat, he sat especially erect and formal. "Rear Admiral Paulson had second thoughts about the SEAL operation. Apparently, he expects a lot of heat from Washington about the loss of Chief Magrue and the AT3 rockets."

"I understand your frustration. I received the same instructions from my own naval staff. They, too, were very upset that the Russian rockets were still in the Rung Sat. Being military geniuses the day after the battle, they now think I made a bad decision sending the SEAL's on the intelligence mission."

Blake felt disappointment, but his job was to keep the Vietnamese motivated. He jerked his body even more erect, tightened his jaw and lifted his chin. "I still think the mission was necessary. As it turned out, we would have come up empty-handed anyway. We must now go all out to find the rockets."

Even though command of a destroyer was on the line, Blake procrastinated in carrying out Paulson's order to fire Duc-Lang because as he had in the past, the Dai Ta had responded in a positive way. He ordered an increase in search intensity. He even offered a substantial reward for information, and he ordered the PRU to search every village. Squads of troops were airlifted into every corner of the Rung Sat where they methodically probed for any clue.

But the guerrillas and the rockets had vanished.

*****

The approach of November elections back home brought thoughts of peace. But Blake's thoughts cycled from the local Rung Sat situation, to the ongoing gunfire investigation, to Beverly and the kids, to Peg Thompson and back to the rockets. Murphy's Law seemed to be in control of his world.

Beverly's letters contributed to his feelings of depression. They arrived with their usual frequency, twice a week, but they were without feeling, as if an obligation written on the run. He admitted his were no better. At least, according to her sparsely worded letters the situation with the kids hadn't gotten any worse.

Even his infatuation with Peg had subsided. After learning Mark had seen Peg off to Singapore, he wondered what she was all about. *Could she have been bartering for the best offer?*

The dry season would bring a welcome change from the rains of the summer, and maybe a solution for one or more of his dilemmas.

THIRTY TWO

TUESDAY, OCTOBER 31, 1972, NHA BE BASE

Another month came and went and the mood of the base worsened. Like a mortuary it was both sad and tense.

The morale of the combined force of RVN Army, Navy, and Air Force still on stand-by after having been assembled to attack following the SEAL operation sank to new lows. Blake watched helplessly as people became irritated over very minor changes to the routine. The Vietnamese went about their methodical duties of cleaning weapons and standing sentry duty, but sneers and barks replaced smiles and laughter.

Blake's morale was no better. One morning during the search for the rockets, Blake made his way to the advisors' mess hall for breakfast. Quickly filling his tray, he drew a cup of coffee and took a seat at the table where Mark, who had already finished his powdered eggs and rice, was having coffee with Gunny, Doc, and Sergeant Trieu.

"Heard anything from the TOC? Anything new on the rockets or the guerrillas?" Blake asked.

Mark's deep set eyes showed a hint of dejection. "Tell him, Gunny."

"Yes, Sa. The VC hit ammo dumps and tank farms all around Saigon last night."

Blake shifted in his seat. Turning his eyes from a plate full of "shit on the shingle," he focused on the Marine Sergeant. "Did they get Dutch World?"

"No, sa. But intel says the VC are on the move in the Rung Sat."

Just then Private Marquell came into the mess hall and advanced to stand respectfully near Gunny Johnson.

"Here comes shit bird," Doc said.

At first Gunny seemed to ignore him, but finally asked, "You get him settled down?"

"Yes, Sir."

"Don't sir me."

"Yes, Gunny."

"All relaxed and friends?"

"Yes, Gunny."

"Good. Take off."

"Yes, Sir, I mean Gunny."

Blake took a sip of coffee, then asked. "What was that all about?"

"Couple of advisors blew up at each other in the mess line," Gunny answered. "Had Marquell take the hot-head out and cool him off."

Blake wasn't surprised. Everywhere spirits were low and it was no different for the U.S. advisors. Go to battle, call it off. Stand-by. Cease fire, no cease fire. Marines and Navy men waited for the unknown.

"Gunny's got Corporal Marquell sing'n our tune," Mark interjected.

"He's doing alright," The sergeant said. "Still snivels, but brig time did him good. He's com'n around. Even think he's off the drugs. I check his gear every day — so far, nothing."

"You hear about Gunny's girl hav'n a baby, commander?" Doc asked.

"No. Last to get the word?" Blake winked at Mark.

"Tell, him Gunny. Born two weeks ago, Commander and I'm the Godfather."

"My girl in the vil, she had our baby." Gunny shrugged.

"Well, congratulations," Blake said reaching to shake his hand. "Got a name?"

"Yes, sir. Bokassa... Bokassa Johnson.

A Navy cook named Putnam with a balloon belly and a face like a waffle interrupted. "Phone call, Commander Lawrence. Saigon."

"Thanks, I'll take it in the galley office."

Blake passed through the glistening clean galley filled with stainless steel pots and pans to the solitude of a small office.

"Commander Lawrence."

"One minute for the Admiral."

The phone clicked, "Lawrence?"

"Yes, Sir."

"What's new on the rockets?"

Assuming it was another of the many tiresome inquiries he had received over the last several months, Blake responded tersely. His tone verged on disrespect. Blake knew his dad wouldn't approve, but he wanted to tell the voice to f— off, although he still didn't abide that kind of language. He wanted to say that if he found them Paulson would be the first to know. "Still work'n on it, sir. Everyone's..."

The Admiral cut him off before he could finish, "All hell broke loose last night. Can't tell you any more about it on the phone. Sent you a personal with the details. Should have it by now. By the way, you know that today was to have been the signing day. The beginning of the cease fire, but President Thieu wouldn't agree. Nixon's called it off. Doesn't want it to look like he's selling out just before the elections, not with the new offensive and Thieu backing down."

"Bad news." Blake said, thinking about the already poor morale.

"Bad news or not, you're in the catbird seat, Blake. We're counting on you."

Blake didn't know what the Admiral meant, but he said, "Aye, Aye..." As he was still adding the word, "Sir" he heard the Admiral's receiver slam.

Blake left the mess hall. Commenting only to Mark about his destination, he went directly to the TOC where he picked up a copy of the secret message Paulson had dispatched. In his office he read:

SECRET
FLASH
PERSONAL FOR COMMANDER BLAKE LAWRENCE
SUMMARY:
NORTH VIETNAMESE BREAK THROUGH AT AN LOC.

END SUMMARY.
A MAJOR FORCE OF NORTH VIETNAMESE REGULARS AT-
TACKED THE WESTERN BORDER CITY OF AN LOC.
SOUTH VIETNAMESE REGROUPING.
GUERRILLAS ATTACKING ENTIRE VICINITY SAIGON.
MANY AMMO DUMPS AND FUEL DEPOTS BLOWN.
LOGISTICS LOW. FIVE SHIP RESUPPLY CONVOY DEPART-
ING VUNG TAU EARLIEST TIDE AM AFTER TOMORROW.
SUPPLIES URGENTLY NEEDED SAIGON.
REPEAT SUPPLIES URGENTLY NEEDED.
PROVIDE MAXIMUM PROTECTION LONG TAU CHANNEL.
PAULSON

Somehow I knew it would happen this way. Like out of some dime store novel. Paulson's put it on my head — made it my responsibility to save Saigon. Sure hope Duc-Lang's troops can get back into it.

Mark, who sensed battle like a hungry bear smells steak, entered Blake's office. "What's the Admiral up to, Commander?"

"Look at this," He handed Mark the message. He motioned to the map and pointed. "North Vietnamese broke through the RVN here at An Loc last night. Pushing for Saigon. Thieu backed out of the cease fire deal. According to Paulson, the defense of Saigon and maybe the entire peace is riding on a major convoy coming through the Rung Sat."

Blake stood side-by-side with his Marine assistant analyzing the chart. Mark made a few benign suggestions about extra chopper flights and PBR patrols when Blake, who was still thinking about Paulson's last remark said, "Wait, Mark." Lights went on. Words spilled like a fountain. "Mark. It's the convoy. Sure! It makes sense. North Vietnamese Army attacks An Loc. Pushes for Saigon. At the same time COSVN orders the fuel and ammo dumps blown up. They know we'll send a convoy. They don't know exactly when. It's the convoy — that'll be Colonel Tu's target and he'll use the AT3 rockets." The stream of thought continued. "He's got spies and he'll get the word. He'll attack the ships. The RVN can't turn this thing around without that convoy. If we can push the Reds back — take the heat off Saigon — Thieu will probably go along — at least with a cease fire. Got to protect that convoy. But this time we'll trap ol' Colonel Tu! Use the convoy as bait. Just like he used the rockets. That son of a bitch! We got him!"

"You could be right, Commander. But Tu could hit anywhere along the channel."

"What do our intel people know about the VC activity? Where were they last seen?"

Mark Harris glanced at the chart. "PRU got a report from the village of Nhon Trach. Some movement near the rubber plantation and the adjacent jungle. A boatman made the other report. He said he saw some sampans near the place where China Fox got hit."

Blake snapped. "Get some recon choppers up while I go to see Duc-Lang."

*****

At the Special Zone headquarters Blake found Duc-Lang and his deputy, Lieutenant Colonel Phat already at work. Duc-Lang explained he had just learned from his side of the breakthrough at An Loc. He said his Admiral wanted to call in American troops to help protect the channel. The short, chubby, Vietnamese Captain stroked his chin. Attempting to disguise his anger with one of his dimpled smiles he said. "But, I refused. Our Rung Sat forces don't need help." Then he added bitterly, "American politics are beginning to control our struggle."

Blake felt his eyebrows raise. Anger raced to the nape of his neck. He snapped, "The American people have paid just as dearly, in dollars and lives."

The sharpness of Blake's response had stiffened Duc-Lang and his next words reflected regret, "Don't misunderstand me, Cô-vân. You are my friend. I feel I can talk to you in confidence. We are grateful. But this is our war. We need your help, but it should be fought our way. With our own forces. I often disagree with my superiors in Saigon. We have known for some time you Americans would leave Vietnam, and we must continue the fight without you. I agree with President Thieu. He has done the right thing not to sign the truce. The North Vietnamese are pushing toward Saigon. When we repulse them — then we can talk."

"Looks like we'll get our chance to prove you can take care of yourselves." Blake said as he handed Duc-Lang Paulson's message. Moving to the wall map of the Rung Sat, he pointed to the checkpoint at Can Gio, near the mouth of the Long Tau. "By this time the day after tomorrow the convoy will be about here. It'll take about another six hours for it to get to Nha Be."

"Of course," Duc-Lang said dejectedly. "I'm sure Tu's already found out about the convoy."

"Okay. Let's assume he has. The question is what can we do? Think!" Blake challenged his counterpart. "Where will he attack?"

Duc-Lang stared dejectedly at the river and shook his head. "Anywhere."

*****

That night a nervous figure moved from shadow to shadow along the fence line that separated the base from the village of Nha Be. At the place where the fence extended into the water, that black sulking form stopped and waited. Then, as if slipping secretly in and out of the base was familiar, the clandestine shape moved hand over hand around the end of the fence, dropped lightly to dry ground on the village side, then faded among the buildings.

THIRTY THREE

Blake joined Duc-Lang in his smoke filled command center. It again became their temporary home. The two drank tea and listened to reports from patrols returning from the search for Colonel Tu and the AT-3 rockets.

Like a caged animal, Duc-Lang roamed back and forth in front of a wall map of the Rung Sat. His head sagged. His eyes reflected dejection. As if playing some Oriental chess game he began to think aloud. "Colonel Tu can't attack just anywhere on the Long Tau. His target for the wire-guided rockets is logically the convoy, but..." He paused. "He could have more than one target. He could also attack Dutch World."

Suddenly his bearing straightened. His body language expressed determination. The grimness previously shown in the lines of his face changed to a hardened expression that sent a message he intended to beat Colonel Tu at his own game. Duc-Lang's eyes brightened to their normal sparkle. Words spilled. "But he'll know exactly where to position the rockets." Turning to Blake he off-handedly said. "I never told you this before, but Colonel Tu was with Giap at Dien Bien Phu in 1954. He's an artillery expert."

Blake watched as Duc-Lang transformed. Fierce qualities previously disguised behind the body of a fat, pompous looking naval officer burst into reality. This last survivor of the Nguyen family, a reincarnation of Prince Anh who at one time had also been the lone survivor of that same ancient dynasty gripped his fists toward the sky. "I must think like Tu!" He paused in front of the chart. "Let me see. There are only two places that were not totally defoliated, where the guerrillas could have any opportunity to escape."

Duc-Lang pointed to the area where China Fox had been hit and then to the place across the Saigon River from Dutch World. "That means he must hide some of his forces here across the river from the tank farm. There is really only one other place he can hide long enough to fire on the ships. Here, near the place where they attacked China Fox."

Blake got up from his chair and joined his counterpart in front of the map. "That correlates with our intelligence, but would he split his forces?"

Duc-Lang shook his head, "Yes, guerrillas sometimes do that. They go in small bands, then form for an attack. I wonder in which group Colonel Tu would most likely be?"

"Maybe they're right in Saigon." Blake said. "Maybe we do think too much about him. Let's forget Colonel Tu for the moment. Concentrate! Only on the convoy! Couldn't we also split our forces?"

"Forget Colonel Tu? Never. I will never forget that... But yes, we can split the forces and he won't expect me to do that. I can send part North and part South, *Cô-vân*."

"Can you control two operations at the same time?"

"Of course. We can be airborne. That way I can fight Tu wherever his guerrillas show up."

Blake continued to press him. "Can we get the troops ready? Is there time to stop Tu before the convoy gets here? How can we keep our plan a secret?"

Duc-Lang agreed to seal the base immediately. Except for Eric's SEAL team which would come in from Cat Lai, no one, not even Blake or Duc-Lang, was to enter or depart for twenty-four hours. They would also issue an immediate warning order to the troops. The operation would kickoff the next morning, at dawn.

Blake's fears about Duc-Lang's men proved unfounded. Fighting men the world over are the same, difficult to motivate for a drill, but easy to arouse when there's a chance for a fight. So it was with the Vietnamese and their advisors when they learned they were to go on short notice. Weapons were test fired, equipment was checked and packed, and briefings were held. Duc-Lang told his officers to have their men turn in early. "They must be rested and ready for a major battle."

The Dai Ta didn't listen to those officers who suggested they couldn't be ready in time. "Rise to the occasion," he told his leaders. "Be ready. We will go, ready or not!"

The night before the operation was to kick-off, a Command and Control boat, accompanied by several PBR's, patrolled the river areas adjacent to the operation. All watercraft, suspicious or not, were detained for twenty-four hours. All sampans were checked for contraband, weapons, and false I.D. cards, then towed to a central collection point.

Waterborne guard posts also got underway. Eric Morris and his SEALs went with the ambushers. Eric would to be the advisor to the Vietnamese Army Captain in charge of the guard posts.

As Blake and Duc-Lang watched the ambush boats set out on their dangerous journey, Blake remembered the story of Prince Nguyen Ahn and his French *Cô-vân*, Pigneau the Priest. *Wonder if those sixteenth century warriors looked like Eric and the rest of the ambushers?* They looked more like woodcutters or fishermen than soldiers as they climbed into a strange assortment of sampans, ski barges and Boston whalers. There wasn't an exact boat for the ambush job. The only criteria was that they have shallow draft and be seaworthy. Blake knew it would be the most dangerous, but potentially most productive part of the operation because they were to stealthily find their way to positions on the northeastern streamlets and silently wait. These ambush boats would position quietly behind the suspected guerrilla positions in order to cut off their escape routes.

Duc-Lang's northern attack force would move in the morning. Using boat assault groups, they would land at three areas across from the tank farm and attack along three lines parallel to the long axis of the mangroves and rice paddies. A Marine advisor was attached to each of the three northern assault groups. Lieutenant Strode and Doc would go with the commander of Company 361.

Mark and Gunny would go with the Southern attack group with Private Marquell as their radioman. Mark told Blake that the southern operation was so important that he had to go in with the troops himself instead of staying airborne. Blake didn't argue because he knew wild horses couldn't keep Mark from a good fight.

That evening, Duc-Lang stood before his subordinate leaders to give his final talk. He began in a quiet tone, but as he spoke the round cheeks flushed and his eyes flashed. His right hand pumped high in the air like a football coach giving a speech before the big game. Blake listened intently as Sergeant Trieu translated Duc-Lang's Vietnamese words. "We must stop the use of the new Soviet weapons against the convoy and the tank farm. If you do not, Saigon could fall. It is important to our country. Fight well! The North cannot sustain an invasion of our land if we deny the guerrillas the Rung Sat. Drive them from our land. Find the Viet Cong. Give them no quarter." He shouted, *Sat Cong!*"

And his troops responded in unison: "*Sat Cong!*"

That night Blake developed a nervous stomach similar to the adrenaline-fed tightness associated with fear. But this wasn't fear, it was excitement, the challenge of fighting Tu. Blake and Duc-Lang had agreed to put finding the North Vietnamese Colonel out of their minds. But under the veneer of not caring, Blake knew Tu would be there and the AT-3 rockets would be there.

The hell with Admiral Paulson. Both have to be stopped.

THIRTY FOUR

The morning of the attack, Blake dressed quickly in his camouflage fatigues, put on his black beret, and left his room carrying a flight helmet and CAR-15. The pockets of his jacket were filled with enough survival gear to make it for two to three days in the jungle. Blake even took the extra precaution to strap on, under his fatigue jacket the snub-nosed .38 he had used in the Can Gio temple.

At the waterfront, troops went aboard boats taking on fuel alongside piers. Other boats circled in the river waiting to be called to load.

Blake and Mark walked among the assembling troops. "Runty-looking bunch aren't they?" Blake commented. "Steel pots flopping over their ears makes them look like a bunch a kids."

"Yah, like big-headed gnomes. Don't be deceived, though. They're damn good fighters, especially in the mud." Mark responded after a puff from his ever-present cigar.

Readying the troops on short notice had been strangely easy. Those who were used to the methodical pace of the Vietnamese would have said it couldn't be done. But now, in the dark of the morning, the soldiers nervously but obediently waited, then quietly boarded the boats.

After the northern attack force loaded, Blake joined Duc-Lang, remaining in the background as the *Dai Ta* had his final talk with his commanders. He spoke quietly, yet forcefully. "I'll be overhead in my chopper. Keep me informed of your progress. Be aggressive and don't wait for my permission. Find them and attack!" They shook hands and bowed. Faces strained by the vigorous preparations blended with jaws set for action.

The boats maneuvered into the basin where the three rivers joined at Nha Be. Some circled, others lay idle in the current, waiting. Slowly a ragged line formed with a command boat in the lead and the armada began to move. At first, until the line gaps were filled, the strange brown water naval force struggled, but then it picked up speed and they were underway.

The Rung Sat forces were well out of sight when Blake and Duc-Lang walked from the empty piers toward the helo pad. They knew it would take hours of cautious maneuvering before the northern attack force would be near the landing areas, nevertheless they wanted to be overhead in a chopper to make sure the assault went well.

The path from the piers to the helo pad took Blake and Duc-Lang near the Rung Sat Commander's office. As they approached, a familiar image caught Blake's eye. A man sat under the flag pole with the weight of his body resting on his hands which were tied to a stick and cruelly stretched behind his back to an extended position higher than his shoulders. In this inverted "V" position, a noose about the man's head forced him to look directly into the sun.

Blake's thoughts raced backward in time. *Duc-Lang must know how I feel about this kind of punishment. I've seen this before. I told Lieutenant Colonel Phat that I don't condone this kind of public humiliation. Is he defying me?*

Guards stood on either side occasionally prodding the man with bayonets. On closer inspection, Blake saw that this man's clothing had been stripped of all rank. Blood dripped from sliced skin and lay in pools mixed with mud.

As Blake and Duc-Lang came closer, cowardly round eyes blinked as if sensing danger. The prisoner had the look of a caged wild animal. It was Duc-Lang's Deputy Commander, Lieutenant Colonel Phat.

"Here is one of our spies, *Cô-vân*," Duc-Lang sneered.

Blake smiled. In his mind he saw the bloody body of Ace Magrue impaled in a jungle pit of stakes. Revenge. "How did you catch him?"

Duc-Lang slapped Colonel Phat across the face. "I suspected him for a long time, but he was clever. Caught him making contact with an agent."

Duc-Lang spat in Phat's eyes and slapped him viciously again. "He is the spy, but he did not tell where we would attack because we caught him before you and I decided on the plan. He will remain here without water, in the sun, until we return. The agent we caught in the village is still being interrogated by the PRU. They will both be tried by our military tribunal. Phat will die for a thousand loyal Vietnamese and Americans!"

By the time Duc-Lang, Blake and Sergeant Trieu arrived at the helo pad, Duc-Lang's Command and Control helicopter was already turning up. The *Dai Ta* ordered his pilot to hold his chopper until the sixteen troop-configured 'slicks' took off. Mark, Gunny and Marquell were already aboard the lead aircraft of that squadron.

After the last Huey was airborne, Duc-Lang gave his pilot the traditional thumbs up and the helicopter carrying *Dai Ta* Duc-Lang and his *Cô-vân*, Commander Blake Lawrence began to move. Climbing quickly to cruise altitude, it flew close to the line of troop-carrying choppers. As they passed each of the helos, Duc-Lang stood at the door. Wind blasting his uniform and wrinkling his face, he gave the thumbs up sign to his troops.

The assault choppers continued toward the southern battle area, but Duc-Lang's bird turned north in the direction of the brown water armada. In the brightness of the morning, his C&C chopper flew at water level passing alongside the line of boats as they forged ahead through the muddy water.

Duc-Lang had the pilot hover momentarily next to each boat and again he showed himself. To Blake, it wasn't hot dog, it wasn't politics, and it wasn't modern management theory. It was good old schoolbook leadership. Duc-Lang changed from his image of a Mandarin money changer to that of a fierce Asian warrior.

Having displayed himself as their commander leading them to battle, Duc-Lang ordered the chopper to climb to 2000 feet. There Blake could again see the Rung Sat and the Killer Forest. To the North he could see waves from the armada wash against the river banks. Black, sleek shaped PBRs, the destroyers of the Vietnamese brown water Navy, raced back and forth in the van.

Next came the brown water battleships. Called "Commandments", these bulky craft converted from LCM hulls looked like Civil War monitors. They led the way with their 20-millimeter gun turrets, 81 MM mortars, and .30 and .50 caliber machine guns.

The cruisers came next. These were the dark Assault Support Patrol Boats (ASPB's) a river boat specifically designed and constructed for use in the Mobile Riverine Force. They were armed with an assortment of 20's, 50's, a 7.62, and two M-60 machine guns. They also carried grenade launchers, 3" inch rockets, and a 60mm mortar.

Following them came the troop transports — the Armored Troop Carriers (ATCs) especially armored to shield against heavy fire, and the LCM-6's and LCM-8's armed with 20-mm and .50 cal machine guns. Every space on every boat was filled with troops.

Compared to blue water task forces of aircraft carriers, cruisers, and destroyers, this armada moved slowly, but considering the treacherous Rung Sat tidal currents and narrow waterways, ten knots was high speed. The line of boats marched along the river, leaving a wash on either side of their wake, and as he watched, Blake was reminded of the World War II documentary Victory at Sea. In the excitement of the moment he quietly whistled a few bars of its theme song.

To the south he saw the swing and curve of the Long Tau Channel and the assault choppers flying in combat formation. In the distance, coming from the ocean, he could see the convoy of giant merchant ships as they plodded their way from Vung Tau, one behind the other. China Fox was among them with Peg Thompson aboard. *I'm still not sure if it was just a war-time infatuation, he thought. But I do care about her — as much as I now care about this little country and Duc-Lang's task of driving Colonel Tu from the Rung Sat.*

Harassment and Interdiction fire from the 105's at Nha Be and Tan Thon Hiep pounded the southern attack area. Precisely on time, fixed-wing bombers and Huey gunships out of Tan Son Nhut circled.

As soon as the H&I fires were complete, tactical airstrikes began. Fixed-wing aircraft dove then pulled out as their bombs plummeted toward smoke-marked targets. The jungle exploded with red fire and gray smoke as the peaceful forest became a war zone. Huey gunships flashed their rockets and strafed the trees, then climbed out to join other aircraft waiting for another run. Again and again the attack planes and choppers came, unloading their ordnance into the chosen areas of jungle and mangroves. Trees fell and mud splashed high as bullets slashed and rockets buried deep, then exploded.

The airmobile 'slicks' of the southern attack force orbited in the sky waiting permission to land while the line of assault boats of the northern attack force kept marching through the water. When the air strikes were complete, Duc-Lang put the microphone to his lips and pressed the key. "*Tan-cong! Tan-cong!*, Attack! Attack!"

To the north, the PBR's raced ahead, with the ASPB's following behind. They riddled the jungle-landing area making pass after pass. Finally the landing craft pushed their bows into the mudbanks, dropped their ramps, and the troops vaulted ashore.

To the south the assault 'slicks' dropped to their landing zones and Vietnamese troops dashed from the doors. Blake had been told Vietnamese were natural mud soldiers; their lightness allowed them to move more easily than their American advisors. For him the proof was seeing them race to set up perimeters more on top of the mud than in it. At first, progress in the South was good. Duc-Lang's soldiers made their way easily through the mangroves and nippa palm. Blake watched as troops ran for fifty paces, then sent out small patrols like the leafs of four-leaf clovers spreading out from the stem. But after about a half-hour the pace slowed.

In the C&C chopper Blake questioned Duc-Lang, "Why no contact yet?"

"Be patient," the crafty, battle-experienced naval officer responded.

The first contact came in the form of a few rifle shots, followed by an occasional claymore. Then the exchange became more aggressive and before long it was evident that the guerrillas would stand to fight.

*****

On the ground, Mark Harris was at the front of the Southern advance with the Vietnamese ground commander, a Lieutenant Colonel. Gunny was with him as a small unit tactics advisor and Marquell carried a radio strapped on his back. As the fighting crescendoed to furious heights, Mark's unit began taking mortar rounds as well as automatic rifle fire, and the casualty rate climbed. Corpses sprawled in strange positions, arms blown away, pieces of flesh torn open, blood on mud-stained clothes. The battle became a stand off and the southern force bogged down, but the VC were still within AT-3 rocket range of the convoy as the logistics ships crept closer along the Long Tau Channel.

Mark, Gunny, and Marquell lay in a small ravine pinned down by fire. Mark shouted to his counterpart, "Call in airstrikes. Tell them to pile on the ammo. Tell them to bring it in on top of the bastards."

Doing as his advisor requested, the Vietnamese Lieutenant Colonel grabbed the radio-telephone and spoke excitedly to the C&C chopper flying high above them. When the Vietnamese in the controlling chopper questioned the mission, Mark grabbed the microphone from Marquell's backpack. "Let me talk directly to Commander Lawrence." There was a pause. Then from the C&C helo came, "Roger, Mark. What's up?"

"For Christsakes, Commander, get that fuc'n air controller to bring in the fire power. Pile it on, like in football. Dump everything on this fuc'n place. We'll put up smokes to mark our front lines. Get every fuc'n bomb and rocket you can in on top of the VC."

"Roger, Mark. Just wanted to confirm that you meant on top of the VC. We don't want another Can Gio incident. Over."

Mark chomped the end of his cigar and spat on the ground then screamed, "Of course I mean on top of the fuc'n VC."

Plane after plane dived for the ground unleashing bomb loads. A series of massive explosions literally ripped the canopy off the jungle and when it was complete the Rung Sat soldiers moved forward pushing the guerrillas back. Soon Mark and his Vietnamese troops were among the VC, fighting tree to tree, bush to bush. Mud and dirt filled the air as earth smells mixed with sulfur and gunpowder. The battle increased in intensity as uniformed soldiers swung bayonets at guerrillas charging with machetes. The VC fought from well camouflaged bunkers and dugouts connected by tunnels. Some of the make-shift bunkers were above ground, but the dugouts were difficult to find and it was not unusual for troops to go right by the only entrance, a small hole in the ground.

Mark, with Gunny and Marquell, moved with their counterparts into an area which had been used by the guerrillas as a temporary base camp. Mangled bodies of two or three VC lay nearby. Screams of pain blended with the sounds of groaning wounded.

The remaining guerrilla force had rallied just ahead at the edge of the jungle. Marquell set up the radio and Mark laid out his maps on an old tree trunk. The Americans and Vietnamese began discussing how to best attack the last of the VC.

Mark saw her about the same time Gunny and Marquell did. She wore loose black pajamas and had a bright red bandanna tied across her forehead. She came out of a hole in the ground and stood erect defying death.

She made an easy target, but Gunny didn't do anything. He shouted, "Co Tahn?" He just stared at her in disbelief.

"Take her out!" Mark shouted. "Gunny, Marquell! Look out! She's got a fuc'n grenade!"

But Gunny remained frozen. He said, "Co Tahn? You were going to Can Gio to be with your mother? Where's Bokassa?" He didn't move as the girl ran toward them crying out in Vietnamese, "*Sat My! Do Van Nghi, toi sat My.* (Do Van Nghi, I kill the Americans)," then threw the black egg-shaped explosive.

Bullets from Mark's CAR-15 pocked the ground as they raced toward her then blew away the belly from which she had given birth to Bokassa Johnson. His weapon stayed on her even after she was on the ground belching bloody meat that matched her red bandanna.

But it was too late.

The grenade bounced near Gunny, and the earth shook from the explosion. Dirt and debris flew. The air was filled with thick brown smoke. A Vietnamese soldier took the full blast, but Gunny and the village chief's aide, a *Dai Uy* (Lieutenant), were also hit.

The concussion jarred Mark, but when he saw Gunny's bloody flesh he ran to the dugout, slammed a banana clip in his weapon and emptied it into the hole. Then he threw in three grenades, stepped away until the fire, smoke and explosion cleared the opening in the ground, then reversed the banana clip and fired again. He ran back to the still bodies of his friends and screamed at his Vietnamese counterpart, "Asshole! Have your troops do a better job searching those goddamn dug-outs!" Mark pushed Marquell aside and grabbed the radio. He called to Blake, "Gunny's hit — bad. Got to get 'im out, fast. Don't know if he'll make it. Get a chopper in here!"

"Roger. Fire a smoke." There was a pause, then Blake said, "Okay. Got your smoke. The *Dai Ta* ordered one of the gunships in. There's a clearing — on your right — bomb craters. Move him there. We'll give it cover!"

Vietnamese medics placed the two wounded men into makeshift stretchers and a squad of troops moved them out to the clearing. As they waited, Gunny groaned and opened his eyes. He looked around, then focused on Mark. He couldn't talk at first, but finally gurgled, "Sorry, sir. My fault. Should 'a shot. Couldn't move. She was Co Tahn — my girl. She had my boy Bokassa. She was a fuc'n VC, a fuc'n spy?"

"No, Gunny. I shoulda got her," Marquell said. "My God, I'm sorry." Gunny never heard. He had passed out again.

Mark Harris on hearing Marquell's statement to Gunny said in mean guttural tones, "You sniveling son-of-a-bitch. You could'a taken her out before she threw the grenade. I don't know what your fuc'n problem is, but you better grow some balls."

The craters provided a place for the chopper to hover then touch down long enough for Mark and the two stretchers to get aboard. It lifted off and climbed to altitude as China Fox, leading the five-ship convoy, passed the place where it had been hit once before. This time there were no rockets.

As the chopper raced for Nha Be with Gunny's mangled body, the convoy continued its journey on the way to "Hanging Tree Bend."

Blake made contact with Mark. His voice sounded tight as if he were holding back emotion. "She must have stayed behind when the other guerrillas pulled out. A fuc'n fanatic. What pisses me is our troops went right by the goddamn dugout. Gunny saw her. Had his weapon ready but didn't react. Christ, he just stood there. I've seen him act like a merciless killer. He didn't this time and he took it. Claimed the VC was the same girl who had his baby! Christ, he wanted to marry her! I'll be back as soon as I get him to the medics." A pause, "Say a prayer for him."

THIRTY FIVE

THURSDAY, NOVEMBER 2, 1972, AIRBORNE OVER THE RUNG SAT

Blake watched from the back of Duc-Lang's Command helo as the chopper carrying Gunny Johnson skimmed the tree tops in its race against time. "What was the situation on the ground in your area?" he questioned Mark over the Command and Control net.

"VC're on the run," Mark's gravel voice responded. "Moving toward the northeast. They'll try to hold out 'til dark. Make a get-away by water. Keep the pressure on, Commander. Eric and that sampan group are in the right position. Left Marquell with the District Chief. Better pick him up and take him with you. Be careful. He was sluggish back there. May be on the shit again. Back as soon as I can."

After picking up Marquell, Duc-Lang ordered his chopper to turn north. He explained, "I doubt if Colonel Tu was with the southern guerrillas. More likely he's with the northern group. From there he could escape back to the jungle near Nhon Trach."

As the helo approached the northern area, Blake saw a small puff of smoke at a point across the river from Dutch World. He watched as a rocket trailing blue and red flew across the water. When it hit in the middle of the giant tanks he saw a flash, then an explosion followed by billowing fires. Vietnamese men rushed feverishly to fight a growing oil blaze.

Damn! Blake thought. *I hope Joanna and Tony are in Saigon. The ammo ships'll soon be in range as they pass on their way to the piers at Newport, north of the Capital City. Tankers like China Fox, with fuel for Dutch World, will have to slow and even anchor while pilots maneuver them to the piers. They'll be sitting ducks. The explosions could devastate Dutch World.*

Duc-Lang decided to direct the fighting from the ground. "Now I will fight Colonel Tu on my terms. You might learn why Vietnamese naval officers must know something besides ships and oceans."

*****

Their chopper landed in an LZ near the main battle. There was an ugly stench to the layered air. To Blake, it smelled like a mixture of medicine and burnt flesh. Lingering brown haze and smoke from bombs and rockets blurred the visibility. Ahead, Blake heard the noise of rifle fire and explosions. He winced as he watched one of the Rung Sat mud soldiers carried away on a stretcher.

Blake and Duc-Lang were met by a hatchet faced Vietnamese Colonel whose deep set eyes and lined face marked him as a man near exhaustion. The grimy, mud-covered officer snapped an aggressive salute. "The northern forces are stalled." He reported. "We made excellent progress at first, but now we're checked. The VC have dug in."

Duc-Lang returned the salute with a wave of his hand and immediately asked, "What's the body count so far?"

The Colonel's eyes brightened when he said, "Thirty-four VC, Sir." His eyes dropped in dejection. "Six of our men."

"Have we identified any of them? Did we get any of their officers?"

Blake knew the question's implication. Duc-Lang hadn't asked directly about Colonel Tu, but it was understood by his officers that a major part of their mission was to capture or kill the guerrilla leader.

"No, Sir. No officers, yet. But we're still moving bodies to the boats where we can take a closer look. Won't know anything for awhile. I do have something interesting for you." The Colonel reached inside a sack, pulled out a VC flag, and presented it to Duc-Lang.

The Dai Ta took it and held it open, then he pointed to the numbers and Vietnamese writing in the upper right corner. "This is Doan 12's battle flag. Colonel Tu is here."

He handed Blake the ragged piece of red and blue cloth with a gold star hand sewn in the center. "Take it as a souvenir. Remember this day. When you were in jungle combat like a mud soldier."

To Blake the flag looked more like a rag, but as he held it a feeling of fierceness swept over him — a mixture of hatred and excitement. "Tu nearby?" The words burst. "You sure? Shouldn't we be pushing to get him?" Colonel Tu had always been Duc-Lang's invisible enemy, but now Blake understood why the man was so dangerous — the reason why Duc-Lang hated him. This ruthless man who tortured pregnant women and sent assassins who killed Girl Scouts had also become Blake's personal enemy. Because of him, Ace Magrue was dead and Gunny was wounded so badly he would probably die. Blake had a mystic desire to see Colonel Tu — in a body bag.

Duc-Lang laid his map of the area across a portable table. As he and the Colonel discussed alternatives, Blake considered the situation. *How strange. Only a few months ago I was aboard ship, shooting projectiles from the 'blue water'. Here I am on the ground, trying to develop tactics to stop guerrillas from firing rockets to sink ships.* Blake also thought of Paulson and he knew exactly what the Admiral would do — forget Tu — save the ships!

That was when Blake saw it — the concept. No longer lacking confidence in his ability in ground tactics he posed the idea, "Shouldn't we hold the right column and push the left across this stream to join the center?" Pointing to the chart, he added, "Wouldn't the ships be out of range of their rockets? Couldn't we then bring in the airmobile troops from southern area to cut them off?"

"I agree. That's it!" Duc-Lang responded. After a moment he added, "In this case it is better that we split up, *Cô-vân*. You join your Marine advisor on the left and I will go to the right. From there I will call in the airmobile forces. Of course, I will now be without my Pigneau." His eyes glistened at his own joke.

"Unless we hurry even that Frenchman couldn't help. Let's go! The ships are getting close,"

Duc-Lang and the Colonel departed with the squad of troops and Blake made his way toward Lieutenant Strode, with Sergeant Trieu at his side and Marquell following with his radio. For the first time Blake was alone in a combat zone without seasoned jungle fighters like Duc-Lang, Eric, or Mark. But, by now he actually felt comfortable. He said to himself, "I'm finally getting the hang of this stuff."

They ran up a small rise to the top of the only high ground. Blake looked at the sky. Even though it was the dry season, there were still menacing clouds in the sky. He raised his binoculars and scanned the rugged country. The terrain ahead was typically mangrove and nippa palm with small areas of brushwood among the rice paddies. Up ahead he could see the stream. The land on the near side was flat and relatively clear. On the other side he saw heavy jungle. He heard the crack of rifles and the rattle of automatic weapons. He saw also the intermittent smoke of mortars fired from a spot on his side of the stream, probably where Strode's outfit was located.

"Get Lieutenant Strode on the line," Blake ordered.

"I got him, Commander," Marquell said after a moment.

Blake took the hand set from him. He stood with feet wide apart, field glasses now hanging by their strap about his neck. He looked in the direction of the action ahead, then dropped to one knee and spread his chart. "Strode. This is Commander Lawrence. Just got here. I'm behind you with Marquell and Sergeant Trieu. On some high ground." Blake searched the map until he found the spot and gave the grid coordinates of his location. "Is that you where I see mortar fire? About 075483?"

"Yes, Sah, that's me." The Southern voice responded. "Glad you're here, Commanda. Pushed the VC out of their base camp. Try'n to keep the heat on 'em."

"Which unit's on your right?"

"Company 809. 361's on the left."

"Duc-Lang gave orders for 361 to cross the stream — to flank them. Are they moving?"

"Ah know, Commanda. But ah can't get the *Dai Uy* to move." The voice sounded frustrated. "Says it's too dangerous to go 'til we get some close air or artillery."

"Have you called for any?"

"Yes, Sah. Sent a message back to the TOC, They relayed to Tan Son Nhut. But you know how that goes. We can get the VC. Ah know we can get em 'cuz they'a standing ground for a change. Our guys won't move without some heavy stuff."

The noise of three choppers passing overhead caught Blake's attention. He asked Strode, "You think rockets from those choppers could help?"

"Hell yes, but, sah... I'm not in contact with them. Don't even know they'a frequency."

"Did you say you're in the VC base camp now?"

"Yes, Sah and you should see this place. Like Christmas in November! Captured a hell of a lot of those new weapons."

Okay. Finally got some of the rockets. Paulson'll get off my back. Now we can go after Colonel Tu!

"I'll walk in there in a few minutes," he said to Strode. "Before I do, I'll see if I can talk those choppers into shooting up that area across the stream, Lawrence out."

"Marquell. Get those choppers on the line for me."

After a short pause, the Private responded, "All I can raise is Lieutenant Strode, Sir."

"Did you shift frequencies?" Blake shook his head. He remembered Mark's comment about Marquell's sluggishness.

"No, Sir."

"Well," Blake said impatiently. "Shift to 36.45."

Marquell swung the portable radio off his shoulders and twisted the dial to the correct position.

"What's his call sign, Sir?"

"Damn it! What's wrong with you? Use Moonriver One! We're Moonriver. That's SOP."

Seconds passed while Marquell repeated, "Moonriver One, Moonriver One," over and over into the handset. After a longer pause the radioman said slowly, "I've got someone, Commander. Maybe one of those Vietnamese pilots."

Blake grabbed the handset, "Moonriver One, this is Moonriver, Commander Lawrence speaking. Is Major Harris flying with you? Over."

"Roger, Moonriver. He is in the back. Over." A heavily accented Vietnamese voice responded,

After a short delay a deep voice said, "This is Moonriver One."

"Roger, Mark. How's Gunny? Is he going to be Okay?"

"Don't know. Medics at Nha Be are working on him. What in the hell are you doing on the fuc'n ground? Over"

"No time to explain. Need your help. Do you have contact with those other choppers?"

"Yes, Sir. My pilot can talk to them, Over."

Blake reviewed the tactical situation with Mark, then asked, "Have you got rockets? We wouldn't have to wait for fixed wing out of Saigon if your choppers can do the trick."

"Roger, Moonriver, I checked with the pilots. We're loaded. We can do it. Let me read back the coordinates. Rockets north of Song Dong Hoa, at 075485. Friendly front lines south of Dong Hoa stream, left and right of coordinates 075483. Is that correct?"

"That's it, Mark. I'm behind Strode. Moving up right now."

"Commander," the gravel voice sounded concerned. "You shouldn't be on the ground. That's what happened to Commander Weeks. He tried to be a Marine. Stay out of the action down there. It's not your bag."

"I'll be alright, Mark," Blake said as his eyes remained fixed on Harris' helo. He followed it until it turned in the direction of the other choppers. Then he looked at his radioman. Marquell had a hangdog look. No longer sympathetic to Marquell the boy, Blake barked, "Let's go! Move out — and act like a man!"

Marquell seemed to stand a little taller as he swung his radio pack to his shoulders.

As Blake neared the front lines, Lieutenant Strode came to meet him. Even in the jungle setting, Strode had a scholarly look with inquiring eyes behind horn-rimmed glasses. He reminded Blake of an anthropology professor on an important dig. As he saluted, words spilled from Strode's mouth. "Ah understand Gunny took a grenade. He gonna make it?"

Blake shook his head. "Don't know. Major Harris got him back to the base. Hope for the best."

Strode led Blake to a pile of crates near a dugout that had been blown out. "These 'a the rockets. Like the one that got China Fox. Ah found about 15 in the camp. Mah guess is that's the reason the VC stood their ground. Try'n to move 'em. Ah think our operation was a surprise, because they finally picked up and ran."

Blake examined the rockets and even lifted one to his shoulder. As he was putting it back into its case he spotted a file folder filled with rice paper. He stooped and picked up the folder then handed it to Trieu, "Looks official. Better hang on to this."

"Quite a haul — Russian rockets, ain't they Commander?" A new voice said.

Turning, he recognized the tough-looking medic wearing the green beret of a Marine advisor. "Doc, I didn't know you were here."

"Yes, Sir," The Navy corpsman responded. "Came in to help with the wounded. Heard about Gunny. He gonna be alright? Any word on his condition, Sir?"

"Not yet, Doc. Keep your fingers crossed." Blake pointed to the Vietnamese soldiers lounging nearby. "Who are those men?"

"That's the *Dai Uy's* reserve, only a squad." Strode responded. "Got the rest deployed as fire teams, on line, up ahead. Were you able to get through to the choppers, Sah?"

Blake looked up at the circling helos. "Yes, in fact it looks like they're about to start their rocket runs. Get 361 ready to move. Let's get closer, I want to meet the unit commanders." Then in icy tones he said to the Marquell, "Stay up on frequency."

As Blake went forward to join the Vietnamese officers, he said privately to Strode, "Thought we had Marquell straightened up."

"Gunny told me he's been do'n bett'a, Sah, but I wouldn't put it past him to be on someth'n."

Doc pulled Marquell aside. The corpsman put his face close to the Marine Private, "I see you're on the shit again. Listen mother-fucker, I heard what happened to Gunny — Understand Co Tahn got him. Grapevine has it you fucked up again. If he dies it won't be because of the gooks. You better hope he lives. Cause if he doesn't I'll have your ass."

The Vietnamese officers knew that Blake was *Dai Ta* Duc-Lang's *Cô-vân*, and as each came forward they bowed deeply. Blake reviewed his plan and told them he expected the three choppers to shoot-up the area on the other side of the stream any moment. "Have your men in position, ready to move across the river."

Off to the north the choppers formed a clockwise circle. To Blake they seemed to be orbiting aimlessly, as if merely sightseeing. Their dark profiles against the sky reminded him of giant hawks drifting in large circles over a meadow on a hot summer's day. As if to conceal their intent, the lazy circle dropped altitude easily and changed to a concise oval. Without warning, the lead helo raised its nose, then pushed over. It seemed to fall out of the sky as it picked up speed on a line directly toward the target. It flew faster and faster with no indication that it intended to pull out. Like talons of a giant hawk reaching out for prey, two rockets, followed by two more, shot from pods under the fuselage. The rockets flew until they buried into the mud with a dull thud followed by a plume of dirt and dust and smoke and a bellow of deafening sound. The chopper continued to fly toward the target, but at the last minute, it throttled back and circled the target. Mini-guns flashed. Hundreds of bullets reached out, as if the hawk had the head of a woodpecker: rat-tat- tatting, in rapid bursts at the enemy. Red tracers raced into tree tops and tore at foliage that crashed to the ground amid the sounds of ugly screams and smells of expended ordnance.

Blake watched that first chopper climb back toward the oval as the next helo pushed over and followed the same routine: four rockets, then during a tight turn about the target area mini-guns fired. The third chopper came and did the same, then climbed back to join the orbiting formation.

On the second pass the lead chopper, in a tight left turn lurched and shuddered. At first Blake thought a mini-gun had misfired then caught up to itself as they sometimes did. But the helo shuddered again and tried to climb. As the nose came up the engine stopped. Then it began to auto-rotate in strange convulsive arcs. Blake realized it had been hit by ground fire, but he felt helpless. It would be touch and go whether the chopper crashed on the South side, near him, or on the North side near the VC. With a lurch, probably caused by an air pocket or an internal explosion, the chopper changed direction, autogyroing as it fell. Parts of rotor blades and weapons flew in every direction. Miraculously there was no fire and the chopper fell on Blake's side, near the stream.

"Is Major Harris in that chopper? Marquell, check it out."

THIRTY SIX

THURSDAY, NOVEMBER 2, 1972, THE RUNG SAT BATTLE

Blake reacted instinctively to the possibility of Mark being in the downed chopper. "Radioman. Get Major Harris on the horn."

After a pause, Marquell responded, "No answer, Sir."

"You on freq?" He said to Marquell in an agitated voice. "Try again, damnit."

Marquell's voice jumped an octave. "Major Harris. Calling Major Harris — Still nothing, Sir. Honest."

"Lieutenant Strode, bring that squad and follow me." Blake snapped. "Major Harris is in that bird. Doc, you come too."

They were within shouting distance of the downed chopper when they heard shots.

"Take cover!" Blake ordered.

The men dove for the ground and crawled for any cover higher than their heads: a paddy bank, a small broad-leafed bush or, a clump of ferns.

"Bastards are firing at the chopper, Sah!" Lieutenant Strode said as he crouched next to Blake.

"Did the *Dai Uy* get 361 across the river yet?"

"No, Sah. Not yet."

"Damnit," Blake said, slamming his fist on the ground. "361's got to risk it. We've got to push the VC out of range of the ships and we've got to get to that chopper. Strode, take off," Blake ordered. "Get 361 across. Take the pressure off this area. We've got to get to that helo." Then with a forward motion of his arm Blake signaled the troops to follow. "I'm taking this squad in close," Blake shouted as Strode hurried away in a crouch.

Blake, leading the squad, inched along. Bellies in the mud, bodies supported on alternating elbows, they pushed their weapons ahead. As they neared the chopper, Blake signaled part of the squad to maneuver to his right. Then, like a squad leader fresh out of basic, he began to direct a fire-and-maneuver operation. First the left fired volley after volley into the area across the river as the right crouched and ran about ten paces, then hit the ground to find new cover. Then the left was up quickly, staying low as the right fired their weapons.

Slowly his squad of Vietnamese soldiers drew close to the downed chopper. Heavy fire from the other side continued to hit near them as well as into the fuselage of the Huey. One of the Vietnamese soldiers took it and Blake signaled the squad to hold their positions.

Above the noise of the battle, Blake heard a groan. It came from the downed helicopter. "It's Major Harris," Doc said as he instinctively started to get up.

"Stay down, Doc!" Blake shouted. "I heard automatic weapons. 361 got across. Should be there in a few minutes. Then we'll be able to get to whoever that is."

Doc scrambled closer to Blake. "Someone's alive in there, Sir! It's got to be the Major and I can make it. Just give me cover."

Blake shook his head. "Not yet, Doc! Stay down!"

The waiting seemed an eternity and the groans grew louder. After their initial success of getting across the stream, 361 couldn't seem to make any progress.

"Sir, I can make it," Doc pleaded. "Once I'm there, I'll be protected by the nose of the chopper."

"No! Stay here!" Blake growled. "Marquell. Get Lieutenant Strode on the line. Find out what the hell is going on with 361."

But before Marquell made the call, Doc was up and running. As if someone had said, "Follow me," Marquell went with him.

Blake was caught by surprise. Not by Doc's action because he knew about Doc's previous bravery and that Mark had been his Company C.O. up North. But he never would have guessed Marquell would also take off.

"Fuck you, Charlie," Marquell screamed. "Semper Fi, Gunny. This is for you. Got ya covered, Doc. Save the Major." He shucked his radio to the ground, grabbed a bandoleer of grenades, and raced in a zigzag pattern toward the VC. Firing his M-16 he mowed down a group of guerrillas who were trying to hit Doc. Marquell stopped twice to heave grenades, slammed in another clip, then continued firing his weapon as he charged toward the small stream. Explosions took out several more Cong and his bullets hit others. He kept running at full speed as if he intended to cross the water.

Blake jumped to his feet and signaled the South Vietnamese squad to follow. He shouted, "Fire into the forest across from the helo. Cover them!"

Marquell continued to charge the guerrillas as Doc zigzagged toward the wreckage in a low crouch. Dragging his medical kit as he ran, Doc weaved a path for the right side of the chopper. He was still about fifteen feet away from cover when he dove headfirst and slid the rest of the way. Doc wasn't hit by the rain of VC bullets, but just before Marquell got to the edge of the stream he took a hit in the face. Blood sprayed into the air as his blond hair turned orange. Another hit his chest and spun him. Blake saw Marquell's jaw half hanging, half detached under the place where his nose had vanished. He fell, face down in the mud.

Doc lay still for a few minutes. Then, using the tangled wreckage as cover, he disappeared into the chopper.

Blake's small band arrived at the stream at the same time 361 charged the VC forcing the guerrillas to retreat. By the time Blake got to Doc he was bandaging Mark's head.

The pilot moved and groaned. Doc said, "The gunner and co-pilot are dead. Pilot should live."

"What about Major Harris?" Blake asked.

"Don't know. He's still out. Patched a small section of his scalp where it was torn. Could be okay. Got to get him to Third Field right away. If he lives, it'll be because you took that VN squad and provided cover."

Blake looked at the changed skin coloring of his Marine companion. Mark's lips were chalky and except for splashes of blood, his face was ashen gray. "Can he be moved?"

"Yes, Sir," Doc responded.

Blake shouted to Sergeant Trieu who was now carrying Marquell's radio pack, "Trieu, get a chopper in here. Now!"

Within minutes a "slick" dropped out of the sky. Airborne troops jumped clear and spread out to form a perimeter.

A soldier's blouse covered Marquell's body as two soldiers carried it to the chopper. Only a shock of blond hair was exposed. Blake thought of his decision to keep Marquell in country and his sharp remarks to the young radioman. Until now he had been too busy to think of his own confused situation — a troubled son growing up at home but even that flashed through his mind as he felt a mixture of sorrow and remorse.

Blake sent Doc in the chopper with Major Harris and Marquell's body. Blake's words to Doc before the helo lifted off were, "I want to know about Major Harris and the Gunny. Get word to me from Third Field as soon as you can.

"And, Doc," he pleaded, "don't let 'em die."

THIRTY SEVEN

FRIDAY, NOVEMBER 3, 1972, RUNG SAT BATTLE

The curtain fell on the tragedy titled "Duc-Lang's Revenge." The Rung Sat Commander and his American advisor had correctly diagnosed the Colonel Tu's plan and sprung the trap. The guerrilla leader had split his forces to attack both the convoy and the tank farm. Tu must have forgotten that he and Duc-Lang had gone to the same military school in Hanoi. He underestimated Duc-Lang's flexibility. Had the Vietnamese Captain's airmobile force not struck in the Southern operational area when it did, Colonel Tu might have been successful in his attempt to sink the ships with his Russian rockets. On the other hand, if Duc-Lang had placed all his forces in the South, Colonel Tu's Northern attack force could also have done the job. If Tu's guerrillas had been successful at either place the channel would have been clogged and Saigon deprived of vital petroleum and ammunition for its defense.

The battle was winding down in the southern area when Duc-Lang's troops pushed the VC toward the back rivers where Eric Morris and the ambushers waited. In the north, Blake's pincer maneuver was successful. When Duc-Lang shifted the airmoble force from the south to the northern battle, the guerrillas became trapped in a dense wooded area too far from the channel to use their remaining rockets against the transiting ships. The noose tightened and the fighting continued. The danger for the ships passed and, from his position with the ground forces, Blake could see China Fox approach the dock at Dutch World.

Blake and Duc-Lang remained in the field directing the battle in their respective areas. At dusk, exhausted, they went aboard a command boat at anchor on a stream a short distance from the battle lines. Resting in hammocks rigged between stanchions, they listened to radio reports from the field commanders ashore. The damage reports from Dutch World indicated that two tanks had been hit and fires were still raging at several locations — the entire plant could explode. The most disturbing news was that the main house had been hit by rockets, but he could get no information about the Marbos.

Vietnamese rivers are desolate places at night. The only sounds Blake heard were jungle echoes, rushing water, and the background crackle of radios. Everyone was tense about the troops ashore. Duc-Lang told Blake that when guerrillas were trapped they typically attempted to fade into the night by filtering through enemy lines. Only on rare occasions did they counterattack in order to break out in force.

At about 0230 hours Blake and the *Dai Ta* were awakened. A Vietnamese naval officer reported in English. "There is action at the Southern ambush sites."

Blake could hear the rattle of automatic weapons in the distance. They came from the direction of the sampan force where Eric and his SEALs were waiting. Blake and Duc-Lang huddled near the radio. At first there were no reports, just the sound of sporadic firing. Then the report came. Sergeant Trieu translated for

Blake: "A force of about 25 Communists tried to escape across the stream." The Sergeant's reports became more graphic. "American SEALs and South Vietnamese soldiers waited silently along the overhang of the river. They delayed opening fire until the guerrillas were waterborne in their boats or were fording the streams."

Blake's mind visualized the fighting as quick, decisive, and merciless. He could see guerrillas, waist deep, burdened with weapons and equipment carried high over their heads, blown with grenades as they tried to swim, and their sampans riddled with machine gun fire. As if he were there he could see the bodies of the occupants left to drown in the slime water.

The radio reports explained in detail about the guerrillas that were annihilated, but they provided no information about casualties among the ambushers. Blake asked Trieu to press the Vietnamese about the SEALs.

Trieu exchanged words with the radio operators. "One American SEAL and several South Vietnamese were wounded by rifle shots."

"Any killed?" Duc-Lang asked.

"None killed."

Blake woke the next morning to the smell of fish and rice cooking on a small stove in the boat's makeshift galley. Blinding brightness came as the Rung Sat sun broke over the trees and onto the river. He couldn't remember when he had fallen asleep, nor when he had slept so soundly.

Duc-Lang and his Vietnamese officers were smiling when Blake joined them. "It worked," the Dai Ta said. "The guerrillas in the South did the predictable and we killed them as they tried to escape through our lines, but the guerrillas in the northern area did the unpredictable. They dug in and held during the night. We have them surrounded. I have ordered the net closed and our troops are advancing. I expect total annihilation."

Throughout the day reports continued to filter in and Trieu translated, "Battle in the South over. Troops in area ordered home."

In the North the battle became a standoff until attack bombers and choppers from Tan Son Nhut saturated the area. Eventually Duc-Lang's men were able to move forward until they had the guerrillas in a small pocket. Radio reports told of bloody fighting and many casualties on both sides. Duc-Lang ordered his troops to police the battle area for holdout guerrillas. Only when he was satisfied that none of the VC had escaped did he order his troops to bring out the dead and wounded and pull back to the waiting amphibious craft for the return trip.

*****

Duc-Lang and his American *Cô-vân* Blake Lawrence had seen the sailors and soldiers go and were there when they returned. They stood side-by-side on the pier at Nha Be, watching as the boats made their landings and deposited sailors tense from river operations and soldiers black with mud. Vietnamese troops bowed respectfully as they left the craft and passed the Dai Ta. Then they slumped again, as soldiers do, on their way to barracks and sleep.

The two leaders stayed until the last boat returned. Duc-Lang ordered the dead guerrillas not be buried until he personally looked at each one. He told Blake he wanted to verify that Colonel Tu's body was among them. Blake went along with Duc-Lang to the base hospital, where they talked to doctors about the wounded. In preparation and in battle Duc-Lang had been ruthless, but now as Blake walked with him, the Dai Ta seemed more like a compassionate father with a sick child, caring but helpless.

After the last jungle fighter slumped into a bunk, Blake and Duc-Lang climbed into a jeep and headed for Saigon. They were tired but there was still unfinished business. The *Dai Ta* intended to make a report to his superiors and then go visit his children. Blake would go to Third Field to visit Mark and Gunny.

*****

Doc met him at the head nurse's desk and rattled off his report. "Gunny's pretty bad, Commander. He needs special surgery. He'll have to be medevaced to the States. Major Harris isn't nearly as bad as I first thought. He was just knocked out. The thing that saved him was a good helmet, a hard head, and a professional patch job by the best medic between here and Chelsea."

Blake was relieved to learn Mark was not seriously hurt, but he wasn't surprised. He expected Mark to bounce back, like a cat with nine lives. Blake followed Doc into a room that had the heavy smell of alcohol and disinfectant. The two wounded marines were asleep. Mark's face had good color, but Gunny lay like a dead man. He was covered with bandages and hooked to several life-support machines. The grayish hue of his skin caused Blake to wince as he touched his hand compassionately. He whispered, "Hang on, Gunny — You can make it."

Blake was still within his thoughts when he heard a female voice arguing, "No. I'm not a relative. I'm his bloody girlfriend and don't get in my bloody way, because I'm going in. Don't try to stop me, Yank."

Peg wore a handkerchief tied around her forehead, her face was smeared with dirt, and she was wearing the working clothes of a merchant sailor. Blake thought she looked older, probably because of the deep circles under her eyes. As she came toward him Blake felt a tug at his heart, but held his feelings in reserve and waited for her response. Peg ran to him and as she threw her arms around him she asked, "How is he?"

Blake wanted to continue the embrace but instead stepped away. She was worried and he understood. *If she wasn't always Mark's girl, she is now.* He gently touched her raven hair. "It's going to be okay. The medics say Doc Crow's field treatment made the difference. Doc not only saved Mark's life, but was so good Mark'll probably be back on the job after a few weeks rest. Can't hurt a war-horse like him. Our Sergeant Johnson wasn't as lucky. A grenade got him pretty bad."

"Did you hear what happened at Dutch World?" she asked.

"Not yet. I was planning to stop there on the way back to the base."

"Rockets hit the house. Blew up just like China Fox. You know, a little hole and a big explosion. Joanna was killed." Peg's head shook and her eyes again showed pain. "She died instantly. Tony's already left Nha Be. He's somewhere in Saigon making arrangements to take her body back to England."

"Joanna dead? Damnit." He felt the hurt inside and out. His temples throbbed and the pain in his heart drove tears to his eyes. "My God."

Then he said to himself what his calling would not allow him to say publicly: *I've really grown to hate war, not just this war, but any war. Before coming to this land, from my blue water ship I had seen guns fire and bombs dropped and I thought I understood that war had a purpose. Now I've lived the results of the madness. Here I am standing between two wounded Marines that I care a great deal about, and learned about the loss of Joanna one of the most beautiful people I've ever known. A human who cared only for others. How naive I've been, cruising around in the blue-water, thinking there were winners and losers. It was easy — dinner in a wardroom by candle light — guns firing at an enemy you can't see — shielding many of the best naval officers from this kind of duty — never letting them feel or see reality — never letting them understand there are no winners, only losers.*

THIRTY EIGHT

After seeing Peg back to her ship at Dutch World and paying a visit to Tony Marbo, Blake returned to base. It took the Vietnamese staff three days to sift through the results and prepare an after-action report. He sat next to Duc-Lang for the final battle briefing listening as Vietnamese officers gave the analysis in terms of statistics: so many of this, so many of that. *How numbers oriented they are. We've so sensitized them and ourselves to statistics that we're satisfied when the numbers sound right. That's what happens when you fight a war sitting on your backside in a defensive position.*

Blake raised his hand and stopped the numbers game, "An Loc? What happened at An Loc?"

The briefer responded matter-of-factly. "Oh, the South Vietnamese Army rallied and successfully pushed the North Vietnamese back to their sanctuary on the other side of the border."

"Do we know if we got all the wire-guided rockets?" Blake asked.

The briefer seemed bored with the questions from the American advisor. After all, he had given the statistics, done his job. "Yes, Sir. Our count of the captured rockets correlates closely with intelligence."

"What about Tu?" Blake blurted. "Senior Colonel Tu — did we get him?"

The briefing officer glanced at the Dai Ta who had a strange look on his face. Duc-Lang touched Blake's leg, the way a Vietnamese touches a friend. He spoke in quiet tones, "The papers you picked up in the base camp confirmed that Senior Colonel Tu was in the battle. You know what he did to my wife and family and how I feel about him. I personally looked at the body of every guerrilla. There were several that looked like I remembered Tu, and who fit the description given by the prisoner Tam Ha: an older man with moderately long graying hair, neatly trimmed mustache and a chin beard. But the faces were disfigured I couldn't be certain. One of them must have been Colonel Tu. It is done. I consider my family avenged." Duc-Lang signaled the briefing was over. Colonel Tu was now buried in that strange cavern — the Asian mind.

Blake closed his eyes. Who was he to argue with Duc-Lang. But was the *Dai Ta* really satisfied, or was he just saving face? Oriental culture still wasn't Blake's strong suit. If it were true — that Tu was dead the world and the Rung Sat would be better off, but he actually felt flat because Duc-Lang was all too nonchalant — Blake sensed an air of uncertainty in his words.

Doc pleaded with Blake, "I hate to bother you, Commander. But, I just came from Third Field and the doctors say Gunny's wounds'll be stabilized enough to travel soon, maybe in a week. Can't you do something to expedite his decoration? It's been sidetracked in Saigon and he ought to get it before he leaves country — once he goes he may never get it. Major Harris usually handles this sort of thing. But he's still on R&R in Singapore."

"Frankly, I got so involved in the wrap-up of the operation, I lost track of the paperwork. I was under the impression everything was going along smooth. What seems to be the hang-up, Doc?"

The Navy Corpsman had taken Gunny's decoration problem as his own. Head tilted, hands extended to the ground, shoulders pulled forward in exaggerated roundness, he said. "Not sure, but I think some of those turkeys in Saigon think he doesn't deserve it because he had a baby by a VC. But he didn't know, Commander — he was in love with Co Tahn. He wants to adopt Bokassa and take him to America. Anyway, Sir, someone's sitting on the papers."

Blake stroked his chin, then ran his fingers through his hair. "OK, Doc. I'll look into it and do my best."

Gunny's decoration turned out to be a horror story. Just as Doc Crow said, the doctors at Third Field decided he had to be medevaced to a hospital in Oakland, California, for a special operation.

Blake made several trips to Saigon trying to solve the problem. On the one hand, some American staffies had at first recommended Gunny not be decorated at all. But when Blake appealed that Gunny was a courageous advisor in the field, Saigon relented but down-graded the decoration from a Silver Star to a Bronze Star Medal. The Vietnamese government also agreed to decorate the Sergeant.

The other problem turned out to be red tape and that looked hopeless. "I don't know what else to do." Doc complained. "We're down to a lousy form here and another there. They take so fuc'n long. Everything has to be handwritten, even the copies. Little people, sitting at little desks, writing meticulously on little pieces of paper. Then the paper goes into a big pile with other papers to wait for reading and rereading before it goes to another big pile for signature. Gunny leaves the day after tomorrow. I've tried everything. At this point money won't do it.

The following morning Blake heard Major Harris in the outer office. He knew Mark was fully recovered when he heard the gravel voice grouse to the Navy Yeoman, "Fuc'n gook taxi drivers. Tried to charge me too many piasters. Boss in, Yo?"

"Yes, Sir," the petty officer responded.

"Welcome back, Mark, how was Singapore?" Blake wasn't surprised to learn that the doctors couldn't keep Mark in bed. Other men may have used the crash and the head wound as a ticket out of Vietnam, but, true to form, Mark wanted to get back to his duties as soon as possible. When the doctors said they wouldn't sign his release from the hospital unless he agreed to an R&R, he surprised them and didn't put up a fight. What they didn't know was China Fox was going to be in Singapore getting a fresh load of fuel.

He had a toothy smile and his bass tones reflected enthusiasm as he said, "Super! Just super!" Mark looked rested but was still wearing a bandage on his scalp. "We stayed at the Raffles. Has a great bar — very British. What a great three days. I'm in love, Boss. Peg was able to get off the ship the entire time China Fox was there. I'm gonna marry her."

"Marry?" Blake said unemotionally. "Why, that's wonderful, Mark."

"Peg and I've known each other for over a year, now. That's longer than most, and we both think it's the right thing to do. Remember, she was the reason I extended over here in the first place. Anyway, my next duty station'll be in the States. This way I'll be able to take her with me." Mark began to tell about his three idyllic days. "Singapore's an old place, about as big as Chicago. It's got narrow streets and it's bustling. Too many fuc'n poor people, though, mostly Chinese. And hot! I've never been so hot. But the Raffles was great, old but great — thank God it was air-conditioned."

Blake heard the voice but his mind drifted. *Should I care if Mark marries Peg? Should I tell him about us? Of course not. The same thing happened to Peg that happened to me. She'll be a good wife. Better than I am a husband.*

A feeling of guilt settled over him. It kneaded his stomach. He became angry with himself, with Peg, with his own self-image. He began to rationalize. *It's the war.* He wanted to say, the fuc'n war, but even though he had adopted that over-used expression in his mind, he still couldn't bring himself to say the word out loud. He remembered the Dutch World Operations manager argue that war made madmen. People did crazy things. Things they wouldn't do if they were back in home-town America. The pressures, the fears, the dreams shattered. Time with Peg wasn't a fantasy, it was real. Now he felt stupid for letting the attraction go too far.

Blake explained the hang-ups he was having with Gunny and true to form Mark said, "Duc-Lang has the power to get things done in Saigon. What's he doing about it?" Even though Mark knew the real story about Duc-Lang — why he spent so much time in the Capitol City, and had seen the man perform well in combat, he had never fully committed himself to trusting him. Blake figured it was deeper than just Duc-Lang. He figured Mark would always be a "hard hat" with built-in prejudices.

Blake took Mark's advice and explained the entire story to Duc-Lang over the phone. The *Dai Ta* didn't sound very optimistic when he questioned, "You mean the decoration for your black Sergeant Johnson, the one who had the VC girl in the village of Nha Be — who gave birth to a Bokassa?"

Blake knew the word Bokassa. Sergeant Trieu had explained that it was their word for describing mixed bloods. He also knew Bokassa Johnson was born in mid-October just before the battle. Nevertheless he was surprised that Duc-Lang knew about Co Tahn and that he used the word not as the baby's name but in the disparaging sense. It was obvious that Duc-Lang was reluctant to help, so Blake reminded the Dai Ta, "Gunnery Sergeant Johnson was my senior non-commissioned advisor. He loved the girl but he was duped." Then he added, "Just as you were duped by Lieutenant Colonel Phat."

Duc-Lang was silent. Blake struck an unfair nerve when he reminded him of Colonel Phat, but by now, Blake pulled few punches in his dealings with his counterpart. In order to soften the loss of face, Blake did add, "Keep in mind, your own soldiers greatly respect Gunny and you know he was wounded during the battle against Colonel Tu."

Finally Duc-Lang spoke. "I will," then added, "As you Americans say — no guarantees."

Early the next morning Blake got a call from Duc-Lang's new deputy. The *Dai Ta* was in Saigon and would not return to Nha Be until late afternoon, but he had Gunny's papers. If somebody could meet the *Dai Ta*'s driver at Vietnamese Naval headquarters at noon, the Gunny's decoration should be ready.

Mark would meet Duc-Lang's driver and get the papers to the hospital in time for the ceremony. He also had to grease the skids with the sergeant major at Marine headquarters to process Gunny's American decoration quickly. It would go down to the wire.

*****

Doctors, medics, and nurses clicked their tongues and shook their heads because their territory was invaded. They nervously warned not to disturb the other patients. Blake tried to convince Gunny's doctor to delay the medevac plane but the surgeon said. "If he doesn't go now he'll lose the arm and have internal problems the rest of his life."

Blake watched as Gunny's bed was raised so he could see everyone without putting undue pressure on his wounds. Doc stood next to the bed.

But Mark and Duc-Lang were unable to pull it off, because it was too late in the day. The civilian staff had gone and Blake was told it isn't good to rush those kinds of things.

The race against time continued. Gunny was to be transported to the airport the next morning at 0800 hours for a take-off an hour later. Mark would go to the Marine advisory headquarters while Blake would meet Duc-Lang at Vietnamese HQ. They would be on the doorsteps first thing in the morning.

*****

Doc walked with Sergeant Trieu as the stretcher bearers carried Gunny to the medevac plane. Mark and Blake were nowhere to be found and Doc offered, "I'm sorry that we couldn't get the paperwork done in time, Gunny."

Gunny shrugged painfully and said, "Not your fault, Doc. They call it 'city hall' back in Detroit where I come from."

Doc started to make a joke, something about how lucky Gunny was to be going home early, but it didn't sound right even as he said it, so he didn't finish. His eyes were moist and he squeezed his friend's hand. "Okay you fuc'n Marine. Take care of yourself. Don't worry about the Co Tahn thing. You'll get over it, right, Trieu?"

"Everything will be alright," the skinny Sergeant said.

"Doc, don' you gimmy that fuc'n Marine stuff. I'll come out of this stretcher and kick yo ass. Goodbye, Doc. Goodbye, Trieu. Be good."

At that moment two jeeps raced across the airstrip. Mark drove the lead jeep and Duc-Lang's driver with the *Dai Ta* and Blake were in the second.

Blake jumped from the vehicle and spoke momentarily to the doctor in charge of loading the plane, then joined Major Harris and *Dai Ta* Duc-Lang at the side of Gunny's stretcher.

"Sorry Gunny. It was impossible to get adoption papers in time," Blake said. "But we're okay with the decoration."

The words were read: "exceptionally meritorious conduct," "courage," "devotion to duty," "brave actions," and "in the highest traditions of the United States Marine Corps."

When the brief ceremony finished, Gunny signaled he had something to say to the officers. The Marine Sergeant winced in pain as he spoke, "I wanted you and the major to know I'm sorry about Marquell. If I hadn't insisted on squaring him away he would have been home safe now."

Blake shook his head. "No, Gunny. I was the one that made the decision to keep him with us, but, thanks to you, he died a Marine."

"That's for sure. Don't worry about that other stuff, the shit — we all did a little Cracklin' Rosie out here. I have two things I'm gonna do. I'm com'n back for my boy Bokassa as soon as I can, and I'm gonna visit Marquell's folks. In this world every little bit helps. I want them to know their boy died a hero. I think he ought to get the Medal of Honor for what he did."

FORTY

The day before Christmas on a sun-scorched athletic field at Tan Son Nhut Blake sat with Mark among a sea of camouflaged bodies. The remaining American advisors watched the dancing and singing of Lola Falona. They whistled wildly when Miss America blew kisses from the stage of the ninth and final USO show.

Bob Hope had them holding their sides with laughter as he fired one-liners. He joked about the cease fire. "We came out here prepared for peace. Not only did they fail to reach an agreement in Paris, but now they're fighting over the hotel bill."

Christmas dinner at Nha Be was prepared by a handful of Vietnamese cooks under the watchful eye of an American. Blake joined his advisors in the mess hall where they ate the traditional foods: turkey and rice, cranberries and rice; mincemeat pie and rice.

Soon after the battle for An Loc had been won, President Thieu agreed to a cease fire. Soon after that, President Nixon announced "Peace with honor." But stopping the war was another matter. Marquell wasn't the last American to die. Blake learned it was a guy he knew — the Senior Advisor at An Loc, Army Lieutenant Colonel Bill Nolte from Onaway, Michigan. He had gallantly fought through the siege of that city and was passionately dedicated to rebuilding the devastation. He was killed by artillery at about midnight on the last day of the war.

For the Americans in the field, the final weeks were both nervous and comical. Blake watched them anticipate the end by packing and shipping their belongings. Then they wandered about thinking that there must be something else to be done.

One of the PBR Advisors told Blake, "I feel like the tail-end man. I was tail-end of the draft so I joined the Navy. I was the tail-end coming to Vietnam, and I made the tail-end river patrol. I guess I'll be the tail-end going home, but I won't believe that until I'm on the plane."

As soon as Blake received the official word that the Americans would be leaving the Rung Sat, he went to visit Duc-Lang in his quarters. Blake's pudgy counterpart was working behind his desk, but rose to greet his *Co-Van*.

Blake clasped his friend's hand warmly. "I suppose you've heard the news. An agreement has been reached."

They sipped cool drinks on a small veranda overlooking the Long Tau Channel where it joined the Song Nha Be. It was the middle of the dry season, and without the rain the Long Tau had more blues and greens, less muddy brown. Boat traffic was heavy, mostly small sampans but also a few junks.

Duc-Lang's cheeks were dimpled in his usual friendly smile, but his eyes had lost their twinkle. By now Blake could tell when his counterpart was irritated. "Yes, but it will be a fragile peace. By the terms, the North Vietnamese are not required to pull back their troops."

"You sound pessimistic."

Duc-Lang's eyes, always expressive, always honest, spoke before his lips said the words. "It is not mine to say, but a fish woman could have struck a better bargain. We Vietnamese have bartered all our lives, so we know. Yes our government had a say — President Thieu agreed, but his hands were tied. There must have been great pressure on your President to accept terms that left the enemy in South Vietnam — on our soil, ready to strike whenever it suits them."

Blake bristled. "Now wait! It's a complicated peace plan and negotiations have been difficult. We Americans'll go home and our prisoners in the North'll be released."

The *Dai Ta* nodded his head slightly then stared away to the river. In his brittle sounding English he said, "So sorry. Please, excuse me. I have learned frankness from you Americans. We will miss you in the Rung Sat and I am happy for the release of your prisoners of war. But I don't understand why they are so important. There are only a few hundred prisoners. Is it because there are senior officers among them?"

Blake didn't want the relationship to end badly, so instead of lashing out he said, "There's nothing more I can say in defense of the negotiations or our values, *Dai Ta*. Our cultures are different. Let's leave it at that." To soften the moment Blake changed the subject. "According to the terms, a commission will administer the country until you have free elections."

Dropping his gaze in apology, Duc-Lang shook his head. In overly precise English he said, "You know it is not normally in the Vietnamese character to make definitive statements when they can be avoided. These are very emotional times. I am sorry that I spoke as I did about the American POWs. But, how can we join hands with the enemy to govern this country? We fought them as Viet Minh and as Viet Cong. We saw the French come and go and now the Americans. Nothing changed. They are Northerners, Bac Ky, dog eaters. You Americans never understood this was a civil war about more than just Communism. It will go on because it is about independence. We have always wanted independence from the Europeans. That may finally happen. It is also about Communism and we will never naturally adopt that system because we have a deep attachment to family and property. It could happen, but only for a few years. But most important it will go on because we are Southerners, Nam Ky. Elections will never work!"

It was over. There was nothing more Blake could do except console his friend. "For the welfare of your country I hope you have elections. And I hope they do keep the peace. But I came to tell you the Rung Sat advisors are leaving in a few days."

"So soon?"

"There's no need for us here any more. We've turned over our equipment to you, and the Rung Sat is secure."

As if offering a prophesy Duc-Lang said, "The Rung Sat will never be secure."

FORTY ONE

The morning the advisors left Nha Be, the Rung Sat was as dark as black marble. Blake felt a chill as he gazed at the Nha Be complex. He thought of the sign hanging above the bar when he left the club the evening before. It said hot dogs 10¢, potato chips 25¢, Coke 25¢, and whiskey 10¢. He visualized the base at the height of American involvement, bustling with aggressive fighting men. He saw Navy Sea Wolf choppers lifting off the pad to buzz the rice paddies in search of Cong, and braggadocio sailors staggering back to barracks ships moored at the piers, surrounded by dark grey PBR's. He thought of the good times, the laughs, and the strong talk, like "get those slope heads," and "let's kill a few fuc'n Cong." He also thought of the thousands of men who would never make their final airplane trip home. *If nothing else, I hope their lives left the mark of freedom on this country. Otherwise, win or lose, they died in vain.*

Trucks and jeeps stacked with sea bags and suitcases were arranged in a line ready for loading. Duc-Lang came to the advisor's compound and stood with Blake and Sergeant Trieu.

"There are a few decent pieces of furniture in my room. I suggest you move them to your quarters," Blake offered his counterpart. "Will you stay in the Rung Sat?"

Duc-Lang smiled and shrugged his shoulders. "Yes, I know the region. Only this morning I learned the guerrillas struck a small hamlet near Can Gio."

"Here's something else I won't be needing it." Blake said as he handed his .38 cal. pistol to Duc-Lang. "It's the weapon I used down in Can Gio. Might come in handy for you." To disguise a surge of emotion Blake turned and shouted, "Mark, mount up — get the men aboard the vehicles."

Then Blake took Sergeant Trieu's hand. Giving it a long, sincere shake, he said. "I'll miss you, just as I'll miss the *Dai Ta.* Thank you for all the hours you so ably served as my translator. Goodbye."

Trieu, as was his habit, touched his wire-rimmed glasses and bowed. "*Chao* (Good Bye) and good luck, *Cô-vân* Lawrence."

Duc-Lang spun the cylinder of the snub-nosed 38 then shook hands with his American advisor for the last time. Each looked hard at the other. The *Dai Ta's* eyes were sad as he said, "You remember the story of Pigneau? The French Priest? You were my Pigneau. I will miss you, my friend. Good bye, *Cô-vân.*"

Blake gave a broad smile and a quick wink American style. As if the parting would only be temporary, Commander Blake Lawrence, United States Navy saluted Captain Nguyen Duc-Lang, Vietnamese Navy, and simply said, "*Chao.*"

At first it was just a job to do. Then came the common challenge of Colonel Tu. Now I feel a lasting bond to Duc-Lang. He felt the surge of emotion again and the beginning of a tear. Turning quickly, again to cover his true feelings, he shouted the cliche from a horse opera. "OK, Mark. Move 'em out."

As the caravan pulled away Blake looked back for a last glimpse. Nha Be was ominously deserted except for Duc-Lang, Hootch Maid Rosie, Sergeant Trieu and a few junior Vietnamese enlisted who loyally waved goodbye. There were no soldiers on parade when they passed through the compound and the village shopkeepers went about their business hardly looking up from their chores. There were no pretty Vietnamese girls waving goodbye and no little children shouting, "Okay, Okay, Okay," as they did when he had arrived.

*****

Blake and Mark were the first to arrive at the place the American Navy called the Annapolis Hotel. They checked in with the local staff and saw to it that their men were settled. They were told that out-processing wouldn't take long and the Nha Be advisors were scheduled to fly out the next day.

"You're on your own to handle final affairs," Mark told the men. "Just don't miss the plane."

A sailor laughed. "Miss the plane back to the world? You gotta be shit'n me, Major!"

*****

Blake's final call on Rear Admiral Paulson was short. The aide de camp ushered him into the paneled office where the Admiral sat working on some papers at a side board. His back was to Blake and he didn't turn until Blake cleared his voice. Without looking up the Admiral said, "Have a seat."

Finally Paulson swung his swivel chair and as if surprised at Blake's presence he said, "Oh, Blake. Trying to clean up this goddamn war. Didn't hear you come in. So you're headed home. I'm damn busy and I don't want to hold you up. Besides, you probably have lots of things to do here in town before you go. I'm surprised you're not taking your destroyer command. You can have her now, if you want." As an after thought he added, "Oh, by-the-way the Convening Authority dropped the naval gunfire investigation after Marquell, the key party, was killed."

Blake shrugged. *Hell, that was months ago and the bastard is just getting around to telling me about it.* He knew Paulson wouldn't understand why he elected to go home to his family and a shore duty job instead of the destroyer. Blake knew his dad, a sea dog of the old school wouldn't either, and there was a time in Blake's life when even he wouldn't have understood, but not now. Not after the Rung Sat. Instead of trying to defend his decision, Blake gave Paulson a summary of the turnover of the Special Zone and the base at Nha Be to the Vietnamese.

The meeting ended unceremoniously when the Admiral's phone rang. Paulson picked it up and began a dialog that lasted several minutes. When it was clear that the conversation would continue, Paulson signalled Blake with his head and offered his right hand for a shake. Between nods of his head and replies "a-ha" and "that's right," he said, "Take care, Blake. See you in the States?"

As he left the office Blake thought, *Not even an attaboy for getting the rockets. Will I become as insensitive as that if I hang around the Navy?*

*****

After some last minute shopping, Blake and Mark met in the clubhouse restaurant at the Saigon golf course.

"How'd it go with Admiral Paulson?"

"You know as well as I, the Chameleon's a legend in his own mind," Blake said with a grin. "When I told him we turned over the American compound and all the equipment in good shape and that Vietnamization was a reality, he seemed pleased. I also told him the Rung Sat was as secure as it could ever be, but I don't think he understood what I meant. He'll never understand this rice paddy war. Would you believe he told me they finally dropped the investigation of the Can Gio gunfire incident." Blake shook his head in disgust then took a sip of his beer. "You get everything done?"

"Mostly, still a few odds and ends. No bargains left in this town. I'll be better off to wait and buy the things I need in Singapore. Peg's waiting for me there. Quit her job with the steamship company. Sure you won't come down for the wedding? You could take a few days before you go home."

To cover his eyes, Blake tilted his beer bottle and took a sip. "No, my schedule's pretty tight. Got to get home to the kids."

"Singapore isn't going to be a big deal anyway. We'll stay there for a few days, then fly to Australia to meet her folks. Then on to Pendleton."

"You've been out here for a long time."

"Seems like forever. Wouldn't change it though. The only war we had. Like it or not that's what Marines do. What better place to do it than the Rung Sat?"

"I never told you – don't know why, but I'm from Pittsburgh, too."

Mark sat back in his chair. "Getoutahere? You're from my home town and never mentioned it? What part?"

"South Hills."

"Well, isn't that something. One for the books."

They laughed when they both decided to order the same thing, a hamburger and a cup of rice, part American and part Vietnamese. They had eaten so much Vietnamese food in the villages and outposts they had gotten used to it. "I refuse to eat any more Nouc Mam." Mark said.

After a while the two men became quiet and pensive. They had run out of things to say.

Finally Blake said, "Ah, Mark." He hesitated then continued. "This'll probably sound dumb but, ah, well, we got along okay. I appreciate how you helped me." Then he laughed, "I guess you don't get too many opportunities to teach a sailor how to fight in the jungle."

Mark coughed before he said, "Hell, that's not dumb. I know what you mean. Listen boss, it came out alright. Don't know what'll happen over here after we're gone. But hey, we gave it our best shot. If those guys in the Rung Sat are any indication, South Vietnam should do okay."

They stood to leave. Their grips were strong. Blake wasn't sure when the bonding took place. Maybe it was the day he jacked Mark up about his language or maybe it was when Mark took his side against Paulson. He knew it had when with a wry grin, Mark Harris, for the first time, said his first name, "Take care, Blake."

FORTY TWO

It was another black granite morning when they assembled for their 5:00 a.m. boarding. Sleepy-eyed Rung Sat advisors sat on benches in one corner of the building. Some were still hung over from a party the night before. The loud speaker vibrated the announcement: "All personnel ticketed on Pan American flight number F2A4, have your orders and boarding passes ready and proceed to gate number one at this time."

"We have everyone?" Blake asked one of the advisors.

"All except Doc. Nobody's seen him since last night at the party."

The Rung Sat group decided to wait together and be the last to board, just in case Doc got there in time. One of the advisors crawled under the barrier and went to the door for a last look up and down the street.

"Here he comes! You should see what he's got with him!"

Doc Crow stepped out of a cab with two Saigon hookers. One was wearing the Corpsman's black beret. The other was carrying two BUFE's and wearing a pair of fatigue trousers with the pant legs rolled up to her knees. She had a pair of combat boots slung over her shoulders. Doc staggered to the door with one arm around each of the girls. "How'm I do'n? On time?" he slurred. Doc wore a lipstick grin from ear to ear.

A sailor said. "You better get your ass in gear, Doc. We're supposed to be boarding right now."

"Come here, hot lips," Doc said as he kissed each boldly. "Goodbye, you beautiful honeys." Then he squeezed the hookers for a last time.

Doc started in the terminal door when one of the girls ran to him and whispered something in his ear. "Money for a cab? Hell take this darlin'," Doc stripped his wallet of its final bills and handed the girl a fistful of paper. He said loudly. "Easy come, easy go, Saigon!"

It was 6:00 a.m., February 11, 1973, one day before the first POWs were released from Hanoi, when the aircraft taxied to the north end of the runway and waited for clearance. Blake's advisors were surprisingly quiet now that Doc was strapped into his seat. In fact, all the people in the plane became silent when it began to roll. Daylight was breaking as it picked up speed. Runway markings, sand bag bunkers and telephone poles all began to blur as it raced toward the end of the tarmac.

The airplane lifted off. At the same time Blake heard the wheels slam with finality into the wells there was a spontaneous outburst. The noise was like the sound of thunder and it shook the aircraft. They stomped their feet and their arms went into the air as if praising the Almighty. They shouted over and over and when the shouting subsided everyone wanted to talk at once.

"Goodbye, Vietnam!"

"Didn't leave noth'n back there!"

"Hello, world!"

"Yahoo!"

"Go'n home!"

Blake even said out loud, "Fuc'n war." *I still don't like using that word, but this time it fits.*

Doc gazed through the window and said, "Hey, look. There's the fuc'n Rung Sat and the Long Tau Channel down there! Now I know I'm go'n to heaven, amigos, 'cause I've spent my time in hell."

The morning sun broke full and bright and ahead Blake saw the light green seas off the coast near Can Gio and Vung Tau where the ocean deepens into blue infinity. Then he looked down. From that altitude the Rung Sat rivers with their light oranges and reds streaked with blues blended with the browns, and blacks of the jungle. But it was the greens that he would remember. Greens that were more brilliant than he had ever seen before. Brighter than he would ever see again. He saw the intertwining, snakelike rivers and the Long Tau Channel superimposed on menacing swamps and mud. Once before, while standing with Mark Harris at the helo pad before his first chopper ride, the image of the Rung Sat on the chart had reminded him of the human brain. Now it reminded him of a heart.

His thoughts exploded. *I didn't want to come to Vietnam. I was bitter and I didn't care about the war or this little country. Now a part of me wants to stay. It's crazy how I feel now.*

I'm sad, because I already miss the land and my friends Duc-Lang and Sergeant Trieu. I'll miss the excitement of flying around in choppers and riding the rivers. Maybe subconsciously everyone who came in-country feels that way.

I'm still bitter because I've lost Ace, Marquell, and maybe my own wife. I still can't get the image of the Girl Scout and the village Elder out of my mind and the thought that it was Gunny's own girl who tried to kill him.

I'm curious, because I might never know the true impact of Gunny's wounds — those from the bullets and those from having his love turn out so tragic, or, for that matter, my own infatuation with Peg and where that might have gone had I acted differently.

I guess I'm satisfied about how it all turned out, because I believe the South Vietnamese can fight on and survive. No, that's not true. I don't feel satisfied. I still feel flawed. Because I'm not sure that this war will lead, as my grandmother said, to a more peaceful world.

Blake picked up the souvenir red and blue flag he had carried aboard — the Viet Cong flag with a gold star sewn in the center. He looked at the rag closely. Duc-Lang told him it was Tu's battle flag. *Wonder if we really got Colonel Tu?*

Epilogue

In the spring of 1975, two years after closing the base at Nha Be and flying home, Blake Lawrence stood on the deck of his own destroyer, in the South China Sea near the city of Vung Tau and the mouth of the Long Tau Channel. It was evening, but the weather was clear and he saw Cape Saint Jacques and the light house on top of Nui Nho mountain. Images formed of the days when he directed naval gunfire at guerrillas attacking advisors and of his days in the Rung Sat. He held several messages that further stimulated his memory.

SECRET
OPERATIONAL IMMEDIATE
SUMMARY: THE NVA HAS LAUNCHED A TWO DIVISION SIZE ATTACK ENDING THE LULL IN MAJOR MILITARY ACTIVITY. END SUMMARY.
TWO DIVISIONS, POSSIBLY THE 425TH AND 304TH DIVISIONS OF THE NVA IV CORPS WITH ELEMENTS OF THE 5TH AND 18TH ARMORED BRIGADES, LAUNCHED A TWO DIVISION SIZE ATTACK NORTH OF LONG THANH, IN AN APPARENT EFFORT TO CUT ROUTE 15 BETWEEN BIEN HOA AND VUNG TAU. AT TIME OF REPORT ARVN DEFENDERS ARE HOLDING.
TO THE SOUTH, PHOUC LE, TEN MILES NORTH OF VUNG TAU, IS REPORTED UNDER HEAVY ATTACK.
SOURCE OF INFORMATION: CAPTURED DOCUMENTS AND PRISONERS.

The images grew and Blake responded silently to his torn heart. *Two divisions? Armor? They're cutting off Saigon.*
He read the next message.

SECRET
OPERATIONAL IMMEDIATE
SUMMARY: 500 AMERICANS REMAIN IN CAPITAL, NEGOTIATIONS CONTINUE. END SUMMARY.
SOURCES ACKNOWLEDGE THAT LATE NEGOTIATIONS WITH NORTH VIETNAMESE REPRESENTATIVES IN SAIGON AS WELL AS WITH SOVIET REPRESENTATIVES ARE CONTINUING. TOTAL WITHDRAWAL OF REMAINING 500 AMERICANS AND OUSTER OF PRESIDENT THIEU DEMANDED.

Damn! They've got to hold. Thieu can't throw it in.

SECRET
OPERATIONAL IMMEDIATE
SUMMARY: SAIGON SURROUNDED, RVN UNITS RESIST-
ING. TAN SON NHUT UNDER ATTACK. END SUMMARY.
UNITS OF THE NVA SECOND, THIRD AND FOURTH CORPS
AS WELL AS THE NVA 232ND TACTICAL WING HAVE
MOVED TO CUT OFF SAIGON.
NVA ARTILLERY IS POUNDING AIRFIELDS AT BIEN HOA
AND TAN SON NHUT, AND IT IS REPORTED THAT OTHER
ARTILLERY HAS BEEN MOVED TO AN AREA CALLED
NHON TRACH ON THE NORTH WESTERN EDGE OF THE
RUNG SAT SPECIAL ZONE WITHIN RANGE OF SAIGON.

Blake saw clouds building above the horizon, and an occasional gleam-
ing rod of lightning. He remembered those skies. It was the beginning of
the wet monsoon, and his mind flashed back to the same time in 1972, three
years before, when he first heard the words. Rung Sat and Nhon Trach. *This
is damn serious. With big guns firing shells at Saigon from Nhon Trach, the
city could fall at any time.*

He wanted to put the pedal on the floor and race up the Long Tau to
duel the Nhon Trach artillery. But his ship was a unit of a greater armada in
an operation called Eagle Pull. The ships of the evacuation force had to
remain on station, patiently waiting the results of final negotiations.

Blake took a lonely vigil in his bridge wing chair, his eyes staring off in
the direction of the South Vietnamese capital. From time to time he could
see smoke rising toward the cloudy monsoon skies and as the evening
changed to night he could see flashes of gunfire to the North of the city.
Explosions, like fireworks, lit up the sky in bright oranges and reds as flames
from burning oil and ammunition burst against the pitch backdrop. The
weather at sea was unusually good, but Blake knew the rains could begin
any time. He said to himself, "If the South Vietnamese could just hold out a
few more weeks, the monsoon would stall the NVA in their tracks. Trouble
is, the enemy also knows that, and they'll be pushing hard."

Joe Voit, the operations officer, came to stand next to Blake's chair. The
sandy-haired Lieutenant wore a ball cap with the ship's name. He had binoculars looped around his neck. "I've got a friend on the amphibious flag-
ship. Been talking to him by flashing light. He says heads up. The evacuation might begin at any time. Negotiations have stopped. The North will
accept only a military solution. A general by the name of Dung has given an
ultimatum for Saigon to surrender. We have until Monday, 28 April, to get
out of the country."

Even though the war was within miles, information was limited and
had to be pieced together from sparsely worded intelligence summaries.
The news penetrated Blake's mind. For him it was unacceptable. He felt a

mixture of anger and depression as he pounded his fist into the rail. *Get out of the country? Damnit, Damnit. Driven out? How could it happen? Why don't we help the ARVN?*

"My friend says there are several options for evacuation," Joe continued. "We'll take out the remaining Americans and a few Vietnamese. He says we've sent in a small Marine unit to protect our people. The Ambassador's in the driver's seat, but he's try'n to hang in. Try'n to bolster South Vietnamese morale, I guess. Everyone was supposed to pull out and fly home out of Tan Son Nhut, but now artillery's shoot'n up that place so it'll have to be a chopper extraction. Messages are flying back and forth from Washington. The White House wants the Ambassador to pack it and get out."

"Damnit, Joe. If the Communists take over, the VC and the North Vietnamese'll be unmerciful. It'll be a damned blood bath."

Blake left his chair and stood at the starboard wing. He gripped the rail until his knuckles showed white, and his nails grooved the wood. Few of his crew were aware he had served in South Vietnam. He supposed fewer still had any idea what that meant. None could really know the deepness of, or reasons for, his strong feelings because early in his career he had learned to disguise his emotions as though they were shrouded in a cocoon of steel. To the unknowing he probably seemed an indifferent, totally bland professional. Now his mind exploded with thoughts of the past. He speculated on the meaning of the messages in terms of the people. He thought of those loyal to the South, with years of democracy under the French and Americans, people like his friends Duc-Lang and Sergeant Trieu.

Blake's hands were still riveted to the bridge rail, his eyes gazing at the land that had such lasting effect on his life, when he was approached again by Joe.

"Excuse me, Captain. Got another intel message." Blake took the paper and stared at it but his thoughts were still sifting Mark Harris's last remark, "South Vietnam should do Okay." Both men had grown to care about the Rung Sat, South Vietnam and the people, so much so that Blake didn't want to believe the whole thing was crumbling. Finally the blurred letters formed into words.

SECRET
OPERATIONAL IMMEDIATE
SUMMARY: THIEU STEPS DOWN. END SUMMARY.
IN A TWO HOUR ADDRESS TO THE NATION PRESIDENT
THIEU ANNOUNCED HIS RESIGNATION FROM OFFICE.
GOVERNMENT TURNED OVER TO VICE PRESIDENT
HUONG.

President Thieu finished? The futileness finally settled like a black shadow over Blake's mind. *I supposed I should have seen it coming.* Thinking back to his own homecoming in 1973 he remembered the neutered uncaring feeling when the the plane carrying his Rung Sat advisory team landed at Travis. There weren't any brass bands or Generals to shake their hands, they just squeezed each others, split up, and dispersed to their homes or new duty stations.

Blake had boarded a plane for San Diego where he was met by Beverly and the kids. As they drove from the airport through the city it was the same thing, no flags, no steamers, and no confetti. Although the world didn't care, he knew the war was not lost and as far as he and Mark were concerned, it need not be.

Blake had gone to his shore duty assignment instead of his cherished destroyer. There he suffered through two years of a dull desk job. He wasn't a hero and didn't want to be treated like one, yet he had assumed there would at least be a modicum of respect for having fought in Vietnam. He soon learned the "age of aquarious" had left its mark. The civilian population ignored the war and the Navy was passive about it.

The time at home did provide an opportunity to develop a new closeness with his children. But, from the beginning Beverly resented his interference with the kids and often reacted, "That's not the way we did it when you were away."

He soon realized the marriage was irreparably damaged. As the months passed she became more and more distant. She kept her job in La Jolla and avoided official Navy functions and parties. They passed each other in the mornings and evenings, but they just never could click. They went away once, but that ended in his drinking too much, and almost no conversation. It terminated in an early return caused by mutual boredom.

A scene was in the making. They both knew it and avoided it for as long as they could.

Finally one day Beverly said, "It just isn't going to work. I'm drowning in a pool of staleness trying to live a life I'm not good at — I don't want to be a Navy wife and I do want to work at my career. Do you understand?"

"What can I say."

"You can say alright."

"Alright to what?"

"You know it's not going to work."

"Don't you want it to work?"

"Oh, shit. Why do you always do this — it's always me that has to act. You avoid."

"What do you want?"

"You were gone too long. It was almost two years."

"History," he shrugged.

"I'm not like you — can't just write it off. I did my duty, but..."

"What can I say. You did — maybe better than me. Those days weren't Disneyland." He shrugged again. "You got to do what you want."

"Blake, I can't believe your macho mind let you say that. I do want my own life."

"We all change. You have a right. "

Beverly took a small apartment and spent more and more time away. Finally she pulled out. The kids went reluctantly, and Blake was left alone to fend. It was all very civil. He and Bev remained friends and he saw the kids. It was just over.

At one point he again considered leaving the Navy. His thoughts about war were pitted against the practicalities of continuing his career. After a period of indecision, he stayed in. It was what he knew and fear of having to look for a civilian job overbalanced his hate for war.

During the rest of his shore duty assignment and now as captain of one of the Navy's newest frigates, he kept himself too busy to think about Vietnam. But now by all the cliches: "twist of fate"; "quirk of the gods"; "truth stranger than fiction," his life had again become intertwined with that country and its war.

Blake stayed on the bridge all night and in the morning Joe returned to deliver what turned out to be the final message. Blake took it and held the paper but not seeing. As if he were in a trance, the faces of Beverly, Ace Magrue, Gunny Johnson, Sergeant Trieu, Duc-Lang and Mark with beautiful Peg Thompson burst in balloon-like images across his memory. Finally his eyes focused on the written words. It was an order from the Commander-in-Chief which simply said:

EXECUTE OPERATION FREQUENT WIND

Blake's destroyer was stationed on the Western edge of the armada, in the van, closest to South Vietnam. It was an anti-submarine ship and had a small flight deck for its own helicopter.

The evacuation of the last Americans from South Vietnam began with Blake standing on the bridge of his ship staring toward the mouth of the Long Tau Shipping Channel.

At first they came in ones and twos, like specks on the horizon. There was one fishing boat. It was followed by a daring Air America helicopter then another small boat. As Blake watched from his vigil high on the superstructure of his ship, he saw them come in threes and fours. Finally they came like locusts over the Mississippi Valley. The Rung Sat rivers spilled boats into the ocean like black ashes dumped from a bucket. Vietnamese Air Force Hueys and Air America birds filled the sky, aimlessly looking to land on any ship with a clear deck. Blake hurt inside as he surveyed the scene. *They're running for the unknown, so running must be better than staying.*

The first evacuation chopper flew near, wobbled her rotors and even made a pass as if to land, but it was waved off in the direction of the aircraft carriers. Unable to communicate, it circled several times, then continued toward the larger ships farther at sea.

Blake ordered his own chopper airborne, and it took a position near Vung Tau to act as shepherd. Soon Blake's ship became the beacon for every Vietnamese boat and helicopter leaving Saigon. They would circle until they understood the frantic hand signals from crew, then continue toward the larger ships with more space.

Marine helicopters which had been launched at first light from the amphibious ships returned to the fleet from Saigon followed by still more Vietnamese helos.

"Look at those choppers — stuffed with people. No other way to describe it, sir." Joe said.

Blake nodded. "Stuffed too tight. Way over safe operating limits." He could see Vietnamese men hanging dangerously from the skids.

At one point eight Huey helicopters circled Blake's ship. One at a time they were directed to come aboard. The Vietnamese pilots had no experience landing on a rolling deck at sea, so the first to come was an Air America bird whose pilot claimed to be ex-Navy. Fortunately the weather was clear, and almost as if God had willed it, the seas were flat. Blake figured they would have come anyway. The Air America Huey flew straight up the ship's wake, hovered, then settled near center deck and began to off-load passengers. People were quickly ushered clear of rotor blades to a safe location below decks.

As soon as he was off-loaded and his aircraft refueled, the Air America pilot gave a thumbs up and lifted off for the return flight to Saigon. "Keep the airport lights burn'n baby, I'll be back," he shouted to one of the deck crew. He did return, four more times, but not a fifth. Blake's sailors nicknamed him, "Ole nuts and guts." Blake assumed his chopper had crashed somewhere in the jungle of the Rung Sat.

Some of the Vietnamese pilots were convinced to fly on to the larger ships, but many followed the example of the Air America pilot and landed. The Vietnamese had no intention of returning for more evacuees and their abandoned helicopters would have fouled his deck for future landings.

In order to clear the small platform Blake ordered each H-1 Huey, in some cases so new they had been in use no more than three weeks, pushed over the side. He watched as resourceful sailors wedged pipes under the skids and rolled the chopper to the deck edge. With a mighty heave by a dozen men, over it went landing upside down, rotor in the water.

Blake shook his head. Shame. *The most versatile fighting machines of that war. Sinking slowly to the bottom of the South China Sea. Nothing we can do — no room.*

Blake watched as the people off -loaded from the helos. They were a mixed bag of women, children, Vietnamese Air Force officers, and CIA agents. Most were Vietnamese civilians who had worked for the Americans. Except for the clothes on their backs most had no personal belongings. Some had bags of gold hanging around their shoulders and others were armed to the teeth with inlaid French shotguns, matched dueling pistols, or Swedish automatic machine guns. Blake ordered them disarmed. *They won't need weapons in America.*

Two American civilians asked to join the commanding officer. One was a small, dark-haired man with equally dark eyes. He was polite enough but Blake suspected he could do damage if cornered. The other was tall and skinny with heavy blond hair and a large nose. His eyes were set deep and had a cold-blooded look which marked him as a mercenary.

"Do you mind if we watch from here, Captain?" the short man asked.

"Not at all, glad to have you. You with the State Department?" Blake asked, suspecting otherwise.

"CIA." The tall man answered curtly.

"What's going on in there—in Saigon?"

"It's a goddamn zoo and the fuc'n keepers are gone." The tall agent answered.

"What do you mean?"

The tall mercenary sneered as he pointed to a passing LCM-8 full of soldiers. "Fuc'n ARVN bolted and ran. First at Danang, then all the way South until they couldn't run any more. Look at them in those boats. Those bastards, they probably threw women and children overboard to make room for themselves,"

The short agent bristled angrily at his tall friend and shook his head. "Horseshit. They're not cowards and it's not that simple. Oh, sure there was some poor leadership, but the Vietnamese were caught in a dilemma that caused a loss of confidence. The military had been brought to peak fighting condition and they could have won if they were supplied. The ARVN really folded because they ran out of logistic support. Not enough gas for the tanks and bullets for the guns. They were trying to consolidate their forces in the southern part of the country, to make do with what they had, when the North struck. The people lost confidence when no country would support the army. When that happened everybody began looking out for themselves. For a mere 700 or 800 million bucks the South Vietnamese could have held—at least until the rainy season bogged down the Russian artillery and tanks they were up against. Hell, our Congress pisses that much down the drain every day."

The shorter CIA agent turned to his taller friend and said. "You never listen to the news, but you should have heard President Thieu's speech the day he stepped down." Turning to Blake he said. "Thieu gave a humdinger—mostly sour grapes but it makes you wonder. He said he never would have signed the Paris agreement except he was threatened that all aid would be cut off. He questioned if Watergate and special interest groups hadn't destroyed the resolve of our politicians. He said it was the leeching of land that finally did them in. Also, the North Vietnamese who were allowed to remain in the South as a result of the poorly negotiated treaty. Who knows? But 'it's bad news at Black Rock' today."

"Well, the Vietnamese Marines didn't run!" the tall man boasted.

Blake smiled at the shorter man. "Bet he was a Marine."

"Had two tours over here." The blond haired man bragged. "One as an advisor with the Vietnamese Marines before I got smart. I'll tell you those little bastards got guts. They held at Danang. Took casualties do'n it. They only fell back when they were the only ones left. They're still hold'n their own near Saigon," the tall mercenary sneered.

Blake wanted to rebuff the tall agent by telling him he also knew something about marines. Instead, charitably he asked, "Did I see you carrying a small child off the helo?"

"Not me. It was him. I wouldn't marry a squaw." The man said contemptuously. "Just use one when I need to."

The other agent looked angry, and embarrassed, "Don't mind him, Captain. We call him 'Callous Carl'. He was in the mountains with the Montagnards too long. The girl's my daughter. Her mother was with us until we got on the helo, but she handed me the child and jumped off at the last minute when she realized her mother hadn't got on board with us. I tried to tell her there was only room for us three but she wouldn't listen. I hope she and her mother made another chopper, but if she didn't I'll get her out."

"Where's your daughter now?" Blake asked.

"A couple of your sailors are looking after her — having a ball. Last time I saw her she was eating ice cream an' cake in the mess hall."

*****

The evacuation continued into the night and the next day and the next. Blake took cat-naps in his sea cabin but otherwise was there to watch the massive collection of refugees. He saw hundreds of small boats dotting the horizon. There was every conceivable type of boat, PBR's, M-6's and M-8's, fishing junks, and sampans; whatever would float long enough to get them to the waiting Navy ships. The boats teemed with people and Blake was certain that most of them had no understanding of the perils of the ocean. They knew only that it was the way to freedom.

One of Blake's men counted 40 barges, each with hundreds of people. Blake knew some would be lost but most saved. It was a tragic sight. Sailors exchanged stories by flashing light about men and women trampled to death trying to get aboard waiting Navy or merchant ships.

On the last evening of the evacuation a small fishing junk flying the yellow with red stripes of South Vietnam approached. Its diesel engine sputtered. It had just enough speed to cause an embarrassing seamanship situation. There were so many people on board the boat wallowed. It rolled slowly and hung with her gunnel almost awash before slowly rolling in the other direction.

Blake cautioned the conning officer. "Careful, Tip, that one looks like a heavy wave could sink her. Too many people. Don't get too close!"

The rules established for the evacuation fleet were clear. If the craft had propulsion, enough food, water and medical supplies and was seaworthy, the people were not to be taken aboard. The seaworthy boats were to make their own way to safety. If Blake had his way they all would have been picked up, but there just wasn't sufficient room for everybody aboard the Task Force ships.

From his vantage point on the bridge it was obvious to Blake this boat had stability problems, but she wasn't taking water and she was under her own power. He suspected a decision either way might be a good one. A closer inspection was required. He watched as the boat maneuvered slowly alongside and sailors went aboard. In his heart he hoped that the on-scene inspection would give him the evidence needed to bring the people aboard.

"What's it look like, Tip?"

"No word yet, Captain. The corpsman and the executive officer are still checking it out."

Blake groused to himself. *Hurry! The ship shouldn't be stopped too long — more helos might arrive any moment. Got to get underway. They'll need wind for their landings.*

"The executive officer says there are close to 150 refugees on the boat, Captain."

"150? On that small craft? What in the hell is taking so long to decide?"

"Wait, Sir, more's coming now."

"Wait? We don't have time to wait!" Blake barked in an uncharacteristic state of agitation. He knew he should have followed his instincts from the beginning and was ready to order the people aboard when Tip shouted, "Captain, the boat has a leak and the engine just died. The XO recommends embarking the passengers and sinking the boat."

"Make it so!" came the crisp words of command.

Sailors jumped aboard and lifted mothers to safety, then handed the babies to other waiting arms. People poured over the fantail and quickly the boat was emptied.

A Machinists Mate poured gasoline among the old wooden timbers and a Gunners mate lofted grenades into her bilges. The derelict wallowed in smoke for a few minutes, then burst into flames, exploded and sank.

The crew ushered the boat people into the ship and Blake returned to his vigil.

For Blake, Marine pilots from the amphibious ships were as crazy as the Air American pilots. They flew into the night but finally were forced to stop after a third helo got shot down, one with 155 people on board—no survivors.

The Vietnamese Navy was the last to leave Saigon. Blake watched as they came out of the Rung Sat through the Long Tau Channel.

He read the summary message.

FORTY-FIVE THOUSAND PEOPLE ABOARD SEVENTEEN SHIPS. FLAG OF THE VIETNAMESE CHIEF OF NAVAL OPERATIONS FLYING FROM THE LEAD SHIP A WORLD WAR II RADAR PICKET DESTROYER.

Blake could see the ships formed in a long line like a slow wagon train. The Vietnamese national ensign still flying proudly in their sad retreat.

The evacuation was over by 30 April 1975. Many thousands were saved. Many died, but many more would have died had the seas not been calm and the Task Force not been there waiting.

As he looked at the mass of U.S. and Vietnamese ships scattered across the horizon, for the second time in his life Blake had the urge to whistle the theme song of the World War II movie Victory at Sea, but this time it didn't fit. It was a proud day for the United States Navy, yet Blake recognized the irony of it all. Over 55,000 Americans had died in the war to preserve that little country. There was no cheering now for the job well done.

The American fleet was ordered to withdraw. Slowly the ships formed naval formations and began to sail away. Blake's ship, still on the most Western edge of the naval disposition, lingered among the last to leave.

Blake, who had been at his vigil on the bridge for over three days and three nights, finally went below to survey the scene at close hand. Refugees had found resting places wherever they could. He walked the topside decks where mothers held crying children and men sat hunkered Vietnamese style in small groups, nervously contemplating their future. As he passed they looked up and he saw it in their eyes. They had lost something precious, their homeland.

He went below to the same scene. He saw American sailors feeding children, helping the old and tending the sick. He saw sad-faced people nervously sitting in small groups, protecting the few personal belongings they had been able to bring. Many, talking quietly among themselves, stopped their discussions long enough to bow respectfully when they recognized him as the Commanding Officer of the ship that surely had saved their lives.

Blake was passing through the galley area where the ship's cooks were serving a long line of refugees when he thought he heard a timid voice say, "Cô-vân."

He continued his inspection of the food then began to walk toward the ladder leading back to the bridge when he heard someone say the Vietnamese word meaning advisor. "Cô-vân, Cô-vân."

Was he imagining the words — words from a different time and place. Blake stopped and listened. The Vietnamese word came again. This time it was louder, but still with the timidness of indecision.

"*Cô-vân* Lawrence?"

He turned to see a slender Vietnamese man bowing, hands clasp together Buddhist style, then stand erect and adjust his wire-rimmed glasses.

"Trieu! Sergeant Trieu! How? I didn't know you were aboard! Can this be true?"

Overcome by the emotion of the staggering events of the past few days, and now at seeing his friend from the Rung Sat, Blake felt a tearlet form. He took the skinny little man in his arms and clasped him warmly. Then they held each other at arm's length for a few moments each stammering to speak at once. Trieu most humbly said, "I did not know that you were captain of the ship. When I saw you I could not resist calling out."

"You were on board that old hulk?" Blake said feeling awkward, having so much to say and not knowing what to say first. "My God, I'm glad you did call out, otherwise I wouldn't have known you were here. I can't believe this. Like a grade 'B' movie. On my ship? You alone? Where's your family?"

"They are with me. We were most fortunate. My wife and children were able to come with me."

The sounds of the words were so familiar—the brittle almost too perfect pronunciation of English — the sometimes awkward sentence structure in sing-song tones.

"I have so many things to ask, but first let's get your family settled. Where are they?"

"In the back. We have found a small corner."

Blake said to a passing petty officer. "Go with this Vietnamese man. Find his family and bring them all to my cabin."

Before Trieu and the sailor went aft, the Sergeant paused to look at the photograph of the person Blake's ship was named after. Hanging in a prominent place in the center of the ship's mess hall, the picture showed a Marine in his end-of-boot-camp pose. Trieu turned to Blake and commented, "Private Marquell looks different in his dress uniform."

"Like the Naval hero he was." Except for Gunny or Major Harris, few Americans would connect Blake to Marquell. Trieu could, but he didn't know enough about the American Navy to question. Blake knew it was strange and even hokey that he ended up commanding a ship named after one of his own men. But stranger things had happened in the U.S. Navy. Blake also knew what an unlikely hero Marquell was. Just another irony of that kind of war — the war that wasn't a war — that a ship was named after a drugger. No one would ever know how good or bad Marquell might have been. All the world knows is he did an unselfish and courageous thing and was posthumously given the nations highest medal.

In the process of commissioning the ship, Blake had even met Marquell's father and mother. What he couldn't tell Trieu, or anyone else for that matter, was that although his act was very brave, ordinarily it wouldn't have been enough to name a warship after him. Marquell's father had friends in D.C. They were powerful and had votes to bring enough pressure on the Navy department.

On all but the smallest naval ships the Commanding Officer has two cabins, one called the "sea cabin" and a larger one called the "in-port cabin." Blake made Sergeant Trieu and his family guests in the in-port cabin, where they were given preferential treatment.

After they were settled, Trieu joined Blake on the starboard bridge wing where last-minute preparations were being made to leave the vigil and join the Task Force for the transit to freedom.

From their vantage point the two men could still see the outline of the mouth of the Long Tau Channel and the eastern edge of the Rung Sat.

"Tell me, what was it like? What happened? Tell me about Nha Be and the Rung Sat."

Blake remembered Trieu's habit of adjusting his glasses before he spoke and the Sergeant, true to form touched them, before answering. "After you left, life continued much as before. I was transferred back to Province where I was given clerical duties. That ended my direct involvement with the activities at the Rung Sat headquarters. I kept somewhat in touch because I had left my family at Nha Be near the many friends we made there. I was able to return most weekends to be with them."

"What about *Dai Ta* Duc-Lang and the Long Tau? Did the channel remain secure? What about VC activity in the Rung Sat?"

"Oh, yes. The *Dai Ta* stayed as commander of the Rung Sat. You know he had a very sad family problem. They say the people in Saigon were very happy to keep him there because of his long association with the area. The Long Tau remained secure, because the Navy patrolled it. But there was always guerrilla activity of some form going on. I did not find it too dangerous for my family; however, there was one event which you would be interested in. One of the oil tank farms got blown up."

"Blown up? Which one and how?"

Bowing slightly, Trieu said. "The one nearest Nha Be. I think it was called Dutch World. There was a great sapper attack in the fall after you left. It was completely blown apart—a great fire. For a time there was a shortage of fuel and more ships had to come up the river."

"We're there any injuries? Who was in charge? Did the Europeans come back?"

"Oh, Vietnamese were still in charge and fortunately there were very few people hurt in the attack. A few guards I think."

"Excuse me, Captain," the officer of the deck interrupted. "We've been ordered to join the fleet as an escort for the Vietnamese Navy. Request permission to come to 15 knots and an Easterly course."

Blake walked across the bridge area and surveyed the situation, then responded, "Permission granted. I guess we can't stay here forever. Keep a careful watch — there are still some small boats around." Then he joined Trieu again at the starboard rail.

"Tell me about the end of the war, Trieu. Why and how did you leave?"

Trieu took off his glasses and cleaned them as he responded. "I was working at Bien Hoa. The Communists came closer and closer. The commander of the military region kept asking for instructions and more supplies. We were told to fight with what we had, but by that time we had heard the terrible stories from Danang. The Communists there took people who had worked for the Americans out to the beaches. They raped the women and killed everyone. The Army surrounding Bien Hoa kept falling back and even though I was an administrative person, I was given a rifle and ordered to fight. The Army held for a while, but the Communists had Russian tanks and more artillery than we did. We fought for a time there, but were ordered to fall back to protect the city and that's when it happened. Too many men became worried about their families and began to desert.

"We learned a famous artillery commander from the battle for Dien Bien Phu came out of hiding in the Rung Sat to join General Dung, the Commander of the North Vietnamese forces. It was Senior Colonel Tu of the Hanoi Trinh family, and because of his intimate knowledge of the Nhon Trach area it was he who directed the positioning of artillery for the shelling of the capitol. His artillery became the pistol at the head of Saigon."

Blake shook his head, remembering Rear Admiral Paulson's lack of concern for the guerrilla leader. "So our battle for the AT-3 rockets wasn't successful, we didn't get Tu after all!"

As U.S.S. *Marquell* picked up speed and swung in a long curve to her new course Blake heard the helmsman call out, "Steady on 066 degrees true, Sir." The lee helmsman shouted, "Engine room answers engine ahead standard, 15 knots, Sir."

From their position on the starboard wing of the bridge the two men began to lose sight of the land so they moved quickly to a new position on the port wing, where they could watch the Rung Sat fade from sight.

Trieu took off his glasses. He cleaned them, put them over his ears and carefully adjusted the wires. When he was finished the ritual he said, "I could have stayed. My involvement in the war was minor and there is always a need for teachers. But Gunny once told me about the freedom in your country. I stayed until I heard the Americans were going to leave, then I found my way to Nha Be and gathered my family. I decided if we could get on a boat we would try to get to the ships we heard were waiting just off the coast. Being an Army man, I didn't know much about the sea so I took a bold step. I went to Captain Duc-Lang and asked for his help. The *Dai Ta* was still in control of all river traffic from Saigon through the Rung Sat. To the very end his PBR's protected the barges and boats that went down the Long Tau Channel to the sea. He wanted me to stay and fight, but he did not stand in my way when I told him I wanted to take my family to America. He understood when I said I wished only to raise my children in the freedom Gunny told about."

Blake looked at his friend and saw that it was the same for Trieu as it was for the other refugees. The Sergeant's eyes had that same distant look, but Blake knew that because Trieu was a historian the agonizing hurt would be deeper and stronger for him. Blake put his hand on his friend's shoulder and said, "I'm sorry for you, Sergeant Trieu — that you lost your country. I suppose that's our legacy. Maybe if we Americans had stayed longer this wouldn't have happened." A surge of guilt touched his thoughts.

The slender sergeant responded. "No!" He said in uncharacteristicly strong tones. "The American people could do no more. They were not wrong. They had the best of intentions."

The two men stared off to the West. A red glow behind dark clouds and a black silhouette of the Vietnamese coast was all they could see. But from the top deck lookout came the report, "Chopper on the horizon, low, sir."

"Captain, chopper in-bound. Want to vector her to the carrier?" The officer of the deck asked.

"Better not, Joe. Bring the ship into the wind and set flight quarters."

After the Huey settled onto the flight deck, Sergeant Trieu followed Blake back to the after bridge where they could observe what they expected to be the last group of refugees to make it out of Vietnam and also witness the last chopper pushed into the South China.

It was Sergeant Trieu who recognized the first person who stepped from the aircraft. "It's the *Dai Ta*. It's Duc-Lang," he shouted.

Blake hurried down to the flight deck.

"Welcome to America," he shouted to his old counterpart above the noise of the rotor blades.

"Can't be!" Duc-Lang said. "*Cô-vân* Lawrence. Is this your ship? And is that Sergeant Trieu?"

"Stranger things have happened. Get your people clear so our sailors can dump that Huey overboard."

"No. I'm not staying." His eyes were different than Blake remembered. The brightness was missing, replaced by a somber sadness.

"Not staying?" Blake said. "Of course you are. Let me take you to America."

"Please, *Cô-vân*. I have brought out my youngest daughter. Take her with you."

"Of course. We'll take good care of her," Blake assured him.

The girl was already in the arms of one of the sailors.

"I am going back — I must continue the fight."

"Why? Why must you go back — the war's over," Blake said.

"It is not over. For me it will never be over," Duc-Lang said. "When the North Vietnamese announced that Senior Colonel Tu had become a member of the ruling body in the South and the Governor of Saigon, I took the name 'Nguyen Nam Ky' or 'Nguyen of the South.' My new wife — she will bear me another son, my oldest daughter, and many of my Rung Sat fighters, including a few Americans have joined me. We have already begun a guerrilla war against Colonel Tu — the one who is a decedent of the Hanoi Trinhs..."

"Americans?" Blake questioned.

"Yes, don't you know that just as the Japanese did after World War II, some Americans stayed and some came back to make Vietnam their home. Some of those are willing to fight. My base camp is in the heart of the Forest of Assassins very near the place where the SEAL's searched for the AT-3 rockets."

"You are going to fight as a guerrilla?"

"Yes. Come with me as my *Cô-vân*. Be my Pigneau."

The tops of the billowing clouds above the coast were all that Blake could see when he heard Duc-lang's crazy request.

Blake remembered the story of Prince Nguyen Ahn and the French priest named Pigneau who became the advisor and benefactor to the last seed of the Dynasty. Duc-Lang never thought of himself as a mere *Dai Ta*. He was a Nguyen and a Nam Ky. Colonel Tu was a Trinh, Bac Ky, a dog eater. And they were always playing the other game of Dominoes.

Not the humpty dumpty version that the Americans thought they were playing where the pieces all fall down in a line.

Duc-Lang and Tu were playing the one where you match the dots, the game played one dominoe at a time in many directions, the more complicated culture game the Americans never grasped.

"Go back?" Blake said. "Become your Pigneau?"

Memories of those brown water days brought a chill across Blake's shoulders, the kind of excitement he hadn't felt in years.

"Dai Ta, under different circumstances I would go back into the jungle again. I feel strongly enough about liberty to do that. Not about war, but about your little country. But now I'm captain of my own destroyer — I can't leave."

Duc-Lang's eyes changed from sadness to the brightness Blake remembered, "I understand *Cô-vân*. But, there is hope. It may not be in our lifetime, but freedom will some day rise again from the Rung Sat jungle."

The two grasped hands for the last time. Blake waved as Duc-Lang's chopper took off then circled his destroyer before it dipped its nose and headed back toward the Forest of Assassins.

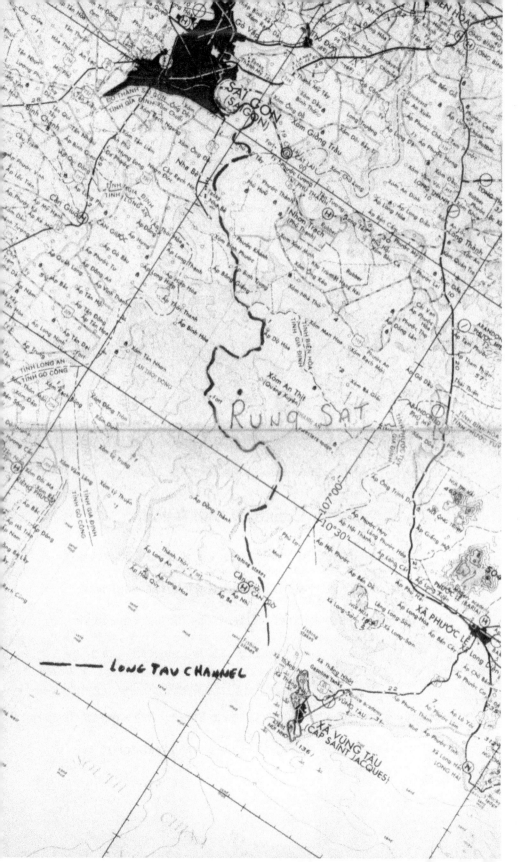

About the Author

Carl Nelson is a decorated navy veteran who rose from enlisted sailor to captain by way of graduation from the U.S. Naval Academy. During a first career that spanned more than thirty years, he commanded five naval organizations including a guided missile cruiser. He served four tours of duty in the Vietnam War, one of which was ashore in the delta as Senior Advisor of the Rung Sat Special Zone. In his second career, Dr. Nelson is professor of international business and author of eight non-fiction books in his field. This is his first novel. He resides with his wife Barbara in Chula Vista, California.

Other Books by Carl Nelson

Your Own Import-Export Business: Winning the Trade Game

Import/Export: How to Get Started in International Trade

Global Success: International Business Tactics of the 1990s

Managing Globally: A Complete Guide to Competing worldwide

Protocol For Profit: A Manager's Guide to Competing Worldwide

International Business: A Manager's Guide to Strategy in the Age of Globalism

Exporting: A Manager's Guide to the World Market